ASCENDED

KENDRA THOMAS

❀ Created with Vellum

To the empty field of dreams that
filled me with possibilities

ONE

SABEARA

"One, two, three, four. . ."

Numbers were all that existed these days. They were supposed to calm me, dissipate the anger warring inside my body.

The numbers were meant to free me.

"Six, seven, eight. . ."

I breathed in a deep breath, imagining the rage bleeding out of me like blood from a tainted wound.

"Nine. . ."

Like rain, rinsing a coal-black sky of smoke.

"Ten. . ."

I opened my eyes. Dusane sat across from me in the grass. His legs crisscrossed with his palms upturned on his knees in a relaxed position. He was watching me perform the technique—his cerulean eyes thoughtful as he gazed at me.

"How do you feel?" he asked.

I answered honestly. Because there were no secrets between us anymore, and I trusted him enough to speak my mind.

"Like I still want to stab someone," I admitted.

Dusane's face remained impassive, but I caught the hint of an amused smile as it tugged at the corners of her lips. I liked that I was privy to what he was actually thinking. At first glance, he would've just appeared indifferent.

"Envorydian, you have to trust the technique."

"I'm trying! But how is counting supposed to help me?" I whined, not bothering to hide my frustration. We'd been at this for three weeks now. We'd returned from the Isles and almost immediately, Dusane had started to train me on controlling my anger. Ever since I'd become an Envorydian and found out about my father's death and Oli marrying Jasper. Well, I guess I was lashing out. Having fits of severe rage that had almost led to me killing Queen Emiress. My emotions were out of control, and I was using fighting to try and fix the situations in my life.

"It's supposed to give you something else to focus on. Give you time to calm down before you do something you'll regret." Dusane shifted his position to scoot closer to me and clasped my hands in his. "Ehren, if you don't give the counting a chance, all of this time spent out here will just be a huge waste of time."

I smiled at him and leaned in a little closer, so our faces were now mere inches apart.

"Well, I wouldn't call it a complete waste of time," I nearly purred and moved to my knees so I could thread my finger into his hair. I let the soft black strands tangle between my fingers and sighed.

His hands immediately found my waist as if it were the most natural thing in the world, pulling me onto his lap. He snuggled me close to his chest, letting out a guttural sound in the back of his throat as he leaned in to kiss the crook of my neck.

"You're trouble," he murmured against my skin.

I sighed, leaning my head back to give him more access. "I know."

"You need to take our sessions more seriously," he warned as he continued his trail of kisses up my neck to my ear and finally hovering above my lips.

"I do take them seriously, Captain." My eyes glittered with mischief. "But sometimes I need a break," I leaned in and closed the gap, kissing him.

He took the liberty of making my head spin for the next several minutes. By the time we pulled apart, I was out of breath and felt like I'd been transported to another planet.

"Hmmm. . . I suddenly don't feel like stabbing someone anymore." I quipped, and Dusane chuckled, shaking his head.

"Come on, let's go back. We have a meeting with the others soon." Dusane deposited me off his lap and helped me to stand.

We were up on the mountainside in a meadow we'd discovered. It was the perfect place to train and was within walking distance of the mansion. Knadiel's mountains perfectly encased the beautiful landscape, and it was becoming one of my favorite places to escape to.

Our hands clasped together as we walked back down. As we neared the mansion, reality began to set in as it always seemed to do when we walked back home.

That day on the ship out in the middle of the ocean, when we'd run into Obsidian's ship. It flashed back in snippets—Emiress and her emissaries escaping, facing off to Obsidian, and Shar nearly dying. Sunn appearing on the other ship, Obsidian fighting to keep her from running to safety, and then Dusane's arrow burrowing in his side.

Obsidian had collapsed, and I'd managed to put the device on his wrist, subduing him. Mid pulled Sunn from his grasp, and luckily she'd been unharmed.

After capturing Obsidian and rescuing Sunn, we had sailed home to Knadiel—Obsidian our prisoner. And now he was in the dungeons of the mansion and we'd been having meetings over the past several weeks to discuss the same, undetermined question.

What did we do now?

~

Everyone was already gathered in the small mapping room when we arrived. Dusane and I took our seats and Oli stood to speak.

"Thank you for joining us," Oli greeted. He looked like he hadn't slept in weeks. But he wasn't the only one. Everyone else in the room also appeared to be feeling the effects of our predicament. Dark circles underneath everyone's eyes were a common sight these days.

I looked around the table, and Rouix greeted me with a friendly nod. Beside her were Embrosine and Shar, who also dipped their chins at me in greeting. Ruby and Knadian were at the other end of the table with Jasper, and as I continued to search the room, I realized he wasn't there. . .

"Captain Whitemane has sent another letter, but it appears he still hasn't seen any activity from Queen Emiress and her people," Oli said.

The mermaid queen that escaped us was nowhere to be

found. Captain Whitemane offered to stay out on the waters and search for her, but with no such luck, it seemed. Not only did we have to worry about defeating the curse but we now had a mermaid queen and her people searching for the compass to take over the land kingdom's that have wronged them in the past. Now we had more than one enemy it seemed we had to be wary of.

I sighed, and Dusane squeezed my hand beneath the table reassuringly.

"They aren't going to risk showing themselves so soon," Shar said, his green eyes brooding as he gazed at the map of our realm spread across the table.

"Has anyone had any ideas about what to do with Obsidian?" Embrosine asked.

Everyone was silent. It was the question we'd been asking for weeks, and still, no one had conjured any good ideas.

"There has to be a way we could use him to our advantage. To help us find the remaining tokens," Jasper mused, so quietly I almost didn't hear her at first.

We now had three of the five tokens. With two remaining, we seemed so close to our goal, but without any idea as to what the last two tokens might be, we were pretty much stuck.

Only two Kings token's remained. Oxtwenel, and Ennsleon. Shar had his suspicions about Ennsleon and that it had something to do with the stars, but the Ethirical was extremely vague and as to where it might be hidden across the realm was a complete mystery. It felt like we'd hit a dead end and none of us knew how to proceed.

"Do you really think he'd submit to helping us?" Rouix asked skeptically.

"He has refused to speak to any of us so far. So it doesn't

seem likely he's going to willingly submit any sort of information," Embrosine said.

"Well, maybe we need to try a different tactic," I urged, and I was the first to broach the idea.

"We aren't going to torture him into helping us," Dusane immediately said, guessing where I was headed.

"Nobody said torture," I said a little hotly. "But we need to at least hang something over his head. Get him to help us in some way." The anger was there, bubbling up beneath the surface of my emotions, always ready to boil over. One, two, three. . .

"He may know if King Elysian possesses one of the tokens. Maybe we could offer him something in exchange for telling us what and where it is." Rouix proposed.

We all fell silent again, thinking about the idea.

"What could we possibly offer him?" Shar asked.

It came to my mind before I could stop it. I blurted out the words for the sake of having no other ideas. "His freedom."

TWO

SUNN

There was something seriously wrong with me. Maybe half of my brain wasn't working correctly—a section of my mind that controlled my thoughts and feelings.

What everyone thought was a monster restraining an innocent young girl from her family was, in fact, not that. Instead, he'd wrapped his arms around me and shielded my body with his because he'd thought they were the threat.

And because saving me would be too twisted—too unrealistic and sickening to fathom, they'd all illusioned their own story.

They sincerely believed he'd had ill intentions.

I let them believe it. Because the alternative was so much worse, that Obsidian had been protecting me.

When the arrow hit his side, I had panicked. And I think my family and friends had perceived my panic as shock. But really, I had been worried Obsidian had been killed. When his body slumped against mine, my heart had dropped into my stomach, and I'd tried desperately to find air to breathe.

I've since reminded myself that I can breathe without him. Even if he had been killed, I shouldn't have been so affected. He was a horrible person, after all.

But no matter how many times I told myself these things. I knew I'd developed some twisted form of attachment to him. And ever since I'd gotten to Knadiel, I'd tried desperately to break it.

But it'd been a month. I hadn't stepped foot in the dungeons where I knew he was being kept. It was basically raising the white flag if I did. I'd be surrendering to the darkest part of myself if I attempted to see him. That threshold was the only thing keeping me from committing a horrendous moral sin.

But today, today, I wasn't strong enough anymore. I'd slowly felt myself going crazy as I tried to stay away. I wanted to know if he missed me as much as I missed him. I wanted to see for myself that he was alive and well. I wanted to hear his voice.

So I'd left my room. And the cold marble floors slapped gently against my bare feet as I made my way to the lower level of the mansion where he was being kept. It was nearly midnight. No one was awake except for the castle guards. And I'd already learned their shift times so I could pass by undetected. I'd done it without even intending to. I'd been planning this for the entire month while lying to myself that I actually wasn't.

As I got closer to the staircase leading down to the dungeon cells, my heart began to beat faster. Should I turn back? I hesitated, stalling in the middle of the corridor. It was so quiet, everything deathly still except for the erratic thrumming of my heart. It was an eerie reminder I was alive.

No, Sunn. You can't back out now. I forced myself to continue. I had to remind myself I wasn't scared of him.

The stairs greeted me minutes later, and I let out a shaky breath before starting down the steps. Lanterns dimly lit the stairs, and the train of my nightgown made a gentle swishing sound as I descended.

The guard that was posted at the base of the stairs was currently gone. He was in the middle of a shift change.

Dear spirits, please don't curse me, I thought as I slipped past the entryway undetected and into the dungeon.

Black iron cells filled the basement of the mansion. But none of them were filled. Except for one.

My pulse quickened as I closed the distance between us. I could see his hunched form, sitting on the cold floor of his cell. His black cloak billowed around him like a protective shadow—his hair shielding his face.

I stopped when I reached the edge of his cage and kneeled beside him on the cool stone floor. I gripped one of the iron bars between my fingertips and dared myself to speak.

"Obsidian," I breathed, and it came out as more of a sigh of relief.

He stirred at the sound of my voice, his head lifting from his hunched-over position.

His eyes met mine—dark, soulless orbs of onyx.

"Sunn."

THREE

SABEARA

The proposition of offering Obsidian his freedom in exchange for helping us had not gone over well. We had all argued for another hour on the possibility.

We had finally captured him, eliminating him as a threat to us. He was lethal and dangerous. Letting him go would be self-sabotage. But what if it was our only way of finding the remaining tokens?

I sighed, walking to my room later that evening and hating myself for even bringing up the idea. But in desperate times, when we had no other options, desperate measures seemed somehow less fatal. Taking a risk was the only way to win.

I opened the door to my chambers and stepped inside, wishing that Liony and Rosen would return from Obscurum already. We hadn't heard from them yet, and I feared the worst had happened.

I threw off my day clothes and exchanged them for a

comfortable nightshirt and pants. I sat in the chair next to my vanity and picked up a pen and the journal Embrosine had given me for my birthday. I'd found it therapeutic the last couple of months to write my thoughts on paper. I always addressed my entries to Liony. She was the only one I really ever wanted to write to.

Dear Liony,

Mid still hasn't shown up to any meetings. What happened on the Isles must have really shaken him. I've tried to ask Shar about what is going on, but he just keeps telling me that Mid will tell me himself when he's ready. I've stopped pressing the matter.

Tonight we had another meeting, and I mentioned offering Obsidian his freedom in exchange for him helping us. Everyone thought it was an insane idea. But at this point, do we really have a choice?

Hope you come home soon.

- Ehren

I put down the quill and closed the journal, stuffing it into the vanity drawer where it slept. Hidden away and destined never to be opened. It was a coping mechanism. None of the words were ever meant to be read.

I crawled into my bed, unable to stop thinking about Mid. Despite telling myself to let it go, I thought of him every evening.

Queen Emiress had changed the color of Mid's heart when we'd been on that island. And something had happened to him. Then we'd arrived back in Knadiel, and Mid had basically disappeared. Shar was the only one who knew what was going on.

I wondered if he was hurt because I'd chosen Dusane or if it was really about Emiress changing him. But I'd had yet to muster the courage to ask him.

At one point, I'd wallowed away and needed my space. It didn't feel fair to take that from him when he'd so freely given it to me.

I gazed out the window, the mountains bathed in the moon's light, basking in its pale luminescence. I'd chosen Dusane. I didn't feel at liberty now to know about Mid's struggles. *He probably wouldn't even want my help,* I thought to myself. I wouldn't want my help if I were him.

I sighed and leaned back against the pillows, trying to fall asleep.

But he kept coming to my mind. Maybe Mid would know what to do about Obsidian. Perhaps he'd have an idea. I tossed and turned in my bed all night, trying to shut out the capricious thoughts.

Maybe he needed someone to push him like Liony had pushed me. Then maybe he would come back to helping us.

Soon my room began to lighten as the sun rose over the horizon—a dim yellow-pink glow saturating the room. I sat up in bed then, shoving aside all of Shar's warning to leave him be.

We didn't have any more time to waste. We needed to take a course of action, and Mid would know what to do. I knew he would.

Before I could stop myself, I threw on some clothes, grabbed my daggers out of habit, and left my room in search of Mid.

I knocked on his door, timidly at first, then more intently when there wasn't an answer.

"Mid, please open the door," I called, inwardly begging that the handle would turn.

I was about to give up when the knob finally rattled, and I froze in suspense as the door slowly swung open.

"What do you want?"

It was the first time I'd seen him since we had returned to Knadiel. And his appearance was the last thing I'd expected. His hair was long, much longer than even when I'd first met him. It fell into his face and around his shoulders in thick dark curls, and his face that was usually clean shaven was tainted with scruff. The dark room behind him seemed to almost swallow him whole.

For the first time since knowing him, I felt like I almost didn't recognize him.

"Mid?" I whispered, too in shock at his appearance to say anything else.

"What are you doing here, Sabeara?" he asked, his tone not welcoming in the least.

I narrowed my eyes at him, not appreciating his attitude. I recovered from the initial shock of the disgruntled sight of him and crossed my arms over my chest.

"I need your help."

"Not interested." He started to close the door, and I reached out to block it before he could completely shut it.

"Let me in, Mid."

I wasn't angry anymore about the kiss on the boat. Or that he'd pretended to be Dusane. Now I just wanted things to be normal between us. I hated the grudge that felt like a thick brick in my chest.

His emerald-scarlet eyes bore into mine, and I met his stare with the same amount of stubbornness. Two could play this game.

Finally, after what felt like forever, he released the tension on the door and opened it fully for me to enter.

I strode into the dark moonlit room and was once again halted in my tracks at what I saw.

There were plants. . . everywhere. On the bed, around the furniture, on the veranda. The most shocking thing was the giant tree growing in the center of the room. Its branches penetrated the ceiling, entangling the chandelier in its leafy embrace. I thought that was shocking until I saw a bird flutter from one branch to another. Then I spotted a small rabbit scurry beneath the shrubbery that was overtaking the vanity table.

"Mid, what happened in here?" I whispered, unable to fully comprehend what I was witnessing.

He laughed bitterly and strode over to take a seat on the couch. He fingered a vine on the armrest not meeting my gaze.

"Why do you even care? I thought you were done with me."

His accusation stung. I had chosen Dusane, but I had never wanted to hurt him. And despite being much happier now that I'd made a decision, it hadn't stopped me from thinking about him every day. I didn't know if I'd ever stop thinking about him —worrying about him.

I carefully stepped around the mess of plants to sit next to him.

"Mid, I may be with Dusane, but that doesn't mean we can't. . ."

"Still be friends?" he scoffed. "Please don't tell me you were about to say that."

I glared at him, hating the way things were left between us.

"What happened to you?" I demanded.

"Emiress," he said simply.

"What do you mean? Are you talking about your heart?" I pointed to his glowing golden heart, now matching the one in my chest.

He laughed bitterly again and I saw something wild, maybe even mad, in his eyes that I'd never seen before. It was sort of terrifying to see him in this state.

"Everything I create comes to life."

"What?" I was unsure if I heard him correctly.

"My illusions. They are all real now."

"You mean, these animals, the tree. . ." I gestured to his creations. "It's all real?"

"There are some limitations. I can't recreate another person, and if it's not a living thing, the illusion won't become something real. It has to be something that is living."

"So anything you create that is a living thing will come. . .alive?"

"And you wonder what's wrong with me?"

"Is this why Shar wouldn't let me see you?"

"I asked him not to let anyone see me till I was sure my new power was safe. I'm still trying to understand it. Come to terms with the fact I can literally create living things."

"Isn't this a good thing?"

He didn't respond for a moment. Then he looked up at me, his gaze serious.

"I never wanted to be a god, Sabeara."

"Then don't use your powers."

"That's like asking me not to breathe," he said.

My jaw clenched. "I'm sorry, Mid."

"I have to learn to control my powers all over again. It's like I was just Granted. I already struggled to figure out my illusions in the first place. Now this?"

I stayed silent, unsure how to comfort him. Then I thought to myself that he probably didn't even want my comfort.

"Well, I know this wasn't the only reason you came here. So what else do you need?" he asked bitterly.

I sighed, just when I thought he was beginning to soften, the prickly walls were erected around him again. I wished he wouldn't see the worst in me. But knowing that it was futile after everything that had happened between us.

"We need to figure out where to search next for the tokens."

"Ennsleon and Oxtwenel have little to no information on what could be their tokens in the Ethirical," he said simply.

"You don't have any ideas on where we should search next?"

"Have you asked the prisoner?" he asked.

"He won't speak to any of us. And Oli refused to let us torture information out of him."

"I see."

"I proposed offering him his freedom. In exchange for helping us."

He looked over at me as I mentioned this. But his face remained impassive.

"Everyone thought I was crazy."

"I don't think it's completely absurd."

"You don't?" I was surprised by his acceptance of the idea.

"No. If it gets us closer to the goal, then I don't see why we don't."

"They think he will turn around and kill one of us."

"Not if we kill him first."

I looked at him, unsure if I was seeing the same Mid I'd known only months before. He'd changed. Everything about this curse made it impossible to avoid being tainted by its lethal tendrils.

"We have to make a decision soon. On what to do next. We are running out of time."

"Are your powers weaker?" he asked, and I pursed my lips.

"Yes, but I think we all still have at least a year or two before we would be completely powerless."

I tried not to think about what would happen if we didn't find the remaining tokens by that time. All the Stone-Hearted slowly losing their powers, decaying away back to mortality. And those who dreamed of becoming Stone-Hearted never experiencing the gift the tree once granted us. . .

"I don't feel it anymore," he said.

"Don't feel what?"

"My powers weakening. It's like when I was changed, my power was renewed. I'm suddenly stronger again."

I glanced down at his heart, unsure how to process everything that had happened to him. I wondered if we'd ever understand what ritual Emiress did to Mid. But it must have been some power we didn't understand yet. I found myself once again aching for more knowledge I worried we'd never find.

A knock at the door sounded and startled me from my thoughts. Both Mid and I turned to see Shar walk through the door.

Shar glanced at me briefly, and I worried he might scold me for coming to see Mid but instead, he gestured for us to follow him.

"You both need to come to the mapping room, now."

"Why, what's wrong?" I asked, worried something bad must have happened for him to need us both.

"Liony and Rosen have returned."

FOUR

SUNN

My real name rolled off his tongue, and I hated that he knew. Which was stupid. Of course he'd figured out who I was.

"You know my real name," I said, my voice almost a whisper.

"What are you doing here?"

He's angry, I thought. *Why is he so angry with me?*

I gripped the iron bar in my hand tighter.

"I. . ." I tried to answer, but the words wouldn't come. "I don't know. . ." I trailed off. Defeated. *Why was I here? This was wrong, and not to mention incredibly stupid.*

He didn't say anything. He turned away and let his long black hair shield his face again—it felt like an inky curtain between us. It was much longer than I remembered, reaching almost to the middle of his back.

"I came. . ." I struggled to admit the words in my head. "I came to see if you were alright."

His head snapped up, his eyes a wildfire now. Fury so bright and pure illuminated his expression. I imagined if I was closer, I could be warmed by their flame.

"Leave. Now," he demanded, jaw clenching.

My eyes narrowed, and I reached out with my other hand, gripping both bars now. Wishing I could snap them in half and release him.

"No."

Unsaid words passed between us. It was the most dangerous and damning silence I'd ever experienced. He knew why I really came to see him. And he was livid.

"I don't know what twisted fantasy you've created in your mind about coming down here. But you and your family are my *enemy*." He spat the words like venom. "If I'd known who you really were, I'd have killed you instantly."

I shook my head, not believing him. "You won't hurt me," I said.

He growled and, as swift as a viper, unfurled from his hunched position—slamming his hands against the bars. The vibration was felt through my fingertips. His face was nearly pressed against the iron, inches from mine. I could feel his hot breath across my face.

"If I had my powers right now, I'd have already drained your heart." There was a promise in his voice, but I was too deranged to believe him.

My eyes flickered to the band around his wrist, subduing his abilities.

"How's your wound?" I asked, ignoring his threats. Confusion flickered across his features until he realized I was really asking about his injury.

He laughed, almost frenetically. "I'm not entertaining this." He turned away, back to his sad, curled-up position in the corner of his cage. He reminded me of a wounded bird. A raven, sheared of his wicked wings.

"I just. . . need to know you're alright," I whispered, hating myself even as the words escaped me.

I heard his breath hitch.

"Please," I begged—shocked by my desperation.

"I was the one who captured your mother and subjected her to months of imprisonment," he suddenly said, and the words hit like a ton of bricks—waking me slightly from the spell I was under. "I've killed people," he added, his husky voice almost pained as he said the words. "Drained them of life."

When I'd found out he'd been the one to capture my mother, I'd been shocked. Then the anger had soon followed. Anger at his actions. Anger at myself for somehow understanding why. He was only doing his father's will. A father that had made him believe his family was the enemy. He's been fighting a war he's felt justified in fighting. Just like my family and me. He was only a child when his father convinced him of the evils he needed to fight. I was sure my uncle Mid and his guardian Shar had killed people before in the battle in Ethydon. I knew my mother had even killed Obscurum soldiers. We were in a war. And everyone thought they were on the right side, including Obsidian.

"Obsidian. Please." I ignored his morbid words. "Just tell me you're alright." I didn't know why I needed to hear him say it. But I wanted to sleep at night. I needed peace only he could give me. I felt sick, disgusted that I needed to know he was alright when I knew I shouldn't care.

He groaned, the sound echoing off the dungeon walls. "I'm fine—*Spirits,* Sunn. I'm fine." His black eyes met mine, pleadingly.

"Thank you." Tears welled in the corners of my eyes as I stood. My legs were shaking, and I wasn't sure why.

He watched me stand, his black eyes never leaving mine.

"I should never have touched you," he said, so quietly I almost didn't catch the words.

"But you did," I answered, and as we looked at each other, we both knew there was no taking back what happened between us.

~

The scent of pines and fresh air enveloped me as I left the confines of the mansion. It was dark. The only light to guide me being the starlit sky and the pale opalescent moon. Despite the fresh air, I found it hard to breathe. I nearly sprinted past the front gates and onto the path that led into the small village. I had to escape. I had to get away from wherever he was.

"Where do you think you're going?" James's voice sounded beside me, and I squeaked in surprise—my heart hurdling into my throat and nearly choking me.

"Spirits, James, you scared me!" I scolded him while picking up my pace again, not bothering to wait for him.

He hurried to catch up and fell into stride next to me.

"You went to see him, didn't you?" he asked casually. Like we were discussing the weather. Like I hadn't just gone to greet one of the greatest villains in the realm, hoping my heart would stop beating for him. It hadn't, by the way. So the entire thing had been futile.

"What makes you say that?" I asked, playing dumb. I gritted my teeth, forcing my face to remain passive.

"Just a hunch," he said, and I could feel him looking at me. His gaze burned a hole into the side of my face.

I quickly came to a halt, and James nearly ran into me. I glared at him in the darkness, hoping he could see the intensity of it.

Since we'd returned from Knadiel, James had taken it upon himself to become like my guardian. Everyone in the mansion had made this mutual decision that James was innocent. Apparently, he'd rescued Sabeara once when she was captive in Severesi. So instead of being subject to the dungeon, like Obsidian had been, he'd graciously been given his freedom in Knadiel, and he'd decided to stick around to help us out in defeating the curse. Lucky me.

"Why do you care, James?" I asked sharply, my tone biting.

"I know something happened between you two on the boat."

I didn't say anything to that. I didn't even know how to admit it to myself, so no way was I going to admit it aloud to him.

"He's dangerous, Sunn," James said, his voice reducing to a worried whisper. His doe eyes, with their childlike blue color, were almost enough to make me crack. But not quite.

"Are you just going to follow me around and keep asking me if I went to the dungeon tonight? Or is there another reason you are following me?"

His jaw clenched, and he sighed, seeing that I wasn't going to be cooperative.

"Are you going to the village?"

"Yes," I answered shortly.

"Then I'll come with you."

"I'm not looking for a lecture. I'm going to the square to think."

"I won't say another word." He pursed his lips together as if to prove he wouldn't bother me anymore.

I sighed and started back on the trail. It was silent as we walked, and I brooded.

I thought going to see Obsidian would break the spell he had over me. That something inside me would see him for what he truly was. A monster, a caged animal that deserved to be locked up for his crimes. But instead, it had only made me miss him more—seeing his face and hearing his voice. Instead of putting to rest the feelings inside me, they had awakened even brighter than before. Now the flame was freshly stoked and blazing anew.

It was one kiss, I tried to tell myself. But it wasn't just the kiss. It was the fact that he'd attempted to save me. That he was suffering, and I knew it. That somewhere deep down, there was a different man than the one he showed the world.

Some masochist side of myself wanted to be the only person who could save him.

I groaned aloud, and James gave me a sideways glance that proved he thought I was crazy. I ignored the look and stormed on to a place I found solace at these late hours.

In the middle of the little village where the people of Aveladon and Ethydon now dwelled, they built an establishment of homes and farms and gradually built up what they once had lost.

We passed by several houses and stores, the windows all dark. The villagers no doubt went in for the night and were sleeping soundly. Then we came upon the pub, the only establishment open at such an hour. A couple of lushed villagers were laughing outside the front doors of the tavern, and I breezed past them to the fountain erected in the middle of the square next to the clocktower. On the weekends, a market was set out in the square where people could trade and sell their goods. But at night, it was empty and quiet. The only sound was the soothing water trickling off the fountain into the coin-strewn water. It was exactly what I needed.

I sat on a bench, and James joined me. We existed in silence for a couple of minutes. My mind wandered to images of Obsidian in his cage, his long hair and black eyes imprinted on my mind.

"I know you think you can redeem him," James whispered, interrupting the silence.

"James," I said.

"Yes?" he answered, the hopefulness in his voice unmistakable.

"Shut up, please."

He sighed, and I wanted to feel bad, but I just didn't have it in me.

"Ever since we've come to this place—" He gestured to the mountains surrounding us on all sides. It was like a giant fortress meant to protect us."You've been acting differently. Your fire is gone, Sunn," he said almost desperately. "I'm worried about you."

"I don't need you to take care of me, James." I wished to take back the words as soon as they left my mouth. The truth was he was my only friend at that moment. Of course I had my family and the Aigoviels, but my parents hadn't been very thrilled with me since the boat incident. When my father had found out that I was missing, he'd gone in search of me. It wasn't until I was found that we were able to send him word that I was safe and in Knadiel with my mother. He hadn't even been able to come to Knadiel to make sure I was alright. He was too busy protecting the Isles from Obscurum and fulfilling his duty to the Sapherine tribe. But I knew he was disappointed in me, and my mother too. I'd worried them sick because of my recklessness. So James was the only person I really felt I wanted to be around at that moment.

He had been there for me since I landed on that wretched ship with Obsidian. He'd stuck by me, and though we hadn't really established it aloud, we were friends. And I was actually really grateful he'd taken it upon himself to watch over me. Because without him, I'd probably do something even more reckless and stupid than going to see Obsidian in the dungeons.

"I'm sorry," I finally said, turning to face him. "I'm just in a. . .weird place."

"I know," he said, reaching out to put a hand on my shoulder. He gave me a comforting squeeze. "And when you are ready to talk about it, I'm here," he said.

I nodded and leaned in unexpectedly to hug him. I don't know what came over me, but for some reason I needed to just be hugged for a moment.

He accepted the embrace and held me tight. I inhaled the scent of him. His cologne reminded me of fall and the forests I used to roam in as a child back in Ethydon.

I was about to pull away when I spotted something over his shoulder. A light in the distance illuminated the dirt road coming towards the village. Soon a group of people could be seen coming down the path. I jumped to my feet and pointed to the group heading toward us, my heart rate accelerating.

"James, look," I said, and he turned to see what I was suddenly so worked up about.

The faces became illuminated in the lamp-lit streets, and that's when I recognized Liony—Shar's sister, leading the caravan back from their journey in Obscurum.

FIVE

SABEARA

We all crowded into the pub. The patrons drinking inside recognized us all immediately, and the room emptied out quickly, giving us our privacy. The bartender hurried to get us drinks as we all settled around a table in the corner of the dim room.

Liony and Rosen had returned. Once Shar told us of their arrival in the village, we immediately left to meet them. Seeing Liony's face after so long was such a relief, tears had filled my eyes.

I sat next to her at the table, and she was still gripping my hand in hers.

"I'm so glad you guys are alright," I said, wiping away the tears that had leaked onto my cheeks.

"I can't tell you how happy I am to be home," Liony said, sniffling. She, too, had tears in her eyes.

"We have lots to tell you," Rosen said. Seeing him again, I was surprised to find that my aggravation towards him hadn't lessened any. His glittering topaz eyes were just as mischievous as before, and I found myself unable to assess him without narrowing my gaze.

Mid and Shar were also at the table, along with Sunn and James who had been out in the village when they'd arrived. They'd been the ones to alert the soldiers in the city to contact Shar.

It was pretty late into the evening, so instead of waking the others, we all gathered in the pub to talk.

The bartender returned with big steins of Lush Fire, Sunn reached across the table for one, but Mid and Shar blocked her attempt.

"Don't even think about it," they both said.

Sunn rolled her eyes at them but folded her arms across her chest obediently.

"So tell us, what happened?" I asked, turning back to Liony. She looked tired, circles under her stormy gray eyes. She looked like she'd been through something dark.

"The plan went very smoothly, actually." Liony's eyes flitted to Rosen, and he nodded at her to continue. I could feel the camaraderie that had been formed between them just by how they looked at each other, but I decided not to dwell on it at the moment and focused on Liony's story.

"We intercepted the Ambassador in her caravan that was going to Obscurum. We managed to subdue her and her men peacefully and took their carriage and other belongings to keep up the facade we'd be maintaining. I pretended to be the Ambassador and Rosen my personal guard."

"She was magnificent," Rosen commented, flashing a sweet smile in Liony's direction.

I glared daggers at him.

Liony took a sip of her drink and continued. "He believed us. For weeks I pretended to be the Ambassador, and it worked. I was able to gain access to obscure parts of the castle and try to discover the king's power. But it took me a while to figure out what his power was because it was so unique," Liony said.

Everyone was on the edge of their seats, listening to her tell her story. Even James stared wide-eyed, waiting to hear what Elysian's power was.

"He isn't affected by anyone's powers," she finally blurted.

"What do you mean? Like he's immune to them?" Mid asked.

"Exactly, no one can affect him."

Silence filled the pub for a moment as this information settled.

"So that would mean he's immune to my illusions then?" Mid asked. "And that he knew all along that the tokens I presented to him back in Obscurum weren't real. He would have known, and he played along?"

A chill erupted down my spine as I thought about Elysian and that day in the throne room when we'd barely escaped. But now we knew he'd let us escape. But why?

"We think he wanted you to get the tokens so that he wouldn't have to. He was planning to make us do all the work, then sweep in once we'd found them and take them from us."

"Then why did Obsidian go in search of the tokens then? If they were intent on waiting till we found them all to strike?" I asked.

"Because Obsidian disobeyed his father," James said. "He wasn't supposed to go in search of the tokens. But he was eager and went after them anyway."

"Have you encountered Obsidian recently?" Liony asked.

"We sort of had a run-in while trying to find the compass," I told her.

"So I'm guessing you must have been able to subdue him then?" Liony asked.

"Ehern, Dusane, and Mid reached the blacksmith in Severesi, and she made a device that we used on Obsidian to keep him from using his powers. He's in the dungeons now," Shar said.

Liony's eyes widened. "And the compass?"

I reached into my cloak pocket, where the compass was always next to me. I pulled it out and showed her the little golden device.

"It wasn't easy to get. We ran into some mermaids too, and it wasn't pretty."

Rosen let out a long whistle. "Sounds like we all have a lot to catch up on."

"But the most important task at hand is getting the cloak of constellations," Liony said.

"The what?" Sunn asked, inserting herself into the conversation suddenly.

"Elysian's power wasn't the only thing we discovered while we were in Obscurum. We found Ennsleon's token."

My jaw dropped open, stunned by this news. "What? You found it?"

"Dusane was right. The dagger wasn't a token. The real token rests on his shoulders. He wears this cloak. It's embroidered with constellations, and he rarely goes anywhere without it. One night I spoke to him about it." She paused, a faraway look stealing into her eyes. "He told me it was the token."

"Do you know what it does then?" Mid asked.

"No, I couldn't manage to figure that part out. I barely managed to get him to admit to me that it was the token."

"We have to go after it," Shar said.

"Don't worry, I have a plan." Liony smiled at her brother, but it was a weak smile tainted by exhaustion. "I caught information about a gathering known as the Dark Fell. It's a private party of sorts for royal guests of the Severesi and Obscurum courts. It's known as the Dark Fell because it resides in the Fell Mountain.

"Inside the mountain?" I asked, confused.

"Its location is only known to those who are invited, and it's very exclusive. I think if we can manage to get inside, we could steal the cloak from Elysian. Going back to Obscurum is too dangerous. His security at the castle is uncanny. At this party, he won't be as heavily guarded, and not to mention, he won't be expecting any of us to show up there."

Liony's eyes brightened, and she looked at Rosen with realization in her eyes.

"And now that we have Obsidian in our grasp, I think I know exactly how we're going to get an invitation."

SIX

SUNN

I followed the others down to the dungeons. James and I took the back of the line. I worried if I said anything, they might send me back upstairs. So I remained quiet, slipping into the shadows to observe. I glanced at James, and he glanced back at me with a worried look.

Sabeara took the lead with Liony, and they reached Obsidian's cage first. Mid, Shar, and the man named Rosen I'd never seen before, stood protectively behind them, ready to defend at any moment if needed.

I stayed back, not wanting Obsidian to see me, in case he was reminded of the encounter we'd had only an hour before, and thought to tell my uncle about it. I wasn't about to get into trouble for seeing him.

"Obsidian," Sabeara said, voice stern. He barely stirred. The only indication he'd even heard her was the soft shift of his inky black hair, barely visible in the darkness.

"We've come to talk to you about a negotiation," Liony said. Her sweet voice was a chilling contrast to the bleak darkness.

"And what could you possibly offer me?" I wondered if it was the first time he'd actually responded to them because Sabeara's soft gasp could be heard.

"Well, I've recently been in contact with your father, and he mentioned something about a Dark Fell party," Liony blurted.

Obsidian laughed huskily "And why would I help you get to the Dark Fell? So you can steal my father's cloak?"

"So you know about Ennsleon's cloak?" Liony asked cooly.

"I know lots of things you don't, sweetheart." A chill ran up my spine, hearing him use that term of endearment with Liony. Something so endearing became vile and vicious on his tongue.

"Take us to the party, help us get the cloak, and we will set you free," Sabeara suddenly blurted.

Obsidian laughed again, and it took him a second to get himself under control.

"I'm sorry for laughing. It's just, why would I ever agree to help you? You think I'd be stupid enough to trust you?"

"Fine. Then we will leave you here to rot away and find the cloak by ourselves," Sabeara growled and turned around to leave, but Liony laid a hand on her arm, stopping her.

"Let's not be hasty," Liony said gently. "What is it you want, Dark Prince?"

Silence filled the dungeon.

"Tell me what you want, and we will give it to you in exchange for your help," Liony said gently, as if she were coaxing the answer out of him. No doubt she was using her persuasive powers on him.

I couldn't help it then. I shifted where I stood, having been standing pressed against the wall for so long my calves were burning. As I fidgeted, Obsidian caught my slight movement in the dim light of the lanterns, and our eyes met.

His dark soulless expression froze me in place, and I took in a sharp breath.

"What I want, you can't give me," he said in a guttural voice. As if he were struggling to say the words.

"Anything is possible," Liony urged.

"So you can make the sun shine in the pits of hell?"

"I've never been one to turn down a challenge," Liony replied easily.

He chuckled, a derisive, cynical laugh, then finally looked away, breaking eye contact with me. I could finally breathe again, and I leaned against the wall to find support for my suddenly feeble knees.

"You really want to risk trusting me after I kidnapped Embrosine? After killing so many of your friends?"

"Why did you take her anyway? What did you have to gain?" Mid chimed in, the anger behind his tone evident.

"To assess the competition, of course. My father knew you'd come for her. And he wanted to see what he was up against. How many tokens you'd managed to secure."

I could almost see Shar fuming in the darkness. But he somehow remained silent, not egging Obsidian on.

"We heard your father was waiting for us to get all the tokens before striking. So why didn't you wait?" Rosen said.

"Because who waits to have all the power in the world? Do you know the absolute glory me and my father could possess if we retrieved the tokens?"

The silence that filled the room must have been answer enough.

"Don't tell me you don't know the consequences of your

potential losses?" Obsidian asked, sounding shocked.

"We know Elysian will become a very powerful Stone-Hearted if he manages to get the tokens. And the rest of us will be left without powers, subject to his tyranny."

"And he can give away some of that power to me. As he has promised. We will both rule side by side. The most powerful Stone-Hearted beings to ever exist."

"Will he want to share that glory now that you've disobeyed him?" Shar asked, speaking for the first time.

"My father will forgive me easily. I'm too strong an asset for him to lose."

"Not anymore you're not," Liony said.

And that's when I knew we had him. I could almost taste the victory in the air. We'd won. Obsidian would have to help us because if he didn't gain his freedom, his father would have no use for him as a shackled, powerless being. And I had a feeling Elysian didn't spend much time or energy on useless things.

"Fine, I'll help you," Obsidian relented.

"Great. We will leave tomorrow," Liony said happily.

"Getting inside won't be an issue because I have an open invitation. But my father rarely takes off the cloak; when he does, it's almost impossible to steal."

"Why?"

"My father's guardian Solvester has this unique ability to sense Stone-Hearted. Even if they are hundreds of miles away from him. So you won't be able to get near the cloak without Solvetser knowing you are there."

"Unless we take someone that isn't Stone-Hearted," I said.

Everyone in the room suddenly turned around as I spoke for the first time, and James beside me made a little noise of protest.

The shocked eyes in the room told me they hadn't known I'd followed them down here.

"I can go, and Solvetser won't be able to track my whereabouts throughout the Dark Fell party."

"Over my dead body," Shar growled.

"I second that. No way am I allowing you to go with us on this mission, Sunn," Mid said.

I could feel Obsidian's heated gaze on my face. He looked just as angry as Shar and Mid for my suggestion. I dared look into his eyes, hoping he'd see my determination.

"I've dealt with him before. I was on a ship with him for several weeks and survived for Spirits Sake. Let me go, please."

"She's got a point," Liony said. Shar and Mid glared daggers at Liony.

"I usually escort women to these parties. I don't go alone. Mind you, they are feeble creatures that follow me like wounded puppies, but it just might work to have her on my arm. That way everyone will think she's nothing more than my plaything." That stung, and he knew it. I felt my breath hitch as he smiled wickedly at me.

"Exactly. Then when I'm the one to get the cloak, I will be least expected," I said through gritted teeth.

"Sunn," James whispered beside me in a warning tone. Obviously, he hated this idea as well.

Shar and Mid looked at Obsidian and seemed almost ready to strangle him... and me for even suggesting the plan.

"Alright, so Sunn will come with us. We will be there to keep an eye on her throughout the party. Though it's risky, it might be our best option," Sabeara finally said.

"Ehren—" Shar protested.

"Shar, this is our only chance at getting the cloak," she said, exasperated, like she didn't like the idea either but didn't have a choice. The two of them must have become close friends because Shar rarely listened to anyone when he was upset.

"Fine, but if she comes into contact with any danger, if there's even a chance she's going to get hurt—"

"We will pull her from the mission, I promise. We will get her out of there if things start to look bad. I swear," Sabeara said.

Everyone was silent for a moment as the plan was contemplated.

"So it's settled then," Liony said, gesturing to one of the dungeon guards. "Release him."

SEVEN

SABEARA

I packed the last of my things into the satchel I'd take on our journey. I was taking the amulet, the compass, and the daggers Shar had given me for my birthday. We had all agreed in our meeting to leave behind Wesoltinece's hammer just so we weren't putting all of the tokens in jeopardy. It wasn't much, but it would have to do. I'd just slung the leather bag over my shoulder when Oli walked in.

"Hey, I wanted to talk to you before you left."

"Sorry I'm leaving again," I said, looking at my best friend, feeling a longing hit my chest. When was the last time we'd spent time together? We used to be so close, but now it felt like we rarely got a chance to talk.

"I'm sorry I can't come with you," he said, concern furrowing his brow.

"Jasper needs you," I said, reaching out to touch his shoulder. "Knadiel needs you."

"I know," he said softly, the worry lines creasing his forehead not disappearing.

"What else is on your mind?" I asked. "You're not worried I'm going to get hurt, are you?" I raised an eyebrow. "I have plenty of people watching over me, Oli."

"That's not what I'm worried about," he bit his lip, and I could see he was struggling to say what was on his mind.

"What is it then?"

"It's about you and Dusane," he said, and I had a gut feeling I knew where this was headed. "I just want to make sure that you two are being—careful," he said, the insinuation behind his tone making my cheeks flush all shades of red.

"Gross, Oli. Didn't you already try and give me this talk when I was like, what, sixteen?" I back away from him, a look of disgust taking over my face.

"Don't push me away. I just know you and your sister don't talk about these things that much, and with your mom gone and now your father—" he let out an exasperated sigh, "I just want to make sure someone is looking out for you."

"I appreciate that, but I assure you, I don't need to talk about anything—" I looked away for him, unable to meet his eyes. He'd been the one to give me the talk when I was a teenager. I was pretty isolated, and Oli was the closest person in my life other than Jasper at the time. So without really thinking about it, he'd been the one I'd asked about intimate relationships. It had been an awkward conversation, and I hadn't looked him in the eye for a month after that. But I was grateful he'd told me.

"So you are taking precautions," he said slowly, and I resisted the urge to put my hands over my ears to shut out the conversation.

"I'm still a virgin, Oli. So there is literally nothing for you to be concerned about," I said. And he blushed, speechless too, it seemed.

"Well, okay then," he said, rubbing a hand across his chin. "I feel a little better now, letting you go off on a trip with him."

"I've been on trips with him many times," I pointed out.

"But not one where you two were a couple."

"You're ridiculous," I rolled my eyes, but a small smile remained on my face. I couldn't help but feel greatful that Oli was still looking out for me.

~

I walked out to the front steps of the castle to see everyone gathered to leave. Obsidian had been let out of his dungeon under the careful watch of Rosen and Rouix. He was free of chains which was unnerving, but we all concluded if he tried to run, it would be pointless because the only people that could open the cuff were me, Dusane, Mid, or Nixie. And because none of us would be releasing him, running would be futile. He'd only get his freedom if he helped us get the cloak. And even then, I hoped it wouldn't come to that.

Obsidian's dark black eyes followed me as I traveled down the steps to Diablo. He sat atop a white horse between Rouix and Rosen. Flanking him on either side with their hands on the hilts of their weapons, ready to subdue him at any moment. I tried my best not to shudder at the sight of him. Obsidian was eerie in a way that brought nightmares into daylight. Remembering what he'd done to Conland and other innocent people flashed into my head, and I gritted my teeth. I would just have to bear his presence for this mission. I didn't have another choice.

Those coming on the trip were Mid, Dusane, Shar, Rosen,

Rouix, Liony, Obsidian, Sunn, James, and me. The others were staying behind to keep an eye on things.

I mounted Diablo and Dusane came up beside me on Elesame.

"You alright?" he asked me, and the sight of him brought an instant sense of relief.

"Yes, just nervous about this whole thing," I admitted.

"We'll get the cloak," Dusane assured me, and I nodded but was still not entirely convinced. Something told me that bringing Obsidian on a trip to capture his father's cloak wouldn't go without some sort of obstacles.

Just then, Sunn came down the steps, her mother beside her with James trailing them. The young man was about Sunn's age. I was shocked to find him on the same ship as them when we'd found them out at sea. James seemed to have taken a protective role over Sunn, which I was grateful for. Sunn was just like the type to get herself into trouble and could use someone watching over her.

Embrosine was saying something to Sunn in an earnest voice while Sunn tried her best to calm her mother.

"I'll be fine, Mom. I promise. Mid and Shar are coming with me. They won't let anything happen to me."

"I know, but I still worry," I heard Embrosine say.

Embrosine was not keen on allowing her daughter to come on the trip with us to help us get the cloak, but Sunn was the only person in the castle without her powers yet willing to accept the challenge. I wasn't surprised by her bravery. She'd always been feisty. Not to mention she survived on a ship with Obsidian as long as she did. There had to be something inside her, a stubborn streak that helped keep her alive. We needed that tenacity now, the kind that refused to let evil win.

Sunn hugged her mother goodbye and then went to mount Ghost. Mid was already waiting for her and helped her onto Ghost's back.

Liony was the last to come down the steps. Dressed in a beautiful brown cloak with a fur scarf and hat, she grinned at the group of us. The tension was thick, and like a lightning bolt striking through a static-filled cloud, she spoke, breaking the silence.

"Everyone ready?" Liony asked.

Not even close, I thought. Not even close.

~

We traveled well into the night and into the next morning before we stopped for a rest. A feeling of awkwardness penetrated the air as we prepared the tents and set up a fire. The only person that seemed unbothered by the situation we were in was Liony. She whistled sweetly as she worked, and I couldn't help but notice Rosen smile at her from across the camp. Something had definitely happened between them, and I mentally made a note to ask Liony about it when I had the chance.

"Are you sleeping in my tent?" Dusane asked me, startling me from my thoughts.

"You scared me," I squeaked, putting a hand to my racing heart.

"Sorry," he said, leaning against the tree and smiling flirtatiously at me. I narrowed my eyes at him.

"I'm sleeping in Liony's tent," I said after catching my breath.

"How disappointing," Dusane pouted playfully and wound his arm around my waist. I would have normally welcomed his display of affection, except I could feel Mid's gaze on us from across the camp, and I nervously laughed, pulling from his grasp.

"You better be careful, Captain. You'll distract me from my mission." I teased.

He smiled knowingly and glanced at Mid for a moment, who was now helping Shar with the fire.

"I see," he leaned in and pressed a quick kiss to my cheek. "I'll just go help Rosen then."

I gave him a thankful smile as he retreated. It wasn't that I was ashamed of our relationship. I just didn't want to add salt to an already open wound. And Mid didn't need anything else on his plate right now, with all the problems with his powers changing and his heart turning gold.

I finished setting up the tent and then returned to the fire. Obsidian was stationed between Rosen and Shar, and he eyed me as I took a seat beside Rouix.

"Have you ever been to the Dark Fell?" I asked Rouix quietly.

She shook her head.

"No, but I've heard stories." She didn't elaborate.

Rouix was usually quiet, but she seemed almost anxious that night. She stared into the fire with her silvery gaze and fidgeted with her fingers in her lap.

"You alright?" I asked her, sensing that something was off.

"Fine," she said quickly. "Just anxious to get this over with."

I nodded in agreement and turned back to the flame.

"Anyone for some bread and cheese?" Liony asked, coming over and carrying a large loaf with a buttery yellow cheese block.

"Or an apple?" Mid said, his hands glowing a bright golden color and illuminating the darkness.

I watched in fascination as a tiny seedling grew from rich earthy soil. A small trunk appeared, and then branches and then thick leafy foliage. A bud bloomed, and then several apples were fully ready for harvest before our very eyes.

It happened in mere seconds. It was the first time I'd seen his live creations.

Rosen didn't even flinch. He reached for one of the crimson fruits and bit into its flesh with a hum of satisfaction.

I could feel Mid's gaze, assessing my reaction to his new powers. I forced myself to stare at the little tree while Liony passed out bread and cheese. I couldn't look him in the eye for some reason.

We all ate in silence after that, and to avoid the awkwardness, I quickly took my leave after finishing my food and headed for the tent. I took one last glance back at the fire and could see Dusane's eyes following me.

"I love you," he mouthed. And I could barely make out his slight mouth movement in the darkness.

I mouthed it back, my heart warming knowing that despite being not so openly affectionate with each other at the moment, he was still there. Protecting me at a distance.

EIGHT

SUNN

After eating our small bread and cheese dinner, I walked over to the tent I was sharing with Mid and crawled inside. I laid down on the blankets and replayed the moment by the fire in my head. James had luckily been the one to catch my fall, but I had seen Obsidian flinch, almost like he would've tried to catch me. Would he have caught me?

It was thoughts like these that continued to make me question my own sanity.

Wind shook the tent, and I could see the shadow of the fire behind the canvas as it flickered, and I shivered deeper into my cloak. We were somewhere in the thick forest between Knadiel and Severesi, and it was starting to get colder the closer we got to the ice kingdom. I already began to miss the warm, neutral weather of Knadiel that was so pleasant.

Mid came crawling through the tent flap a couple of minutes later. He shuffled around a little bit before kneeling beside me and carefully pulling the blanket over my shoulders.

"Uncle Mid, I can tuck myself into bed, you know." I looked at him, raising a brow.

He looked down at me; it was almost like he was seeing me for the first time as an almost adult woman.

"Right, sorry," he blushed and climbed into his side of the blankets. "I forget how old you are now."

"Almost eighteen," I reminded him.

He shook his head at that realization as if he could shake the thought away.

"I used to sing you to sleep when you were a kid. It was our little ritual, do you remember?" he asked.

"I remember," I said, and the memories of his melodic voice whisking me away into dreams was something I'd always cherish. I'd never doubted that Mid adored and loved me. He was my protector when my father wasn't around. But not only that, my friend and partner in crime when I wanted to steal some sweets from the castle kitchen.

"Time has passed by so quickly," he murmured to himself. His head hit the pillow, but his eyes remained open. He looked at me, his green and red eyes assessing me with an expression of nostalgia.

"I'm sorry things haven't been easy for you these past couple of years, Sunn. Leaving Ethydon and being taken hostage on an enemy ship—" he sighed, his eyes now pained. "All of us wanted to keep you from this mess, but we failed."

I shook my head at him. "You can't protect me from everything."

"I know."

"Then all of you need to stop trying."

He pursed his lips, assessing me with knowing eyes. "You've

always been unusually brave and stubborn. It's a very dangerous combination."

"It's in my blood. "I smirked at him, and he chuckled.

"I won't argue with that. Now, get some sleep. We have a long journey ahead of us."

I obeyed and closed my eyes, falling into a dream about a pair of soulless ebony eyes.

~

Before the sun was even up the following day, Mid urged me awake, letting me know the others were packing up. When I stepped groggily out of the tent, James came over to me. My mind was foggy from sleep as I rubbed sleepily at my eyes. I was unsuccessfully tying my cloak around my neck when James took over and helped me.

"Are you alright?" he asked me.

"I'm fine, just tired is all," I admitted, while another yawn escaped me.

"We will be in Severesi territory soon," he said. "Hopefully, only another day or so of traveling."

"Oh goody," I said in a monotone voice filled with sarcasm.

He gave me a smile and gestured towards Ghost and Mid, who I'd be riding with.

"Here, let me help you up," he gave me a leg up onto Ghost, then returned to his own steed towards the back of the caravan.

The camp was cleaned up quickly, and before I knew it, we were on the path again, heading towards the Dark Fell Mountains.

We traveled all day. And I didn't think it could get colder, but I'd been wrong. The temperature dropped more and more with each mile we conquered, and soon it was snowing. Crisp snowflakes floated around us, lightly dusting the forest floor and our clothes. I shivered, burying my gloved hands into Ghost's fur to find extra warmth.

Mid didn't say much as we rode, and neither did anyone else in the group. Except for a couple of directional conversations to ensure we were on the right path, it was mostly silent. And despite being so cold and tired, my eyes stayed glued to the horse Obsidian was riding on. Rosen and Shar were on either side of him, alert and ready for anything that might happen. Obsidian never tried anything, though, not even a flicker of suspicious activity. He simply rode in between the two men, calmly assessing the trail ahead, his expression emotionless.

At one point, I think he could feel my stare on him because he glanced back for a brief second, catching my eye before he quickly turned away again. Just the tiny glimpse of his dark onyx eyes sent my heart fluttering and my cheeks warming. Why was I suddenly imagining what it would feel like to be riding on that horse with him, wrapped in his arms, pressed against his chest—

"Let's stop here."

My immoral thoughts were abruptly cut off when Shar called the group to a stop.

It was getting dark again, which meant setting up camp once more.

I held back a groan as we dismounted and resettled our camp.

With everyone's help, things went faster than anticipated, and soon, a fire was blazing. I joined James, curling up beside him. Naturally, he rested his arm on the log behind me. His extra warmth helped to ease the severe cold that had yet to leave my bones.

"Thanks," I said quietly to him.

He simply nodded and gave me a soft smile.

"We need to discuss our plan for when we reach the mountain," Dusane suddenly said.

Everyone around the fire murmured their agreement.

"Does anyone have any ideas on how we should go about this?" Sabeara pressed, and no one said a word for many moments.

I couldn't help but glance in Obsidian's direction, he caught my gaze, but his expression remained impassive. I knew he must have some idea of what we were about to get ourselves into. I mentally urged him to speak up.

"We will need to split into groups," Obsidian finally said. All eyes turned to him, and the tension could suddenly be felt gripping the air around us. It was the first time he'd said a word since leaving Knadiel.

"A group will stay back with our belongings. Then the rest of us will go into the castle, and from there, we will need to split up. My father will no doubt be wearing the cloak. So the goal will be to get him to take it off during the party, and hopefully, we can steal it."

"How will we get him to take off his cloak exactly?" Rosen asked. He was sitting beside Liony, and I noticed on his arm a flicker of a golden tattoo. It looked similar to the Envorydian tattoo on Sabeara's arm. I wondered where he came from and who this soldier was. I still hadn't quite figured out who all of Sabeara's new friends were, but she was obviously involved with the one named Dusane. He was an intimidating individual, all brooding and dark. But Sabeara seemed very close with him, the two sitting beside each other, hands clasped. I wondered what happened between her and Mid, but my mother wouldn't elaborate when I asked for details. It seemed all of my family still saw me as a little girl and didn't want me privy to family drama. I'm sure I'll figure it out one day, I thought.

"I will worry about getting my father to remove his cloak. But the rest of you will need to watch where he places it once he removes it."

"How will we do that?" Mid asked.

"The ballroom is a circle," Obsidian drew a line in the snow to demonstrate the layout of the Night Fell party. "You will all station yourselves in the upper balconies. So you'll be able to discreetly look down on the party while staying out of sight."

"I thought you said your father's auxiliary could sense Stone-Hearted," Sabeara said.

"He can. But you'll be surrounded by other Stone-Hearted, and he can merely feel a Stone-Hearted's presence. As long as you stay out of sight of my father's aid Sylvester, you should be able to remain undetected."

"Then what?" Rosen pressed.

"Once I get my father to remove the cloak, I'm sure Sylvester will take it to my father's rooms. Once we've found which room he's in, we will send Sunn inside, and she will grab the cloak undetected because she's still human."

I could see Shar's disapproving shake of his head at the idea. He obviously still didn't want me going in alone to get the cloak.

"Alright, so after I've gotten the cloak, then what?" I asked.

"We meet up at a designated location outside of the mountain," Obsidian said.

"I don't like this," Mid suddenly blurted.

"Me either," Shar chimed in.

"Well, it's already decided," Liony said, glaring at her brother and Mid. "We don't have another choice. We need that cloak."

"I can handle myself," I said, and Mid looked about to argue, but then Sabeara spoke again.

"How do we know you won't sabotage the whole operation?" Sabeara asked Obsidian coldly.

"You don't," he said, staring her dead in the eyes with little to no emotion.

"He can't use his powers without one of us releasing him from the bracelet," Dusane reminded Sabeara. "If he wants his freedom, he needs to help us with this."

I still didn't know how they were planning on letting Obsidian free. Once he helped us, would they simply release him? Would he turn on us when he was free and kill everyone? I instantly pushed the thought away. Something inside of me had faith it wouldn't happen. I don't know how it would all turn out, but I had to hope he wouldn't walk away.

I looked across the fire and caught his gaze. Obsidian's dark expression bore into mine, and I felt something in my heart twist almost painfully. The thought crossed my mind faster than I could stop it. I wanted him. Needed him.

Don't leave. Please. I thought to him. I wondered if he could see the desperation in my eyes. Feel my need for him to stay after all of this was over—after he was free.

I watched his jaw clench, a sharp shadow in the firelight, and he looked away, breaking the connection.

I let out a breath I was holding inside my chest.

"Alright," Sabeara sighed as if she hated the risk they were taking trusting him. "We will go with your plan."

"As I said before, Sunn will have to attend the party with me," Obsidian reminded them.

I heard Shar make a strangled noise in the back of his throat across the fire.

"If you so much as think of touchin—" Mid threatened.

"Mid," I glared at him. "For once, stop trying to protect me and think about the good of the Stone-Hearted people. If I have to act like a mindless plaything on his arm at the party to get the cloak, so be it. But I can handle myself, and all of you need to stop worrying about me."

Mid's jaw clenched at my reprimand. I knew he was still seeing me as a young girl, his niece that he'd always protected, and I inwardly begged him to let up.

"She's right, Mid," Liony said, laying a hand on his shoulder. "We need her to do this."

"When we arrive, we'll need to find clothes suitable for the event. I think we could find a guest room and borrow clothes," Obsidian said, ignoring our little dispute.

"You mean steal," Rouix said.

"Whatever helps you sleep at night, darling." Obsidian flashed a wicked smirk at Rouix, and she merely rolled her eyes.

"We will do what we have to do," Sabeara said. "Whatever it takes. We are getting that token."

NINE

SABEARA

We passed the city of Iradence the next day, barely glimpsing its front gates and crystal city inside. We kept as much to the outskirts as possible. We passed miners making their way into the city, and I was once again hit with the realization of how many people were suffering. I hoped we could somehow abolish the system when we lifted the curse, defeat Severesi and Obscurum completely and give these innocent people a better way of life.

Once past the central hub, we traveled for another several hours, and that's when the temperature began to change. A weird mix of sand and snow began to be made present like we were right on the border of Obscurum and Severesi.

"Odd, isn't it?" Rosen asked, coming up beside me with a smirk on his face.

"How can the snow exist here?" It was starting to get warm again.

"Your guess is as good as mine," he winked, and I rolled my

eyes at him. I still didn't trust him, even after he'd returned from his mission with Liony. He and Liony had indeed bonded over their trip to Obscrum, but my feelings for him hadn't improved. There was just something about him. Something that told me he had secrets he was keeping.

"The Dark Fell mountains are directly on the border of the two kingdoms. The weather is going to be unpredictable. We could hit a snowstorm or even a sandstorm." Shar interrupted our conversation, and I felt an anxiousness similar to how I felt when invading the Obscurum castle nearly a year ago.

It was that evening, just as the sun was setting, the mountain came into view. It was so vast we could see it from miles away. It appeared more like a volcano than a mountain. It was made of black rock, with little to no foliage on it. Half the mountain was dusted in snow, the other half barren and scorched from the Obscurum heat.

"The party is being held inside there?" I asked

"There's a mansion within it," Shar said, not elaborating further.

We set up camp in an expanse of trees that would keep us from the view of passing travelers to the Dark Fell. We decided against a fire; instead, everyone retreated to their tents to rest up before the next day when we'd be going inside the mountain.

I lay next to Liony that night and could barely see anything in the darkness. But I did catch a small sliver of her gray eyes. She was looking at me expectantly.

"What?" I asked her, seeing the expectancy in her expression. Why did I have a feeling I knew where this was headed?

"You are mad about Rosen and me," she stated.

I opened my mouth to protest, but nothing came out. I closed my mouth again in defeat. I couldn't lie to her.

"I'm not mad," was all I managed to say. "He just gives me a bad feeling." I remembered the galloway fight. The way he turned things gold and that wicked smile on his face. My thoughts also revisited the time he mentioned a seventh stone called Amberidium. And then a place called Pendilore.

"He's not what you think, Ehren," Liony insisted, her persuasive voice smooth and gentle. She could try, but it wasn't going to work. My discomfort for Rosen ran pretty deep.

"He's a rogue Envorydian. Do you know what that is Liony?" I asked.

"Isn't that blue-eyed captain of yours also a past rouge?" she asked, and my mouth fell open. How did she know that?

"Rosen told me," she said as if seeing my confusion. "So, as you can attest, not all rouges are terrible people."

"I don't trust him," I said.

"I've spent a lot of time with him recently." Liony looked lost in thought for a moment, remembering something from their journey together. "He's a good man," she said. "If you can't trust him, trust me."

I sighed and forced myself to consider that Liony had different knowledge about Rosen after spending several months with him. Maybe there was more to him than just being a rouge. Didn't mean I had to find out for myself, but I could at least give Liony the benefit of the doubt.

"I do trust you," I said and reached out to find her hand in the darkness. She gave my fingers a little squeeze.

"Goodnight, Ehren,"

"Goodnight, Liony."

The next night everyone was on edge, eager to start our mission into the mountain. The entire camp was strung with nervous energy. It was decided that Liony and James would stay back with the camp while the rest of us headed into the castle. From there, Obsidian and Sunn would split off into the ballroom while we surrounded the ballroom on the lookout, waiting for the cloak to be removed so we could locate where the king's assistant, Sylvester, would take it.

I hated sending Sunn into the ballroom alone with Obsidian, but I had to remember that he couldn't really hurt her, not with his powers at least, and we would be watching her the entire time, so if anything happened, we would be able to rescue her.

Rouix had passed us all our cloaks for disguises, and I was now wearing a black Obscurum cloak. Some of the others wore white to represent Severesi.

"Alright, let's go. The party is about to start in an hour," Shar finally broke the silence, and without saying anything else, we all gathered our things and started to exit the small expanse of trees we'd been protected in for the last two nights.

I watched from the corner of my eye as Sunn said goodbye to her friend James.

"Just be careful with him," James told her. "He can be unpredictable."

"I know, James. Don't worry about me. I can handle him," Sunn said confidently.

I wasn't so confident she could and worried her childlike courage was going to get her hurt. But then again, she was only a couple years younger than me. Seeing her so grown up was odd because I still pictured her as a young teenager, riding off on a wild stallion that I had to rescue her from back in Aveladon. But we didn't have much choice in the matter at this point because no one else was still human.

I sighed and turned back around to see Dusane holding his hand out to me.

"Ready?" he asked me. I nodded and placed my hand in his, letting the feeling of our fingers entwining relax me a little.

It was a half-hour journey from where we were camped to the front steps of the mountain. It was a rocky journey up the mountainscape. And the lanterns on the path were the only thing illuminating the darkness. The sun had gone down hours ago. Other Stone-Hearted attending the party fell into steps behind us, and we could hear their excited chatter as we journeyed up the mountain's path to the front doors.

When we reached the entrance, we were greeted with huge metal doors now wide open, revealing a long red carpet leading into a vast foyer with massive chandeliers. We could hear music coming from inside. Obsidian had taken the lead, and when the guards asked for his name, he simply said, "Obsidian Demesne, with King Elysian. These are my friends."

The guards immediately stepped aside to let us through, and I could hear my heart pounding in my ears as we passed inside. I worried they might stop us, but they didn't even glance in our direction after Obsidian announced his presence.

The Dark Fell mountain was almost exactly as I imagined it. Brooding, dark, and reeking of an expensive luxury that no doubt was built with blood. The rich and powerful of the Obscurum and Seversi society dwelled here, and I could feel it. We were on enemy territory.

Dusane squeezed my hand again, and I was grateful to have him by my side.

The room was draped in red curtains and rugs, golden vases,

and elaborate paintings decorated the walls and tables. Plush velvet couches were adorned with guests seated and already drinking Lush Fire as they chatted. I could hear the music coming from the ballroom as we neared.

Obsidian slowed to a halt about a hundred feet from the ballroom doors.

"We split now," Obsidian said under his breath

No one moved for a moment.

"Hurt her. And I will kill you," Shar growled.

Obsidian looked at Shar as he took hold of Sunn's arm, a smirk threatening at his lips. "She's safe with me."

My stomach churned at his words. I didn't trust him. I could only pray to the spirits this didn't end badly.

"I'll be fine," Sunn quickly said, glaring at Obsidian for taunting Shar.

"If something goes wrong, we will stop the operation and get you out," Mid assured her.

"It won't come to that. Now go." Sunn urged them to disperse, and together we split separate ways.

We all followed Shar down another hallway, taking the flight of stairs up to the second floor that would allow us to look down on the balcony below. I couldn't help but look behind me a couple times as we climbed the steps, worried someone might be following us.

"Relax, Envorydian, no one knows we are here," Dusane said under his breath beside me.

I nodded and forced myself to face forward again.

We finished climbing the last steps, and the ballroom came into view. I looked down over the balcony's edge, leaning against the twirling, ornate banister. From up here, we could see the people in gowns twirling and dancing to the band of musicians.

The eerily beautiful violin song only added to my anxiety as I gazed around the stunning room filled with chatter and mingling. It was all black and white cloaks. Each of them had hearts of silver and gold, a couple with violet or blue. This was for the elite. The only people without such colored hearts were the servants around the room, passing out food or Lush Fire. My eyes took in the entirety of the Dark Fell until I finally found the throne at one end of the floor. My heart stopped for a moment, and I realized no matter how many times I saw him, I would be afraid. Seated in a massive chair draped in velvet crimson was King Elysian.

TEN

SUNN

We didn't go into the ballroom right away. Instead, Obsidian began leading me down another hallway and up a flight of stairs.

"Where are we going? I thought we were supposed to go into the ballroom?" I asked.

"Dressed like that?" Obsidian gestured to the grungy clothes I'd been wearing on the journey, only marginally covered by my white cloak.

"You need to dress the part if we are going to pull this off," Obsidian said.

We roamed down a hall with doors until Obsidian chose one, pushing it open tentatively to see if anyone was inside. Once he found it empty, he hurried inside and motioned me to come in after him.

We were abruptly bathed in darkness. I couldn't see anything except for the shadowed outline of the furniture. I heard Obsidian fumbling around for something then suddenly, a soft glow illuminated the room. He'd lit a lantern on one of the bedside tables.

It was a guest bedroom. Someone was obviously staying in for the party. A lady's purse rested on the bed, and a man's coat hung over one of the chairs by the vanity table.

Obsidian didn't waste any time. He hurried to the closet and pulled out one of the suits to change into. He undid his cloak, threw it onto the floor, and then started for the buttons on his shirt.

I found myself frozen in place, unsure of what I should do.

His fingers paused on the button he was undoing—already halfway down his chest. He must have seen my hesitation.

"Here, put this on." He ripped a dress off the hangar nearest him and threw it at me. I caught the silky purple fabric just before it could hit the floor.

"Is there nowhere else I can change?" I asked nervously, looking around the room and finding that the closet was definitely too small to change inside of. I was trapped.

"Sunn, just take your clothes off," he growled. Just as he said this, his shirt fell into a heap on the floor.

My cheeks flushed twenty shades of scarlet.

I'd seen him shirtless briefly on the ship, but it had been a small glimpse. He wasn't stocky, but tall and lanky. Lean muscles banded down his chest and stomach, the sharp angle in his hip bones jutting out dangerously. He was so pale, but it was oddly beautiful on him. The stark contrast of his pearl skin and dark hair was enough to make me dizzy.

He reached for the waistband of his pants next and I was just quick enough to look away as he dropped them to the floor. I waited a minute before turning back around to find him thankfully dressed again and buttoning up his suit coat.

"Sunn, what are you waiting for?" he asked impatiently. When I still couldn't find the will to move, he stormed across the room towards me, and I instinctively took several steps back from him.

"Will you at least turn around?" I asked, my voice failing me and coming out as a whisper. *Where was my courage? Spirits, I needed to be lushed to do this,* I thought. *Someone, please get me a drink,*

"It's nothing I haven't already seen before," he smirked wickedly, sending my heart into even more erratic beats.

I tried to protest, but then the wall hit my back, and I stilled.

He reached me seconds later, his fingers finding the tassels of my cloak and untying them. The white fabric fell to the floor in a heap, and I felt my heart stop.

"Obsidian," I whispered.

"I'm not afraid to undress you, Sunn. So either you do it, or I will. We don't have much time."

"And I'm not afraid to punch you, so back off." I glared and finally found the willpower to shove his hands away from me. The glimmer in his eyes blazed as if he liked that I was fighting him.

I hurried to undo the buttons on my shirt, but my hands shook with his dark gaze on me.

He sighed and turned around, finally allowing me privacy.

Quickly, while he was being vaguely gentlemanly, I changed out of my clothes and managed to slip the dress on. It had buttons going up the back though, and I could only get two or three of them by myself.

"I got it."

I jumped when I suddenly felt his fingers come into contact with my bare back.

Gradually he started to button up the back of my dress, and I struggled to find my breath for a moment.

I forced myself not to speak. But I wanted to beg him to keep touching me. To turn me around and kiss me. But it was extremely wrong for me to want that. Finally, his fingers left my skin, and I was set free from his touch.

"The party is in the main hall. Follow me," Obsidian was already heading for the door, and I hurried after him.

The gown was a bit big on me, the sides not super snug and the hem a bit long. But it would have to do for the time being. I just picked up the skirt to walk better and hoped I wouldn't trip in front of everyone.

We entered the dimly lit hallway again and traveled down three flights of stairs towards the ballroom. The buzz of chatter could be heard as we got closer, indicating where the party was being held. The dimly lit hallway eventually revealed two guards at a grand entrance into the ballroom, and my heart rate increased as Obsidian halted us in the shadows. He was staring at the double doors going into the ballroom. Light cascaded into the dark hallway. Once we passed over that threshold, there was no going back.

"Are you ready?" he asked me.

"I think so."

"You'll be acting as my date to this party," he reminded me.

"I know that," I said snappily.

Obsidian's black eyes bore into mine, and I thought I saw a slight hint of reluctance in his eyes. Like maybe he really didn't want to do this. This would help him gain his freedom. This shouldn't be hard for him, I thought.

"I don't think you have even the slightest idea of who I am to become behind those doors," he said suddenly, and the comment shocked me. Was he warning me?

"Show me your worst." I dared.

~

He took my hand and laid it on his arm so he could escort me. I could feel how tense he was as we walked toward the ballroom doors together. He stared straight ahead, jaw clenched, his emotions not wavering in the slightest.

I could tell he was concentrating, and I couldn't help but feel nervous about what awaited us when we entered the party. What would it be like to act as the woman on his arm? What facade would he show these people?

But I realized I wouldn't be acting when we were out there. I wanted to be near him. I wanted to talk with him and have him twirl me around on his arm. Which made me feel even more sickened with myself. What was wrong with me?

I stole another glance at Obsidian and admired his long dark locks, falling across his forehead into his soulless black eyes that were more beautiful than any night sky. I took in his gold-trimmed suit, black cloak, and glowing golden heart and felt more of my morals dissolve.

He was too stunning to ignore.

As we passed over the threshold into the light, I took in all the faces. It was thronged with guests. Black and white cloaks intermingled in the beautiful room adorned with dripping crystal chandeliers and flickering candles. Tables were spread across the black marble floors that clicked beneath my heels. The crimson curtains on the floor-to-ceiling windows were drawn back, revealing the twinkling night sky. The perfect backdrop to a nightmarish event. So why was my heart fluttering with excitement at the scene?

Several people took notice of us as we entered, and their eyes widened when they spotted Obsidian. I tried to keep my chin held high. But it was hard to be confident amongst the grueling stares.

My palms began sweating as Obsidian guided me through the crowd, his confidence radiating off of him, and I knew everyone near him must have been able to feel it. A smile now replaced the glare he'd been sporting only moments before. He nodded to those he passed, flashing them a simpering sweet smile. A charming devil was now the one guiding me through the party, and I couldn't help but notice that even those who smiled back at him seemed utterly terrified.

Obsidian guided us to a table at the very front of the hall, and that's when I spotted his father.

King Elysian.

He, too, had dark hair like Obsidian, but his eyes weren't dark. They were bright blue, glittering like sapphires. He was sitting next to a couple other men, wearing the cloak of constellations, conversing with a glass of lush fire in his grasp. The crown on his head was a little crooked, somehow fitting the rather twisted situation perfectly.

I thought I would be fine witnessing King Elysian for the first time. I'd gone over this moment many times in my head. Preparing for it. But the nerves began to overtake me when I realized I was literally in the enemy's den. I gripped the sleeve of Obsidian's cloak, trying to remain calm.

"Relax, Sunn." Obsidian said, so quietly I almost didn't hear him. "I won't let him hurt you."

When Elysian spotted his son, I could see the immediate

surprise that flashed across his face before his gaze hardened with anger.

"Father," Obsidian greeted with a smirk, bowing slightly at the waist. I quickly offered a curtsy, but the king didn't even look at me. He was staring at his son, the fury on his face all too evident.

"Obsidian, what are you doing here?" Elysian asked, a tight smile on his lips now. He was trying to save face in front of his friends.

"I wouldn't miss a Dark Fell party, you know me, father," Obsidian purred, and Elysian's eyes narrowed even further.

"You've been gone. I thought you wouldn't be back in time." The unsaid conversation passing between them was intense. I could feel the tension thick in the air.

"Well, when I didn't find anything out on my expedition," Obsidian emphasized the word expedition. "I thought I might as well come home."

Elysian glowered. He hadn't authorized Obsidian's little journey to the Isles.

"Well, you'll be sure to tell me about it after the party. We can discuss matters then," Elysian said, and it sounded almost like a threat. My eyes zeroed in on the glittering token gracing his shoulders. The item we'd come for. My fingers itched to grab it and run away with it. If only it could be that easy.

"Of course, father. I'll find you after the party." Obsidian flashed one more wicked smile to those at the table who were watching in wide-eyed astonishment at the encounter. I guessed the only person who could play with King Elysian's emotions was Obsidian. The only one capable of walking into the fire and coming out unscathed.

Obsidian guided me away from Elysian's table, and I could

finally breathe evenly again as the distance between him and us increased.

We retreated to an empty table far from his father, for which I was grateful. A vermillion bottle of lush fire was set out with glasses. Obsidian sat down and immediately started filling himself a drink. I started to sit in the chair next to him, but he stopped me.

"Girls I bring with me to these parties don't sit in chairs next to me," he said, and he seemed disgusted with himself. He threw back the entire contents of his glass before saying, "they sit on my lap."

My eyes widened, and I thought for a moment he was joking. But when his dark, now glassy eyes remained hard as stone, his nostrils flaring, I realized he wasn't kidding.

"Okay," was all I managed to whisper before he took me by the waist and guided me to his lap. It felt all too natural when my arms fell around his neck to steady myself, and his hand gripped my thigh.

"Is this really what you do?" I whispered nervously. Never having been so openly affectionate in public before with anyone.

He gave me a practiced smolder that reeked of lust and leaned into me so his nose grazed my neck. Goosebumps erupted down my spine, and I tried not to gasp at the sensation. I reminded myself that he was pretending, putting on a show for those around us. But I couldn't ignore that I was unsettled by how easily he played the part.

My eyes flitted nervously to those around the room, and I caught several pairs of eyes. Was Mid and Shar in the shadows witnessing this? The thought sent panic surging through my veins. I sure hoped not.

"I told you. This is who I am," he murmured as his lips

pressed against my neck, so softly I barely felt it. But even the whispering brush sent my heart stammering.

"Then why does it seem like you are forcing yourself?" I asked, and I sounded completely breathless. He stiffened, and his lips paused against my skin. "If you claim to be so heartless, why do you have to be lushed to touch me?" I added, knowing I'd hit a nerve when his hand gripped my thigh. But the smile remained on his face, because he had to keep up the facade he was giving to those in the room. He didn't answer me. But his silence was enough.

He tilted his head back to look up and meet my gaze. I wished suddenly that I could drown in the dark pools of his eyes.

"Do you ever actually like any of the girls you bring to these parties?" I asked, changing the subject. "Or are they just objects in your mind that you like to play with?" I raised an eyebrow at him.

He leaned in to nip the side of my mouth with a teasing growl.

"They are nothing but pawns in my game," he assured me, and I felt my stomach roil. "I like bringing women to taunt my father and embarrassing him in front of those he wishes to impress." He gave the corner of my mouth another gentle brush with his, and it was the closest to a kiss we'd gotten since the one he'd given me on the ship. The memory of how his lips felt was still alive in my mind as if it had happened yesterday. I wanted him to kiss me so badly. I almost whimpered and asked him to stop teasing me.

"I thought you and your father were on the same side," I said.

"We are. But sometimes, we have—differing opinions."

"I see," I said, not even comprehending what we were discussing now.

"Taunting him isn't the only reason, though. I bring women because I like the company too," he added. The glimmer in his eye was meant to stab me. He was saying these things to prove that he hadn't changed. But I wasn't convinced.

"Kiss me then," I said boldly.

His nostrils flared. "No."

"You don't want to mess up the mission, do you? Doesn't your father need to believe that you'll bring women into his court and make the guests uncomfortable with your tactless displays of affection?" I was putting on a brash, bold front. But he wasn't the only one capable of putting on a good mask.

I ran my fingers into the hair at the nape of his neck and tugged him closer to me.

"Shouldn't we make your father believe you're the same heartless, vindictive prince you've always been?" I enjoyed the thrill of taunting him far more than I should have. That rush of not knowing how he would react was absolutely addictive. "We wouldn't want him catching onto us, would we?"

His black eyes were filled with fire now. He was fighting internally with himself, and I could see it.

"Or are you finally going to admit you're not the same man you once were?" I whispered.

I could see that something inside of him snapped.

Reaching out to grip my chin in his hand, he crushed his lips to mine.

ELEVEN

SABEARA

We all picked our stations and split into pairs. Mid and Liony, Me and Dusane, Shar and Rosen. We located an exit to keep and eye on, spreading out across the top floor.

Dusane and I found a table on the balcony, and I stole two glasses of lush fire from one of the passing servants. I sipped the contents of my glass eagerly.

"You shouldn't drink on the job," Dusane said, his intense blue eyes on King Elysian and his assistant. We had been waiting for Sunn and Obsidian to enter the ballroom, but they still hadn't come in yet. I was starting to get edgy and needed some Lush Fire to soothe my panic before I really started to worry.

"Where are they?" I asked, ignoring his reprimand.

"I'm sure they'll be in soon. If not, we will find her. Don't worry."

"What if things go badly," I whispered, hating that I was

fearing the worst. My foot was tapping impatiently beneath the table, and I felt edgy.

"Ehren, you need to relax." He grabbed my hand across the table and began rubbing his thumb soothingly across my hand. I looked at our clasped hands, then up to his eyes, where I found myself anchored by his gaze. My anxiousness eased.

"I'm sorry, I'm trying. It's just been a while since we've done anything like this."

"I know," he said calmly.

Just then, the ballroom doors opened again, and Obsidian and Sunn came walking inside. My attention turned solely to them. So grateful to see she was still alive and safe.

She wore a different outfit now. Beneath her white cloak, she now had on a beautiful purple gown with golden embroidery on the bodice. Obsidian had changed too, into a black suit coat with golden buttons and trim. They both looked stunning, and the entire ballroom looked over at them as they entered.

I gritted my teeth, hating how well they looked beside each other. It disturbed me though, that Sunn seemed so calm. She didn't look the least bit concerned that she was on the arm of a killer.

She held her head high as they walked in, her bright fiery red hair standing out amongst the crowd. They were headed straight for King Elysian. I held my breath as Obsidian began talking to his father. Elysian looked very irritated that his son was at the party, and I hoped a fight wouldn't break out. Luckily those around the room lost interest fairly quickly and returned to their chatter. King Elysian seemed to think his son was not worth the hassle and dismissed him. Obsidian and Sunn headed to an empty table.

I watched curiously as Obsidian sat in his chair and Sunn hesitated before sitting in his lap.

My mouth dropped open, and I instantly shot a look across the ballroom to Mid who looked about ready to kill someone.

"He has to stay calm," I said to Dusane. "He'll ruin the operation." I worried Mid wouldn't be able to hold it together. I glanced at Shar and he had a similar look on his face.

"They'll be okay," Dusane assured me. "They won't risk hurting her by stepping in."

I hoped he was right. Obsidian had warned us she'd be acting as his date, but I hadn't really contemplated what that would entail.

The two talked amongst each other and I watched Elysian's reaction. He was obviously irritated with his son being there. It was moments later when I glanced back at Obsidin and Sunn and gasped when I saw them kissing.

Obsidian had his hand in Sunn's hair, his lips melded to hers, while his hand snaked around her waist in a possessive grip. Sunn had his lapels in her hands, clutching them almost desperately. And that's when I finally saw it. Something I wished I'd never caught sight of.

The way Sunn was kissing him back.

"Oh, Spirits," I said. The blood drained from my face and I suddenly felt faint.

Dusane's jaw clenched, and I heard a raucous of glasses shattering nearby.

What had happened on that ship? Because we obviously didn't have the whole story.

TWELVE

SUNN

Stars exploded behind my eyes when our lips met. He demanded entrance to my mouth, grasping my bottom lip between his and stroking his tongue with mine. His kiss was wonder and darkness. Sin and seraphic. A conflicting symphony of emotions that elicited a painfully beautiful song. I had no doubt it would torment me with its melody after it ended.

When he pulled away roughly, I gasped for breath, already needing to feel his lips back on mine. It wasn't enough.

"Why do you insist on tempting me?" he asked as if he was in pain. His fingers still gripped my chin—forcing me to remain looking at him.

"Because I know you feel something for me," I dared to say.

"You're wrong."

Just then, a new song began to play, and it was as if Obsidian was pulled from a trance, remembering why we had come in the first place. The cloak. His fingers fell from my chin, and he lifted me off his lap and grabbed my hand roughly in his. He led me onto the dance floor and pulled me close to him.

His arms wound around my waist, and my hands fell onto his shoulders.

Still dizzy from the kiss, I gripped his suit coat in my hands, trying to remain steady.

I asked, "what's your plan to get the cloak?"

"My father is a very competitive man," he said, his gaze flickering to his father across the ballroom. "He can't say no to a fight he knows he might win. So if a fight breaks out, he'll most likely remove the cloak so as not to damage it."

"You're going to start a fight then?" I asked, taking a guess at his meaning. "How?"

Obsidian jaw clenched. "It won't be me starting the fight. It will be him."

I was confused by what he meant until I saw him coming toward us in the crowd.

Shar.

Obsidian gently pushed me out of his grasp and behind him as if to shield me from what was about to occur.

Shar had seen the kiss.

And he was not happy about it.

Fear sent a tremor through me. I had a feeling things were about to get really ugly.

Obsidian grabbed another glass from a servant's passing tray, chugged the entire contents of the glass, then threw it to the ground, letting it shatter into tiny pieces on the marble floors. Then without even a pause, Shar met him in the middle of the dance floor and swung his fist straight into Obsidian's jaw.

THIRTEEN

SABEARA

I tore my eyes away from the scene of Obsidian and Sunn kissing to the source of the crashing noise. An entire cart of Lush Fire had been shattered, I don't know how it was managed, but I turned to see Mid being held back by Rosen and Rouix. The three were struggling against each other.

Dusane and I stood from our seats, hurrying over to them, wrestling one another.

I grabbed Mid's right arm while Dusane grabbed the other to assist Rouix and Rosen.

"Mid, calm down," I said through gritted teeth. His emerald-scarlet eyes were trained on the ballroom floor, a rage unlike anything I'd ever seen ignited in his expression.

"Operations over. We need to get her out of here," Mid growled.

"It's an act, Mid. You have to calm down," Dusane said, his cerulean eyes darker than I'd ever seen them.

That's when I realized Shar was nowhere to be seen and that something really bad was about to happen.

"Where is Shar?" I asked Rosen, a new fear turning my blood cold. His topaz eyes were grim for the first time since I'd met him. He merely gestured with a slight nod to the dance floor below us.

I ran to the edge of the balcony, just in time to look down and see Shar throw a punch straight into Obsidian's jaw.

I gasped.

"Spirits," I heard Rouix say beside me.

The operation was basically being blown to pieces. So much for being discreet.

I turned back to see Rosen release Mid and the two glared at each other. Mid's hands were flickering with the gold light as if he was trying desperately to hold himself back from seriously injuring Rosen.

"Pull it together," Rosen commanded.

"Mid," I snarled. "I know she's your niece, but getting upset right now isn't going to help."

Mid seemed to slowly realize this and thankfully didn't make another attempt to follow after Shar. Instead, he watched with a steely gaze down at the fight that was now happening in the middle of the dance floor. People had surrounded Obsidian and Shar as the two were battling in hand-to-hand combat.

"We have to get out of here," I whispered, hating that Shar had lost his cool. Out of all the things to lose it over, it had to be a kiss.

I looked up at the chandelier a couple yards away from me on the balcony. I glanced down at my cloak and hurriedly undid the ties.

"What are you doing?" Dusane asked me.

"I'm getting down there to stop this fight," I growled, swinging the onyx fabric with all my might. I flung the edge so it would loop around the chandelier. Climbing up onto the balcony, I took both edges of the cloak in my hands and tugged on it to check its strength, then I jumped.

The free fall sent my stomach dropping and my heart plummeting as I swooped down to the floor, landing on both feet with only a slight pain in my ankles.

Both men turned to me. Obsidian had blood pouring from his nose into the crevices of his teeth, making his smile that much more eerie. I saw the amusement in his eyes and knew he must've been planning this.

Shar was unlike I'd ever seen him—hair wild and free from its ponytail, showing the sharp angles of his face. His nose was bleeding too, and he quickly swiped at it, leaving a trail of crimson on his white sleeve.

"Come to join the party, cousin?" Obsidian asked, grinning.

FOURTEEN

SUNN

Sabeara swung down from the chandelier, landing between Shar and Obsidian.

I was too terrified to move—couldn't make my limbs listen to my brain telling me to run from the scene.

"Come to join the party, cousin?" Obsidian said, grinning wildly at her.

Sabeara didn't get the chance to answer.

Shar shoved Obsidian roughly; the two stumbled into the middle of the dance floor. Shocked gasps came from the women around the room. While excited murmurs came from the men.

I looked over at Elysian. He was glaring at them from his seat, all too aware it seemed of what was happening.

Obsidian threw another punch, but Shar dodged the blow and landed a nice fist to Obsidian's gut. I watched in horror as the two continued to go at each other until some guards stepped in, pulling them apart.

Obsidian turned on the guard holding him, wriggling free from his grasp and swiftly taking the guard's sword from his side. His eyes were wide with excitement, a wicked smirk on his now bloody lips.

"Want to join too?" Obsidian asked, while swinging the sword dangerously at the guard. The guard jumped back right before his arm could be sliced off.

"Seize them!" Elysian boomed, pushing his way through the crowd. And my panic was quickly replaced with triumph. In fact, my heart soared when I saw Elysian remove the cloak of constellations and pass it to his auxiliary. I watched in awe as his right-hand man took the cloak out of the ballroom, slipping away from the commotion and out of sight, just like Obsidian predicted.

Then my attention was pulled back to Obsidian. His father was joining the chaos, his face red with fury. Elysian had noticed Sabeara and Shar, and the guards started to close in on them.

I need to run, I thought. I really need to run.

"Come on, Father, I'm only having a little fun," Obsidian teased. And I had the bizarre thought that he looked absolutely stunning this way.

I was taken aback by his disheveled hair, skin aglow and flush from the fight. His chest heaving, the buttons on his suit coat set free, revealing the golden color of his heart. His black eyes held a lightness that was rare to see. He was enjoying this. And it was wrong of me to be enjoying the sight of him. But there I was, drinking him in and getting more intoxicated than if I'd been drinking Lush Fire.

Elysian growled angrily, pulling a glittering violet dagger from its sheath—his guards flanking him dangerously.

A couple people screamed, and soon the entire ballroom was in commotion.

Shar and Sabeara also pulled out their blades. More black cloaked guards flooded the party while Elysian headed straight for his son.

At this point, I had enough sense to move out of the way.

I ran as fast as I could, but somehow it felt like I was in a dream, moving slower than I would've liked due to the fear that was freezing my limbs.

My back hit the wall as people ran all around me, fighting to escape. Elysian and Obsidian were now head to head, his father with his glowing purple dagger fighting Obsidian while he wielded an ordinary sword. Obsidian didn't appear to be afraid. But Sabeara and the others definitely seemed concerned. Together they fought off black cloaked figures that were reigning down on them. Their teeth clenched, and brows furrowed.

My heart sped up in my chest, fearful for my friends and family's lives. Mid, Rosen, Rouix, and Dusane had all managed to make their way down to the floor now and joined quickly in the fight. But they were severely outnumbered.

Realizing I was useless just standing flush against the wall, I gathered my courage and found a serving plate that had clattered to the floor. Picking it up, I let out a wild battle cry and began hitting as many black-cloaked guards as possible with it.

I knocked one man out cold, and immediate victory swelled in my chest. Moving off of adrenaline, I swung for another guard that spotted me and hit his arm pretty swiftly. The man cursed and cradled his hurt arm, wincing in pain. I swung again, ready to take him out completely, when he put his hand up, stopping the blow. He ripped the serving plate from my fingertips and sent me sprawling to the ground.

I groaned when the marble hit my knees, and my dress made a ripping sound upon impact. Now the dress had a slit clear up to my waist, my entire thigh revealed along with my black and blue knees.

I looked up at the man I was fighting. He bore down on me, closing in for the kill when he was suddenly stabbed in the side.

The blood gushing from his stomach was the last thing I'd expected to see staining the marble floors. And then I looked to the culprit of this man's sudden death and found Obsidian wielding the weapon that had taken his last breath.

"Time to go," Obsidian said to me, his eyes so black now I had an inkling to be afraid of him. But too bad I was broken when it came to my survival instincts. Instead of cowering away, I reached out my hand to him.

He helped pull me to my feet, and that's when I looked behind him to see his father being lifted up by his guards. He had a large wound on his chest, no doubt from Obsidian.

Mid charged towards him, and I watched in awe as his fingertips glowed a beautiful gold color, and a flock of birds appeared in the air at the tips of his fingers, swarming Elysian.

Elysian and his guard's shouts of protest could be heard as the birds overwhelmed them, and the caw of the dark black ravens echoed across the high ceilings of the ballroom. I'd never seen anything quite like my uncle's ability, but it was magnificent.

"What about the others?" I asked. "And the cloak?" I desperately looked to find them still fighting off the Obscurum guards in the room.

"They'll meet us out at the camp," Obsidian said. "As for the cloak. We're going to get it on the way out."

His tone told me not to ask questions. He took my hand and pulled me out into the foyer. He seemed to know exactly where he was going. Now with the chaos happening in the middle of the ballroom, no one would be able to stop us from grabbing the cloak and running.

We ended up in a small windowless room. It looked like a library of sorts with a bunch of bookcases lining the walls and withered spines of old volumes muddling the shelving.

"What are all of these?" I asked, unable to help my curiosity.

"Ancient books that are forbidden to be read," Obsidian said quickly.

"Forbidden? Why are they here."

"Well, I shouldn't say forbidden. No one understands the language."

"An ancient Stone-Hearted language? How old are these books?" I stared in awe.

"A couple thousand years old?" Obsidian was distracted as he spoke. He was pulling back a bookcase that was actually a door, and behind it was draped Ennsleon's cloak on a stand.

It was stunning. A piece of almost sheer fabric with twinkling constellations woven into the dark blue with silvery strands. It was a masterpiece—a work of art. And immediately, I wondered what it could possibly do.

"Hello, old friend," he said to the token. Pulling it from its resting place, he stuffed it into his pocket and grabbed my hand again. "Ready?"

I didn't get to answer before he was tugging me back out into the foyer and to the front doors where we'd originally entered.

Of course, our exit couldn't be effortless. When we got out

onto the front steps and began descending the volcanic rock back to the camp, more guards came running up the path, letting all the other partygoers run past them, their eyes glued to Obsidian and me. We had the cloak, and they wouldn't be letting us leave without a fight.

FIFTEEN

SABEARA

I became consumed by the rage again. After all those months of struggling to keep myself in check, it came back with a vengeance.

I fought off guards left and right, my body soaring with the feeling. *So this was what it felt like to be free.*

I swung, grunted, and sidestepped until my heart felt like it would beat out of my chest. Sweat formed on my brow, and every little cut a guard managed to land on me filled me up like a drug.

I kept Obsidian and Elysian in the corner of my eye, seething still that he'd managed to make everything turn into chaos. But honestly, what had I been expecting? Obsidian was known for causing trouble.

Obsidian finally landed a significant blow to Elsyian's side, and then he ran over to me while his father struggled to compose himself.

"I'm going to get the cloak and take Sunn back to the camp."

"You hurt her, and I will make sure you suffer," I said to him, and he simply grinned.

"As much as I'd love to experience your attempt, I will be delivering her safely to James and Liony."

"I'm trusting you, Obsidian," I said, desperation in my every breath. I knew I couldn't trust him. So why was I doing it anyway? Maybe it was the way he'd kissed Sunn. Perhaps it was how I'd caught a glimpse of something more than just putting on a show as their lips had touched. He cared for her. And that was the only sure thing I knew at that moment. Yes, it brought on a whole plethora of new complications, but at least it gave me some semblance of security. For now.

"See you soon, cuz." He winked, and then he was heading back toward Sunn.

I turned back to the chaos—ravens flying all around the room, Rosen turning people to gold—I pushed it all to the side and focused on getting to Dusane's side to help him with the three men he was warding off.

I helped him eliminate one man, and his blue eyes turned to me with a grateful expression.

"Thanks," he grunted, swinging his dagger.

"No problem," I said. The two of us were now back to back, and the thrill of the fight bubbled inside my veins.

"Are you managing the rage?" he asked, and I let out a cynical chuckle.

"Let's just say I'm not exactly calm."

Just then the guard he was fighting managed to get a blow to his arm and Dusane hissed.

I took down my opponent with a swift swipe to the shoulder, then turned to help Dusane, who was holding his wounded arm.

"You alright?"

The guard let out a battle cry and swung to hit him again. I quickly hindered the man, but my eyes remained on Dusane.

"Yeah, just a nasty cut." Dusane slowly recovered, holding his wounded arm to his side.

"We need to get out of here," Dusane said, and I nodded in agreement. Though everything inside of me wanted to keep going and take down every last one of the black-cloaked figures in the room, I knew he was right.

I caught Mid's eyes and gestured to the exit, he told Shar, who was beside him, and then Dusane and I ran into the hallway.

We were almost to the foyer when a figure came running up to meet us.

My eyes widened when I took in the individual standing before me.

I knew those eyes. Dark green eyes. I'd left the memory on the snowy mountain that day—never expecting them to return.

"Jade?" The name fell from my lips like a gasping breath.

Dusane's jaw clenched, seeing the rouge Envorydian that had almost killed him on the mountain all those months ago.

"What are you doing here?" Dusane asked.

"I should be asking you the same thing." Jade smirked, not at all worried it seemed by the two-on-one that was about to go down.

"I thought we killed you," I said, glaring at the man before me.

"Sorry, sweetheart, still very much alive." Jade let out a spine-chilling laugh.

"You're working for him," Dusane said, eyes widening.

"I work for whoever pays me the highest wage," Jade said, raising his eyebrow. "And if I remember correctly, you did at one point too."

Dusane growled.

"Tell me, is the princess paying you to sleep with her too?"

That's when he snapped, and Dusane lunged for Jade.

The warrior captain within him emerged, and he was using every skill imaginable to fight the Envorydian before him. I had to admit, it was impressive seeing Dusane fight. He was so lithe and quick, his every move practiced and precise. It was like he was doing a dance.

Jade matched him almost perfectly due to the fact they both had similar training.

I forced myself to focus. Trying not to let the shock of Jade being at the party affect my focus. If he was here, that would mean that other rouges were probably working for Elysian as well. Dusane had once said he didn't believe Jade was working with him. But obviously, that prediction had been wrong.

I grabbed the hem of my dress and ripped it so it wouldn't get in my way. Fighting in a dress was not ideal. I ran at him then, jumping for momentum. I locked my legs together and put as much weight into my body as possible, so I could hit Jade down like a pin in a game.

His eyes widened as if not expecting me to come flying towards him at such a speed.

My shoes landed on the center of Jade's chest, and he was flattened to the floor. Dusane stumbled in the aftermath. Thankfully, he managed to get up quickly, the brunt of my blow hitting Jades' chest. I landed with only a slight stumble and then proceeded to deliver a swift punch to Jade's cheek.

He didn't stir. He was knocked out cold.

Dusane looked down at his past comrade and raised his dagger to finish him off.

"Dusane," I said, shaking my head. "Let's just go."

He was hardly a threat. if we'd managed to take him down twice, he wasn't worth the extra effort. Killing him would only make me more of a killer.

Dusane nodded, following me as I stepped around Jade's fallen body and to the foyer.

Soon we were out the front doors back onto the volcanic rock of the front steps when Shar, Rosen, Rouix, and Mid came running up behind us.

"Where's Obsidian and Sunn?" Shar asked, his green eyes seething.

"There," I said, pointing to the two of them. They were on the front steps we'd initially ascended—surrounded by nearly a dozen guards. They were obviously trying to keep them from leaving the mountain.

Red blurred the corners of my vision as I prepared for yet another fight. I looked over at Dusane and he didn't stop me, didn't tell me to calm down. Instead, he lifted his dagger and pointed toward the cluster of black cloaks.

"Let's fight, Envorydian."

SIXTEEN

SUNN

Soon the others joined us on the steps, and we weren't the only ones facing off to the new swarm of black cloaks barreling straight for us.

I glanced at Obsidian, fear forming in my eyes. I wanted to be strong, but my instincts told me to run. I'd fought giant, poisonous sea creatures on a boat before, but Obsidian had been the one to save me then. And he'd had his abilities. With the bracelet on his wrist, he was completely powerless. He was as good as mortal.

Obsidian put himself in front of me just as the first guard attacked. I cowered behind him, searching for a rock on the ground I could use as a weapon. I finally found one that looked sharp enough and turned to slam it into one of the guard's head.

A sickening sound emanated from the man's skull as I landed a vicious blow. But I knew it was absolutely necessary we escape, so I swallowed down the bile that rose in my throat.

The guards weren't interested in any of the other party guests who had all but fled at that point. They only wanted us.

I feared what would happen if we couldn't escape. What Elysian would do with all of us in his grasp. I pushed the thought aside, refusing to entertain the possibility of us not making it out alive.

Then the ground began to shake, loose rocks tumbling down the mountainside. I struggled to stay upright at the sudden shivering of the earth beneath us.

I looked up to see Mid concentrating, using his ability to create giant vines to shoot up from the earth, capturing the feet and ankles of the soldiers fighting us. Their cries could be heard as they were wrestled to the ground by the dark green foliage.

A couple managed to hack themselves free, but most of them were subdued.

Finally able to breathe, I looked over at Obsidian who at the same time reached for me.

"Let's go," he said, breathing heavily from the fight.

Just as he took my hand, I heard a scream, and it wasn't from one of the guards. It was from Sabeara.

I turned around, my eyes wide with concern.

The vines had managed to grasp almost all the Obscurum men. But the guards on the steps were untouched, it seemed. Elysian had managed to escape the ballroom again, still standing with the heavy wound in his breast. I was unsure how he was standing, but he was. Small bits of flesh were taken out of his skin where ravens had pecked his skin. He looked torn up, yet he was smiling still.

Goosebumps erupted across my skin.

His right-hand man that had managed to avoid the tether of

the giant vines, was holding onto Dusane. His hand gripping his shirt collar, dragging him down the other side of the mountain.

Sabeara and Mid tried to run to him. Mid's hands already glowing gold, ready to produce some sort of illusion that would hinder them. But then they disappeared.

Vanished.

Gone.

Nothing in their previous place.

Elysian, torn and bleeding with his two men and Dusane at their side, completely vanished. Someone had an ability that we were unaware of and Sabeara screamed again in rage, turning desperately left and right in search of him.

"Where did they take him?" she shrieked.

"There! I can see their tacks," Rosen said. His skin was glowing with some sort of gold protective plating I'd never seen before.

He ran over to some of the rocks that had been displaced. They were somehow invisible, but they were moving.

"They're taking him," Sabeara hurried after the tracks but then stopped abruptly and turned around to face us. Her eyes locked on Obsidian. "Get her back to the castle. Now. Or you'll never see your powers again," she threatened. Her sapphire eyes held a fire in them that scared me and I was honestly seeing her for the first time. A warrior now, no longer the gentle princess I'd met all those years ago.

Obsidian didn't waste any time. He took my hand and continued to tug me down the mountain.

"Wait we can't just leave them!" I said desperately.

"Don't fight me, Sunn," Obsidian warned.

"I don't trust him," I heard Shar rage behind us.

"Shar, we don't have time to argue about this. They just

kidnapped him!" Sabeara seethed, angrier than I'd ever heard seen or heard her in my life.

I caught a glimpse of Mid and Shar staring after me as Obsidian began guiding me back down the mountain to the camp where Liony and James awaited.

"We have no choice. I need you to help me find him," Sabeara said to them, pleading now.

Obsidian helped me through the Obscurum guards that laid on the mountain side, entangled in giant plant limbs and hordes of volcanic rock. Some were bleeding, others crying. They grunted and yelled at us as we passed.

I felt myself hyperventilating a little as we were enveloped by the trees again.

Dusane had just been kidnapped.

Somehow Elysian and his men had turned invisible and escaped the raid.

Where were they taking him?

SEVENTEEN

SABEARA

They'd vanished. Just like that.

One second we were fighting side by side. Then Mid was making the ground erupt with giant stalks of green vines that had imprisoned the remaining men on the mountainside.

Then I turned around and Elysian had Dusane in his hold.

It was my worst nightmare.

I thought he'd been taken care of in the ballroom. After the knife cut to his chest and the flock of birds that had all but consumed him. I didn't think he'd be able to get up, let alone walk outside to finish off the fight.

But he'd been there, his skin dotted with scars from the pecking he'd endured. And the wound on his breast dripping droplets of crimson onto the ebony rocks.

Then his comrade, Sylvester, smiled, and they vanished.

Dusane along with them.

Luckily they'd not been transported, just turned invisible,

because I could hear their footsteps as they raced across the rocks. Loose stones tumbled down the mountainside as they left, and I knew we'd still be able to track them.

I sent Obsidian and Sunn back to the camp. I needed at least some of us to get home safely. They needed to tell the others at the castle what had transpired. And I'd also never forgive myself if something happened to Sunn.

I turned to Mid, trying not to succumb to the utter terror that was overwhelming my bones.

"We need horses," I said, and he nodded, jaw clenched.

He didn't even hesitate. He closed his eyes, arms shaking from the effort after already fighting so much and using his ability to create so many things. But somehow he managed to produce three steeds that we could all ride on together.

He mounted the white animal, and I jumped up behind him. The others followed suit. Rouix with Rosen, and Shar by himself.

We raced off after the tracks we'd managed to glimpse, trying our best to head in the direction we thought they'd gone.

I wrapped my arms around Mid's waist, my stomach sinking. I could only hope we'd find their tracks, that somehow whatever vanishing magic they had hold of would wear off and we'd see them again.

We hadn't foreseen someone with such abilities. I worried that it had something to do with Jade being at the party. The king must've been working with The Mantle. The Envorydian group of rouges that Dusane had once been a part of.

Of course things just couldn't go according to plan. Of course something bad had to happen. Like the mantle working with Elysian. We'd killed the others on the Niafell mountain in

Severesi, but I knew there had to be more rouges that existed. Was Elysian recruiting them?

I berated myself for being stupid enough to take on such an undertaking in the first place.

I couldn't even think about the cloak at that moment. I didn't even know if Obsidian had retrieved it or not.

But I didn't care. The man I loved had just been taken. And I needed to find him.

We left behind the Dark Fell and the Obscurum guards entwined in the volcanic rock and foliage. And headed towards the other side of the mountain to an even bigger nightmare.

EIGHTEEN

SUNN

"We have to get out of here." Obsidian was quickly packing up the camp, grabbing at items and stuffing them into the packs lying around the fire. I'd never seen him move so quickly.

We'd relayed the story to James and Liony. Liony looked sick after telling her about Dusane being taken, and James's baby blue eyes were wide with shock.

"Sabeara told us to get back to Knadiel," I said.

"They are going to find him. They have to," Liony said more to herself than to me. She shook herself from the stupor she seemed to be in and began helping us clean up.

"Can you guys get back to Knadiel by yourselves?" Obsidian asked after we'd packed the last of the tents. He looked at Liony expectantly.

"I know the way if that's what you mean," Liony said, confusion furrowing her brow.

"I'm taking Diablo, and Sunn is coming with me."

"What? Why?" I looked at Obsidian, shocked by the unexpected demand.

"I told Sabeara I'd get you back to Knadiel safely."

Obsidian grabbed my hand and began pulling me in the direction of the black winged steed waiting patiently in the trees.

"Hold up, not so fast." James put a hand on Obsidian's arm, and the look that Obsidian gave James might as well have seared him. "We should travel together. It will be safer."

Obsidian shoved James back, causing him to stumble. Liony quickly went to steady him and nearly fell over too.

"Obsidian!" I yelled.

Obsidian ignored me and smirked at James, a dangerous gleam in his eyes. "I was told to get Sunn back to Knadiel or my freedom would be compromised. So excuse me for being less than civil. But if she doesn't get back to the castle, this—" he gestured to his cuff "—doesn't come off. And that just doesn't work for me."

James glared at Obsidian, a hatred so thick in his expression it created a tangible tension in the air between them.

"You're not taking her anywhere." James reached for me, pulling me towards him.

James had his hand on me for a mere second before Obsidian grabbed Jame's outstretched wrist and twisted it at an uncomfortable angle, forcing him to let go and fall to his knees. James groaned, his face furrowed in pain, gripping his wrist.

"Touch her again, I dare you," Obsidian threatened.

"Obsidian, stop it!"

Liony knelt beside James, cradling his hand in hers and then looked up at Obsidian with a shocked and fearful expression.

Obsidian stepped in front of me, stopping my attempt to go

to James.

"Don't make this hard, Sunn," Obsidian warned, the dangerous fire in his eyes still ablaze.

I glared at him, my fists clenching angrily at my sides. "You can't just hurt my friends like that." I tried to shove past him, but his arm shot out, stopping me.

"Get on the horse, Sunn." There wasn't room for discussion in his tone. "I'm taking you home."

"Why are you acting like this?" I asked, hating that he was rescuing me but also being a huge jerk in the process. His tactics were all twisted. Yet I don't know what I was expecting from him. This was Obsidian. Being a gentleman wasn't in his makeup.

"It feels good to be the bad guy," he smirked, but his eyes were dark when he said it. "Now, I'm only going to say it one more time. Get on the horse, Sunn."

I looked desperately over at Liony and James. Liony looked up and nodded grimly at me. Telling me to listen to him.

"Go, Sunn, we'll be okay," she assured me.

I hesitated, wanting to fight Obsidian more on the matter, but knowing he was stronger than me.

I huffed angrily, feeling furious tears prick the corners of my eyes, but I eventually relented, turning on my heel and heading towards Diablo.

Obsidian got on first, then reached down a hand to me. I felt I was betraying myself and everyone else by taking it and joining him.

Obsidian's arms enveloped me as he reached for Diablo's mane.

I looked over at James, imploring him to forgive me as Obsidian urged Diablo upwards, taking off into the sky.

NINTEEN

SABEARA

The thunder of hooves matched the pounding of my heart. I could see nothing but the path in the distance, begging it to lead me to Dusane. My body shook from clinging to the steed's body for so long.

The rage that Dusane had tried so hard to dampen in my blood now roared like a ferocious lion. I was angrier than I'd ever been.

Flashes of the party came back as we rode. Hitting me like a fresh blow to the core with every image. Obsidian kissing Sunn, Shar starting the fight. Mid and the crows with their black wings flapping against my skin. Then Jade entering the party, who I'd thought we'd left behind in Severesi. I could still see Jade's eyes in my mind and his body knocked out cold on the Dark Fell floor. And lastly, the most vivid image of them all, Dusane vanishing with Elysian.

"Ehren, stop," Shar called to me, but I could barely register he was speaking to me. I was too engrossed in the torment my mind was relaying.

"Ehren!" he growled, and next thing I knew, he was galloping up beside me, grabbing hold of my horse's mane and tugging us to a rapid stop.

It was so abrupt that I lost my balance and went sprawling into the dirt and forest briars. I let out a grunt as I somersaulted through an array of sticks and leaves.

When I found my footing I stood up, the cuts and bruises I acquired in the fall already healing.

I turned on him before I could even consider counting to one.

"You did this!" I screamed, not even recognizing my own voice as the screeching yell scorched my throat.

Shar also fell off his steed in an attempt to get me to slow down, and he grunted as he stood to face me.

The others slowed to a standstill around us. I ignored them, my eyes trained on Shar.

"Ehren, please, can we slow down and talk about this," Shar pleaded, his voice gentle and cautious as if he was trying to calm a wild animal.

"You just had to fight him, didn't you? You couldn't have held it together just a little bit longer?" I stalked towards him, seeing red in the corners of my vision. I had never felt the urge to hurt someone close to me before, but he'd gotten Dusane kidnapped, and all I could think was that hurting him would make things better.

"You don't understand, Ehren—" Shar said, and he had the decency to look ashamed for once.

"Oh, I think I understand completely," I said darkly, and before I could think about the consequences, I took a swing at him, landing a punch square to his jaw. His head snapped to the side with the impact, blood spattering to the dirt floor.

"Ehren, please," Shar didn't fight back, probably because he knew he was in the wrong. He simply looked up at me, clutching his jaw where blood from his split lip trickled onto his fingertips.

"I swear to the Spirits in the tree Shar, if he's dead because of you, I will kill you." I don't know what urged me to make such a threat. "I'll kill you!" I screamed and lunged for him again, only to be hindered by a large body stepping between us.

"Sabeara." The voice penetrated my rage for a split second, but then I tried to move around the person holding me, needing to hurt Shar as much as he'd hurt me. "Sabeara, calm down." The voice came again, and it did something to me. It tugged at a part of me I had buried. It stirred something from my past that I had refused to believe still existed.

It rattled me for a moment, and I looked up to see Mid holding me back, a look in his eyes I'd never seen before when he'd looked at me.

Fear.

"Get off of me," I growled, shoving his hands away. But I couldn't deny that the feeling of him still lingered. Something got through the rage. And when I looked into his emerald-scarlet eyes I didn't have the strength to admit that it might have been him.

"If he hadn't started that fight, Dusane wouldn't have been taken."

"Fighting about it isn't going to help us find him any faster," Mid reasoned with me, and he was bold enough to take another step towards me. Reaching out carefully, he cupped my cheek in his hand. "We're going to find him," he assured me, and I froze, feeling emotions wrack my body I didn't want to feel. I bit my lip, fighting back the tears threatening to overtake me.

"He's going to be alright. We will get to him. I swear it," Mid whispered gently, pulling me towards him.

I refused to break down. Refused to allow myself to crumble in that moment. But his arms around me were so comforting. I couldn't deny that I needed him. I buried my head in his chest. Letting silent tears course down my cheeks. He held me tightly to him, rubbing my back soothingly.

"We'll find him," he whispered, his lips brushing the crown of my head.

TWENTY

SUNN

I'd never ridden on a Pegasus before. It was terrifying and exciting all at the same time. We soared high into the night sky, the swoosh of Diablo's wings guiding us closer than I'd ever been to the stars and constellations. Ascending up above everything made it feel like we were in a different world, that the land below us was so much farther away than it really was.

We didn't talk. I was too angry about what had happened with James, and more than a little furious Obsidian had basically kidnapped me.

My mind was a mess of thoughts, replaying the events at the Night Fell, then the forest with James and Liony. Then the moment we kissed in the ballroom, and Shar getting upset.

Obsidain said he had meant to start a fight so his father would get involved. Did he kiss me just to start a fight?

The air grew cold very quickly and I couldn't resist the shivers that wracked my body as we passed through Severesi territory. I curled into my cloak and unwillingly into Obsidian's warmth that his body was providing.

His arms tightened around me, and my body betrayed me, my stomach erupting with some twisted feeling of excitement and desire. I inwardly shouted at myself to pull it together and stop reacting to him.

"Are you okay?" he asked me softly, and the unexpected gentleness in his tone made me furious.

"Why would you care?" I snapped childishly.

"Sunn," he murmured, his tone reprimanding me and melting me simultaneously.

"Why did you kiss me?" I asked, the anger adding an edge to my tone.

"Because you asked me to remember?" he said simply, and the way he answered the question without hesitation only made me angrier.

"I'm not so sure that's why," I said.

"We weren't going to get out of there without a fight, Sunn. My father would never have taken off his cloak unless by force. When you suggested a kiss, I thought it would be the perfect thing."

"You knew we wouldn't get out of there without a fight? That would have been nice to know in the meeting before we went into the Night Fell."

"It wasn't what Sabeara or the others wanted to hear."

"So you lied." The anger began to boil, hotter and hotter in my blood. I wasn't cold anymore. My skin was suddenly flushed, hot from the fury that was raging inside of me. The audacity this man had.

"I did what I had to do to secure my freedom," he said, his voice hard. Remorseless. Unforgiving.

I could no longer be near him. It was too much. The party, the kiss, the way he'd treated James. I had reached a point, and I was ready to snap.

"Bring us ," I demanded.

Obsidian hesitated at the tone of my voice. "Sunn—"

"Land on the ground, Obsidian, or I swear to the spirits in the tree I will jump."

He sighed at my dramatic demand and, without further argument, guided Diablo down from the starlit sky towards the snowy forest below.

Diablo's hooves landed in the blanket of alabaster snow minutes later. And I didn't waste another second. I dismounted and angrily stomped through the powder in the opposite direction of where we'd landed. I had no idea where I was going. I only knew I was so livid I couldn't be near him another second.

"Sunn, where are you going?" Obsidian asked, sighing with exasperation.

"I'm walking home," I yelled.

"You can't walk home," he said.

I spun around. "I can't stand another minute with you!" I screamed across the expanse of trees. The pale light of the moon illuminated the forest around us with a soft glow. Even though I yelled, my voice was muted in the snowy landscape. The white fluff coated everything. It was quiet and peaceful, unlike my feelings at that moment.

He shoved his hands into his pockets and looked at me as if I was a child throwing a tantrum.

"You'll freeze to death,"

"So be it then!" I growled.

"Sunn—" he said again.

"Do you even think about the consequences of your actions?"

He opened his mouth to speak again, but I interrupted, needing to say my peace.

"And the way you hurt James. You know what he means to me! How could you do that to my friend?"

"I don't know why you're surprised by all of this," he blurted.

I huffed and turned around again, going further into the trees. I was done with him.

"Okay, I'm sorry," he yelled, causing me to halt in my tracks. "I'm sorry for not telling the others about my plans. And for hurting James," he said, obviously irritated he was even saying the words aloud.

I waited. Still not turning to face him.

"I'll apologize to James," he said, sighing.

I finally faced him again, my arms crossing over my chest.

"You're just saying that so I'll get back on Diablo."

He shrugged. "Maybe."

I reached for the snow before I could contemplate what I was doing. I gathered a fistful in my hands, moulding it into a tightly compacted ball before throwing it at him. When it hit his chest, exploding against his black cloak in sparkly white flakes, he looked up with a stunned expression.

"Did you just throw a snowball at me?"

"Have fun showing up in Knadiel without me." I started to walk away from him. But then something cold and hard hit my shoulder—icy powder peppering my neck. I froze, taking a couple of seconds to process that he'd thrown a snowball back.

TWENTY-ONE

SABEARA

We had to travel through Obscurum. That's where the tracks were leading us. I hadn't returned to Obscurum since we raided the Obscurum castle to save Embrosine. I'd once flown over the dreaded city, but had yet to step foot inside its walls.

"Do you think they're taking him to the castle?" Rouix asked as we treaded through mounds of sand.

"No, I think that would be too obvious," Shar said.

"I'm sure there have been rumors of them traveling through the city. Let's see if we can get someone to fess up to where they might be taking him," Mid said.

"And if no one has seen them?" I pressed, hating that my mind was even going there.

"We will figure something out, don't worry, Ehren," Shar assured me.

The sand seemed to go on endlessly until the dark walls of

the city came into view. They were so much bigger up close. I couldn't deny the fear I felt while looking at them.

The city had a gated entrance that let civilians in and out, I didn't know how we'd get inside, but I just trusted we'd find a way.

Sure enough, as we got within a mile of the city walls, Mid voiced a plan.

"I can make us appear invisible for a couple of minutes while we pass through the gates, but I don't know how long I'll be able to hold the illusion on their minds."

There was a line of civilians leading outside of the city gates. There were a few guards, and holding an illusion on multiple people's minds was a lot harder than one from what he'd told me of his abilities.

"We will be quick," Shar assured him.

We held our heads high as we neared the gates, and then just before coming in sight of the guards, I caught Mid's hands glowing. Then we walked right in, not a single one protesting as we passed.

We were careful to weave past the other civilians until we were inside the city, then he dropped the illusion.

We all wore black or white cloaks, so we weren't completely out of the ordinary. But I wasn't prepared for what I saw when we passed through the front gates.

It has similarities to the prison I'd once been entrapped within, only much darker and more eerie. The courts had a light to it I couldn't explain. Though the people were imprisoned, they had actually seemed happy. The Sethen Courts hadn't felt like a prison. But here, this was what I imagined the Sethen Courts should have been like.

People crowded the streets, most people in grungy clothes

and black cloaks that were torn at the edges from constantly dragging on the cobblestone streets layered with sheets of sand. The people looked distraught and hopeless. We passed beggars on the streets and many tents with vendors claiming to be fortune tellers and seers. There was a wildness in the people's eyes that scared me. Like they were close to going mad if they stayed another second behind these dark walls.

The buildings were all crammed close together, much like the courts had been. Metal roofs and scrap pieces made homes that were barely big enough to fit a couple of people inside. Animals also roamed the streets, wild cats and dogs.

Obscurum soldiers riding on Crykon surveyed the streets. I saw multiple encounters of soldiers subduing innocent civilians only to hit them with the butts of their swords. It felt dangerous here. I wondered where they could've taken Dusane in a city like this.

The murmur of nightlife surrounded us, just as loud and rambunctious as the day, it would seem. I thought these people might be winding down after a long day, but it seemed to be the liveliest time for them. We brushed shoulders with Stone-Hearted, pushing our way through the market square. We were just about to the other side when a hand landed on my shoulder, imploring me to stop.

I turned to see a little old woman grasping my arm. It was a shock to see her age. It wasn't every day a Stone-Hearted showed signs of true age. It meant she was hundreds of years old. Her bright violet eyes narrowed on me accusingly, and I was taken aback by the sudden hostile expression.

"You're the monster who burned the tree," she hissed at me. Her words slurred with anger as her leathery tongue accused me.

"Excuse me?" I asked, barely audible because I couldn't believe this woman knew who I was.

"You brought the curse onto us. You burned down our salvation!" She gripped my arm tighter, no doubt causing blood to draw where she clawed me.

I tried to tug my arm out of her grasp, but she was quite strong. My eyes narrowed on her, my heart beating so fast I could hear it in my ears. How did this woman know who I was?

Just before I could manage to fight back, a hand clamped down on the woman's arm, wrenching it from where she had her vice-like grip on me.

The woman grunted in pain, and I looked to my right to see Mid, the one who had stepped in.

"Touch her again, and you won't be seeing your last days," Mid growled.

I was still in shock that this woman knew my crimes. I was grateful Mid had stepped in, otherwise her fingernails would have probably reached my bones by now.

"What's going on here?" Shar came up behind me, his eyes narrowing on the old woman and Mid, who still had her skinny arm between his large hand.

"This woman, she knows that I burned down the tree," I whispered. I wondered what sort of rumors Elysian had spread to his people about me, how they knew my face. What if it wasn't Elysian at all? What if this woman was some sort of mind reader or future seer? I didn't know how she knew, but I now felt even more unnerved being in the streets of this city, knowing that people might recognize me.

"We need to find a place to stay for the night. We can't have you out on the streets," Shar's jaw clenched, and I hurried to follow after him and Rouix. Mid reluctantly let the woman go and followed behind me, his large presence reassuring me as we made our way to a place we could stop for the night.

A run-down inn came into view, and we hurried inside. The smell of fire and dirty bodies filled the room as we went to the counter to ask the keeper for a room.

"Got one room," the woman said, not even glancing up at us. She was reading a book, her spectacles lazily resting on the bridge of her nose.

"We'll take it," Shar said, and once he had the key, we hurried up the wooden staircase out of sight and into the dingy little guest room.

"Rouix, Rosen, you're coming with me. We're going to go and search for anyone who might have seen Dusane. You two, stay here," Shar said.

"I want to come with you," I said, gritting my teeth.

"Can't always get what you want, princess," Rosen said, smirking at me. I glared at him, feeling like I might just rip his head off with my teeth.

"Ehren, now is not the time to argue. If we are ever going to find Dusane, we have to see if anyone spotted them passing through. But if people in this city know you as the girl who burned down the tree, we aren't going to get very far. You need to stay here," Shar said.

"How did she know who I was?"

"I don't know, but Elysian could have plastered your picture in the churches or around town, for all we know. Or she's just a crazy woman. Who knows, but I'm not taking any chances. Stay here with Mid. We will be back as soon as we can."

I hated feeling useless. It was the worst feeling in the world after trying to be of use for so long. But I didn't argue anymore. Shar had a point. I would be more of a distraction if people kept recognizing me, and I didn't want to slow down our chances of being able to find Dusane.

~

Staying behind was much worse than being out in the city where I could be caught, because all I did was sit and worry. I paced the floors, working a pattern into the carpet as I walked back and forth across the small room.

"Ehren, you need to sit down. Eat something," Mid said. He was sitting on the only chair in the room, his arms crossed over his chest watching me anxiously pace.

"I can't sit down and eat when I know Dusane is out there probably being tortured by the hands of Elysian and maybe even rouge Envorydians. I saw Jade at the party. It must mean Elysian is working with rouges."

"Jade? You mean that Envorydian we fought on the Niafell Mountain? He's working with Elysian?" Mid suddenly asked.

"It looks like it. Dusane said he doubted those rouges we met were working for Elysian. But we were obviously very wrong."

"How did Dusane even know them?"

"Dusane used to be a part of their group. It's called the Mantle." I shook my head, still trying to process that at one point in time Dusane had been a rouge Envorydian. He'd worked for whoever paid him the most, and killed for others just like Elysian.

"So Elysian could be controlling this group of Envorydians? Why do they want Dusane?"

"I doubt they want him for anything other than to use him as bait in order to lure us into their trap." I growled in frustration. "Any chance Elysian has to put us off our game, he takes it."

"Great. First there is Elysian, then mermaids, and now lethal Envorydian clans. Things just keep getting better." Mid sighed, and I stopped pacing, forcing myself to sit on the edge of the flimsy bed.

"Just when I think we're going to get a step ahead of him, he throws a new obstacle into our path."

Silence spread between us for a moment as I continued to overthink and stress.

"You really should get some rest," Mid urged. "If we happen to catch onto Dusane's trail, you'll want to be as rested as possible for whatever fight awaits us."

I knew he was right. I just couldn't imagine sleeping, knowing he wasn't safe.

"Fine, I'll try."

I laid down, pulling back the covers and reluctantly crawling inside.

"What about you?" I asked, looking at him in the chair that didn't appear at all comfortable.

"I'm fine right here. You just sleep."

I wanted to argue but didn't have it in me after the night I'd just had. Closing my eyes, I was surprised that I welcomed the darkness. I was so exhausted my bones felt heavy and weighted with fatigue. I drifted into the blackness, sleep enveloping me—and then the nightmares came.

TWENTY-TWO

SUNN

I turned slowly to face him, irritation boiling in my veins.

"You did not just do that," I growled. Knowing full well that I'd just done the same to him. Except he deserved it.

Obsidian smirked, his dark eyes playful yet also holding some lingering threat.

"Two can play this game, Sunn. And let me assure you, you won't win."

He scooped up another handful of snow and threw it. It hit my shoulder, bursting into a flurry of crystal powder.

I gasped, shocked. Yet I also scolded myself for expecting anything less than retaliation.

But I wasn't about to let him get away with it.

I reached down, gathering another ball in my hands to throw at him. Soon we were in a full-fledged snowball fight. And each throw became a bit more emotional than they should've been.

I was angry about the kiss and scared for my friends. And

throwing the snow at Obsidian honestly was making me feel better. I probably should've felt some sort of guilt for making him my punching bag, but I felt none at all. If he wanted to be demanding and difficult, I would be too.

I growled aloud when I was hit for the third time on the back and I rushed to hide behind a pine tree.

I took several deep breaths to gather myself before I went into the line of fire again. Just as I was about to peek out from behind the tree to attempt another throw, I was tackled to the ground.

"Spirits!" I cursed as his body fell atop mine, both of us collapsing into the snow.

"Give it up, Sunn," he growled in my ear, and I gasped, struggling against his hold as he pinned me to the ground.

"Let go of me," I gritted out between clenched teeth, trying to shove him off me. It was a futile attempt. He was much bigger and much heavier. He wasn't going anywhere.

His hair fell into his eyes, creating a little shield around our faces in the cool night air. Our hot breaths mingled like puffs of smoke in the space between us.

"If I let go, you need to get back on the horse with me," he demanded in a hushed tone.

"It's a pegasus, genius. Not a horse," I spat angrily, and he rolled his eyes.

"I know you're afraid right now, Sunn. And I know you're acting like this in an attempt to stay sane. But I promise everything is going to be okay if you come back to Knadiel with me."

I let out a scoffing laugh. *Did he really think I was so stupid?*

"I know the reason you want to get back to Knadiel, and it's not to help me. It's to help yourself."

"Sunn. . ." he murmured, and his expression turned offended.

His jaw clenched, and he trailed off after saying my name. Then he reached up to brush back the wet locks of hair from my face. I was drenched in snow, and against my fervid skin the crystal ice was melting.

Suddenly with our faces so close together the memory of the kiss that we'd shared in the ballroom came rushing back to me all over again. It stung, knowing he'd only kissed me as a show. I wished I didn't care, and of all the things to be feeling right now anger and hurt over this kiss was not the one I should've been feeling the most. My friends were going after Dusane, who'd been kidnapped. I should be most concerned about them.

But my chest was aching and my heart felt like it had been stabbed a little after learning of the plan he'd had, and how he'd used me.

"Is this about the kiss?" he suddenly asked. Then he leaned down so his nose brushed my cheek, and I shuddered.

"Obsidian—"

"You're mad that I kissed you to start a fight," he said confidently, then he moved to the space just below my ear and gently pressed his lips to the sensitive skin there. I jumped at the sensation.

"I'm not mad," I managed to choke out, shivering beneath him and not because of the cold.

"I kissed you to start a fight. But that doesn't mean that I didn't enjoy it," he murmured, moving his hand from my cheek to the spot at my waist. His grip tightened.

My head fell back into the snow, and I tried desperately to regain control of my mind and body. *Was the world spinning?*

"My sweet, feisty girl," he said with a hint of a smile in his voice. "If you only knew."

I barely held in the whimper that threatened to leave me.

"I'm not mad about the kiss," I dared to say, even though it was a blatant lie.

"Then get back on the horse with me," he challenged, and that's when I looked back into his eyes. I could see the hunger mirrored in his expression. A tension was thick between us that I was scared and also curious to acknowledge. But I knew nothing good could come of it.

I forced myself to push on his chest, and he willingly backed off and helped me stand.

I brushed off the excess snowflakes clinging to my cloak, and then I marched back to Diablo. I hoped he couldn't see that my legs were shaking.

I mounted first, and he followed. Swiftly swinging his leg over, his hands wound around my waist and gripped Diablo's mane in his fingertips.

Nothing else was said as he kicked the pegasus up into the sky, and we flew away from the snowy forest.

TWENTY-THREE

SABEARA

The nightmares were a rendition of our fight at the Night Fell. Only we didn't make it out in my nightmares. We were trapped inside, every one of my friends left dead with vacant eyes and pale faces. I woke with a start, shaking, sweat dripping down my brow.

It was dark. The candles in the room extinguished. It took me a moment to remember where I was, that we were in Obscurum, searching for Dusane.

It was all my fault. If I had just stayed with him, insisted on not going down to break up the fight. Maybe I would've been close enough to stop them from taking him. If I had just let him return to the Sethen Courts like he wanted to originally, he wouldn't have been dragged into any of this. Into my mess.

All the guilt and regret weighed against my chest as I blamed myself, even though, logically, I knew it wasn't my fault.

My breath came in and out in short gasps, and I felt like my chest was closing in. My fingertips began to tingle, going numb, and losing sensation. I was getting caught up in some sort of panic. It was overwhelming my body, running through me like an unstoppable poison, and I felt almost like I was outside looking in on myself.

I knew I was probably overthinking because of everything that had happened. I knew logically I could breathe, but in that moment, it seemed impossible to make my body listen to my brain.

My hands flew up, clutching my throat.

"Mid!" I cried. *I can't breathe. I can't breathe.* "Mid," I yelled again, tears coming to my eyes as fear overwhelmed my body.

I could see his figure stir in the darkness. He must've fallen asleep on the chair. Suddenly a candle was lit, and the light softly illuminated the room.

"I can't breathe," I gasped, still clutching my neck, trying to get in the air that just didn't seem to fill my lungs anymore.

He knelt beside the bed, taking my face in his hands, wiping away the tears that were pouring down my cheeks

"Shhh, I'm here," he murmured, stroking my hair. "Try and slow down. Focus on breathing," he instructed.

"I can't—I can't breathe." I hiccuped a heart-wrenching sob. Wanting to be strong because crying and falling apart in a panic was not what I did. Neither was getting so angry I almost killed people. This wasn't me.

I reached for him, wrapping my arm around his neck and clinging to him. Needing an anchor. Needing something to take the fear away.

"You're having a panic attack, in and out now, sweetheart. In and out. Breathe with me," he said gently. He took in a big lungful of air, and I did my best to follow his inhale and exhale. It was a painfully long five minute before I started to calm down, and the fear began to subside. The feeling came back into my trembling hands.

Still clutching his shirt in my hands, my head buried in the crook of his neck—I knew I was safe. I also knew I should be embarrassed I just broke down and panicked so intensely. But this wasn't my Envoy captain.

This was Mid.

"That's it," he whispered, still giving me soft, soothing caresses, running a trail up and down my back. "Breathe."

"I'm sorry," I said, feeling tiredness seep into my body as I came down from the epic panic.

"Don't apologize," he said sternly. "Never apologize for your emotions."

Silence stretched between us for a couple of minutes as I gathered myself.

"Mid, why do you think Elysian is doing this?" I asked.

"I don't know. Forr power, most likely. Revenge against Aveladon, maybe. If he gets the tokens, he will become the most powerful man in the realm. Is that not enough incentive?" Mid looked sad like he wished he knew why too.

"He killed my mother. Why would someone kill their own sister?" I dared to say the words aloud. It crossed my mind alot. But there were no answers. With my parents dead and no one else with the full story of what happened all those years ago, I had only memories of that night in the sitting room, when I'd heard what my uncle had done.

"You haven't asked him, have you?" he whispered. "Obsidian?"

I shook my head. "I haven't spoken to him."

"He may know the reason," he said softly.

"I can only imagine the lies Elysian fed him. Why would I

have any reason to trust him?" I put my head in my hands, still trembling slightly from the panic attack.

"It might help you to come to terms with things."

A mocking laugh escaped me. "You know I didn't remember who Elysian was until I saw him again in that throne room."

"Oli told me," Mid said, his eyes sad.

"It all came flooding back to me, Mid. Like a giant wave." Tears filled my eyes again. "For years, I'd known he was the one who'd killed her, but I'd blocked it from my memory."

"You must not have been ready to face it until then."

"We were friends," I sniffled. "Obsidian and I." The vague image of us as children running through the woods behind the castle came to my head. It was blurry, so faint, that if I chased after the memory, it seemed to only disappear faster. "I remember spending time with him. I know we trusted one another." I paused. "I just wonder if it really had to come to this," I whispered. "Our family feud elicited a war." I looked up at him, trying to grasp the knowledge of that thought.

"It wasn't just your family," he whispered. "Obscurum wasn't the only kingdom that pleaded severance from Aveladon. My own ancestors left and created Ethydon as well. So it's not only the fault of your family. This separation, this war. . . It was inevitable."

"I feel like I'm breaking under the pressure," I whispered, daring to admit it aloud.

"You've been so strong for so long," Mid said to me, brushing back a strand of hair that was stuck to my cheek, wet from my salted tears. "You expect too much of yourself."

"I don't want to be that girl again," I admitted. "That girl that had to be rescued because she was so weak. I want to be capable of rescuing myself."

Mid's eyes appeared pained at my words. His jaw clenched, and he sighed.

"Just because someone has to come to rescue us every once in a while doesn't mean we are weak."

"What does it make me then?" I gestured to myself. "I'm nothing short of an anxious mess."

"It makes you human," he whispered. "And despite what you may think, just because your appearance is perfect, your senses are sharpened, and your body can heal from any wound inflicted upon you, does not mean that you're immune to pain and heartache. Deep down, underneath all of that beauty and strength is still a human girl. You don't just get to erase that part of you when you become Stone-Hearted."

I didn't want to believe he was right. I tried to erase every weak part of myself until nothing of Sabeara remained. But maybe that just wasn't practical. Maybe that weak and powerless girl would always be a part of me.

"Is it horrible that I don't want Dusane knowing how messed up I am?" I whispered. "If he saw me like this." I gestured to the tears on my face. "I can only think he'd be ashamed."

"I don't think anyone could ever be ashamed of you," Mid whispered.

I didn't know how to reply to that. I knew Dusane loved me. But he also expected things from me. Control and level-headedness were in the contents of our training. What would he say if he knew there were more fissures and cracks in my soul than he could count?

"Do you want me to help you dream?" Mid asked quietly.

I should've said no. I was with Dusane, and having another man calm me down from a panic attack and then whisk me off into pleasant dreams didn't seem very platonic, or safe.

"Please," I whispered, hating myself for the plea that left my lips, but knowing it was the only thing that would keep me from falling back into another panic. At that moment—I needed him.

I moved over in the bed, and he sat next to me, not attempting to get beneath the sheets. He leaned against the headboard instead, crossing his arms over his chest.

"I'll stay until you're asleep," he assured me. "Where do you want to go?" he asked softly.

"Take me to the garden," I said, and no explanation was needed.

"Okay," was all he said, then he stretched out his hand, feather-light as he touched my cheek. His palm glowed that familiar golden color and my eyes drifted close, transporting me to a world of soft red petals and crimson trees.

TWENTY-FOUR

SUNN

A knock sounded, waking me from a nightmare. It wasn't until moments later that my surroundings came to me. I spotted the white bedsheet and the veranda doors that held the view of Knadiel behind them, and I realized the nightmare had been real.

I sat up in bed with a gasp, just in time for the door to open and for my mother to come in.

"Sunn," she whispered, her voice choked with emotion. We hadn't had a proper reunion the night before.

"Mom," I replied, so relieved to see her that my heart ached.

She ran across the room and pulled me to her. I was still groggy, and the tears stung my tired, dry eyes.

We'd returned to Knadiel the night before. After a long flight, we'd landed on the mansion's front steps. I vaguely remember guards taking hold of Obsidian before hauling him away again. Then my mother and grandparents had come running down to meet me, and they'd ushered me up to my room. I'd told them what happened while half asleep, giving them as much information as possible until I could no longer keep my eyes open.

"Dusane was kidnapped, and the others went after him." I was saying it more to myself to remind myself that it was real. "We barely made it out of there."

"I'm so glad you're alive." She hiccuped a sob that nearly tore me in two.

After a moment of holding one another, she pulled away to look at me and then ran a hand down my wild red hair.

"Are you okay?"

"I'm fine. It's so good to be home."

"I don't know what I would've done if I had lost you. I'm still sick over the fact that Obsidian was the one to bring you back. So many things could've gone wrong, Sunn."

The thought of causing my mother more worry made my heart hurt. She'd already been through so much.

"Sabeara told him to get me back here if he wanted the cuff removed."

"We're lucky he listened."

I hated that I was lying to her. If she only knew how I really felt about the enemy living beneath the same roof as us.

"Are you okay? Did he harm you at all on the journey home?"

"No, mom. I'm fine. I told you, I lived on a ship with him for weeks. I know how to deal with him."

"I don't want you to have to deal with that monster, Sunn." Her words stung. And a part of me wanted to defend him, but I stopped myself before I could make that mistake.

"Well, it's over. And we have the cloak. So I guess it was all worth it."

"Nothing is worth risking your safety. It was wrong of me to allow you to go off with them like that. I should've known something would go wrong."

"No, don't say that," I pleaded with her. "I wanted to go. I needed to go. I hate being couped up and unable to help."

Her eyes spoke more than her words ever could. I would be lucky if she ever let me out of her sights again.

"You should rest more. I'll let you know when James and Liony arrive."

She kissed my forehead and then got up to leave. When the door closed behind her, I put my head in my hands and sighed.

~

James and Liony returned the next day. When I heard word that they were inside the castle, I rushed to James's room.

I was praying he would be there when I opened the door, and a huge wave of relief washed over me when I found him at his writing desk next to the window.

"Sunn," he greeted. His clothes were dirty and wet still from the long journey. He looked tired and fatigued, making guilt seize my chest. I could feel his quiet anger radiating off of him. He was most definitely still mad about what had happened.

"James," I said, taking a seat on the chair next to his bed and curling my feet beneath me. "I'm so sorry."

"There wasn't much you could do."

"Still, I'm sorry. He shouldn't have treated you like that. You were only trying to protect me."

He didn't respond for a moment. And I could feel that he wasn't ready to accept the apology.

"Do you know where they took him?" James suddenly asked.

I looked away, unable to meet his gaze. "The dungeons, I presume."

James shook his head, his jaw clenching and unclenching again. "He's in his own room."

"What?" My eyes widened.

"Liony thinks he is on our side now. After he helped us out of the castle and aided in your return to Knadiel safe and sound, she believes he's no longer a threat."

"That's a bold assumption."

"Oli isn't buying it, and he's livid that Liony is fighting him on the matter. But King and Queen Knadian agreed to no longer keep him in the dungeons, but in a guarded room in the east wing."

Silence emanated between us, and I could feel James's irritation radiating off of him.

"Please don't go see him," he suddenly said, his voice almost pained.

I looked up in surprise at his plea. "What makes you think I was going to?"

"I know you agree with Liony."

"When did I ever say I agreed with her?" I said, irritation flaring in my blood. I was still shocked Liony had advocated for Obsidian, after everything he'd done. Why she would do something like that, I wasn't quite sure.

"You didn't have to. You got on that horse with him. That was answer enough."

"He made me get on Diablo!" I growled, hating the accusation in his tone even though it was completely true. My heart beat for Obsidian. But no one needed to know that. "You don't know anything." I stood up and started for the door.

"Please, Sunn, be careful. He's not what you think he is."

I halted with my hand on the door handle. "What is he then? If you know him so well?" I narrowed my eyes accusingly.

"Exactly what you don't want him to be. A monster."

My nostrils flared. I was really getting tired of people calling Obsidian a monster.

"Just, please. Don't go near him. I don't want to see you get hurt," James begged, but it only made my anger at his words thicken.

"Come get me when you're ready to talk about the cloak." I shut the door behind me with a resonating slam, hoping that would get my point across.

James could try all he wanted to make me stay away from Obsidian, but little did he know I'd already tried to tell myself no. I'd scolded, berated, and rebuked my own insane attraction to this ungodly prince. But no one, not even myself, could stop my heart from wanting him. So I was done fighting.

My common sense had slowly been beaten to a pulp by my darkest desires, and my willpower was now a bleeding, battered mess left on the granite floors of the Dark Fell halls. There was no stitching up my reason. He had unraveled me. And I desperately never wanted to be put back together again.

~

My feet made their way to the east wing on their own. It felt like I was outside my body as I searched for Obsidian's room and ended up in front of the only door with a sentry stationed outside of it.

"I need to speak with Obsidian," I told the guard.

He eyed me warily. "Only King Olivine is permitted to—"

"Let me inside soldier. You don't want to mess with me," I

said and raised an eyebrow at him. I was ready to make additional threats, but he didn't need much convincing, it seemed, because he moved aside and opened the door for me.

I spotted Obsidian almost immediately. He was standing by the window, his black cloak absent from his shoulders, dressed in a white shirt and casual black pants. He didn't even bother turning to face me when I entered.

The room he was in was small and quaint. No decor was in his room like the other guests' rooms. A bed with a plain comforter was against the wall, and an old wooden vanity rested on one end of the room next to the closet. Despite its drab appearance, it was a definite step up from the cold dungeon he'd been in previously.

"Looks like someone needs to do some redecorating," I said casually, taking a seat on the edge of the bed. Despite my nonchalant tone, my heart was racing, my stomach a ball of nervous energy at the sight of him.

"What are you doing here, Sunn?" he finally asked, and I sighed, wishing he'd have played along, even if just for a moment.

"I think we should talk about what happened. Liony thinks you're no longer against us because you saved me back at the Night Fell. She was even bold enough to say that you're on our side now."

"I wouldn't say that exactly." He turned away from the window, and his black eyes met mine.

"What game are you playing?" I asked.

"Oh, you know. The one where I convince your family to trust me, then I kill them all in the end." His eyes gleamed with sinister promise.

"Sure." I gave him an incredulous look of disbelief.

"Don't say I didn't warn you."

I raised an eyebrow at him and stood from the bed. I walked over to him and felt this sudden pull to reach out and touch him. Why did I always want to be close to him? He was like a drug or a glass of Lush Fire but with far more addictive qualities.

"You could have left me to die back there. But you didn't."

"You wanted to be rescued." He flashed a knowing smirk. He was antagonizing me, and it made my heart flutter.

"Maybe I did." I reached out and touched his arm, he didn't pull away immediately, but his smirk faded. I suddenly felt brave enough to be blatantly honest with him. I tried to hate him, I tried to tell myself I was insane for being attracted to him. He was infuriating, and demanding, and yet I still wanted him so severely.

Maybe it was time to stop fighting the insanity.

I ran my fingers up his arm and dared to twirl the edge of one of his long locks between my fingertips.

"I like your hair," I commented abruptly, unable to hold in words after thinking them for so long.

His nostrils flared, and I swear I saw a glimpse of untold desire in his eyes. Then he stepped away, breaking the contact I had with him.

"You should leave," he said.

"Why?" I asked boldly, not moving an inch.

"Because if someone finds you in here, you might get in trouble."

"Worried about me, are you? How sweet." My words dripped with honeyed sarcasm.

"Get out," he said, demanding this time.

"Make me," I said, my blood running hot as fire as I took a dangerous step towards him again, invading his space. *Fight me, kiss me, put a knife to my throat,* I inwardly begged like an insane person. *Just please, touch me again.*

He looked about, ready to take me up on the offer, when a knock at the door sounded.

"Your majesty, is everything alright in here?" It was the guard I'd threatened, the fear in his eyes evident as he gazed at the two of us. He was probably checking to make sure I was still alive. If I died on his watch, he would definitely have to endure the repercussions. Obviously, he wasn't willing to risk that.

"Everything's fine. She was just leaving," Obsidian spoke for me.

I smirked at him and turned on my heel to leave the room. Just before leaving I stopped in the doorway and turned to say over my shoulder, "I'll see you at noon in the study tomorrow. You'll need to tell Liony how the cloak works."

"Why would I do that?" he asked,

"You're on our side now, remember?"

TWENTY-FIVE

SABEARA

Rouix, Rosen and Shar returned with a lead on where Dusane may have been taken. The two had spoken to a group of men that labored in the city at night and said they'd seen a group of men in dark cloaks carrying an unconscious man. Shar asked which direction, and they said towards the water.

"So they're going through the city?" Rouix said. We were all sitting inside the small inn room. I was too nervous to sit, so I paced the floor.

"Probably planning on passing through," Shar said. "Wherever they're taking him, it's not the castle and most definitely not somewhere in the main city."

"What's beyond the city walls?"

"More sand and more water," Rosen said. "There's not much in the Obscurum kingdom other than the city Elysian has built. The rest is desert, untouched and unclaimed."

"You're sure about that?" I pressed, hating that we were so clueless on what lay beyond Elysian's kingdom.

"Well, there is one place," Shar said, and he looked grim. "There is an island off the coast of the Severesi waters that border Obscurum seas, where the Mantle has been rumored to train their youth."

"Xevaria," Rouix whispered, her face turning pale.

"Oh spirits, I forgot about Xevaria," Rosen said.

"So you think they may be taking him there?" I asked.

"Wait, since when does the Mantle have an island?" Mid asked.

"Not many people have been there. The only person I know that's been on the island before is Dusane and. . ." Shar glanced at Rouix, who looked as if she'd seen a ghost.

"Rouix, do you know where this place is?" I asked.

She nodded slowly, her eyes vacant of emotion as she stared off across the room. "I was raised there."

A silence filled the room as this news settled.

"Wait, I thought the Mantle was just a group of rebel Envorydians that had bad blood with Dusane. Since when do they have a place where they train up Envorydians?" Mid asked.

"Obviously, Dusane hasn't gone into much detail on the reality of the Mantle," Shar said, biting his lip.

"He said that the Mantle was a bad group of Envorydians and that he'd made enemies with them long ago. He never really told me anything else," I said.

"The mantle is the most vicious Envorydian tribe in the entire realm," Rouix whispered. "They have Envoy techniques dating back to Wesoltinece that have long since died among other Envorydians. On Xevaria they raise and train Envorydians from childhood, so they are more vicious than the others. Dusane has bad blood with them because his loyalties weren't always solid. Dusane worked for many people in the past, and he betrayed the Mantle at one point."

When I got Dusane back, he would be explaining to me what happened with the Mantle. I'd obviously not asked enough questions because everyone else seemed to know my boyfriend's past life except me.

Shar's jaw clenched, obviously not liking that Rouix was talking about the Mantle.

"Would the mantle really side with Elysian just to get revenge on Dusane?" Mid asked.

"It's more than that, I'm sure," Shar said, "I bet they are siding with Elysian because he offered them money and Dusane's head."

"Two things the Mantle can't resist. Revenge and Money," Rosen said. I didn't want to know how Rosen knew about the Mantle, so I didn't ask.

"Okay, so you grew up there?" I asked, looking at Rouix. "Your parents were part of the mantle."

Rouix laughed darkly. "No, my parents weren't on the island. They sold me to the Mantle when I was a baby."

"Sold you?" My eyes widened, nausea overtaking my stomach.

"I think we should focus on finding Dusane. We don't have much time," Shar interrupted, cutting off the conversation abruptly. He obviously didn't want us to press her about it. I looked over at him, but his sharp green eyes didn't reveal anything more.

I decided that it could wait. I'd ask her later if the time felt right.

"Let's head towards the island then. It seems like a logical place he might be," Rosen said, a somber expression on his face.

"Now that you mention it, I think it's the only place he'll be," Rouix said. "Knowing that Jade was at the party too, it's very likely Elysian and the Mantle are working together. I think it's our best guess." The fear in her eyes made me realize just how serious the situation was. I don't think I'd ever seen Rouix with fear so openly in her expression. Which could only mean they were in for a lot of trouble.

TWENTY-SIX

SUNN

The next morning I entered the study, Liony was already waiting for me. She had a cup of tea in her hand and was blowing on the steam gently.

"Sunn, you wanted to meet?" Liony asked, and I sat down beside her trying to look relaxed.

"I spoke to James yesterday," I said, and Liony merely raised an eyebrow. It was what I had always loved about Liony. Her ability to act calm in any situation. She was the most nonjudgmental person I knew. I'd grown up with her because her brother Shar was Mid's guardian. Liony was family to me.

"He said you talked the others into letting Obsidian out of the dungeons. Why would you do that?"

"You and I both know that Obsidian isn't going to hurt anyone."

"Do we know that?" I asked, raising an eyebrow.

"He wouldn't risk hurting you," she said confidently.

I paused, not sure if I liked how much Liony was seeing.

"I talked with Obsidian, too. I told him to come here. I thought he could tell us about the cloak.""

"Your mom doesn't want you getting involved with the curse stuff after what happened at the Night Fell. She'll be really upset with me if she finds I am in here talking to you about it."

"My mother can't keep treating me like a child. Please, Liony," I said, my eyes pleading.

Liony sighed, then slowly, a small smile tugged at the corners of her lips.

"Well, I figured if we were going to study this cloak's powers, we might as well do it right. I invited Jasper as well."

"What?" Panic threaded through me.

"She has possession of the cloak now, for safety purposes, of course. I told her we'd be getting together to test the cloak out in the study once you asked me to come."

"But what if Obsidian doesn't show up?" I started to feel more nervous now, knowing the queen of Aveladon would be attending this study session to figure out the powers of the constellation cloak.

"Oh, he'll show," Liony said, her tone sure.

I didn't have time to react to her comment because the door to the study opened and Obsidian walked through the door. Two guards flanked him, one of them being James.

Obsidian's face gave nothing away as he sat down on the other end of the long study table. The study was a quaint little room in the mansion, with books on all sides filling dark wooden shelves. It was dim, only lit by the light of a small window that gave view of the Knadiel village.

"You asked for me," Obsidian said, his eyes on Liony.

Liony smiled and gestured toward me. "She seems to think you know what the cloak does."

Obsidian didn't answer, his eyes shifted to me slowly, and he raised an eyebrow. "Does she?"

The study doors opened again, and Jasper walked through the doors. She looked as regal and refined as ever, a long blue dress gracing her body with the red Aveladon cloak around her shoulders. Her beautiful blonde hair was pinned back from her face, and I couldn't help but look down at my shirt and pants and feel slightly out of place.

"Good morning," Jasper greeted, giving us all polite nods.

She came to sit beside Liony, who smiled sweetly at her.

"Glad you could join us, my queen. Obsidian here was just going to tell us what he knew about the cloak," Liony said sweetly.

Obsidian's jaw clenched, and Liony smirked at him.

"I helped you get the cloak. Shouldn't you be setting me free now?" Obsidian asked, and I couldn't help but notice that James had refused to look at me since we got into the study. He was eyeing the books on the shelves, looking as if he was trying to do anything but tune into the conversation we were having.

"Well, we can't really set you free yet because Sabeara and Dusane are halfway across the realm. And considering they won't be back for a while, why don't you just help us to know what the cloak does in the mean time?" Liony said, her sweetness suddenly seeming almost lethal as her silvery gaze bore into Obsidian.

His eyes narrowed, but after a moment, his onyx eyes softened and he sighed.

"Whoever wears the cloak gets a complete knowledge of their powers and how to use them."

Silence spread throughout the study as we all took this in.

"But I already know what my power is and how to use it," Jasper said, confusion furrowing her perfect brow.

"You may think you know how to use your power, but a Stone-Hearted can take many years to master every aspect of their power. And even then, some die never knowing their full potential."

Jasper pulled something from inside her cloak, revealing the constellations cloak, and set it on the wooden table for all of us to see.

"Shall we try it then?" I asked. "I can't use it 'cause I obviously don't have any powers. But Jasper?" I gestured towards the cloak. "Maybe you should try?"

The queen hesitated for a moment before nodding and taking the cloak and wrapping it around her shoulders. The guards that followed her in hovered around her, looking concerned she was putting the piece of clothing on.

"Relax, I'm not going to be harmed," she told the two guards, and they took one step back, a wary look still on their faces.

After she fastened the cloak, she looked at Obsidian. "What now?" she asked.

"Now try using your power," he said.

Jasper nodded. Hesitantly, she closed her eyes, and after a moment, a soft breeze filled the study. Jasper looked to be in serious concentration as she summoned her air power.

The air in the room shifted, turning into a soft breeze that ruffled my hair, and Jasper gasped aloud.

Soon we were in a whirlwind. The air around us picked up into a mighty sweeping swell, causing books to start flying off the shelves and the windows to rattle.

The two guards took hold of Jasper, worried for her safety.

"My queen, maybe you should stop!" One guard shouted over the whooshing noise of the wind.

But Jasper didn't stop. Her eyes remained clenched shut, the wind getting even stronger. I had to grip the study table so as not to be knocked over, the wind was so strong.

And then something miraculous happened.

The air in the room started to form dark grey clouds all around us in the small study, a musky scent surrounding us. Then I felt a water droplet hit my cheek, and I gasped, looking up. Suddenly it was raining in the study.

Small storm clouds above us shed raindrops into the study, and a small lightning blot gave a flash of light.

She'd created a storm.

Jasper opened her eyes, and let out a sweet sounding laugh.

"I never knew," she whispered in amazement. And then slowly, the storm dissipated, the clouds evaporating, and the wind calming. Soon we were back in the study, all of us slightly disheveled and damp after the episode.

Jasper took the cloak off her shoulders and put it on the table, looking at the token with wide eyes.

"I could understand my power completely. It was like reading a language I've been trying to understand for years."

"That was incredible," Liony said, wringing out her short black hair over the table.

"We need to tell the others," James said, his wide eyes still transfixed on the cloak.

I nodded, also entranced by the token and the glittering constellation pattern embroidered across the navy blue fabric.

We now had four of the five tokens.

Only one more to go.

TWENTY-SEVEN

SABEARA

We emerged from the tree line, and my eyes took in the icy sheet of ocean before us. Though we stood on hot, nearly burning sand where the shore met the water, it became cold as stone.

We'd been traveling for half a day, following Rouix's directions to the shoreline. It had brought us to a sandy shoreline pressed up against a frozen sea.

Being on the border of the two climates was particularly interesting. How it was possible, none of us were sure. But we looked out at the icy landscape, and I could see the fear in my friend's eyes.

"Do we have to cross the ice?" I asked.

"You can see the island in the distance," Shar said, pointing to the horizon.

I squinted my gaze, as did the others.

It was hard to see so far out, but after a moment, I finally spotted the dark speck that must've been Xevaria. There was definitely something out there amidst the icy terrain.

"I see it," Rosen said, holding up a hand to his eyes to block out the sun.

I walked across the sand and placed my boot on where the ice began. I put light pressure on it, testing it to see how strong it was.

It didn't budge, not a crack in sight, so I stepped on with both feet. A relieved breath escaped me.

"We'll have to be careful crossing. We don't want to fall through," I said to the others.

Shar came up beside me, also stepping onto the ice.

"We'll be careful then," he said, his jaw set determinedly.

We spread out in a line, following each other with a bit of distance between us to disperse the weight across the ice. We walked slowly, so slowly it was almost painful.

I wished so badly I could run, run until my lungs burned and my heart ached.

I just wanted to get to Dusane as quickly as possible.

At one point in the journey, a chunk of ice gave way beneath Mid's shoe and his right foot plunged into the icy water. He pulled it out with a curse, and my heart jumped into my throat.

"Mid!" I yelled, fear coursing through me.

"I'm fine," he assured us, but his teeth were gritted. It must've been freezing. He pulled his sopping boot out of the hole in the ice and proceeded forwards again.

I turned back to face the island reluctantly. It was closer now, and I could see trees poking up on the small bit of land, blanketed in ice.

I glanced back at Rouix, checking if her face showed the fear I had seen back on the shore.

Rouix appeared impassive, her red eyes assessing the island ahead with sheer determination. That brief moment of fear I'd seen in her eyes was gone now.

She was ready to face her demons.

TWENTY-EIGHT

SUNN

I stared at my reflection the next morning, my fingers working on the crimson strands as I plaited my hair down over my shoulder. My mind wandered to thoughts of Ennsleon's cloak, and all that we had discovered. I had felt nothing with the cloak on my shoulders. But Jasper had. She'd had an epiphany of sorts. The cloak told her more about her powers than she could have thought possible. But when she took it off, she retained none of it. The cloak seemed to give the user the ability to access the full height of their abilities. It was an unusual weapon, but a weapon, no doubt.

A knock at the door sounded, pulling me from my thoughts.

"Come in," I called.

The door swung open, and James appeared on the other side. He strolled into the room, holding a small sponge cake with brown frosting on the top. It looked absolutely delicious.

"Good morning," he said politely, setting the cake down in front of me.

"What's this?"

"Don't you know what day it is?" he asked, his brow furrowing with disappointment.

"Uh, care to enlighten me?" I swiped some of the frosting with my finger and sucked it with delight. It was chocolate. My favorite.

"It's your birthday," he said, gesturing to the cake.

My eyes widened. I'd forgotten. With everything else going on, my birthday was the last thing on my mind.

"I thought you were mad at me."

"Truce for today, then?" James asked, and I was grateful to see that he was in better spirits.

I laughed at my own memory lapse. "I almost forgot, you know?" I said. "Eighteen isn't really that special if I don't get any powers."

James frowned, reaching out a finger and stealing a taste of the frosting.

"It's still special. You're technically an adult now."

I rolled my eyes. "Sure. Tell that to my parents, and my grandparents, and Mid, and Shar—"

"Okay, okay," James raised his hands in surrender. "So it means nothing."

"I appreciate you saying that," I said with sarcasm, smirking. "Because I am no more an adult than I was yesterday, according to them."

"Being the youngest in the family makes them protect you needlessly," James said.

"You're not family and you protect me needlessly," I pointed out, raising an eyebrow.

James flushed and distracted himself by throwing away the remains of the cake I'd now dissected after only eating the frosting.

"Okay, so maybe you're just the type of person people want to protect. Stop being so—protectable."

I rolled my eyes. "I'll do my best. Now tell me the truth, does my mother have something planned?"

James bit his lip. "Maybe."

I stood from the vanity with a groan. "I have to stop this now before it gets out of control."

James followed me out of my room and down the hallway to the dining room. My mother and grandparents were seated at the table, along with Jasper and Oli beside them. They had a stack of papers in front of them, talking amongst themselves quietly. When they saw James and me enter the room my mother stood immediately and came to embrace me.

"Happy Birthday, sweetie."

"Thanks, Mom," I managed to say with a forced smile.

She pulled away, and the excitement in her eyes was unmistakable.

"I have some fun thing planned today and—"

"Can we not do anything?" I blurted, cutting her off.

Jasper's tea spoon clanked loudly in the sudden silence.

"You don't want to do anything for your birthday?" My grandmother asked, and it would be impossible to miss the dejected tone of her voice.

"Uh, well, you see, I'm just not really up to celebrating due to the whole not receiving my powers thing," I admitted. "And I'm a little stressed knowing that the others are out there searching for Dusane. It sort of kills the desire to celebrate when people I care about are in danger."

"But honey—" My mother started to argue.

"I understand, Sunn. How about instead of having a party, you come to the village with me later today?" Jasper suggested.

"What are you doing in the village?"

"I have to grab some supplies."

"Sounds a lot better than having a party," I admitted.

My mother sighed but nodded her head. "Just be safe, and take James with you." My mother raised a brow at him. "I trust you will keep her out of trouble?"

James blushed and gave my mother a small nod. "I'll do my best."

~

The village in Knadiel reminded me much of the city that once existed in Ethydon before it was attacked and destroyed.

The buildings were all made from wood, harvested from the forests around Knadiel, and brown and red flags waved from the balconies.

I sighed, looking around at the people milling about the village square. The people seemed happy, content even. The population of Knadiel wasn't very big. Most of the people that used to live in Aveladon and Ethydon had died in the war. I didn't remember much detail from that time. I only remembered traveling through the woods with Sabeara and meeting my father on the docs. I remembered being afraid.

"You should buy something, Sunn," Liony said. She had agreed to join us when she found out we were headed into the village for supplies.

"I don't need anything," I replied easily.

She rolled her stormy gray eyes, and Jasper, on the other side of me, smiled. Jasper was always quiet and only spoke when it was necessary.

"It's your birthday. You have to get something for yourself. How about this?" Liony stopped outside a shop selling beautiful hair clips. The owner had made them out of twigs and flowers, creating gorgeous leafy designs that could be put into your hair.

"I don't really do hair clips," I responded and she sighed. Hooking her arm with mine, she guided me further into the square where a beautiful fountain rested. A couple children were throwing in coins and laughing together.

"You're boring me," Liony said.

"We came here for supplies, not to shop for me," I reminded her.

James was holding the bag of paper and ink we had bought. He trailed behind the three of us, observing for threats or anything that might jump out around a corner. Too bad there wasn't much to protect us from. Knaidel was safe. Extremely safe. I wasn't worried anything would happen.

"Okay, well, you can't stop me from buying something for you. How about this?" Liony pulled up to another shop window. It was a dress store. In the window were gorgeous gowns of various colors, sparkling and glistening with rhinestones and jewels. Liony gestured towards a gorgeous black dress with a sparkling bodice.

"When would I ever wear that?" I asked, my brow furrowing. But I would never let them know that I really liked the design. It reminded me of Obsidian's black eyes. I wasn't known to make fashion choices over people's eyes, but I wasn't known for being attracted to evil princes either. There was a first time for everything, I guessed.

"Whenever you want! There need not be an occasion to dress

up and feel beautiful, Sunn. Remember that," Liony pointed a finger at me. Then, without asking for permission, went into the store and bought the dress. Before I could stop her, it was put into a bag and passed to James, who without complaint, carried it for us.

"It's a lovely gown," Jasper said, giving me a kind smile. "I think it will look great on you."

"Thanks, Jasper," I said, hating to disappoint the queen of Aveladon. I smiled kindly at her and didn't make any more fuss about the dress. If it went unworn, so be it. At least Liony and Jasper were happy.

We wandered around the square for some time. Jasper stopped to talk with some of the people. She obviously knew them well. They spoke as if they were old friends. She ensured that things were running smoothly and that people were happy and healthy. She was a perfect queen.

Our afternoon shopping spree in the village didn't last long. I began to feel guilty that we were enjoying ourselves while Sabeara and the others were on a mission to rescue Dusane. Every day they didn't return, the worry seemed to deepen. How could I enjoy myself when my family and friends were still in danger?

Soon we headed back and we stepped into the mansion again. I thanked Jasper and Liony for the afternoon and retired to my room.

James followed me upstairs and dropped the dress bag onto my bed while I sat down with a sigh into the comforter.

"How was shopping, you two?" my mother asked as she came walking through the door.

"It was nice to get out," I said, trying to plaster on a fake smile.

"It was a lovely afternoon," James said. "I should get going, though. Make sure I'm not needed somewhere else." He bowed at the waist and then quickly left the room, leaving my mother and me alone.

"What did you get?" She gestured towards the bag.

"Oh, Liony bought me a dress," I showed her the beautiful ebony gown, and she smiled.

"Well, the thing I got you will go perfectly with it." Her eyes shone with excitement as she passed me a small little bag.

"Mom, you didn't have to," I started to say.

"You're my daughter. I have to spoil you. It's my job."

I smiled thankfully at her as I began opening the gift. Then I pulled out a beautiful black shawl. She was right. It would go perfectly with the dress. It sparkled and shone just like the gown, with beads that dangled from the edges of the beautiful piece of clothing.

"Wow, it's amazing. Thank you." I hugged her tightly, thanking her for the gift.

"I know things aren't ideal right now. But I want you to know how much I love you. And someday, you will get your powers, honey. I promise." She brushed back a strand of my wild red hair, and I felt a lump form in my throat. I suddenly felt emotional.

"When is father coming home?" I asked her, wishing so badly that he didn't have to care for Arradale so we could be together.

"I don't know honey, probably not until the curse is over and Obscurum is defeated," she whispered, and I could see she was hurting too.

"I just want this all to end," I said, looking down sadly at the shawl pressed between my hands.

"Me too." She kissed my forehead.

"Mind if I have some time to myself?" I asked her, "Eighteen seems to be hitting me a little harder than I thought." I gave her a weak smile.

"Of course." She stood from the bed and walked towards the door. "Happy Birthday, sweetie."

TWENTY-NINE

SABEARA

Despite being able to see the island, it was an infuriating speck for most of the journey.

When we finally could make out all the details on the island, I couldn't help but sigh with relief.

But the relief was short-lived. Now that we'd survived getting to Xevaria, we had to get Dusane off of it.

An icy castle-like structure was surrounded by large trees glossed over in sheets of ice. Surrounding the icy treescape were caves that dripped with icicles.

"Do we head in blind?" Mid asked.

"We don't have much of a choice," Rosen said, his jaw clenching.

"Rouix, do you remember how this place is mapped out?" I asked and she shook her head.

"A lot of the memories are blank now."

I felt immediately horrible for pressing. She'd been sold to the Envoyridans on this island. What had happened to her?

The only thing I knew for certain was that it would have been traumatizing for her if she'd blocked it all out.

Shar nodded grimly and stepped into the first cave.

"If we encounter the enemy, we'll just have to fight our way through."

A chill went up my spine, followed by a rush of the rage that so frequently hovered above the surface of my self-consciousness. A quiet thrill also went through me at the thought of a fight.

Nothing would be sweeter than avenging Dusane. Dark images of seeing people bleed for taking him from me bombarded my mind and I had to fight them back.

You're not a killer. I told myself.

We entered the dark caves on the island. They reminded me much of the way Severesi was built. Nearly translucent, our hearts illuminating off the surface in an array of rainbow colors.

It was beautiful but also cold and oddly eerie.

We stayed in a tight line, assessing our surroundings carefully.

I clenched my dagger in my hand. Jumping at even the slightest noises—water dripped down from the cave walls and ceiling, the thud of someone's boot scuffing up the icy floor.

We blindly wove our way through the icy tunnels until we took one route and ended up face-to-face with five Envorydians.

We all halted in our tracks, our breaths catching in our throats. Everything was still for a few seconds, and then we lunged for them.

It was a swift fight.

We each took one of the Envorydians guarding the entrance

to the tunnel. A battle cry echoed around us, and the cry was from my own lips.

I dug the tip of my dagger into the shoulder of the man I was zeroed in on.

He was covered in tattoos, his heart a bright violet. He must've been at least a foot taller than me. But I didn't allow myself to be intimidated.

He let out a cry of pain when my blade met his flesh, and fresh crimson blood spattered the cool white ice—tainting its crystal sheen.

I dug it deeper into his flesh for good measure, then landed a kick to his stomach.

He doubled over. I pulled out my dagger from his shoulder. I wiped the blade on my pants and then turned to face the others.

They had already taken down the other four, and we all were catching our ragged breaths in unison.

"Let's keep going," Shar instructed, not missing a beat.

It felt criminal leaving those men behind in the tunnel, bleeding out onto the snowy floor.

But nothing was going to stop me from getting back Dusane.

We emerged from the tunnels a few moments later. We expected more resistance, but there was no one to be found.

It felt oddly like a trap. Like they were leaving the tunnels open so we would come onto their territory.

It was like they'd left the door open and invited us in.

I knew it couldn't possibly be so easy.

We emerged from the other side of the tunnel, the sun still high in the sky. And that's when the castle-like structure came into view.

It was in the very center of the island. Encased in the tropical trees that were blanketed in thick alabaster snow.

I scanned the three stories with my eyes and knew that they must be keeping him inside there. Where else would they be keeping him?

"We need to get inside that building," Rouix said, her jaw clenching. "I think I know where they are keeping him."

THIRTY

SUNN

It didn't take me long to find a bottle of Lush Fire and attempt to drown my disappointments.

Eighteen. A day I had dreamed of since being a child. But our realm was cursed, and I was destined to remain human until all of this insanity was sorted out.

I'd put on the black gown Liony had purchased for me and the shawl from my mother. They fit perfectly, and I had to admit I loved the way I looked.

I lay on the carpet in a pile of glittering black silk, staring at the ceiling, while everything felt fuzzy and numb. I drank straight from the bottle, taking another sip, and some orange liquid dribbled onto my cheek.

I wasn't usually so dismal. I usually saw a bright side to most things. But tonight, I felt like wallowing. I'd entertained my mother and friends for the day. It was my turn to do what I really wanted. And that just so happened to be getting lushed in my bedroom while staring at the ceiling.

My thoughts strayed to my uncle Mid and the others on a rescue mission to get Dusane. I worried for their safety—wondered if they would indeed find him or if something far worse was awaiting them. I hated this worry, this stress that was strung throughout my body day in and day out. I wished I could go back to being a kid when I didn't have to face such things.

I sighed and sat up, the world spinning for a moment as I got to my feet. I exited my room and started down the hallway that shimmered like a moving picture. I knew exactly where I was headed and knew I shouldn't, but in my drunkenness, I didn't have the common sense to stop myself.

When I got to his door, I was lucky enough that the guard stationed outside was fast asleep. So much for keeping the evil villain from escaping. Obsidian could have easily ran. *Why hadn't he? Was he really on our side now?*

I stepped over the guard with surprising gracefulness and opened the door without bothering to knock.

My eyes found him almost instantly. He was sitting shirtless on his bed, leaning back against the headboard, a book splayed on his lap.

Spirits, he's beautiful.

His eyes widened at the sight of me. "What are you doing in here?"

"Your guard is a horrible sentry." I ignored his comment and swayed over to the sofa, bottle still in hand.

"Are you drunk?" he asked me. Setting his book aside, he looked at me with a furrowed brow.

"I'm not drunk," I stated, my lip jutting out in a pout. "I'm just a little tipsy, is all."

"Uh huh." He didn't look convinced.

Then he seemed to notice what I was wearing, his eyes

running down the length of me, taking in the black dress and the way it hugged my body like a glove. I shouldn't have enjoyed the way he was admiring me, but I liked it. I liked it alot.

"Like what you see?" I asked, smirking at him.

His eyes snapped up, and his jaw clenched. "You shouldn't be in here."

"And you shouldn't be so grumpy all the time," I said, tossing back another gulp full of Lush Fire, my throat burning with the fiery bubbles.

He sighed, pinching the bridge of his nose as if he was getting a headache just having me in close proximity to him.

"Since when do you read?" I asked him, gesturing to the open book.

"Is there something wrong with me reading?" he asked, his tone clipped.

I smiled at him, not bothering to hide the sultry longing in my eyes. "No, it's just not something I imagined you would enjoy doing."

"And what do you assume I do with my free time?" he asked, raising an eyebrow.

"Oh, I don't know. Plan ways to prey on the innocent. Plot your revenge against Aveladon." I paused and looked at him with playfulness in my gaze. "Sleep with beautiful women."

He made a surprised noise in the back of his throat, almost like a scoff and a chuckle mixed together.

"And how do you suppose I'd do those things while locked away in here?" he asked, humoring me. I loved when he humored me. It made my heart flutter and my skin tingle with a heat that was addictive. I wanted his words to melt me. His gaze to burn me. Inside and out. Like a moth to the flame, I didn't care what happened to me if I got close to him. As long as I could have this feeling.

"Well, the first two you can do easily in this limited space." I gestured to the small room he had been trapped within for a week now.

"And the last one?" he asked, raising one dark eyebrow, his onyx eyes boring into mine. Daring me to respond. "Finding a woman to share my bed with isn't so easy when I'm being kept prisoner."

I hated the sudden image in my head of him with other women. The jealousy that ripped through me was raw and real. I don't know what I'd been hoping for, that he wouldn't speak so nonchalantly in response to my accusation. But then again this was Obsidian. I should've learned long ago not to expect anything from him.

I set down the bottle beside me, the liquid courage like a drug in my veins. I loved feeling invincible.

I slowly stalked toward him, doing my best not to stumble in my haze. He simply watched me patiently as I neared. I didn't hesitate to reach out and touch his arm. His pale skin was so soft.

"I'm sure there's at least one woman in this castle willing to break the rules for you."

His eyes flickered to my hand on his arm.

"Are you offering?"

I giggled, not able to help myself. I stumbled away from him, back to the safety of the sofa. He had no idea just how much I was offering.

"I'm not giving my virtue to just anyone," I slurred. "I'm seeking a noble, gentlemanly prince that is going to sweep me off my feet and make me his jewel." I fanned myself, pretending to look off into the distance, a whimsical look passing across my features.

To my surprise, he laughed. And the sound was felt down to my bones.

"Oh, sweet girl, nobility is an illusion."

The nickname fell from his lips, and I felt my heart stop in my chest. He'd called me that same name back in the snowy forest too, and it took me a moment to remember to breathe again.

I looked over at him, trying to see if he regretted his term of endearment. But the playful wickedness still shining in his eyes told me he didn't.

"An illusion?" I asked, sounding sort of breathless even to myself.

"All men are the same," he assured me. "You may find one willing to entertain a noble front for a time. A man that feigns to seek your company. But really, men only want one thing."

His eyes ran up the length of my body, and I couldn't stop the goosebumps that rose on my arms.

"You're disgusting," I said, sticking my tongue out at him. "That can't be all men want."

He raised an eyebrow as if daring me to defy his opinion.

"Maybe not all men. I mean, some of us want to be left alone, in our solitude, to read." He smirked and gestured to his book.

"Today's my birthday, you know." I ignored his attempt to get me to leave, and he sighed.

"I didn't know." He didn't offer a happy birthday.

"Eighteen isn't very fun without getting my abilities. That's why I'm drinking this." I lifted the bottle up for him to see. It was almost empty now.

"Seems like a healthy alternative to facing your disappointment."

I glared at him.

"You're one to talk," I grumbled.

This surprisingly elicited another chuckle from him, and the sound of it made my bones even warmer.

"You have a pretty laugh."

He raised an eyebrow. "I think you should head back to your room now. Wouldn't want someone to find you here."

"Scared someone might figure out you're not as scary as you let on?"

His dark eyes narrowed. "I think you're delusional. I've never given you any reason to believe I'm anything but lethal."

He would really do anything to keep up his villainous facade.

"Does it ever get tiring? Lying so much?"

He rolled his eyes. "You're relentless. Please go to sleep."

It wasn't healthy, but I greatly enjoyed seeing him so bristled. He was beautiful in every form. But when his emotions would rise, it gave him a different kind of beauty. A dark, addictive beauty that I wanted to drink.

Definitely drunk, I thought. *How could I possibly be thinking about drinking him?*

"Fine. I'll go to bed. But you're going to miss me." I stumbled to my feet, wobbling to the door.

"I'll be positively nostalgic when you're gone."

I giggled, walking out the door and back into the hallway. I don't remember anything else after that. The Lush Fire puzzled my thoughts and made me wonder if the encounter in his room had been nothing but a blissful, lushed dream.

THIRTY-ONE

SABEARA

The plan was to scale the mansion. Which sounded easier than it actually was.

"You sure that he's up there?" I asked Rouix.

Her blood-red eyes assessed me, and they narrowed a bit at my skepticism.

"No, I'm not sure. But I think it's our best bet," she replied.

"They're luring us onto the island. If they wanted to stop us, they would've tried by now," Mid said, his features tense.

"We just have to hope we can escape the trap once we fall into it," Shar said with a sigh. Reaching down to his side, he pulled two knives from his holster. Then with a grunt, he stabbed the sleek blade into the ice, lodging it in place so he could begin climbing.

"You don't like this," I said, looking at the tense expression on Shar's face. The fact that we'd walked onto the island with little to no resistance so far was a huge red flag. They expected us to come after Dusane, and they'd let us walk on to Xevaria so easily there was no way it wasn't a trap.

My stomach twisted with nervous anticipation.

"I don't have another choice. And I hate not having another choice," Shar admitted, and then he began climbing.

He was faster than I expected. Using all his strength to pull himself up by stabbing his knives into the ice, ascending towards the window on the third floor.

I looked at Mid, and he gestured for me to go ahead of him.

"Worried I'll fall?" I asked him, sensing that he was going behind me in case.

"Is it so horrible that if you fall, I wanna be there to catch you?" he questioned, raising an eyebrow.

My heart did a weird little flip before I suffocated the emotion and forced myself to focus on the task at hand.

I reluctantly went next, taking out two knives from my pack. I followed Shar's example and began slamming the blade of my knives into the icy wall one at a time. Climbing as fast as my muscles would carry me.

Mid, Rosen, and Rouix climbed beneath me, and with heavy breaths, I watched Shar above me, gauging my speed and forcing the burning in my arms to the back of my mind. Three stories were higher than I anticipated.

At one part of the climb, I didn't embed one of my knives into the wall deep enough so I slipped, and Mid caught my foot.

My breath left me, and fear seized my whole body for a few seconds while I reinserted my knife.

"Thanks," I said, looking down at Mid for a moment. He nodded, his jaw clenched, and we continued the grueling climb.

Eventually, I pulled my body over the sill, my stomach

scratching on the cold, icy stone as I tumbled through the window.

Shar was already there, and as I stood up, regaining my balance to join him, my heart stopped again in my chest.

Standing in the room were a dozen or so Envorydians. They each had emblazoned a plethora of tattoos on their bodies, the rouge Envoy tattoo the only one I recognized.

And then, standing in the middle of the group of guild fighters was Elysian.

Mid and Rouix tumbled in behind me, and they also stood. I knew the moment they realized we were surrounded. I heard both of their breaths hitch, and Mid cursed under his breath.

"Where is he?" I demanded, and Elysian's face broke into a wicked grin.

"No need to fret. He's not far," Elysian patronized, pointing out the window behind us. "See for yourself."

And sure enough, I turned around and looked out the window. When climbing, I hadn't been able to look behind me at the view.

But I could see it plain and clear now.

Beyond the snowy trees was what looked to be some sort of training arena. It wasn't visible when you first looked at the island from afar.

Inside this arena were dozens of other Envorydains, and a small figure in the center, tied up on what looked to be some sort of platform. The dark hair and the way he stood immediately gave his identity away.

Dusane was on the island. But he was not in the castle. No, he was in the middle of some Xevarian arena and looked to be the source of their next show.

THIRTY-TWO

SUNN

Trying to get rid of the pounding headache from my previous night of drinking, I visited the stables. I figured maybe some sunlight would assist in rejuvenating me, but it seemed to be making the ache in my temple worse.

There were really not very many things to do in the mountain fortress that was Knadiel. Now that we knew what the cloak was capable of, Jasper and Liony were constantly in the library planning together. But it wasn't fun to sit by and watch when I didn't have any powers of my own to experience the phenomenon of the cloak for myself. It wasn't like the Isles here. I couldn't just hitch a ride on a nearby ship to get a change of scenery.

I tried to read through the Ethricial, but most of it seemed like another language to me. I wanted to be of help, but I also had my mother's voice in my head, telling me to let the others take care of it.

I sighed, entering the barn and allowing the smell of straw

and dust to overwhelm my senses. It helped clear away some of the discomfort in my head. I brushed the soft nose of a couple of the horses as I passed through. I thought I would want to ride, but I eyed the saddles and felt nervous at the thought. The last time I'd ridden on a horse by myself, the creature had taken off, and it had been one of the most terrifying experiences of my life. Luckily Sabeara had been there to save me, or I think I would have definitely been injured.

A pang of sadness went through my heart at the memory. That was back when Aveladon still existed. I still remember traveling to the beautiful kingdom. It had been a dream come true to go there with Mid to court Jasper. As a young teen, it was unreal to be in the beautiful Aveladon castle and involved with all the royal fanfare. So many things had changed since then.

I sighed and made my way across the fields behind the mansion. It was very lush and green. The air felt nice. It was never too hot and never too cold in Knadiel. I picked a couple wildflowers as I ambled along. Then I spotted a little pond in the distance. I always saw the little pond from the dining room window. It sparkled in the mornings, reflecting the sun like glass. It was so clear. A river that came down from the mountain kept it full of crystal blue water. Fish flitted in and out of the rocks beneath the surface, and I dipped my feet inside, sitting in the marshy grass at the edge, not caring that it was soaking my day dress.

I reached down and let my hand fall beneath the glassy surface, watching the way my fingers moved beneath the water. I became entranced, but was pulled from my thoughts when I felt an odd sensation on the back of my neck.

It felt as if someone was watching me.

I looked around, trying to see if anyone was in the distant

forest, but the treeline seemed vacant of life. The only hint of movement was the rustle of leaves from the breeze.

I looked back toward the mansion, still feeling the odd sensation, and that's when I spotted him.

On the third floor, the balcony doors to his room were open, and he sat casually in a chair, a book in his lap. He wasn't even pretending not to watch me.

We looked at each other for a moment, his obsidian expression just as intense from a far distance.

He looked stunning in the morning light, lounging lazily in his chair reading. He almost looked normal. It was an odd way to see him. Obsidian belonged in the dark. It was unusual to see him in such a bright light. It was almost jarring. Seeing him in the daylight made him more real. He wasn't just a figment of my forbidden imagination or the lovely monster that haunted me while I slept. He existed, and seeing him now was an unexpected reminder.

He wasn't allowed to leave his room. So I imagined his balcony was the only place he had access to fresh air.

His gaze didn't waver, and something in my stomach started to feel warm with how he looked at me.

I hadn't been proud of the conversation we had the last night when I was drunk. But to say that my feelings were all because of the Lush Fire would be a lie. The drink had only made it easier to voice what I felt. It made me bolder, but I think deep down, my thoughts were already bold. The Lush Fire had been the key that set them free.

I smiled up at him, but his expression remained impassive.

I didn't think before doing what I did next.

I stood from my crisscross position by the pond, reached for the hem of my dress, and pulled it over my head. I had a pair of flimsy undergarments underneath, so I wasn't completely naked. But the breeze definitely was more prominent now, a little chillier than I had been with my dress on. Goosebumps appeared on my pale, freckled skin, and then the whole time, still holding his gaze, I stepped into the water. Soon the water was up to my waist, and then it was clear up to my neck.

I watched the expression on his face, but it was unreadable. Then I swear I saw him give me a slight shake of his head.

I leaned back in the water, letting my body float on the cool surface. I spread my arms out and stared up at the baby blue sky and watched the clouds as they slowly drifted. It was odd that I never noticed the clouds were moving unless I stopped to take a moment to really look at them. What a beautiful creation I forgot to admire because so many other things were taking up my mind.

Everything was quiet in this position, the water filling my ears and muting everything around me. It was just me, the water, and the heated sensation of Obsidian's gaze on me. It thrilled me to know he was watching me.

I knew I was crossing invisible lines.

But I wanted to eradicate them. I was tired of lines and unwritten laws that I wasn't allowed to want someone like him.

I righted myself then, a smile still playing on my lips.

I looked up at the balcony expecting to see Obsidian still sitting watching me.

But my heart sank.

The doors were no longer open, and the chair was empty.

THIRTY-THREE

SABEARA

"What are you doing to him?" Shar growled, seeing the scene below in the arena.

It looked much like the Galloway back in the Sethen Courts. Memories from that day when I fought for my freedom made a whole new level of fear zip through my body.

"Stalling for time, I guess you could say," Elysian said casually, like he was talking about nothing more than the weather.

He began pacing the floor to the small room we were all crowded within. The stares of the other Envorydians bore into me, but I didn't look at any of them. My eyes were glued to Elysian.

"Stalling?" Rosen asked, and I hated that we were playing Elysian's stupid game. We were in his hands like clay, and he was doing with us as he pleased. I wished so badly we could've had the upper hand.

Mid moved behind me, and I could've sworn that a golden light shone from the corners of my eyes. I gestured with my hand behind my back for him to stop. We were up against dozens of other Envorydians. We needed to play this very carefully. We were severely outnumbered.

"You see, when I found out about my son's little—adventure," he paused on the word adventure, and I knew he was talking about the episode out at sea.

"I was angry at first. He wasn't supposed to go searching for tokens without my consent. But I figured he'd come home empty-handed soon enough, and he would learn his lesson not to disobey orders."

I hated how he was toying with us. Speaking like we were old friends just having a conversation, while Dusane was chained up down in the arena. I was about ready to throw a knife at him but knew it would get us nowhere. The best thing to do at the moment was to play his game.

"But when he never returned, I figured something had happened to him. And then I got word that you had him captured."

"How did you know that?" Shar growled.

"I have eyes everywhere. You think you're safe in that little kingdom of yours, but I've known you were there all along. I've just been biding my time. Watching, waiting until you retrieve all the tokens so I can take them from you."

"What sort of game are you playing? Telling us your whole plan?" I asked, my voice laced with venom.

"Just trying it keep things fair," Elysian smirked, his blue eyes so hauntingly like my mother's that it made me nauseous to look at him.

"Fair?" I asked.

"You take something of mine. I take something of yours."

"Obsidian," I said, my heart racing in my chest.

"He could've left with you at the party. I'm sure you have a way to get that bracelet off of him," Shar said matter-of-factly.

"Which is why I'm upset, you see," Elysian sighed. "It seems that my son may have turned against me."

Mid snorted, not at all convinced.

"You don't think so?" Elysian asked, raising an eyebrow.

"I think you're just an evil man," I said simply.

Elysian grinned. "You may be right about that, Sabeara."

The name stung my soul. I wished it didn't, but it brought back parts of me like an old wound. It had healed, but sometimes there was phantom pain, and it elicited with the sound of that name.

"Maybe I'm tired of this game of cat and mouse, and I want to eliminate the competition," Elysian said.

"You're not going to wait until we find all the tokens, then?" I asked coyly.

"There's only one left to be found. Can't be too hard, can it?"

It was then I caught sight of Rouix standing beside me, looking at the man standing just to the right of Elysian.

"Ahh, I see you've noticed my friend," Elysian's gaze had turned to Rouix. "This here is the leader of the Mantle. Meet Ezra."

This man Elysian introduced us to was tall and built like a warrior. His blonde hair was cut close to his scalp, and his eyes were dark brown and lethal. He had swirling tattoos on his cheekbones—matching tattoos to those on Rouix's cheeks.

Something cold and dark stirred in my core.

I could clearly see the terror on Rouix's face, and never in my life had I seen Rouix afraid.

This must be the person that she had been sold to.

Ezra smiled at Rouix and took several steps toward her.

"I thought you'd flown away, Little Bird." He spoke softly to her, crooning like he was a lost lover.

Ezra reached out to touch Rouix's cheek, and she smacked his hand away as fast as lightning.

"Tsk, tsk, tsk," Ezra scolded, but he looked to be enjoying himself immensely. The same evil delight in his eyes as Elysian's. "I see you have changed so much from when I raised you up."

Rouix barred her teeth, her body quivering with rage.

"It's so good to have you home."

"This isn't my home," Rouix spat, and she looked ready to sink her teeth into him.

Ezra eyed her thoughtfully and once again I was overwhelmed with the curiosity to know what occurred on this island and where Rouix came from.

Rosen stepped in front of Rouix then, coming nose to nose with this Ezra man.

"Take us to him," Rosen demanded.

"Glad to see you're all ready for a fight," Elysian said happily. "I'd love nothing more than some entertainment before you all die on this frozen paradise."

I gritted my teeth, knowing that getting Dusane free and getting back to Knadiel was going to be a lot harder than we planned.

"No one is going to die," Mid assured him, but Elsyain just smiled wider.

"We'll see about that."

THIRTY-FOUR

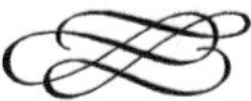

SUNN

"We're leaving," Liony said.

I was in the dining hall the next morning with James at my side. My mother, my grandparents, Oli and Jasper, were also at the dining table—a spread of fruit, eggs, and other brunch delectables on the table. I paused with a strawberry halfway to my mouth.

"Where?" I asked suddenly.

"We've heard word of another group of wanderers that need rescuing."

Ever since the war, there had been groups of Ethydon and Aveladon people that had gone into hiding since the entire kingdom had been burned. A large population had made it to Knadiel, but some stragglers still remained. And it wasn't safe for them to be wandering the other kingdoms. But Knadiel's location was kept very secret, so to try and rescue as many people that hadn't made it to Knadiel, they had been staging rescue missions for some time now.

"I'll be going with Liony and Jasper," Oli said.

"And what about you three?" I asked my grandparents and my mother. "Are you leaving too?"

Ruby looked at Knadian before answering.

"We will be going to look for information on the last token."

I knew everyone was trying to be super secretive about their plans with the curse, but I honestly hated how they treated me like I was made of glass.

"Let me guess, I'm not allowed to come?" I asked, my eyes narrowing.

"It's for your own safety, Sunn," my mother chided.

I rolled my eyes. "Whatever, fine. Go search for stuff about the curse without me."

"We think it might be good to get a head start on where the last token might be. Especially with the others out searching for Dusane. We want to make sure we aren't abandoning our mission to find the tokens and lift the curse," Ruby said, her gaze sympathetic, almost as if she wished she could include me but couldn't.

"I get it. The fate of the world is in our hands," I said, biting angrily into my strawberry.

"James will stay here with you, and there will be many guards patrolling the castle," my mother said.

"Sure you want to leave me alone?" I asked, smirking. My mother's eyes narrowed on me.

"You better be on your best behavior, Sunn. I don't love that we will all be out of the castle for a few days, but I trust that you'll be able to handle yourself here with James and the rest of the guards on duty."

"I'll be fine," I mumbled dismissively.

"We shouldn't be longer than a couple of days," My mother said. "The people in need of rescue are said to not be far."

I allowed my anger to be pushed aside for a brief moment. Knowing that where they were headed could be dangerous.

"Be safe," I said. And my mother reached out to give my hand a squeeze under the table.

"We will."

~

I watched Knadian, Ruby, and my mother leave down the front path the next morning from my bedroom window.

"Can you believe they are leaving me here?" I asked James, who was lounging on the chaise at the end of my bed.

"I think everyone is anxious to figure out the last token."

"Where do you think they are headed?"

"I heard your mother mention that she knew someone that might be able to tell them what the token might be."

I huffed and crossed my arms over my chest before turning back around.

"I hate this," I said, and James sat up, giving me a sympathetic look.

"I know, I do too."

"I'm sorry you're stuck watching me," I said, sitting down next to him.

"Don't worry about it. Beats working for Obsidian," he admitted, and I went quiet.

"I don't think I've ever asked you why you were on his ship," I said, feeling guilty that I hadn't ever pressed.

"I needed the money for my family," he said. And then sighed.

"I joined the Obscurum army to support my family. And once I had money, it was too late to escape the clutches of Elysian."

"Where is your family now," I asked quietly.

"They are still in Obscrum, and I don't think they would be able to leave the city even if they tried."

"They couldn't come to Knadiel?"

"Obscurum isn't the type of place that allows you to leave without reason," James said, not making eye contact now. "They work for Elysian closely, and let's just say they are quite valuable. He would know if they decided to leave, and I don't think he would be gracious enough to allow that."

Silence spread between us.

"I'm sorry, James."

"I'm sure they are managing without me. King Olivine has managed to help me smuggle in funds to them even now."

"He has?" I asked, my eyes widening in surprise. "I had no idea."

"I only hope it reaches them."

"You hate him," I said, hating myself for the feelings I had no control over.

He looked at me, his blue eyes piercing. "More than you know."

I bit my lip and couldn't hold his gaze any longer. It was an accusing look as if he were asking me to explain why I felt the way I did for him.

"I'm so sorry, James," was all I could say.

"I wish I could be angry with you, Sunn."

"You can be," I said, giving him permission.

"I don't think this is your fault."

"You think he's tricking me."

"I can't say for sure."

"I wish I could hate him like you do, James." It was the truth. I didn't know why my heart longed for Obsidian, but it did. I had tried to deny it but failed. I was a slave to him now more than James would ever know.

James sighed. "Let's not talk about this, Sunn."

"Fine," I said, my jaw clenching. "We won't talk about it."

His green eyes looked sad as I shut down the conversation. I felt hurt and guilty all at once.

"I've got to go check the guard posts. I'll be back soon," he said, standing and heading for the door.

I didn't try to stop him. And the door shut with a soft click.

~

The castle was eerily empty with most everyone gone. I looked around the dining hall, a breakfast spread before me that I was unable to finish by myself. The long table with dozens of chairs remained absent except for me at the very head.

A pang hit my chest thinking about everyone out doing something useful while I sat in the mansion doing absolutely nothing.

I huffed and stood up, no longer feeling hungry. I headed for the courtyard, thinking I could use some fresh air. It was out in the gardens amongst the flowers and the trickling of the fountains where I found a moment of serenity.

Instead of sitting on the bench amidst the hedges and flowerbeds, I climbed right over the daffodils, stepped into the patch of blooming daisies, and laid down amongst their soft petals. I stared up at the pale blue sky and sighed. A bee buzzed above my head, and I could feel flower stems squishing into my skin and clothes. No doubt they'd be stained with pollen once I stood, but I didn't much care.

I don't know how long I lay there in the flowerbed, staring at the sky. But I didn't get up until I heard hoofbeats in the distance.

Thinking it might be Liony or maybe my mother returning to the castle and that it was much too soon. I stood up and used one of the benches to peer over the big hedges of the garden.

What I saw instead made my blood run cold.

A dozen or more black horses galloped across the stretch of grass leading to the mansion. These dark creatures were like a rolling black cloud across the bright yellow fields—men in matching black cloaks sat astride them, heading straight for us.

I thought maybe I was dreaming for a moment, but then the hoofbeats began to make the earth hum, and I could feel the vibrations beneath my feet. This wasn't a dream.

We were under attack.

How did they get into Knadiel?

I gasped, fear seizing my chest. I stumbled down from the stone bench I'd used to peer over the hedge and tripped on the brick pathway, trying desperately to reach the mansion.

"Obscurum!" A scream tore from my throat, and my heart hammered in my chest—adrenaline pouring into my blood like wildfire.

I burst into the foyer, gasping for breath. The guards at the door looked at me with bewilderment as I barged inside —frantic.

"Obscurum is attacking," I said desperately, rushing around the room. "Call all the guards, anyone who can fight. The mansion is being attacked!"

I don't know how I got the words out, but somehow I did.

Sill consumed by sudden shock and fear that we were being charged and the mansion would be raided any moment. I felt my knees buckle.

"Princess, Princess," I heard someone say. One of the guards in the foyer reached for me.

I'd fought giant creatures on the ocean, creatures that squirted poisonous venom. But this, for some reason, felt ten times scarier.

They were disrupting a sacred place that had been safe for so long. Never had I imagined they'd get inside.

A memory flashed into my head when we'd been raided in Ethydon. When Aveladon had been burned, and I'd been taken to the Isles. It was like a part of my adolescent brain had hidden the feelings deep within, and with this sudden realization that the same scenario was happening again, it was too much for me.

I fell onto my hands, hitting the wood floor with a painful smack as I tried to find air.

"Sunn," James's voice penetrated the sudden fear that had seized me, as he was helping me to my feet. "We need to get you to safety. Obscurum is attacking us."

"Everyone is gone. What are we going to do?" I started to ramble, "What if we die in here? What if they come back and find us all dead? What about the village? Did they attack the village?"

So many questions and so many concerns. I was feeling faint.

I started to fall backward, and James's eyes widened, reaching for me, but then a pair of arms wound around me before he even needed to get me. The warmth of this person's touch was familiar, and my body knew instantly who it was.

"I got you," he murmured, pulling me to his chest. Suddenly I was being cradled in his arms. I looked up in shock to find Obsidian holding me.

"How did you get out?" James asked angrily.

"Do you really think that if I wanted to get out of here, I couldn't get past those puny men guarding my door?" Obsidian asked James with a droll stare. "Gather your men. They'll be here any second."

"Care to explain why they are attacking?" James asked, rage in his eyes.

"I would guess it's because my father is trying to rescue me."

My eyes widened, my hand still slung around his neck. He was so beautiful up close. And he smelled of amber and sandalwood. I wanted to breathe him in, but now was not the time to be getting intoxicated by his scent.

"Rescue you?" James growled angrily.

"Don't worry, kid. I'm not planning on letting them take me back. But they're not going to leave without a fight. So are you going to gather your men or not?"

James glared at him, seething with rage. "Let her go. I need to get her to safety."

"I got her," Obsidian insisted, and as he started to head toward the hallway, more guards came flooding into the foyer, hearing the news of the attack. The two that usually guarded Obsidina's door were a part of the entourage. They skirted past him as he walked towards them with me in his arms.

"We're sorry, sir, we tried to stop him," one of the guards said to James, a stutter in his desperate words.

"You're not taking her anywhere," James reached for his arm, ignoring the two guards that had let him go free, but Obsidian quickly pushed James off, his hold on me immovable.

"I'll help you fight, but let me get her upstairs first," Obsidian's black eyes narrowed on James, who used to be his servant. James didn't seem to like taking orders from him, especially not now that he was free.

"I'll kill you if you hurt her."

Obsidian rolled his eyes. "James. Please. Protect the mansion. I'll be right back."

James' eyes flitted to me, but I had no power to stop this man from taking me wherever he wished. I was weak. Something in my body was retaliating against me. This sudden attack was too much for my mind to handle. I slumped against Obsidian's neck, and James' green eyes went cold.

"Fine." James turned on his heel and began barking orders to all household guards.

I had no idea if the villagers were alright, but I had to hope that James would be able to handle the situation.

Dread consumed my stomach as Obsidian began climbing the stairs up to his chambers.

"I need to fight," I mumbled against him. Gosh, I was being so cowardly. Why was my body shutting down in fear? Was I shaking?

He entered my chambers and set me down on the bed. Then, kneeling before me, he reached up to brush the wild crimson curls from my face.

"Breathe, love," he commanded, and I stared into his black eyes, forcing myself to take in a breath. "Good girl," he murmured, running the back of his hand down my cheek. "You're okay. I'm not going to let them hurt you."

"But James and the villagers. What about my famil—"

"Where's my strong warrior?" he asked, slight amusement in his eyes. "You once defied me on my own ship. What are a few Obscurum soldiers?"

"They attacked the mansion in Ethydon. The wedding. . ." And that's when I realized that Obsidian had been part of that raid when I was a young teen. The one where I had to escape with Sabeara to the docks. I had felt like a young child at that moment during Jasper's and Mid's wedding. Paralyzed by the chaos that had overtaken my innocent life.

This very man before me, calming me, telling me that nothing would happen to me, also had created demons deep within my soul. How twisted was that?

"Shhh. . ." he said, and somehow he calmed me. "I'm going to go help them stop this fight. But you have to promise me you'll stay here."

"I want to help," I pleaded, but my body was saying the opposite. For some reason, I was afraid. He was right. Where was my courage after everything I'd endured?

"I know," he said, a small smile tugging at the corner of his mouth. "But it will help me if you stay here where I know you won't be harmed."

"Why do you care?" A little bit of fire suddenly flickered to life in my chest.

"You and I both know I can't answer that."

THIRTY-FIVE

SABEARA

We didn't fight them.

Not yet, at least.

Until I knew we had the upper hand, I wasn't going to attack. And I could see that the others were smart enough to follow along.

There were just too many Envorydians on the island to attack with just us five.

They didn't try and lay a hand on any of us, thankfully. But they did surround us as we were led down to the arena where Dusane was being held.

I kept my eyes on Elysian the entire time. Hating that I was willingly allowing myself to be led into his trap. It went against all my fighting instincts not to just attack him right then and there.

I took several deep breaths and thought of Dusane to get through the rage that threatened to consume me.

They guided us through another set of sleek icy tunnels until we emerged into a giant arena.

Loud cheers became a chorus all around us as the bystanders watched us enter. There were Envorydians seated throughout the oval shaped arena. Our feet left the slick tunneled floor, and suddenly it felt like I was walking on sand.

I looked down to find tiny ice crystals creating a gravel floor for the arena. I perused the diamond-like pebbles, watching them glisten in the sunlight.

I looked up again, stunned to find an almost replica of the Galloway. What was it with Envorydians and fighting in arenas?

But this arena wasn't nearly as large as the one that existed in the Sethen Courts. And standing in the center of it was a large column that Dusane was trapped against.

My jaw clenched at the sight of him. He looked beaten and bruised, hanging his head low like he couldn't hold it up anymore.

All my instincts told me to run to him, but Mid reached out a hand as if to stop me. He shook his head sharply, and I had some sense left to listen to him.

We were on their turf. We had to play by their rules.

"He's hung on longer than I expected he would," Elysian commented above the buzz of the rowdy crowd. The way these rouge Envorydians screamed from their seats was anything but playful. They wanted us dead.

I could see it in their angry, hate-filled expressions as they yelled obscenities at us.

Rouix looked like she saw a ghost as she looked around at everything.

"Let him go," Shar demanded, and Elysian smiled.

"Unfortunately, I can't do that," he started walking up a set of steps leading to a throne-like chair in the front row.

"But that doesn't mean I won't let you try and win him back."

I glared at him with as much hatred as I could muster.

"If you can reach him and undo his chains, you are free to go."

I glanced from Elysian to Dusane. There was nothing in our path but a hundred or so feet of crystal ice sand. There had to be more to it than just running over to him and removing the chains.

An obstacle of some sort that he was planning to put in our path.

And then, just as I had the thought, a giant roar reverberated through the arena.

We all took several steps back on instinct when four dragons appeared from more icy tunnels.

They were fierce-looking creatures. One a bright cobalt blue, another a deep red. The third was stark white and the last a dark green. They had scaly bodies and giant talons. The jaws of these creatures were also utterly terrifying. The teeth were as long as my arm.

I'd never seen a real-life dragon before, which made fear bubble up in my veins.

Elysian laughed manically at the expressions on our faces. "Well, what are you waiting for?"

THIRTY-SIX

SUNN

I was alone in the room, Obsidian's words still ringing inside my mind. *You know I can't answer that,* he'd said. Then he'd left, back out the door.

I thought about chasing after him, but I was still feeling dizzy. I did the cowardly thing and stayed behind.

I rushed to the window, trying to steady my heartbeat. One part of myself told me to be brave, and the other was shutting down. Bodies were funny that way. Sometimes we've got no control over them. And I personally despised the feeling.

I threw open the balcony doors, taking in the scene of several dozen black cloaks dispersed across the mansion grounds. Knadiel guards were fighting back, keeping them at bay. Thank goodness it seemed to be a fair fight.

King Elysian could've called his whole army and taken over the entirety of what was left of our kingdom. But he'd sent just enough to get his son back.

I tried desperately to understand why he wouldn't just end it.

If he knew where our hiding place was, why he hadn't just massacred our kingdom.

The tokens.

It was the only explanation. He couldn't find them on his own. And he needed Sabeara and the others to remain alive to get them. Then a bloody battle would take place. It was the only explanation.

I searched the chaos for Obsidian but couldn't find him amidst the fighting. I squinted my eyes, trying to spot his tall, lanky form, but when an arrow came flying through the window, nearly taking off my ear, I stumbled back inside with a petrified squeak.

"Spirits!" I cried.

Deciding it was too dangerous to keep watch, I scurried into the closet, some part of me shutting down even more. Memories bombarded me of that night back in Ethydon when everything was ripped away. Why did I suddenly feel like a small child?

"Spirits," I cried again, hating that I'd kept it together for so long and now I was cracking.

"Go down there," I scolded myself aloud. "Help them."

But I was useless. Powerless. Afraid.

Tears filled the corners of my eyes, and I desperately pushed them back. If something happened to James, or Obsidian, or any of the other guards on the premises. . .well, the thought was just too much. I'd already lost friends out at sea and had too many close calls recently to feel comfortable with another attack.

It felt like hours before someone came back into the room. And at first when the door opened, immediate fear coursed through me, thinking it might be Obscurum guards coming to kill me.

I screamed when the doors to the closet were ripped open. I

was huddled amongst dress clothes and pajamas, trying to stay hidden.

Appearing on the other side of the closet doors was Obsidian. Blood peppered the skin on his arm, and his shirt was ripped. He was breathing heavily, and his eyes were bright with an intense fire.

He looked furious.

"Come here," he said, his voice surprisingly soft despite the expression on his face.

A whimper escaped me as he pulled me from my hiding place and to his chest.

"You're alright," he murmured as I buried my face into the crook of his neck, clinging to him.

The anxiety in my body eased almost instantly, which was positivity insane. Because this was the man that had caused so much havoc in the past, he'd been the captain of the demons that I now faced, yet somehow he was soothing those same demons with his arms around me.

I was losing my mind. Something was wrong with me.

"Is everyone alright?" I asked, and just then, the door burst open, James barreling inside.

"Sunn, are you okay?" He hurried over to me, and I detangled myself from Obsidian's arms so I could also embrace him.

"What happened down there? Are there more Obscurum men coming?"

"My father was trying to retrieve me," Obsidian explained. "I don't think he's sending more."

"Why didn't you go back with him then?" James asked. Blood stained his clothes, and his skin was slicked with sweat. A couple bruises graced his forehead, and he had cuts on his forearms. He'd taken a beating for sure.

"Let's just say I wasn't ready to return home just yet. I'm sort of enjoying my vacation," Obsidian said sarcastically, his lips twitching with a wicked smirk.

"Because of you she could've been killed!" James growled, moving me behind him. He stalked towards Obsidian.

"James!" I warned. "Haven't we had enough fighting for one day?"

"Some of my men were close to death today. You're lucky everyone made it out." James pointed his finger into Obsidian's chest, angrier than I'd ever seen him.

"You're naive if you think my father wouldn't have attacked your kingdom eventually, with or without my presence," Obsidian said. "Now at least I helped you defeat them, and my father will now get the message that I'm not coming home anytime soon."

"You are not our ally. You're a prisoner," James spat angrily. "You think you have an alliance with us in some way after the Dark Fell, but let me make this clear. We are *not* on the same side."

I put a hand between them, and James eased off a bit, but he was still coiled to pounce. His eyes glued on Obsidian like he wanted to see his lifeless body on the floor.

"We must warn my mother, my grandparents, and Oli and Jasper of what happened here. We need to get them back here as soon as possible," I reminded James.

"I have soldiers that can go," James said, turning back to face me, his eyes still bright with fury.

"I'm fine, James." I knew without words being said that he was avoiding leaving me here in the castle alone with Obsidian while he went to find the others.

"I'm not leaving you here!" James yelled, and it was the first time James had ever raised his voice at me.

I took a step back, not expecting the sudden volume change.

"Yell at her like that again and see how long your heart remains beating," Obsidian growled, stepping in front of me now.

Spirits in the tree, I thought.

"Stop it!" I yelled at the two of them, my hands shaking from the intensity of the situation.

"James, go send word to the others about what happened here. And have the soldiers that are in good enough shape check out the village. We need to stand ready for another attack just in case."

A painful expression replaced the anger in Jame's gaze, and I knew he was more hurt than ever. Me trusting Obsidian was a whole different level of pain for him. He couldn't understand it. And unfortunately, I couldn't either.

"I'll be fine!" I said more forcefully. "He's not going to hurt me. Now go!"

James looked about ready to argue more, then clamped his mouth shut. He didn't say another word. He simply glared at Obsidian and then stormed out of the room.

As the door slammed behind him, I sighed and turned back to face Obsidian.

"What has gotten into you?"

His jaw clenched, and he walked away towards my bathing room. I followed after him, still strung with stress after the fight.

When he didn't answer immediately, I started to ramble with anxiety.

"I should go downstairs and assess the damage. They probably need help—"

"You're not going anywhere," he said, his tone unyielding.

I glared at him, hating when he ordered me around.

"I think you've let your freedom go to your head. You don't control me, Obsidian."

He grabbed a few towels down from the cupboards in the bathing room and carried some soap to the bathtub.

"You're going to stay in here and calm down after what just happened. Last thing I need is you going downstairs and seeing the mess that was made and fainting on me."

"You think I'm that weak?" I glared at him. "Do you not remember I was on that boat with you when the Ocular attacked us?"

He let out a huff. "Sunn, this raid triggered some emotional response for you. And this doesn't have anything to do with whether or not you're weak. Everyone has moments where they can't be strong anymore." He reached out to grab my hands, which were indeed still trembling.

"See, you're shaking."

My eyes remained narrowed on him as I pulled my hands from his grasp. "I don't need you to take care of me."

His eyes remained emotionless for a moment as he stared at me. The setting sun reflected through the window pane above the tub and made like fire in his dark depths.

"I'm going to start a bath for you, and once you've calmed down, you can go downstairs. But right now, there's nothing you can do. James has it handled, and the guards are cleaning up the mess."

Tears filled my eyes, and I quickly had to squint them away.

Tears wouldn't do well in my argument that I was holding it together.

"Sweet girl," he whispered gently, reaching out to wipe a lone tear that had escaped onto my cheek. "Please don't cry."

"People were so close to dying today, Obsidian," I said, my voice so quiet it barely sounded like me.

His jaw clenched, and he nodded. "You blame me."

"I don't blame you." I quickly said. Because it was the truth. "You didn't send those men. Elysian did."

Obsidian nodded slowly, then let out a sigh.

"I'm going to go change, and I'll be back in a moment."

It was then that my eyes were drawn back to the blood peppering his skin. He didn't appear hurt, but the red caked on his skin from what must've been our enemies made my stomach churn.

"Are you injured?"

He shook his head. "Just a little roughed up," he assured me, then he gave me another intense stare. "Stay here."

I wanted to argue, but he started heading for the door, and something in me was just too tired to fight him. So I watched him leave and then turned to watch the water fill up the tub.

THIRTY-SEVEN

SABEARA

Dusane was tied up in the middle of the arena, his hands tethered with a thick glistening chain. He was the center of their attention. The prize in their bloodthirsty game. And I was brought back to that day in the arena. The Galloway felt like child's play next to this. The dragons snapped their teeth, the most beautiful and dangerous creatures I'd ever laid eyes on. They flapped and threshed their scaly wings, and I could hear my blood pounding in my ears.

In the Galloway they tried to keep people from dying. When someone was injured, they dragged them from the chaos. This fight didn't have any rules. No one to step in and stop things from going too far. This was a game of life or death, and these Envordyians wouldn't be satisfied until our hearts stopped beating.

Several emotions rocked through my body at the sight of the dragons and Dusane in the middle of them. Fear, anger, and a resolve to kill. For the first time in a long time, I allowed myself to unleash the emotions I'd stifled inside of myself. The bright rays of fury poured over me, and I bloomed. Flourishing as I allowed the rage to take over, I willed it to consume me.

I ran, Mid, Rosen, Rouix, and Shar behind me.

We raced toward Dusane. My only concern releasing him and getting him back safely.

The blue dragon charged first, its icy cobalt scales flashing in the bright sun, nearly blinding me as it whipped in front of us, then over our heads, casting a brief shadow across the arena.

"I got this one, you go," Shar called, already pulling his weapon from his side.

His choice for this fight was an axe. It had a thick wooden handle and a sharp silver blade. He threw it with a battle cry, hitting the blue dragon square in the chest.

The creature whined, stumbling into the sand as the intensity of the axe sent it sprawling. Shar closed in on the animal, Rosen on his tail.

Rosen took his turn, touching the dragon, and his power overtook its body, turning it to gold.

I didn't have time to revel in the fact that Shar and Rosen had just taken out the first dragon in a mere couple of seconds. My eyes remained on Dusane, unmoving from my target. But then the next dragon came, sleek and white, with feathers like an elegant swan.

An abrupt image flashed into my mind. I wanted to see its alabaster flesh marred with blood. I ached to see it bleed for me.

"I got it!" Mid yelled, still keeping up beside me.

This whole time the Envorydians in the stands were cheering, booing, screaming obscenities at us, going absolutely wild over the show. But they were so far in the background I barely noticed them. I had one thing on my mind. Saving Dusane.

Mid gave a mighty yell, the light in his hands exploding and a giant animal morphing to life from the bright orb.

Another dragon. Black as night, with eyes blood red, the animal he'd conjured screeched, fire pluming out of its mouth in a vermillion streak so hot I could feel it across my shoulder.

The white dragon was not expecting this. It gave a mighty cry and flew up above the fire, barely avoiding the black dragon's attack— a couple of the feathers on its wings now singed with ash. The black dragon chased after the white one, the two swirling around each other up into the sky, abandoning the arena.

I looked back for a moment, checking on Mid, sweat trickled down his brow, and I could tell the creation of the dragon took a lot out of him. Rouix was right next to him, still keeping up with us.

"Mid!" I yelled. He must've heard the question in my tone.

"I'm fine, Sabeara. Keep running. We're almost to him," Mid said, but our last monster approached—the crimson dragon.

I growled, livid that we had another obstacle to tackle.

The red beast was guarding Dusane, standing awfully close like he was its young, and the dragon was protecting him. It fanned out its wings in warning as we neared.

"What do we do?" Rouix asked.

It opened its mouth, letting out a streak of red fire.

"Kill it," I said simply.

Mid's hands glowed again, and vines came shooting up out of the cold sand, a shower of grainy ice peppering my skin. The thick plants took hold of the red dragon's taloned feet, and it tried to fly away but failed, the vines keeping it secured.

It gave a mighty screech, another wave of fire shooting from its mouth at us.

We barely dodged the flame, and it singed some of the vines that were holding it. We had to act fast, or it would burn the confines and fly away.

The dragon, angrier than ever before, gave another shot of fire, and I felt my right shoulder burn. I let out a scream of agony but kept running.

We were separated now, the fire making us unable to stick close together in our attempt at avoidance.

Mid continued to try and tie down the dragon with vines, and Rouix unsheathed her knives and began throwing them at the creature.

I could really use a dragon on our side right about now, I thought.

Dusane was still behind the crimson dragon. He seemed to be barely registering what was happening. His dark hair fell across his forehead in a matted tangle, and his head drooped against his chest as if he were exhausted. I could see now that I was closer, the indigo bruises on his skin. The blood marring his lip. He had been beaten.

Another wave of fury overtook me.

How could these Envorydians do this to him? To Rouix. To us.

I could only imagine the torture they had put Rouix through in the past. The people they'd killed for other benefactors, such as Elysian. The Envorydians here on this frigid island were not here for peace. They were vile puppets, eager to kill and devour for a price. And Elysian, he was the worst of all. He was the one that fulfilled the payment.

This entire island and the people on it deserved to burn.

And that's when it hit me.

I couldn't burn the island. But maybe I could drown it.

I halted in the sand, taking several feet back from the dragon as the idea came to me. Rouix continued to wound the dragon gradually, avoiding its fire while Mid held it down, conjuring vines to subdue it.

I took the compass from my pocket, my chest heaving with ragged breaths. I held it in my hand, closed my eyes, and willed the creatures of the sea to listen.

I didn't know if I had to be close for them to obey the compass. Especially when the water surrounding the island was under a sheet of ice. I didn't know if they could break the surface and come to my aid. But I didn't have another choice. They had to hear me. They had to obey me.

"Come on," I whispered, imagining exactly what I wanted from the creatures in my mind. Splinters of ice, giant cracks in the opaque surface. I pictured big sea creatures attacking the icy surface, swirling around the island to create seismic waves. I imagined it all crumbling, the surface shattering like glass. I could only hope they'd listen to my command.

The compass began to glow violet and bright, then it happened.

The entire arena began to shake. And a thundering clap echoed around us. The ice was breaking. Then the sound of whooshing waves breaking the surface in the distance followed. I opened my eyes and smiled.

The bystanders in the crowd seemed to notice something was happening the moment they heard the loud cracking of the ice. And that's when the screaming began.

The waves and the mass of sea creatures hit faster than I would've thought possible, overtaking the sides of the arena swiftly. Water surged over the walls, pouring down into the arena, while fins and tails from all sorts of water beasts swarmed us.

Freezing cold water sloshed around my ankles as the waves and fish hit, and my friends turned to look at me, shocked expressions on their faces at the sudden frigid waterfalls spilling in around us.

The dragons screeched at the water, and they flew up above it, flapping their scaly wings in a mad flurry to avoid being splashed.

"Hurry! We have to get Dusane and get out of here, or we'll drown!" I yelled to Mid and Rouix.

Rosen and Shar came running over to us, leaving behind the carcass of the green dragon they'd also defeated. I watched as the water covered it, and a large shark took a bite from it, burying it in the navy blanket of its ocean grave.

"Sabeara, what have you done?" Shar yelled, coming up to my side. The water was at our knees now. Fish swirling in and around our shins. I was already shivering, my teeth chattering.

"I'm flooding the island," I showed them the compass. "I asked for a little help."

Shar's eyes widened, and he looked around at the swarm of sea creatures and the Envorydians panicking at the sight of the water overtaking the stands.

He didn't ask anymore questions, just ran over to Dusane. The red dragon was up in the sky now, roaring alongside the other dragons at the sudden water flooding everything. He used the hammer to break the chain, releasing him. I went to Dusane and put his arm around my shoulder so I could support him.

"Let me," Mid said, taking my place as he was much stronger.

"Now would be a great time to tell us how we're going to get off this island," Rosen said.

I hadn't thought about the how before flooding everything.

"The dragon, he'll come," Mid said confidently.

Just then, the black creature Mid had conjured came swooping down towards us, landing in the water. It screeched at us in greeting, blood glistening on its onyx scales from the fight with the white dragon.

"Hurry, get on," Mid didn't hesitate. He helped Dusane's limp body onto the dragon's back, then Rouix and Rosen. Shar was last, barely fitting along the creature's scaly back.

"We can't all leave on the dragon," Shar said.

"You go, we'll find a way," Mid said

"I'm not leaving you two!" Shar said, looking straight at me.

"Just get him off this island." And my expression must have been intimidating enough because Shar nodded. The five of them disappeared into the sky, and then the water was up to our waists.

"Get the Crykon to come to us," Mid said, swimming through the water now. He looked exhausted, his lips blue from the chill as his teeth chattered. Using his power was taking a toll on him.

I was just about to do as he said when something grabbed me by the neck, suddenly choking me.

I was shoved under the cold water, and the commotion around me was suddenly silenced. Sounds became muted by the depth of the icy underworld I became submerged within.

I tried to scream, but nothing came out except a flurry of bubbles in the water. I tried to fight, but they were gripping me so hard that my windpipe felt like it was being crushed.

Then I was up above the water again, and I was face to face with my attacker.

Elysian.

"You thought you could flood the island and that you wouldn't go down with it?" Elysian growled. His hair was sopping wet, the dark strands falling across his forehead. His lips were cobalt from the chill, matching the color of his seething blue eyes, which were a twisted, villainous version of my mother's. I couldn't respond. Black spots were beginning to dot my vision from his choking hold on my neck.

Mid pulled the sword from his hip, swinging for Elysian. Elysian let me go, pulling out his violet dagger just in time to ward off the blow. The two weapons met, but the violet dagger cut through Mid's like butter.

I gasped for air, stumbling in the water, struggling against the waves as I tried to recover. My fingers were numb. I couldn't feel my legs anymore. If we didn't drown, we'd surely die from the cold.

I knew I could heal quickly, but I didn't know if I was necessarily immortal. It was one thing to think you were immortal and an entirely different thing to try and test the theory.

The other Envorydains were panicking. None of them paying attention to the fight where we were. Most were swimming, trying to find higher ground, or finding pieces of ice to float on, attempting to find a way to escape the flood of water and creatures. But Elysian was determined not to allow me to leave Xevaria alive.

The two sparred in the water, Mid and Elysian, as I regained myself. Mid had to use his power to fight off Elysian and his glowing dagger now that he was without a weapon. He conjured seaweed vines, trying to drag Elysian down into the waves.

I healed slower than I would've liked. But eventually, the spots in my vision cleared, and I thankfully hadn't dropped the compass.

I closed my eyes, begging the Crykon to find us.

Next thing I knew, I spotted sparkling scales in the water. The relief I felt made me feel hopeful for a moment.

One of the water horses neared me, its gorgeous sleek, scaled body coming up next to me. It gave a watery snort, sprinkling me with water. I mounted the glittering purple Crykon, clinging to its finned mane.

"Mid!" I screamed over the chaos. He was still fighting Elysian. The seaweed wound around Elysian's body, finally subduing his hand swinging the lethal dagger. Mid had several wounds from its violet blade. I could see a tear in the arm of his shirt, blood seeping into the fabric a dark crimson.

Another massive wave came crashing over the arena, and the people scrambled to avoid the flooding. It hit Elysian and Mid, breaking the two apart for a moment.

The wave covered me as well, and I clung to the Crykon firmly, not wanting it to take me with it.

When I resurfaced again, still clinging to the mane of the Crykon I felt a hand on my leg beneath the water, and I screamed, worried it was Elysian. Then Mid's head popped up, and he gasped for breath. He was shivering as he struggled to mount the horse behind me.

When I realized it wasn't Elysian, I hurried to give him a hand. Pulling his large form up behind me.

Then I urged the Crykon forward.

Just then another hand reached up out of the water, this time Elysian.

"You won't get away from me," he sputtered against the waves.

"Watch me," I growled, reaching for the knife at my belt and stabbing his hand that gripped my leg. He gasped in pain and fell back into the water. Mid gripped me from behind, and we kicked the Crykon onward.

The horse was fast even in the water, moving almost as

quickly as a real fish. It somehow moved us through the chaos, away from the arena until we were met with the icy edges that hadn't been broken. I could see now a giant slit in the icy blanket that covered the sea where I had cracked its resplendent surface. The crack ran for many miles until it met up with the island.

The Crykon reached the edge of the ice that wasn't broken, and Mid and I climbed off and started at a run back across the way we'd come.

It was slippery, just as bad as when we'd first arrived. But we did our best. I slipped a couple times, but Mid helped me regain my footing. I feared I would freeze to death right on the ice if I stopped.

I didn't dare look back to see if Elysian was following or to see the wreckage of the island.

I just kept going. I didn't stop until Mid tugged me to a standstill.

"Ehren, stop," I was lost in a trance, my eyes hooked on the horizon as the cold stung my eyes and the wind whipped my wet form.

"Sabeara, stop!" he said again, and this time I snapped out of it, slowing to a halt on the ice.

"What?" I turned on him, my teeth chattering. If I lost momentum now I worried for both our lives.

"Your feet," he pointed down to my bare feet. They were bleeding profusely, leaving bloody footprints on the ice. I must've lost my shoes in the water. Mid's boots were luckily still on his feet.

"Let me carry you," he said, and I shook my head

"It'll heal," I said, but the cuts on my feet were deep, and now that I'd noticed them I winced in pain as I tried to take another step.

"Not fast enough, come here," he said, but his arm was bleeding.

"You're injured too."

He didn't ask permission then. He scooped me up in his arms and began running again.

I gripped my arms around his neck and felt guilty for the relief on my body as he carried me.

It wasn't just my feet that were injured, my body was retaliating against me from the shock of the water. My heart seemed to be pounding slower. I think my body was trying to heal several parts of myself, and because my heart wasn't as strong as usual with the curse affecting me, it was taking forever.

Mid's breathing was heavy as he continued to run. How he was managing it being injured himself, I didn't know. It was like he was somehow even stronger than he was before with his golden heart, which I didn't know how that would be possible. But I was the healer. I should've been the one that was helping him.

He was blue and shivering, but he pushed on, running until the sun began to fall over the horizon.

"Let me down, Mid," I said, my feet were finally healed and my body was returning to a normal function now that I was no longer in the freezing cold depths of the water.

He slowed to a walk, and somehow pulled me closer, my head fell into the crook of his neck.

"We're almost there," he murmured.

I didn't protest. I was too exhausted.

Thankfully in the distance I could see land. The beach that we had come across when we first arrived.

He'd run the entire way, half of it with me in his arms.

When his feet hit the hot sand, he fell to his knees and laid me down. My body felt a stinging sensation all over as the hot grains met with my chilled skin. I let out a sharp breath but didn't fight it. The fiery heat felt too good to argue. He fell beside me on the sand. We both laid there, warming ourselves against the hot beach. His arm was resting on my waist, and he gently gripped my side.

"Are you alright?" he asked breathlessly, panting as he tried to catch his breath.

"Yes, but you're bleeding." I sat up, which required quite a bit of effort. I reached out to his arm and conjured up as much strength as I could muster, healing him.

"Thanks," he said, his lids halfway drooped.

"I thought we were going to die back there," I admitted.

"Me too." He put a hand to his forehead and groaned. "I'm so sorry."

"Why are you sorry?" I asked, appalled by his sudden apology. "What could you possibly be sorry for."

"I didn't have enough energy to create another creature. I would've flown us out of there if I had been strong enough."

"Mid, stop," I said, reaching out to touch his hand. "You saved them and us."

"I should've made Shar stay back with me."

"Shar wouldn't have survived," I said. And we both knew it. We were both stronger. Something with Mid's new power was making him more resilient, and I was a healer. If anyone else had stayed in that water for that long, they would've died. "I don't think you could've carried Shar across the ice like that." A small smile tugged at the corners of my lips.

"You're right. He's a lot heavier than you," he smiled back, and then reality seemed to settle back on us unwillingly.

"We have to get going. They will catch up soon."

"What I would do for Diablo right now," I said and sighed

"We can travel tonight around Obscurum, and then I know somewhere we can stop to rest on the outskirts," Mid said.

"Where? Another friend's house?" I raised an eyebrow thinking of the time we met Syd in Eslecaster.

He shook his head. "Not exactly."

THIRTY-EIGHT

SUNN

I stared at the bath he'd drawn. The bubbles smelled heavenly, like vanilla and strawberries. The entire bathing room was coated in a sweet warmth, and a humid perspiration clung to my skin, instantly calming me. I padded across the rug and reached for the soft white robe on the hook next to the basket of towels and lotions. I shrugged into the robe's soft material, loving how it felt on my skin.

I lit a few candles, and I was instantly calmer. Or I tried to convince myself that I was. Underneath my calm exterior was a nervousness keeping my heart beating just a little too fast for normal. Obsidian would be back soon to check on me.

He'd fought during the raid, and he'd made sure I was okay after I'd panicked. He'd nearly attacked James when he yelled at me. What was going on?

I tugged the robe a little tighter around my neck. I was more covered than when I wore that ball gown at the Night Fell but for some reason wearing a robe felt more scandalous and revealing.

I didn't know what he would think when he walked back in and saw me in my robe. He probably thought I'd be done with the bath by the time he returned. But I waited for him. Because I knew deep down, I was hoping for something.

Surrender maybe?

The doorknob turned then, and Obsidian walked back in. He had a tray with tea and cups. He couldn't see the bathing room when he initially walked in. So I watched with labored breathing as he set down the tray and looked around, his brow furrowing when he found the room absent.

"Sunn?" he called. He walked closer to me, and my heart rate increased with every step that got him closer to my view.

It was seconds later that he spotted the bathing room. The tub, the candles, the bubbles on top of the soap-filled water. And me, in a robe.

He froze, his eyes landing on me and taking in the situation slowly. His eyes roamed up and down my body, taking me in.

"I see you've made yourself comfortable," he said. For a second, I thought I saw anger flash in his expression. "Hmm. . .." the sound came from deep in his throat as he walked slowly over to me, his eyes not leaving mine.

"Is everything okay out there?" I asked.

"Things are calming down, thankfully. It doesn't look like another attack will occur. At least not tonight."

I was grateful to know it was over, at least for now. I didn't think I could take any more anxiety attacks.

"Care to join me?" I asked, gesturing to the hot water. He wasn't at all phased by my invitation, it seemed. I was hoping I could catch him off guard, but nothing seemed to affect him. His cold black eyes remained impassive.

"I don't really do baths," he said, stopping just a couple feet away from me.

"Oh, so you do every other extravagant thing, just not baths?" I rolled my eyes, and he actually looked surprised for a moment.

"What do you mean by that?"

"Oh, you know, when we were on the ship together, I recall silk sheets and fancy finger food with wine. Dear Prince Obsidian never wanted to get his hands dirty. You liked putting your feet up and watching other people do the work for you." My words were weapons, and I hoped he would fight back. "I just assumed baths would fit in with all of that," I shrugged, trying to act as if it didn't affect me. But my skin was beginning to feel flushed beneath the robe, and my insides were twisting with anxiousness.

"I appreciate extravagant things," he said, taking a couple more steps toward me with a thoughtful look on his face.

I didn't move, knowing if I ran now, he would win the invisible battle I'd staged.

"It's romance I don't fancy," he concluded, closing the distance so that now there were only a couple inches between us.

"Romance?" I asked, raising an eyebrow. "What makes you think taking a bath has anything to do with romance?"

"Oh, you know. Maybe it's the bubbles and perfume. Or maybe—" his voice reduces to a whisper. "The infatuation I see in your eyes. Tell me, do you feel the sensation of butterflies when I look at you?"

"I wouldn't dare be so cliche." I gritted my teeth, hating that the musky scent of him was causing me not to think straight.

He raised an eyebrow, and a smirk tugged at the corners of his perfect lips.

"You don't even know what it is you want, do you?" he asked, leaning in a little closer. His breath was suddenly hot against my cheek. "I think you can't decide if you want me to take this robe off of you right now, or if you want me to be a gentleman and walk away."

I froze in place as he reached out a hand to touch my waist, his fingers skimming the ties on my robe.

"And I think you and I both know I'm not a gentleman. So that only leaves one option."

Without warning, he tugged the strings of my robe, and I gasped aloud. Before the front of the robe could fall completely open, revealing myself, I gripped the lapels back together and spun around, nearly falling face forwards into the tub.

Obsidian's arms encircled my waist, catching me and pulling me tightly against him. His lips found my neck, and he murmured against my stammering pulse.

"Oh, sweet girl, did you really believe I wouldn't take you up on the offer?"

With haggard breathing, I tried and failed to catch my breath, unsure of what just happened.

His arms slowly released me, and I steadied myself against the side of the tub.

That's when he burst into laughter. He backed away, trying and failing to control his chuckling.

I turned around, my eyes narrowing at him.

"You're making fun of me," I said, my cheeks burning with the heat of embarrassment and shame and maybe a couple of other emotions I couldn't name.

He chuckled all the way over to the tea tray and carried it

back to rest beside the tub. When he finally got his laughter contained, he faced me and gestured toward the bubbling bath water.

"Get in, love. The tea is getting cold."

~

He'd said to get in and drink the tea. And instead of telling him to turn around and leave, I told him to turn around so I could undress and get in. Once I was underneath the bubbles, and my nakedness was obscured, he turned back around and started pouring me a cup. I realized our dynamic was a little dysfunctional. Spirits, it was absolutely insane that I was in the same room with him. But for some reason it also felt extremely right. This was what we were. Beautifully dysfunctional. On the verge of dangerously strange.

"You didn't have to laugh at me," I said, resting my head back against the porcelain and trying to tame my racing heart as he casually poured himself a cup of tea too.

"I'm sorry if I offended you. It was just too funny not to laugh." His eyes were bright with a playfulness I'd never seen before. It made me giddy.

"I'm an innocent young girl. How could you even threaten to take advantage of me like that?" The game we were playing was absolutely intoxicating. I never wanted it to stop. My heart was still racing from the experience. My skin flushed with slight embarrassment. I would probably be a hint of red until tomorrow.

"I think the question is, why would an innocent young girl tempt a man like that? Shouldn't you still be recovering from the shock of the raid?"

I sat up a little bit, the bubbles still clinging to my skin but I watched his eyes flit down with hesitancy for a second, uncertainty in his expression at my movement. I put my arms on the edge of the tub and rested my chin against them and he relaxed a tad.

"I like pushing you."

"Pushing my limits?" He raised an eyebrow.

"How can there even be a limit if you feel nothing towards me?" I raised an eyebrow.

"Tell me about the Isles," he suddenly said.

"What about them?" I asked. I hated that he was changing the subject, but the fact he was even talking to me was enough to allow me to let it go. He never asked me questions.

"What was it like there?"

"It was hot. And the castle was incredibly boring," I admitted. And he let out a husky chuckle that penetrated my bones and turned them to mush.

"Why were you on the ship that day?" he finally asked. I knew what he was talking about. The day he'd taken over Rissen's ship. The day he had captured me. Little did he know since then he had never let me go.

"I had been on the island for almost a year. The only way I could get rid of the boredom was by sneaking onto the ships for a couple days. It made my father crazy, and I got into lots of trouble whenever he found out. But no matter how many times I got yelled at, I continued to go on the ships." Memories of my times out at sea, the ocean, the salty wind in my hair. They would never leave me. "It was the only freedom I ever got, and I craved it."

Obsidian considered this for a moment, his brow pursed in thought.

"What about you?" I asked.

"What about me?"

"Tell me about your home."

He scoffed. "Obscurum?"

"Yes, tell me about it."

"It's sandy and hot. And it's filled with desperate, poor people seeking a way to escape."

The reality of his sentence hit me like a punch in the gut. He was being completely honest with me. A rarity with him.

"It sounds terrible."

"It is," he affirmed. "And I'm part of the reason it's so terrible."

Silence emanated between us. "I don't have a home, Sunn," he said quietly. "The word home gives off the impression of a place where I'm happy and comfortable. I have a kingdom. I'm the prince and heir of a piece of land that I could one day rule. But it is not a home."

"Were you ever happy there?" I asked.

"One time, when I was a child maybe. And my mother was alive."

"How did she die?" I dared to ask. James had told me some of the story on the ship, but no one knew the full extent of what happened. I'd been waiting for the moment to ask.

"I think you already know the story," he said darkly.

"But I've never heard it from you."

He paused, considering it for a moment before finally telling me. "My father told me that my mother was killed by my uncle, King Cassian. I was told as a child that she was taken prisoner and died in Aveladon's dungeons due to neglect and starvation."

The image I was picturing nauseated me. "What crime did she commit?"

"My father doesn't believe she ever committed the crime. But it was rumored that she committed treason."

"Treason?"

"They say she tried to poison Cassian at a gala."

"You don't think she did," I said.

"I'm not so sure now," Obsidian admitted, looking down at his hands. "It's hard to believe that the woman that raised me, that loved me, and cared for me growing up could possibly be capable of such a crime."

"Why are you questioning it?" I asked, my voice a mere whisper.

"Do you want the honest truth?"

More than anything, I wanted to say, but I held my tongue.

"Please," I said in a mere whisper.

"Because of you."

THIRTY-NINE

SABEARA

All I wanted to do was fall down and sleep. But I worried if we stopped we would be attacked by the surviving Envorydians who made it off the island. I hoped that Elysian drowned in the depths of the ocean. But some part of me knew he was still alive. I wasn't going to believe he was dead until I saw it with my own eyes.

We went as far around Obscuruum as we could on the route back home. We didn't dare pass anywhere near the Obscurum kingdom again. So we stayed on the outskirts, treading into the jungle that reminded me of the Sethen Courts. I may have even treaded the same paths two years ago. I followed Mid, who seemed to know where he was going.

"How do you know we aren't going in the opposite direction?" I had trusted Shar and Rouix to guide us on the journey before, but they weren't with us now. And I had a magical compass, but it was pretty much useless unless I wanted to summon sea creatures.

"I used to hunt these lands with my father."

"You did?"

"We never told anyone, of course." Mid turned to give me a small smile. "My mother would've had our heads if she knew we were crossing borders to hunt."

"I can imagine. Is that why you were so comfortable crossing borders when I met you?" I thought about the time we traveled to Eslecaster together.

"Probably." he shrugged. "I figured as long as no one knew I was the prince, I was safe."

We continued walking, treading through the hot leaves and sweaty plants that were so different from the Severesi cold we'd just come from.

My feet were thankful for the warmth. Though sticks and rocks still pierced my bare feet, I endured it. I'd much rather have cuts and scrapes than deal with frozen, bloody feet.

It was pitch black a couple hours later, and I worried in the dark that Mid wouldn't be able to find his way.

"We should stop. I don't want to get lost."

"We're almost there," Mid assured me.

Then, sure enough, I saw something in the shadows ahead, softly illuminated in the rays of the moon that filtered down through the jungle leaves.

It was a little abandoned house shrouded in plants and vines. It appeared to be almost swallowed up by the foliage.

Mid found the door handle that was wrapped in jasmine vines and urged the door open with a loud creak. It gave way with a whine, and then we stepped inside.

It was hot in the little house, the humidity almost suffocating. Mid quickly went to the window and pushed it open, allowing the hot, wet air inside to escape.

There were two rooms. One had a bed with rumpled old sheets and pillows, then the other was a kitchen area with a table and chairs, some pots and ladles on the wooden table top. A couple of hunting weapons hung on the walls, arrows for a bow and spear tips lying around.

"What is this place?" I asked him as I gazed around the room.

"It's a safe house," he said. "Me and my father would stop here when we hunted and needed a rest."

"Did he build it?" I asked.

"We found it one day, abandoned," he admitted. "And we just hoped no one ever came back for it." He grinned, and I shook my head at the look on his face.

"That's where you get your wild streak. Your father."

"Doesn't seem like the type to break the rules, does he?" he asked.

"Not at all," I admitted.

"He was actually quite the rule breaker back in the day." Mid sat down on the chair at the table and then took his shirt off. Peeling off the still damp and bloody shirt over his head and tossing it to the side.

"Was he?" I asked, leaning against the wall to watch him as he wiped the blood off his skin with his shirt, he was examining the wound I'd healed, but the skin was utterly perfect again, not a scar in sight.

"Let's just say my mother tamed him."

He stood up and walked over to the closet pulling out shirts and trousers that were hanging inside.

"Here, put these on." He threw me a new pair of clothes and some socks too. I clutched the musty but dry shirt and pants to my chest.

"Thank you," I went into the other room to change, thankful

to be in different clothes. My skin was finally no longer flushed with the chill from the water, and I was returning to normal again. My feet felt a hundred times better, and I was myself once more.

I walked out to find Mid changed as well, sitting at the kitchen table again.

I went to sit across from him.

"I could probably create us a ride to get us home now. I'm feeling much stronger."

"Could we maybe just sleep for a couple hours? I'm exhausted."

He nodded. And the silence was thick between us for several long minutes.

"He knows where Knadiel is," I said quietly.

Mid nodded, then sighed. "I don't think this isn't going to end without a bloody battle."

I hated the thought. But knew he was right.

"He was angry that Obsidian joined our side."

"I wouldn't exactly say he's on our side."

"I don't know. You saw the way he was with Sunn."

His eyes flashed with an angry fire. "Are you referring to the kiss?"

"Yes, the kiss," I said, and he shook his head.

"He forced that onto her. Which reminds me, Obsidian is dead when I get back."

"I'm pretty sure Shar will beat you to it."

A growl left his throat, and he stood suddenly, pacing the room.

"Mid, I don't think that kiss was forced," I blurted, and he stopped in the middle of his pacing.

"You're joking, right?"

I stood up and gave him a sympathetic look. "I think Sunn feels something for him."

Mid became frozen, still as a statue. "She's a child, Sabeara."

"She's almost eighteen," I reminded him.

"Obsidian is a murderer. Sunn can't have feelings for him," he spat, and I walked over to him, putting a hand on his shoulder to stop his pacing.

"Mid, I know you don't want to think about this right now, but for Sunn's safety, I think we need to consider that she may have feelings for him."

"Easy solution, I kill him, and she'll have no monster to lust after."

I sighed. "You can't kill him."

"Why not."

"Because we need him."

"You just said Shar is going to do it for me." He glared at me as if I were the one pushing the two together. "What makes you think he hasn't already done it?"

"Because he knows how much we need him," I said. "As much as we all hate to admit it."

"This is just great. First Shar and Embrosine, now this." Mid walked over to the bed and sat down with his head in his hands.

I walked in after, approaching him carefully.

"I'm sorry about not telling you," I said softly, and the silence was deafening for a moment as my confession was suspended in the air.

"I wrongly took my anger out on you. Shar should've told me. Spirits, Embosine should have."

"Still," I said. "You trusted me. And I betrayed that trust."

He looked up, and his green eyes softened. "Sweetheart, you

have nothing to be sorry for." Every time he called me that, something in my chest felt warm.

"Shar told me that he and Embrosine were going to figure things out," I dared to tell him.

Mid's jaw clenched.

"I think they might tell Ashelor," I added.

He sighed. "I think Ashelor already knows."

"How?" I whispered.

He looked over at me as if deciding whether or not to tell me something.

"When I was younger, I remember something. An angry fight between Shar and my mother."

"Your mother?"

"They were talking about my sister's wedding." His brow furrowed. "I was so young I didn't really know what they were talking about."

"Do you remember anything about the conversation?"

He nodded and sucked in a sharp breath. "I remember them talking about the consummation."

It took me a moment to register what he'd just said.

"I had just come in from playing outside in the woods. I overheard them talking in another room."

"Do you remember anything else?"

"I remember hearing Shar say he would do it for her."

"Do what for her?"

"I remember the exact words were, I will take his place."

"Take his place?"

And then it all dawned.

"Mid," I gasped, looking over at him, and he nodded as if he'd already put the pieces together.

"I think they were required to consummate their marriage the night after their wedding ceremony. It's a Sapherine tribe tradition. I imagine my sister couldn't go through with it, so Shar somehow. . ." he trailed off. "Sabaera, I think that Shar is Sunn's father."

FORTY

SUNN

I was speechless at his answer and couldn't respond for a moment. I looked down at some stray bubbles on my wrist, and I slowly wiped them away while thinking on his words.

"How did I change your mind?" I asked quietly.

He set his cup down on the tray and crossed his arms over his chest.

"I guess when I met you, it made me see things differently."

"Did I say something?" I asked.

"Not necessarily. I just don't think you are capable of something so horrific. And you were associated with people my father claimed were so heartless."

"They are good people," I whispered.

"That's why it hurt so much, Sunn." His expression was suddenly pained. "I trusted Sabeara and Jasper with everything. That included Ehren and Casimir. We were family. To hear that their father imprisoned my mother and that she died at his hands. It was a betrayal, unlike anything I'd ever experienced."

I was so shocked he was admitting these things. It was almost unreal. Was I dreaming?

"But until I met you and found out who you were. I guess I never stopped to consider that maybe I was on the wrong side."

He abruptly stood from the vanity chair and looked about to say something more, but then he left the bathing room, shutting the door behind him. I sat in the lukewarm water, unsure if I'd heard the words he'd said or just imagined them. *Did Obsidian just admit I changed his mind? That he thinks he was on the wrong side for all these years?*

I stood slowly from the bathtub and stepped out onto the rug. I towel-dried my skin and hair and then put on my night clothes. I took my time. A little scared to go out and face him.

I took a deep breath before opening the door to the bedroom. He sat on the sofa, facing away from me. I carefully walked over to him and sat on the opposite end of the beige cushions.

"Obsidian—" I began, but he cut me off.

"I shouldn't have said all of that." His dark gaze was back to being hard and impenetrable. The vulnerability had vanished.

"No, I'm glad you did."

"Why?" His eyes blazed to life again, an angry fire suddenly ignited in his onyx orbs.

"Because it helps me see you've really changed."

"Is that what this is about? Is this some twisted attempt at trying to fix me?" He stood up, his hands clenched in fists at his sides.

"What? No, I'm not trying to fix you, Obsidian."

"Then what do you want from me?" he asked, and his voice

broke, and I could hear the desperation. An emotion I'd never before heard laced in his words. "Do you want me to bare my soul to you? Is that why you've been trying to get close to me? Is that why you've insisted on making me admit I'm not the same anymore?"

My feelings waged war inside my body. He had no idea how he made me feel. The conflict that I had been enduring for so long. Several months ago, I had seen a different side of him on that boat. And I'd seen it again multiple times since then. A side that wasn't a monster. And seeing that he was capable of softness, of gentleness, of love— it was what made me fall for him.

The reality that I loved him hit me so hard that I lost my breath.

Spirits, I loved him.

I loved him, and I wanted him to love me back.

But he was too scared, too afraid to love someone. And I knew it was because he didn't believe he was good enough.

"I just want you to admit how you feel about me," I said.

His jaw clenched, and he held my gaze for a moment before tearing his eyes away and letting out an angry growl.

"Sunn, I can't."

"Why not?" I stepped towards him, but he just took several steps back, keeping the distance between us.

"You know exactly why," he said darkly.

"I don't think I do!" I felt tears prick the corners of my vision. I was so done fighting with myself and feeling conflicted over the gorgeous yet dangerous fallen angel that I loved.

"Because I'm bad for you!" he yelled, not bothering to hold back. "You may think I'm not a monster anymore, but that's where you're wrong. I will always be a monster. Nothing is going to change what I've done." He strode toward me. Reaching out to clasp my face in the palm of his hands. He looked desperately into my eyes, begging me to believe what he was telling me.

"All I do is take, Sunn. I take and take and take until there's nothing left. And for the first time in a long time, I don't want to do that. I don't want to be the person that leaves you lifeless. I don't want to taint you with the darkness inside of me."

"But that's where you're wrong, Obsidian. I've never felt more alive." I reached out, touching his chest tentatively with my fingertips. "You aren't going to taint me."

"I shouldn't make you feel alive, Sunn. I should make you feel scared. I should make you feel so disturbed that you run the other way." He groaned and stepped away again, obviously struggling. "The spirits are punishing me."

"Punishing you?"

"Every time I look at you, I'm reminded that I can't have you. So yes, punishment is fitting, I would think."

"No one is punishing you, Obsidian! You're punishing yourself!"

"Damn it, Sunn. Please just stop!"

"I can't stop!" I nearly screamed across the room, anger vibrating my bones. "I can't stop because I love you, Obsidian."

He froze as the words left my mouth. The tears in the corners of my eyes escaped, falling down my cheeks. All was still for a moment. Only the sound of our erratic breaths. Our pounding heartbeats.

"I love you." A hiccuping sob escaped me. "I love you, so please, don't ask me to stop."

He looked at me with wide, tortured eyes. My confession was obviously not what he had been expecting and he seemed to be trying to decide which side of himself to succumb to.

"Spirits strike me down," he finally murmured, closing the

distance between us. His hands cupped the sides of my face again, and he crushed his lips to mine.

The kiss was raw and bruising. Nothing was subdued or withheld. A whimper left me, the feel of him and his lips against mine attending an emotional and physical need I'd been craving for far too long.

He groaned, his mouth opening against mine. He gasped, I gasped. The taste of my tears mingled on our tongues, and we fell into each other again.

His hands tangled into my long tresses while the other secured my waist and lifted me off the floor. My legs wound around him, and he pressed me roughly against the wall. He gripped my wrists, tugging them above my head, pinning me in place. I was trapped within his embrace, but I didn't have any desire to escape.

"Obsidian," I said, another desperate whimper leaving me. My mind was a foggy delirium. His skin, his scent, his touch— became my entire world.

"If you say my name like that—" he breathed, his lips falling onto my neck, peppering my skin with mind-numbing kisses. "—I won't be able to stop."

"Please don't," I begged.

The wall fell away from behind me, and he guided me over to the bed. We fell into the soft comforter as he laid me down and caged me with his body. My arms wound around his neck while his hand spanned across my abdomen.

I gripped the fabric of his shirt in my hands, tugging upwards.

He obeyed, sitting up for a moment to remove his shirt, and discarded it to the floor.

His pale, lean body was as I remembered it from catching a

glimpse of it once before. His golden heart shone beneath his pearl skin, the wonder of it taking my breath away. He was muscular, but not so much that he was bulky. His willowy form was so beautiful I didn't want to tear my eyes away.

He leaned back down, grasping onto my bottom lip. He kissed me senseless, until I forgot my own name. Everything about him was euphoric. An eclipse of emotions. The moon meeting the sun.

Needing to feel more, wanting more of his skin on mine, I reached for the buttons of my nightshirt and began to undo them one by one. Before I reached the second button, his hands stopped me.

"Easy there, love," he said, his voice husky.

"Don't you want this?" I asked, and it came out more like a gasp.

"Not like this," he murmured, brushing a wild strand of hair behind my ear gently.

I wanted to argue, but he kissed me again, silencing any arguments I tried to make. His kisses became less fervent, and he pulled back slowly until he finally stopped completely and ended our kiss by pressing the gentlest peck to my forehead.

"I should go," he said. The resistance in his voice couldn't be hidden. He didn't want to go. And I didn't want him to leave. Something monumental just happened between us, and he wanted to leave?

"Stay," I whispered, looking into his dark depths with desperation. He had no idea how much I needed him.

"If someone finds me in here—"

"Everyone is gone," I reminded him. "And James will be out searching until morning."

"I hate how he looks at you," he said suddenly.

I was still trying to catch my breath from our intense kissing episode.

He moved so that he could lean against the headboard.

"He's my best friend," I said.

"He wants to be more than a best friend to you," he said, reaching out and running a hand through my hair and staring at the strands with a furrowed brow.

"He knows where I stand, especially after this morning," I reminded him.

"I shouldn't have snapped at him. I should be pushing you to be with him instead." His jaw clenched.

My eyebrows rose in shock. "You're kidding, right?"

"He is a much safer option," Obsidian said, leaning in and nipping the sensitive skin beneath my ear. "He would never hurt you."

"You're right, because I don't love him." My heart fluttered when I said the words again. I just wished he'd say them back.

He must have read the disappointment in my gaze.

"I can't say it right now. If I say it aloud, I'll never be able to forgive myself."

I leaned my forehead against his and sighed. "Obsidian. . ."

"Sweet girl, I don't deserve to love you." His eyes filled with that same torment I'd noticed earlier before he'd kissed me.

I hated that he thought that. Hated that he couldn't open himself up to me fully. I wanted to push the subject more but knew it was rare enough that he was sitting, touching me, kissing me. Something had just changed between us. Something I couldn't put a name to. The conversation we'd had and then the kiss we'd just shared had opened up a piece of him I'd been waiting to see for so long. I would have to take what I could get.

"Just lay with me then?" I asked, my voice breaking.

His jaw clenched, and I worried he would continue to fight me, but then he simply nodded.

"I'll stay. But just for tonight."

~

Obsidian went to wash up and had been in the bathing room for quite some time. Leaving me alone to think by myself was dangerous, especially after everything that had just happened.

Had I really said that I loved him? And had he really kissed me? Is this a dream? Is he really staying the night?

Anxious thoughts bombarded my mind. I couldn't sit anymore, and I began to pace the rug. I was suddenly so nervous. Now that the games and facades had been brushed aside and we were being completely honest and vulnerable with each other, I felt like an innocent young girl. I'd developed a thick skin against him over the last several months, but now I was completely open, absent of any sarcastic armor, ready to be wounded. It was terrifying.

I groaned, running a hand through my hair.

The reckless, overthinking didn't stop until he stepped out of the bathing room.

I froze when he emerged.

He came out, his shirt still absent, so I could see his glowing gold heart and pale muscled chest. He wore only a pair of pants that hung loosely on his hips. His hair was wet and slicked back from his freshly washed face. His dark black eyes assessed me, and it was like he could read me instantly.

I must've looked as crazy as I felt because he slowly walked over to me, his expression softening as he neared.

"What's the matter?" he murmured, and his husky voice sent shivers down my spine. *What was this man doing to me?* He was slowly unraveling me, and I feared nothing would be left of me if he kept melting me with his voice.

"Nothing," I said hurriedly, even though it was a blatant lie.

"You look like you're about to run out the door," he said, giving me a soft, teasing smile as his hand found my cheek and traveled up into my hair. My hands fell on his bare chest, and I felt the nervous fluttering return full force to my stomach.

"I guess I just realized some things," I whispered, not wanting to admit my erratic, definitely juvenile girl thoughts to him.

"What epiphany did you have while I was washing up?"

"You want me?" I finally blurted.

He pursed his lips. "Was the kiss we just shared not enough proof?"

I blushed, thinking back to the moment on the bed when I started to undress myself unsuccessfully. My cheeks burned red at the memory. "Maybe I need a little more proof?"

He stopped my rambling by leaning in and kissing me again. His lips were so soft, so warm, and I couldn't help the quiet little sigh that left me. His lips moved against mine, grasping and tugging until I was once again breathless and disoriented.

When he pulled back, a lazy smile grew on his lips.

"Sunn, I can't explain exactly what's happening between us. But I don't think we need to figure out everything tonight either."

"So you just want to sleep next to me tonight? That's it?" I asked, confused by this dark prince that owned my heart.

"Is that not enough?"

"It's enough," I said breathlessly.

"Good," he said, gently pulling me towards the bed again. "Then let's get some sleep."

I followed him towards the bed, my shyness returning. *Hadn't I blatantly thrown myself at him multiple times? Why was I suddenly so timid?*

Because this was real, I thought. *This isn't a game anymore.*

He pulled back the sheets and gestured for me to get in. I crawled beneath the covers and waited for him as he blew out the candles around the room, bathing the room in darkness. The only light that remained was the soft golden light in his chest.

I jumped a little when his hand fell on my waist.

"Why are you trembling?" he asked, concern lacing his tone as he pulled me into him.

"Obsidian, a couple hours ago, we were fighting your father's men sent to kill my family. Then we argued until I admitted I loved you, and then you kissed me, and now we are lying in my bed together. I think I'm warranted a little trembling," I said dramatically.

Obsidian chuckled as his fingers began to trace lazy circles across my back. He smelled heavenly, like expensive musk and amber.

"Stop thinking," he said, his lips brushing my temple and causing another shiver to wrack my body.

"That's kind of hard for me."

"Just try," he urged, and I sighed, forcing myself to close my eyes and focus on the beating of his heart.

Gradually I faded into the exhaustion my body was ignoring. And I fell into a peaceful oblivion.

~

I jolted awake sometime in the middle of the night, gasping for air. I'd been dreaming of Obscurum soldiers raiding the castle. There was lots of blood, so much it had turned the marble floors of the castle crimson. I hated dreaming of death.

"Sunn, it's just a nightmare." The horrific images slowly faded as I took in my surroundings. I was in Knadiel, with Obsidian—in my bed.

I looked up into his onyx eyes, he was watching me, and I wondered if he'd even fallen asleep.

"Obsidian," I whispered. The relief that I had been dreaming overtook my tear ducts.

"What were you dreaming about?" his hand smoothed my hair and cupped my cheek where he wiped away the tears I hadn't known I'd shed.

"I was dreaming about Obscurum raiding Knadiel."

"Everyone is alright, sweet girl. You're alright." His hand caressed my neck, landing on the necklace my mother had given me when I was just a child. It was a little sun pendant on a thin gold chain.

"What is it?" I asked.

There was something about having a conversation with someone in the middle of the night, with the moonlight seeping through the windows and casting a blue hue on the room. It was so quiet, so calm. It was so much easier to let go in the darkness to tell secrets and share intimate caresses. It was oddly comforting and serene.

"I like this," he murmured, gazing thoughtfully at the sun pendant.

"My mother gave it to me," I said, loving how his hands felt against my neck as he fiddled with the little chain.

He gazed at it a couple minutes longer, then shifted his attention back to my face. I could sense some sadness in his expression.

"What?" I asked quietly, not wanting to break the quietness.

"Nothing," he said, but I didn't quite believe him.

"Do you think the others will be back soon?" I whispered.

"They probably got word of the attack and are heading back now."

I bit my lip, contemplating this.

"And Ehren?"

Obsidian sighed. "Either they've escaped by now with Dusane, or he killed them."

My eyes widened, and he seemed to realize how blunt his statement was because he rushed to ease me.

"I'm sure they're alive, though. I doubt my father will be able to defeat them. They're pretty resilient."

"You promise?" I asked, hating the thought that they wouldn't make it out.

"I promise. They were skilled enough to take me down. And that's saying something."

Silence passed between us for a moment before I interrupted again.

"Obsidian, do you think we should tell them about us?" I whispered, daring to say what was really on my mind. Is that what we are now, an us?

"They aren't going to accept you and me together, Sunn."

I looked into his dark depths, hating the truthfulness in his words.

"I don't care what they think," I said.

"I know you don't." He leaned in and pressed a kiss to my lips. "I can't just stay away from you. Not after everything, and after tonight and—"

"Shhh." He held my face in his hands, forcing me to calm down. "Let's not worry about this right now."

"But Mid might kill you—"

"Sunn, please," he begged. "Can't we just have one night where we don't worry about the outside?" His dark black eyes were pleading, so warm and full of emotion unlike I'd ever seen.

I forced my arguments aside and tried my best not to look pained at not being able to work through everything that night.

"Alright," I relented.

He pulled me against his chest again, and I melted into him.

"I love you," I whispered, holding my breath to see if he'd say it back. He simply stroked my hair and pressed a kiss to my temple.

"Goodnight, Sunn."

FORTY-ONE

SABEARA

"You think Shar was with her on her wedding night instead of Ashelor?"

"It's the only thing that makes sense."

Silence spread between us for several moments.

"If Shar is Sunn's father. . ." I trailed off.

"I haven't been the only one they've been lying to," he said, his jaw clenching.

"They just need to come out with the truth."

"This would've been incredibly damaging to our family reputation. And not to mention the alliance with the Isles, which is why I think they've been hiding it."

"Will the Isles be upset with Embrosine if she breaks it off with Ashelor?"

"It could render the alliance useless."

"We need the isles."

"Which is why I'm starting to see why they have lied."

"Couldn't they just be together in secret?"

"Who says they haven't been?"

"You know Shar's not that type of man," I said.

"You're right. Which is why I think I caught them kissing that night. I think it was a breaking point for them both."

Silence spread between us. "If you loved me from afar for eighteen years, would you have done the same?"

"I wouldn't have lasted eighteen years, Sabeara," he said seriously. "Loving you from afar is the hardest thing I've ever had to do for the short time I've endured it."

I felt my breath hitch.

"I feel for Shar now. Because I know what it feels like to watch the woman you love be with another man." His eyes were piercing as he spoke his next words. "I don't blame him. Not at all," he said.

"But Sunn."

"Sunn will learn the truth, and when she does, she'll have every right to be angry. But I know she also loves Embrosine and would want her to be happy."

"Do you think Embrosine ever really loved Ashelor?"

"Ashelor has always been gone," he said. "Seeing him was a rarity. So I don't think there was much of a relationship as you might think. I mean nothing romantic, at least."

"An agreement. For the alliance."

"Exactly. And he loves Sunn. Don't get me wrong, he's been a wonderful father to her." He sighed. "But I have to admit that Shar has been around far more than he has."

"What a mess of lies."

"Yeah." Mid put his hand to his forehead and began to massage his temple as if a headache were forming.

"If only love weren't so complicated," I said quietly.

"If only," he agreed, looking over at me, his eyes searching mine. We looked at each other for a moment until I could no longer handle the heat of his gaze and had to look away.

"We should get some sleep now," I said, slightly breathless.

"You can take the bed. I'll take the floor." He gestured to the one bed in the little safe house.

I looked back at him and gave him an incredulous look.

"Do we really have to do this?" I said, feeling exhausted all of a sudden.

He looked at me with a puzzled expression. "Do what?"

"Mid, you've slept next to me nearly naked multiple times. Keeping up these pretenses. . ." I gestured toward the bed. "Just sleep in the bed with me."

"But—" he started to argue.

"There's no point in both of us getting a horrible night's sleep after what just happened."

He looked at me almost cautiously. "You're sure?"

"I'm sure," I crawled on top of the musty old covers, too hot to crawl underneath them.

He joined me, keeping a small space between us as he lay next to me.

"Goodnight, Sabeara."

"Goodnight, Mid."

~

I woke the following day, a weight around my waist and Mid's breath against my neck. I paused for a moment and looked down to find his tanned arm warped securely around me. Sun filtered through the murky window onto our tangled bodies, and I carefully dismantled myself from his embrace, trying not to wake him.

I gathered my things, feeling much better after a couple hours of sleep.

Hearing my rustling, Mid eventually stirred. He sat up groggily in the little bed and rubbed his eyes.

"Morning already?"

"I think we should get back quickly if you're feeling up to it. I'm worried about the others."

Mid nodded, pushing himself out of bed to join me in preparing to depart.

"I think I'm rested enough to get us home."

When we exited the hut, the humidity immediately greeted us. The caw of birds in the branches resonated above, and the dribble of water running off the green leaves peppered my skin.

I breathed in the misty air, feeling like I was back in the courts.

"A pegasus should do," Mid said, and his hands produced their familiar golden light, a gorgeous white creature forming in the space between the dewy trees.

The beautiful creature whinnied upon its creation, and then we walked over to its side and mounted its back together. Mid took his seat behind me, his arms brushing my sides as he did.

He kicked the creature gently, and then we took off into the air. I was familiar with flying, so it was nothing to me when we emerged above the alabaster clouds, and the jungle below became but a speck.

We headed towards the mountains where Knadiel resided, and I desperately hoped that after the previous day's events, that everyone was now safe and back where they belonged.

FORTY-TWO

SUNN

Fluttering my eyes against the brightness of the morning sun, I groaned, stretching my tired muscles. It took me a moment to remember everything that had happened the night before. Then it came to me in a rush, making my heart flutter and my skin flush at the memories.

Obsidian.

The kiss.

Telling him I loved him.

Sleeping in my bed.

I turned over, expecting him to be there, only to find the space next to me empty.

I sat up and ran a hand through my tangled hair. He must've left to be sure no one caught us together.

I got out of bed and changed my clothes, and ran a brush through my hair. After making myself decent, I left my room in search of him.

I checked his room first, only to find that it was empty too.

I went to the main hall next and then to the dining room. There were a couple guards who were cleaning up the glassy remains of the fight from the day before, but no sign of Obsidian.

The panic started to settle in then. Just as I was passing the foyer, James came walking in, several sentries behind him.

"James, is everything alright?"

"Yes, the village is taken care of. And word has been sent to the others to return home as quickly as possible. Thankfully none of the villagers were hurt." He came over to me, worry creasing his brow. "Are you alright? I left you with him, and I was worried about you."

"I'm fine," I said, my voice breathless. "But I woke up this morning, and he's gone."

"Gone?" His brow furrowed. "What do you mean?" I could see the distrust in his gaze, and then gradually, realization seemed to dawn on his features making fear seize my chest.

"Spirits, he ran," James said suddenly, already jumping to the worst conclusion. He turned to the guards beside him. "Search the grounds for Obsidian. I think he's escaped." They immediately jumped into action, the guards running back towards the front doors to the outside.

"You really think he left?" My breaths started to come in and out so fast that I worried I might hyperventilate. I couldn't tell James what had happened the night before. All the things that transpired.

I had told Obsidian I loved him. *Would he really just leave after that?*

The world suddenly felt like it was closing in on me.

"I think I know him well enough that he'd do something like stage a rescue and then use that to escape again."

"But his cuff is still on him. Why would he run if he knew Sabeara would be back to set him free any day now?"

"I don't know, Sunn. And that's what scares me the most. We have no idea what he's planning."

I couldn't stay in the foyer any longer. I ran after the guards, needing to see for myself.

They searched the stables.

The fields.

The gardens.

Every room in the mansion.

But every empty place only further confirmed my fears.

He left.

I ended up in my room. I'd run back to my chambers, James calling after me. Ignoring him, I burst back into my room, where the evidence from our night together still remained. I looked at the rumpled sheets and the memories of his hand on my face when I woke up in the middle of the night, felt like a knife was stabbing me in the chest.

"No, no," I murmured under my breath, not believing it to be real. "You can't leave," I whispered. Hating that I'd walked right into his trap and didn't even see it coming.

I ripped the sheets off the bed, an angry growl reverberating from my throat.

How could he leave me after everything?

In desperation, I ripped the pillows off the sofa, and knocked the entire contents of my vanity to the ground, needing something to break, other than my heart.

I was angry and hurt and, most of all, blindsided.

What was I thinking, falling for him?

I fell to the ground, exhausted from tearing the room to pieces.

The tears came then, and I heard pounding at my door. It was James. I had locked it. And I wasn't planning on opening it.

The pounding continued as I felt hot tears dribble down my cheeks and onto my lap. I held back the sobs, so he wouldn't hear me.

"Sunn, open the door!" James yelled, but I pretended not to hear him.

Biting my lip, trying to hold back the tears unsuccessfully, I looked up and came face to face with the mirror on the wall. My eyes were glassy with tears, and my nose and cheeks flushed from crying. I reached up and wiped the salty droplets from my cheeks. Only then did I notice my bare neck.

I gasped, reaching my fingers tentatively to where my necklace used to be.

The sun necklace my mother had given me was gone.

And so was Obsidian.

PART TWO

FORTY-THREE

SABEARA

When the hooves of our Pegasus hit the ground, I immediately ran into the mansion. Mid didn't even try to stop me.

Everything was a blur, my heart racing in my chest as my feet moved as fast as they could. I just needed to see him. And know that he was alright.

I burst through the front doors and quickly went in search of him. I knew he would be in the infirmary.

When I pushed open the doors to the little healing room, he was already up and out of bed.

Dusane stood by the window and turned around when he heard me enter.

"My little Envorydian," he murmured sweetly as I entered the room.

A sob tore from my chest as I ran into his arms.

"Are you alright?" I immediately asked. Hating that we'd been apart for so long.

"I'm fine, but you're squeezing the life out of me," he said, his voice strained. I immediately let up on my hold and backed away to assess the condition that he was in.

He still had some faint bruising on his cheek, and I immediately reached up to heal it for him. The burning in my chest had never been more welcomed.

"Thanks," he murmured as I took what was left of his healing process and made sure he was whole again. He brushed back a strand of hair from my face and leaned down to kiss me.

His lips met mine, and I sighed into him.

It was a good long kiss, and it made me realize once again just how much I'd missed him.

"I missed you," he said against my lips, and I let out a shaky sigh.

"You don't know how worried I've been."

He let out a weak laugh. "I'm surprised you came to rescue me," he teased.

"Why would that surprise you?" I asked, raising an eyebrow.

"I thought for sure you'd be glad to be rid of me by now."

"Never," I said fiercely, pulling him in for another kiss.

His lips danced on mine, a welcome familiarity fusing us together. Then there was a knock at the door, and someone's throat clearing interrupted our reunion.

"Sorry to interrupt," James entered the room, his cheeks flushed from embarrassment.

"James." I had forgotten everything else for a moment, my sights so focused on Dusane.

"Did you bring her up to speed?" James asked Dusane, and he shook his head grimly.

"We have the cloak," James started, and my eyes widened.

"Did you find out what it does?"

"It appears to help a Stone-Hearted understand their powers so they can utilize them more effectively."

"Interesting," I mused, wondering what such knowledge would feel like.

"That's the good news," James said.

"The bad news?" I asked, turning back to Dusane, who still had his arm wrapped around my waist.

Just then, Mid also came walking through the door, Liony alongside him.

"Knadeil was attacked while we were away," Liony said. "We just arrived a couple days ago, after it happened."

"Attacked?" My eyes widened, shock coursing through me. "They found us?"

James nodded grimly. "Obsidian helped us drive them out, but after the fight, he disappeared. "

"What do you mean disappeared?" I asked slowly." Who let him go?"

James pursed his lips.

"I went to check on the villagers, and by the time I returned, he was gone. All the soldiers were focused on getting everyone to safety. And because he helped with the attack, Sunn didn't think he was a threat anymore..."

"Sunn did this?" Mid growled. "She let him go?"

I looked at Mid, a warning in my eyes. I told him I saw something at the Night Fell. Maybe now he would believe me.

"Don't blame her for this. I shouldn't have trusted her with him. It's my fault," James said.

"She can be pretty stubborn, James. This isn't your fault either," Liony said.

Dusane sighed, kissing my temple. "Things can never just go smoothly, can they."

"But he left with the cuff. So he's still powerless," I said, confusion furrowing my brow.

"No one really knows why he'd leave without being freed first," Liony said, but she looked like maybe she had a theory.

Everyone in the room went quiet.

"Where is Sunn?" I asked.

More silence.

"She's in her room. She hasn't left in several days," James said quietly.

FORTY-FOUR

SUNN

I knew the others had returned. But I failed to participate in the reunion.

I didn't want anyone to look at me with anger, pity, or a mix of the two, and I knew that was all that awaited me on the other side of the door.

Those that had gone to rescue Dusane had finally made it home. And I knew that my mother, Oli, Jasper, and my grandparents were also home.

They'd each tried to knock on the door at least once, trying to coax me out of my room.

I hadn't eaten much in the days I'd stayed in my room. Nothing sounded appetizing. My stomach felt like it was made of stone. I would take sips of water, and every once in a while, when a servant would put food outside my door, I'd pick at some bread or fruit.

I felt so cold since he'd gone. I shivered into the covers where he'd last been with me, and I shamelessly tried to cling to the smell of him for as long as it would remain.

They wouldn't understand.

No one was going to understand.

Obsidian was gone, and he wasn't coming back.

I'd told him I loved him. How stupid could I have been? I was angry and felt betrayed. But most of all, I felt heartbroken. How could he have just left? Without even freeing himself? I worried I played right into his trap.

I couldn't help but wonder if any of it was real.

"Sunn," I heard my name muffled through the door. "Please open up, love."

Shar. I knew it was him.

"You can't hide in there anymore," he said firmly on the other side of the hardwood. "Let's talk."

"Go away," I said, my voice cracking due to lack of use.

"Please, love," he begged.

Shar had always been good to my family. My whole life, when my father had been gone, he'd acted as a surrogate father of sorts. He was strict and sometimes a pain in the ass. But he cared. And I knew deep down that his words would probably be the only words that I could handle at the moment. I could take tough love over pity. And Shar was sure to give that to me.

Sitting up, I detangled myself from the rumpled covers and smoothed out my wrinkled shirt. Then I walked over to the door and ripped it open.

"Go ahead. Scream at me. Yell at me. I know you're all thinking this is my fault."

His dark green eyes burned into mine as he pushed his way into my chambers and then closed the door behind him. His silence was terrifying.

"I know you know I kissed him on that dance floor willingly," I spat. "I kissed him, Shar. And I would let him do it again."

Shar closed his eyes, taking in several deep breaths.

"I'm a traitor. Just say it!" I screamed, somehow finding my voice. All the pent-up anger and rage was stewing in me for so long, and it felt so good to bleed myself of it.

"I stood up for him because I was stupid enough to trust him! And I'm sick and twisted for falling for someone I shouldn't have ever gotten close to! Just say it, Spirits, say it, Shar. Yell at me, lock me up in the dungeons, do whatever you must to make it right." Gasping, sobbing breaths escaped me as tears poured down my cheeks.

"Tell me how to fix this, how to fix me. . ."

I crumbled, and he caught me in his arms. He pulled me to his chest and immediately cradled me.

"Shhh. . .it's alright."

My tears soaked his neck. I couldn't remember the last time he'd held me like this. I was probably a mere child. But I remembered him fixing my wounds as a kid. He was Mid's guardian, but he'd been a guardian to me as well.

"Fix me, Shar. Please."

"You don't need fixing."

"How could I fall for that monster?"

He sighed, running his hands through my red curls gently. "Love is not something we can control."

"You think I'm insane." My voice was muffled against his tunic.

"No, I don't think you're insane. Just human."

I cried harder, hating how dark and miserable I felt.

"He's gone now. And there's nothing you can do to bring him back."

More tears fell.

"I can't pretend it doesn't enrage me to know he touched you."

"I—"

"Let me finish."

I reluctantly let him speak.

"But it's not my place to judge your desires. I only care that you're alright, love. I don't want to see you hurt like this."

"He broke me," I sniffled.

"You're not broken," he murmured, kissing the top of my head. "Now, let's get up and get you dressed. The others have returned, and we need to decide what our next plan of action is."

"You don't need me. I'm useless. You can all have the meeting without me."

"I'm done pretending you're a child, Sunn. Now, if you want to be treated like an adult, stand up and help us figure out what to do next."

"I hate tough love."

"Get used to it. It's the only love I give."

"That's not true," I whispered.

"Right now, it's the truth. Now come on," he helped me stand and reached down to wipe the tears that slicked my red cheeks.

"They're all going to hate me for what I've done."

"Trust me, they aren't going to be upset with you."

"They'll think he tricked me, that I was stupid enough to fall for his games, and they'll pity how naive I am."

His jaw clenched, and he sighed. "Let them believe what they wish to believe. Only you know the truth."

FORTY-FIVE

SABEARA

We convened in the study the next day. Though I was exhausted and tired and could've slept for two days straight, I knew we needed to make a plan.

We all met in the study, a fire licked at a fresh cut of wood in the hearth. Some took spots at the table, while others sat by the orange and yellow flame.

I wondered if Sunn would show up. But just as I thought the words she walked in with Shar at her side.

My sister briefly hugged me before taking her seat next to Oli at the head of the table.

I addressed everyone in the room with my eyes. Nothing was said for many minutes.

"I'm glad everyone is okay," Knadian spoke first. "That's all that matters."

Sunn wouldn't look up from the table. She looked like the study was the last place she wanted to be.

"Obsidian is gone," James said. "We were attacked and we need to prepare for another one."

"We can't stay here anymore," Liony said quietly, sadness coloring her tone.

"Where can we possibly go?" Jasper asked, fiddling with the coin in her palm. The firelight glinted off the golden rim alerting me to the nervous habit she still maintained.

"Does it even matter?" Rouix asked. "They have such a big army now. With Seversi, Obscurum, and the mantle we are doomed to lose in a battle."

"And that is what this is coming to," Embrosine said sullenly.

"We can't give up," Shar said forcibly. "If we give up now, everything that's happened will have been for nothing."

"Shar is right," Ruby said, her poise and grace still in tact amidst the tiring conversation. "We can't give up now."

"So where do we go?" I asked, a lump forming in my throat. Why did I suddenly feel like crying? I must've been more tired than I realized. The last couple weeks catching up to me. I pushed back the sting in the corners of my eyes, and swallowed. "Obsidian has escaped us, and now they know where Knadiel is. It's unsafe to stay here, so we have to leave. But where? Where else is there to go?"

"The isles of Arradale?" Jasper suggested.

"We already ruled that out. They're dealing with attacks from Obscurum on the daily, they've sent hundreds of soldiers to help us already and they aren't very strong at the moment." Embrosine said, her jaw clenching. "The only reason Elsyain hasn't sunk the entire island by now is because he knows that what he truly wants lies with us."

"The tokens," Mid murmured.

"If we go to the isles he'll surely just follow and we'll be trapped on an island with nowhere to go if Elysian instigates a battle."

"Alright, so not the Isles," I said, frustration burning in my veins. Why did it feel like I was in a maze with no way out?

"We could go to Pendilore."

All eyes turned to Rosen, and more fury burned in my blood.

"Not this again," I said, burying my head in my hands. "You don't even know if such a place exists, Rosen. You've never actually been there."

"What's this place you speak of?" Knadian asked.

"It's a kingdom that has answers to our world's powers." Rosen said. "It's hard to explain, but a Reminant I spoke to told me that if I went there I could finally understand my powers more intently. He even said that there was more to our world's history and magic system there."

"He believes his heart is made of a stone called Amberidium." I said, not bothering to hide the disbelief in my tone. "He thinks that it's different from Cirtine, the stone that makes hearts gold."

"What is this Amberidium stone do?"

"I was told it was the life source of our universe."

I glanced to Mid, who was eyeing Rosen with a very thoughtful expression.

"Someone was obviously speaking nonsense to you. Telling you to go find a kingdom with all the answers to our world is just insane."

"Is it?" Rosen asked, looking sort of angry at my disregard for his beliefs. "We barely know anything about our realm, our history, our past. And what we do know is based off this book—" he picked up the Ethirical that rested in the center of the table.

"An extremely vague story of the kings that created our kingdom. It barely explains anything in here. I mean, it's a miracle we've found any tokens at all with how little is explained."

I remembered him speaking of this place when we fled the Sethen Courts. It seemed just as insane now as it did then.

"I think it may be where we need to go," Rosen said, more fervent now. And for the first time it seemed that he was all seriousness. Rosen was usually sporting a conniving expression, a mockery just beneath the surface of his tongue. But he looked completely sobered. His eyes almost afraid as he said his next words. "The Reminant that told me of its existence once told me that it housed the answers so many of us desperately seek. To the tokens, to our magic system, to everything."

"But it is just a rumor," I said, my eyes narrowing. "We can't take thousands of people to find a place that may or may not exist."

"I know it exists, I just haven't found it yet," Rosen's jaw clenched and I sighed.

"We wouldn't all have to journey to find this, Pendilore," Liony said, for some asinine reason she seemed to be entertaining the idea.

"What do you mean?" Oli asked.

"We could hide in the caves on the border of Ethdyon and Aveladon where so many people were found stranded after the Ethydon war. It's where many of my rescue missions have been to. There's a location that could easily house thousands. The caves in those mountains run for miles. Then, if you do find this Pendilore, you could send us word and we could travel to meet you."

"It may not be a bad idea," Dusane finally spoke beside me.

He reached out to take my hand beneath the table and our fingers intertwined "If we stay here we are sure to die. Elysian will come looking for us. And Obsidian could very well be on his way to tell him every little detail he's learned while he was here."

"What happens if we don't find Pendilore?" I asked, hating that it sounded like we were going to go find some magical place that Rosen suggested we go to. "I mean, this place could be a complete story."

"It's not a story," Rosen insisted. "I was so close. . ." he trailed off. "I could feel it. I was so close, but it must not have been the right time when I'd gone searching."

He sounded slightly crazy as he said those words. Like he believed in destiny and fate and other things.

"I just wish there was more proof," I said.

"I have some, but it's small," Rosen said, reaching into his cloak he pulled out a book.

It looked old and worn, much older than even the Ethirical. He laid it out on the table for us to see. The leathery front was cracked and withering away. I worried if we touched it, it would disintegrate.

He opened it to a page with a map, and turned it around for all of us to see.

"This book is thousands of years old. The Reminant gave it to me when I went in search of Pendilore originally."

"Where did this Reminant get this?" Dusane asked, his eyes widening.

"I don't know. It's not in our language, it's an ancient language, but the map is universal. It lays out a lot of our realm and shows us where Pendilore should be."

Rosen pointed to some of the marks on the map. It was true

to the landmarks that our realm had. I could make out the mountain ranges, and several of the rivers and oceans we knew of. I could even spot the Isles of Arradale. The place Rosen was pointing to was high above the rest of the kingdoms, it was further than we'd ever traveled before. It would take us days to get to where he was pointing.

"This is where it should be."

Everyone was silent for many moments.

"How do we know this isn't a fake book?" I asked.

"This doesn't look fake, Sabeara," Dusane said, suddenly onboard with Rosen's idea, it seemed. Which was odd considering the two didn't particularly like each other. "He may have something here."

"Why have you never shown us this?" Mid asked.

"Because we were too busy searching for the other tokens to worry about Pendilore. Also, I didn't know if you'd all believe me or not."

I think I was angry about the whole idea simply because I didn't want to learn everything about our world and our magic. So many awful things had already transpired due to power. I was actually wishing I could go back to simpler times. When I was human again.

I cursed beneath my breathe, not believing I'd just had that thought.

"Fine." I stated roughly. "We'll go in search of Pendilore if that's what everyone agrees to." I looked around the table, and no one objected to the idea.

"We've exhausted all our paths," Jasper said. "If we must go down a new path, though it be blind, so be it."

She said it firmly, but it was impossible to miss the quiver of doubt in her voice. To see the doubt and the fear on everyone's faces.

We'd run out of options. And now I could only hope that Rosen was right and we'd receive the answers in Pendilore that we'd been so desperately seeking.

FORTY-SIX

SUNN

And as much as my mother begged me to go with her alongside Jasper, Oli, and my grandparents to guide the Knadiel people to a safe location, I told her I felt like I should follow Shar and the others.

She'd tried to fight me on it. Said it would be much safer if I went with her to the caves. But I stood my ground. Knowing that I would rather be in the caravan searching for Pendilore. I needed a distraction.

Thankfully after some convincing, she reluctantly let me go.

"I'd rather you stay. . . but you are an adult now. So if you want to go, that's your decision." I could see the sadness in her eyes. The control it took for her to allow me to make this decision by myself.

"Thank you," I said, grabbing her hand and squeezing it. "I'll be fine, Mom."

"Be safe, Sunn. I couldn't forgive myself if you got hurt again.

I love you," she said, emotion clinging to her voice. Then she hugged me tightly.

"I love you too, Mom. And I will be safe. Don't worry."

I hugged my grandparents goodbye as well, then hurried down the front steps of the mansion. I waved goodbye one last time to the others, and then blew a kiss. Knowing it may be a while till I saw them again, I felt a pain in my chest.

But the pain at saying goodbye only urged me onward. The faster we found Pendilore, the sooner I could see my family again.

~

It was pretty quiet and sullen as we began our journey. I rode with Mid atop Ghost even though James offered to let me ride with him on his steed. After everything that had happened, James was being awfully gracious. But I was still feeling ashamed to face him. Like he'd been right all along, and I should've listened to him. Thankfully he was giving me space. I was lost inside my own thoughts for the first part of the journey.

Rosen claimed he knew a place that could help us further the knowledge of the curse. He firmly believed our answers were in this kingdom a Reminant once told him about when he'd sought answers to his powers.

I was ready for the curse to be over. I was ready for everything that happened over the last several months to be put behind me, so I could move on. If that meant seeking out a kingdom that might exist and give us all the answers, so be it. Even if there was also a large chance that it was completely fictional.

It was hard not to think about what happened with Obsidian as we journeyed. So many unanswered questions flitted through my mind. It was exhausting trying to silence all my thoughts. Memories of him and the things he'd said to me, the way he'd touched me. . . I feared he may forever haunt me.

Why he'd left, I was still trying to figure out. And I'd never get my answer, which probably upset me the most.

I could only hope his effect on me would fade with time, that I'd no longer feel the hole of his absence as I grew older. But even as I thought it, I knew it would be futile. I didn't think I'd ever be the same again.

We traveled for several hours until nightfall. When it became harder to see through the trees, we decided to stop and set up camp.

I helped set up a few tents, and then it was decided that I would sleep with Liony. She went to bed almost immediately. And the others followed quickly after. It seemed no one was in the mood for conversation. After everyone had a quick but sparse meal of bread and cheese, they all crawled into their beds. Mid kissed my forehead on his way to his tent.

"If you need anything, you know where to find me," he said gently. Then he paused, a thoughtful expression coming to his face. "Also, maybe you should talk to your friend. He's worried about you." He gestured towards James, who was hanging his pack on a tree by the animals. Then he left me by the fire, not even telling me to go to sleep. I was glad he respected my decision to stay up. I couldn't have slept if I'd tried.

I knew he was right, I needed to talk to James, but I just didn't know if I was ready to admit all my wrongs.

James began walking back from the trees towards his tent, and I stood up, walking over to him. He slowed when he saw me coming towards him.

"Hey," he said.

"Hey," I replied awkwardly. "I'm sorry." A lump formed in my throat.

His green eyes softened, and he reached out to touch my arm.

"You have nothing to be sorry for."

"I don't know if I'm ready to talk about it all yet. But I need you to know that I'm sorry, at least."

He sighed and nodded. "You don't need to apologize for anything, Sunn. And we don't have to talk about anything yet."

His words soothed the ache that seemed to be constantly pounding in my chest since Obsidian had taken a chunk out of it.

"You're my best friend, James."

"I know." He smiled softly. "And you're mine too." He gestured back towards mine and Liony's tent. "Now get some sleep. We've got a long journey ahead of us."

I nodded and watched him leave to his tent before retiring back to the fire. I knew I wouldn't be able to sleep, so I reveled in the quiet alone time and sighed aloud.

"Long day?" I jumped at the sound of Sabeara's voice behind me.

"More like a long few months," I said, while inwardly telling my heart to calm down after being startled.

"Sorry if you don't want company." Sabeara sat down on the opposite side of the burning logs.

"It's alright," I said, but really I wasn't in the mood to talk. I hoped she could sense my reluctance to feign small talk and simply leave me be. I liked being around Sabeara, but knowing that she was related to Obsidian made it difficult to look her in the eye for some reason.

"You haven't seemed yourself since I arrived back." The comment was like a knife jab straight to the chest.

"I'm fine," I said, but it was a complete lie. I'd never felt so vacant.

"I'm glad that you were alright after the Night Fell. I was worried that you wouldn't get out of there."

I didn't respond, not really even knowing what to say in my mood.

I heard Sabeara sigh softly, and it caused me to look up and meet her deep, sapphire eyes.

"Sunn, I know the way you felt for him. And I'm sorry that he left."

Something dark and bitter made its way through my veins at her comments. She had no idea how I felt for him. And I didn't need her pity.

"You don't know anything about him. I know you all think he played me. But he didn't," I said quietly. Hating that I was picking a fight but feeling too hurt not to act defensive.

"He's a trained killer, Sunn. Have you not considered that it might have been all a ploy to free himself?"

My blood boiled with a rage unlike I'd ever felt before. And I very nearly risked yelling across the flame at her. *How dare she.* I clenched my fists at my sides. Barley able to contain my fury.

"You don't even know him. You both have a side of the story the other hasn't heard," I said, not budging from my view of things.

"I figured. But I never had the chance to talk to him. Jasper and I have just assumed Elysian had some sort of falling out with my mother and that he wanted her kingdom. We never really understood why."

"Your father imprisoned Lillian," I said, not caring to shield her from the truth anymore.

"What?" Sabeara's brow furrowed in confusion. "I remember my aunt Lillian passing away and my father telling me Obsidian and his father wouldn't be around much anymore. But I never knew she was imprisoned."

"She died in one of your dungeons, it was rumored she tried to kill Cassian, and she was charged with treason. " I looked her straight in the eye. Daring her to deny it.

"That's why Elysian killed my mother." Sabeara seemed to realize something, and sadness overtook her expression. "For years, I couldn't remember that day." I could hear the pain in her voice. "It wasn't until I saw Elysian again in Obscurum that I remembered them leaving and him telling my father he'd killed my mom."

"Obsidian thinks you knew that his mother was imprisoned and died in your castle walls."

"That's why he hates me so much, why he's taken Elysian's side then."

"Do you know if she really did it?" I asked, hating that so many things had been wrongly assumed. That Obsidian's entire life would've been different if his mother hadn't been killed. "Obsidian wants to believe she didn't."

"Not that I can remember. But a lot of things went on behind closed doors that Jasper and I didn't know about."

"I wish someone was alive that could give us the full story," I said, hating that I felt loyal to both sides. One part of me wanted to support my family, the Aigoviels, and everything they'd gone through. But Obsidian. He was unfortunately caught up in the crosshairs, and it was hard to be angry with him. He'd told me his side of the story, and now I felt torn. I could see both sides and why they thought each other enemies.

"The only person left is Elysian, and I'm sure he's got a twisted view of what really went down," Sabeara said, then she looked at me, a thoughtful expression taking over her features."He must trust you if he told you all these things."

I looked down at my hands, reaching up for the necklace that was no longer there. "He's not who everyone says he is. He was dealt a bad hand. Fed lies since he was a child. He only believed he was on the right side."

"I believe you," Sabeara said. "I wish I didn't have a tainted memory of him draining the heart of my friend Conland. But he killed a close friend of mine. And he participated in getting your mother kidnapped."

I winced.

"I know you've killed before too, Sabeara," I said darkly. "None of our hands are free of blood."

Sabeara recoiled like I'd slapped her. "You love him," she said. It wasn't a question.

"Yes, I do." I looked up at her, showing her with my eyes that I was dead serious.

"I'm sorry he left," she said, but really I could see the relief in her expression that Obsidian escaped.

"It's for the best," I sighed, standing from the ground. Abandoning my vain hopes of solitude. "And I'm sure everyone else thinks the same."

I started to walk away, but I stopped when she spoke one last time.

"I wish things were different, Sunn." Sabeara whispered, and emotion formed a lump in my throat. She had no idea how badly I wished things could be different too.

FORTY-SEVEN

SABEARA

I hated feeling out of control. I hated even more not knowing what we were headed into.

But I tried desperately to bite my tongue and follow alongside the others. As we ventured further away from Knaidel, following Rosen's map, we came into a slightly cooler area. The clear blue sky was suddenly stained with grey. Wisps of dark storm clouds clung to the air but never let any rain fall. I worried that we might get caught up in a storm, but each night we traveled, not even a droplet managed to escape the fog.

I was grateful for the cooler weather. I'd rather have a slight chill than be slicked with sweat.

We stopped for the second time after many hours of silence.

Talking with Sunn on our first night journeying, I'd desperately tried to understand all the events that transpired so many years ago. Sunn's explanation of why Elysian was so angry at my mother now made much more sense. I had always thought he just wanted power, that he might've been jealous of what my family had. But to know it was in retaliation for the woman he loved...

Oh, what I would do to talk to my mother at that moment. Or even my father. To find out what really happened when I was a child that tore our family apart and made us mortal enemies.

There wasn't much to say. It seemed that everyone was tense and not really in the mood for conversation. Our future was in the hands of Rosen, and in this kingdom, that may or may not even exist.

I sighed as I dismounted from Diablo.

Camp was set up quickly. But I ached for a day when I wouldn't have to set up another camp again. I wanted someplace I could call home, a place where I could settle.

Dusane came over to assist me with the tent, and then once we got all the flaps correctly placed, he stretched out beside me beneath the tan canvas, casually putting his arms behind his head.

"You haven't said much since we left," he said. And I looked over at him, into his dark blue eyes that remained so impassive, they appeared almost cold if I didn't know him so well.

"No one has said much since we left," I said, sighing. "Sunn also talked to me last night and told me a bunch of things that Obsidian told her. It's been unsettling to say the least."

"What kind of things?"

"Like why Elysian hates my family. He thinks my father wrongly imprisoned his wife for an act of treason, and she died in our prisons. Elysian blames my father for her death. I always thought she'd just passed away from some unknown ailment. My parents had never told me really why she stopped coming around."

"I'm sorry, Ehren," Dusane grabbed my hand, and our fingers entwined.

"I'm just angry that I don't know everything. That my childhood is this twisted blur. I don't know if I'll ever really know what happened in the past. And no one is alive to give us the real story."

"How are you doing? With the Rage?" he questioned softly, reaching out to run the tip of his finger down my arm. I shivered at his touch.

"I think I'm doing better. Sometimes I let myself slip, but then I quickly correct my thoughts."

"Good, that's good. That you're catching yourself and gaining control again."

"Yeah, I just wish I could stop feeling angry altogether. This news about my family isn't helping in the slightest. I hate fighting it, but I can't help but feel it when more things come up every day that just mess with my emotions. I feel like I can't catch a break." I clenched my fists and stared at my small knuckles. Shocked that such small hands could house so much force now that I'd been taught the Envorydian craft. It was difficult to remember a time when I didn't know how to wield my body to defeat an opponent. When my hands were simply hands and not weapons.

Something in my chest ached at that thought, when I was so innocent and untainted.

"I don't know if you'll ever not feel angry," Dusane said thoughtfully. "It's part of being a person. But you can find a way to bury it, to extinguish it."

I nodded, Dusane's words inspiring me. Filling me with renewed spirit.

"You're right."

He sat up slowly, suddenly so close that his breath could be felt across my collarbone. It was the first time we'd been alone, it seemed, in a very long time. We could still hear the commotion of everyone outside setting up camp, but with him so close, all that noise seemed to drift away until it was just us two.

"Dusane. Can I ask you something?"

"Of course," he said, kissing the spot beneath my ear.

"The Mantle. How were you involved with them?"

He froze, pulling back and giving me a concerned look. "I don't know if it's such a good idea to get into all that."

"Rouix told me that you have some twisted past with them, that they partnered with Elysian because they could get revenge."

"They partnered with Elysian because he could give them money. I don't think it had anything to do with me."

I gave him a knowing look. "Dusane. Talk to me."

He sighed, running a hand through his hair. "I used to work for Elysian. You knew that. I was a personal Envorydian that did his bidding."

"Okay, go on."

"Well, sometimes I'd take outside jobs to earn extra money. I got involved with Jade and others from the Mantle on an odd job. At first, we did well together. Then, they started to trust me."

I felt my stomach sink.

"But I wasn't one to be a part of any guild. I wanted to be on my own. So when things got too close, I broke it off."

"How?"

"I betrayed them. During one of our jobs, I ended up with all the money, and they never saw me again." His jaw clenched. "They've been seeking revenge since it happened. But those in the Mantle are lethal, Ehren. And where they live on Xevaria is even more lethal. I'm grateful I cut ties when I had the chance."

"Why didn't you tell me all this?"

"Because it was a part of my past that I'd honestly pushed aside. I didn't want you judging me either."

"Dusane, you know I'd never judge you."

He leaned in, kissing my temple. "I'm not proud of who I was before I met the others in the Courts. I don't want you to see me as that person."

"I don't." I pulled back to look him in the eyes again. "But Rouix. Dusane, she was sold to the people on that island as a child. She must've been through something horrific."

Dusane nodded sullenly. "She's told me rare stories about her times on that island, and you're right, it was lethal. And her entire childhood and early adulthood were taken from her."

I felt my heart ache at the thought of sweet Rouix being taken advantage of.

"I'm glad I took down the island then," I said, and he pulled me tighter against him.

"Me too." His lips brushed my neck. "I love you," he murmured. "You know that, right?"

I nodded, my eyes fluttering closed on their own accord.

"I love you too," I whispered as his lips finally captured mine.

His hands wound into my hair, his fingers gripping the strands at the base of my neck. I let out a soft moan as he leaned me back against the one blanket we had. I could feel the forest floor beneath us, but I didn't care about the rocks and sticks digging into my spine.

All I could feel was the weight of his body as he gently pressed into me. And the way his hands felt in my hair and ran along my side.

I reached up, my arms wrapping around his neck and pulling him even closer.

He grunted in what appeared to be pleasure and nipped at my lips once, twice, a third time.

"I hate not being able to have you all to myself," he said, brows furrowing in frustration.

"We are alone," I said, kissing his lips again.

"Not completely, and you know it," he said darkly. His hand gripped my hip, and a zing of desire went through my bones.

"Soon," I promised, reaching up to push back the dark black locks from his forehead. "Once we reach Pendilore."

He sighed. "If we ever reach it."

"If it turns out not to exist, we'll still figure things out. We always do."

He nodded, then pushed himself back up again, pulling me up alongside him.

"We should get some sleep."

"Yeah, I'm just going to check on Diablo one more time."

He nodded and laid back on the blanket while I headed through the canvas flap. It was dark, the sun now far behind the horizon.

Everyone looked to be in their tents, except for Mid. He was sitting by himself by the fire, his features dark in the light of the orange flame.

"Hey," he greeted me as I stepped out and walked to Diablo.

"Hey," I checked Diablo's rope tied to the tree and nodded toward Mid politely.

"Need help sleeping again?" he asked casually, but I could see the smirk on his lips. My cheeks burned, and I was glad it was dark outside so he couldn't see.

"No," I bit out more sharply than I intended. "That's not why I got up. I'm just checking on Diablo."

I heard some rustling and then Mid's footsteps came up behind me.

"Do you think we'll ever reach this place?" he asked, leaning up against the tree across from me. I could feel his presence so intently, even when he stood several feet away from me.

"I hope so, for all our sakes." I double checked my knot and then started heading back towards the tent. I didn't feel comfortable alone with him. For some reason, it felt odd after the night we'd spent together on our journey back from Xevaria.

"You alright?" he asked me, and I paused.

"I'm fine," I said, looking back at him. His eyes held mine captive for a few seconds, and I felt my breath leave me.

Dusane was waiting for me back inside our tent. So why had I looked back? Why was I still looking at him?

"You'd say something if you weren't, right?" Mid asked softly, and my brow furrowed.

"What do you mean?"

"I mean, would you tell me, or someone else at least, about what you're feeling? If you needed to get it off your chest?"

It was such an odd question, and for some reason, it felt sort of like an attack.

"I'm fine, Mid. I don't need to talk about anything."

"You know if you bottle your feelings up, they only fester."

I glared at him, not liking where the conversation was headed. For some reason I could feel that he was referring to Dusane somehow. Without even saying his name.

Things had been civil between us for a while now. Mid had been kind to me when we searched for Dusane. Now I worried that civility was coming to an end.

I could see a flicker of something in his eyes. Something akin to a challenge.

"I'm not bottling up my feelings, Mid. I'm just fine."

"You know you don't always have to be in control all the time."

"What are you getting at," I bit out, wondering if he'd overheard our conversation in the tent and hating that I hadn't thought to speak quieter in case someone was listening in.

"I just don't want to see you suffer," he said, his gaze softening, and I could feel the truth in his words.

"I told you, I'm fine."

"He could be wrong, you know," he said quietly, a mere whisper now.

I didn't respond. Knowing he was referring to Dusane. "Trying to stifle your anger may not be the answer."

"You don't know anything. Please. Just stay out of it."

I stomped back towards my tent. Not at all in the mood to hear what he had to say. I had no idea Mid even knew about my rage issues. But apparently, he'd been clued in, or maybe he was just observant. Either way, I didn't want his opinion.

If there was one thing I'd learned about suffering, it was that I preferred to do it alone.

FORTY-EIGHT

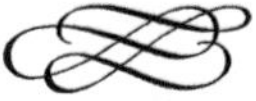

SUNN

The weather changed pretty quick. And it matched my mood.

Rainy. Cold. Miserable.

After my talk with Sabeara I didn't feel any better about the situation with Obsidian.

The worst part was I never really had time to myself to mull it over. I wished I could've been alone. To mourn like the pathetic broken-hearted girl I was.

I should've seen it coming. And I think that's why it hurt the most.

So when it started to rain, and Ghost's paws began to sink into the muddy path, I figured it was the perfect omen.

Even the environment was catching onto the way that I was feeling.

It got increasingly harder to wade through the terrain when the rain turned into an all-out storm.

"We should stop and take cover," Shar suggested. His long

blonde hair was soaked, dripping down his eyelashes and onto his lips.

"I agree," Rosen said, looking up at the dark black sky that was mercilessly pouring down on us.

We convened off the path, taking cover beneath the big branches of a large tree. It helped to shield us from the rain a bit, but it didn't stop the river of water that seemed to be moving downhill, creating a stream down the path we'd been trekking.

"I hope it lets up soon," Sabeara said, curling into Dusane's side to avoid the rain better.

"I've never been to this part of the realm before. Maybe rains are common here," Shar said.

"In this region, they are," Rosen said, brushing back some wet locks of hair from his face. "I ran into quite a few storms the last time I journeyed through here."

I huddled next to Mid and Ghost, my shoes becoming immersed in mud and grime. I could feel it down to my toes, and with each shift of my weight, I could hear the squish of water in my boots.

Ghost whined, his white fur soaked and now so brown he didn't even look like a polar bear anymore.

It didn't stop for a good hour. And that's when things got even worse.

The water got more demanding and the stream gushing down the mountainside started to look more like a river.

"Hang on," Shar said to everyone.

I clung to Mid's shirt, fearful that I might actually be taken with the mud. When my foot slipped, and I started to get pulled by the muddy terrain, I realized how much more severe this storm was.

"Sunn!" Mid reached for me, but he wasn't quick enough.

I slipped, my feet being pulled out from under me. I was taken away from the tree and the tiny bit of shelter we'd been maintaining. I was dragged into the river of mud and water, and fear shot like fire through my bones.

I reached for anything to stop myself from being tugged away, but my fingers grasped onto nothing but loose rocks and roots.

The earsplitting crash of a tree sounded, and soon, the mud was taking down small trees.

I screamed when a tree landed right next to me, the slushy grime consuming it and swallowing it like a mud monster.

"Sunn!" Shar ran beside the mudslide, chasing after me down the side of the mountain.

"I got you! Stay calm!" His green eyes were wide with panic. He grabbed a tree branch from the side of the path and sprinted toward me. He laid the tree branch in my path, and I reached out for it, clasping the lifeline he offered me.

Thankfully I caught the edge of the branch, and he was able to tug me back to semi-dry ground.

He pulled me into his arms, and I didn't realize I was crying. Sobbing actually. I hiccuped, trying to regain my composure.

"Shhh, you're okay," he continued to hold me as I shivered in his arms.

"I almost just died in a mudslide," I gasped. I had grit in my mouth and had to spit multiple times to free myself of the pebbly feeling between my teeth. The shock was freezing my blood, and it all happened so fast that I was still processing.

"You're okay."

Just as my heart began to slow, I heard another scream above the rain and the rush of the river.

Both Shar and I turned to see Mid and Sabeara being pulled into the mudslide.

"Ehren!" Dusane yelled, and he about threw himself into the slide, but Rouix held him back.

I watched in horror as Mid and Sabeara were submerged beneath the mudslide. I searched desperately in the pouring rain for a sign of life, hoping that they hadn't just succumbed to a muddy death.

I let out a sigh of relief when I saw Sabeara's head pop up.

But as soon as the relief came, it went because I suddenly caught sight of a drop-off in the distance. We'd passed a little crater earlier that housed a little grotto. And now the water was gliding right towards it, carrying Mid and Sabeara right into its gaping embrace.

"Spirits," I cursed just as the two of them fell into the hole in the ground, vanishing from sight.

FORTY-NINE

SABEARA

Water, grime, and grit were all around me as I tried desperately to stand in the sludge we'd fallen into.

"Sprits," I cursed, the water to my knees and the mud sucking my shoes so deep it was impossible to move even an inch.

"Are you alright?" Mid grunted, pushing himself up to his feet, the mud making a slick suction sound in the process.

"I'm fine, are you?" I panted, struggling to regain my footing.

"I'm fine," Mid assured me.

I looked up at the dark sky, rain stinging my irises as I searched above us and spotted Shar peering down over the edge. It was probably a good twenty feet up. It was a miracle neither of us were injured.

"You two alive?" Shar called down over the edge.

"We're fine!" I yelled back.

"We'll work on getting you out of there, hang on tight," Shar assured us. Just then, a sad whine sounded from above us. It was Ghost, probably worried for his owner.

I looked over at Mid. His wavy hair and clothes were caked with mud. Then I assessed myself. My dark black outfit was just as filthy and was now a dark cocoa color.

I spit out some sand that gritted against my teeth.

"I hope the others are alright," I said, thinking about Sunn and how she'd nearly gone under the mud avalanche that had slid down the mountain.

"I'm sure we've got the worst of it," Mid said, looking up angrily at the hole's opening.

I sighed and struggled through the sludge to a large rock a couple feet away. I was getting nervous about all the critters that might be lurking in the wet hole and hoped to perch on the rock. I felt better when I managed to heave myself onto the flat surface above the watery sludge.

I pulled my knees to my chest and shivered.

Mid joined me then, huffing with exhaustion as he sat on the rock.

We both took several moments to just breathe and catch our breath.

"I don't think I've ever felt so dirty in my life," Mid huffed.

I let out a weak laugh, too fatigued to make light of the situation.

Awkwardness spread between us. Being in a deep, wet, muddy hole with him was not the most ideal place to be. Especially after the conversation we'd had the night before.

"Sabeara, about last night—"

"There's nothing to be said," I hurried to cut him off.

"I think I may have offended you, and I'm sorry if that's the case. My tongue can get me into trouble at times."

I scoffed. "You know, Mid. I thought we were past this point."

"What point?" he asked, brushing back his hair from his face. His red and green eyes were glowing with eagerness. He wanted to fight.

"The point where we argue about feelings and the past between us."

His eyes widened. "Past?"

"Yes, the past between us."

"You're kidding right?"

"Does it look like I'm kidding?" I spit out another little pebble that I felt between the crevices of my teeth.

"Did I allude to the idea that I'd given up? If so, you're sorely mistaken, sweetheart."

I sat up straighter and narrowed my gaze. "I'm with Dusane now. I thought we'd established that—"

"Oh, you've established that loud and clear. But just because you have moved on does not mean that I have."

"Is that why you made that comment last night? You still assume that I somehow need you or want you?" I asked, my voice raising in pitch.

"I don't need to assume anything," he scoffed, the arrogant, sarcastic prince that had bewitched my younger self returning to the surface.

"You're bold to think that the feelings I had for you so many years ago would still stand."

"The way you kissed me on that boat would argue that they are still alive and well."

I tore my gaze from him, my cheeks flaming as he brought up the kiss where he'd pretended to be Dusane.

"I thought you were Dusane," I spat, hating that he'd tricked me but also feeling shame because I remembered the feeling it had given me. Why was I feeling shameful? I didn't have anything to be ashamed of.

"Whatever helps you sleep at night," he said, leaning back casually on the rock with his arms behind his head.

"I'm not doing this," I shook my head, closing my eyes so I wouldn't have to look at him.

I couldn't believe he still thought that I had feelings for him. After I'd clearly stated, it was Dusane I was in love with.

"You can't possibly tell me you're happy with him. I can see you've got all your emotions tangled up inside, and they're just waiting to be set free."

"What does that even mean?" I glared at him, feeling the sudden urge to hit him.

"You know exactly what I mean. It's like he's trying to control you or something."

"Excuse me? Did you ever think that I want to be in control of myself? And I'm asking him for help?" I sputtered, too many words coming to my mind to say them fast enough. "How do you even know about what I'm going through? You know nothing."

"Don't I?" He raised an eyebrow, all teasing gone from his expression.

"I know you're struggling to rein in your anger. That after everything that's happened to your family, to your kingdom, that you're furious."

My nostrils flared, and my hands clenched at my sides.

"I know he's been trying to help you control your anger. But did you ever think that maybe you deserve to be angry?"

My heart skipped a beat at his words, not knowing how to take them and shocking me a little. Deserve to be angry? Did I deserve to be angry?

"I don't want to kill people, Mid."

"Maybe you wouldn't have to if he didn't try his best to silence you."

"He doesn't silence me!"

He raised an eyebrow. My chest was heaving now, my cheeks pink with fury.

I closed my eyes and began counting to ten.

My eyes flew open when I heard him chuckling.

"Counting? You're counting?"

I snarled, literally snarled like an animal at him. "Don't push me."

"You know what, Sabeara. I want you to yell at me, scream at me. Even better, throw a punch. Come on, hit me."

He gestured to his chest, his eyes alight with something mischievous and dangerous.

"Stop pushing me!"

"Then stop holding back!" he yelled, and I growled, reaching out to smack him on the chest.

"You're the most infuriating man I've ever met!"

"Good. That's it, sweetheart. Tell me how you feel. I don't want you to hide your feelings."

He grabbed my hand where it had hit his chest. He took hold of it, not allowing me to pull it back.

"Let go for me," he murmured, leaning in ever so slightly, so our foreheads were almost pressed together.

His scent overwhelmed the dirt and grime that seemed so pungent in the air. A wave of pine hit my nostrils, and my thoughts wavered.

"Tell me why you're angry. Tell me why you're upset. I want you to stop controlling everything."

I shook my head. Something in my chest was suddenly

feeling funny. Like something might crack if I kept pushing the boundary we were pushing.

"I —I—"I struggled for words, something inside me ached to speak, but another part of me was unsure what I would even say. After so long of stifling my emotions, burying them so deep, I didn't even know if they could be unleashed again after being tampered down for so long.

"I can't—"I was finally able to say.

But before he could argue further, a rope fell from the hole above us, and Shar's voice echoed through the cave-like hole we'd almost been buried in.

"Climb up, you two!" he called down. "Hurry, in case another flood comes!"

I yanked back from Mid's grasp, my thoughts clearing the moment our distance increased.

I nearly dove back into the muddy slush as I tried desperately to reach the rope that was our means of escape.

I clasped the fibers between my soaked and pruney fingertips then yelled to the others.

"I'm ready! You can pull me up!"

FIFTY

SUNN

Thankfully Sabeara and Mid were unharmed. And the rains stopped almost as soon as we pulled them from the grotto.

We were all caked with mud, soaked to the bone, and shivering.

It was a struggle hiking through the mush to find a semi-dry place to set up camp. But thankfully, the mountainside changed from earthy ground to rocky ground soon after. The trees slowly faded behind us, and big gray boulders replaced the muddy soil, and I realized with relief that we must've just passed the worst of it because soon we were all dry, the sun baking us like mud cakes against the rocky surface.

After reaching a cave-like cavern in the side of the mountain, Shar suggested it was time to rest for the day. No one argued with him.

I found a place far away from the others and started to remove my clothes.

The material clung to my skin, and removing the shirt over my head was difficult. A pair of hands assisted me, and I squeaked in surprise.

My head finally popped through, and I found James to be the assisting culprit.

"Thanks," I muttered, hurrying to throw on another shirt over my undergarments. But James didn't seem phased. I guess we'd reached a point where dressing in front of each other was the least of our concerns.

I laid my muddy clothes out on the rocks to dry and felt discouraged looking at the clothes that would probably never look the same again.

"No problem. How are you holding up?" James asked, running his hand down my arm and helping me brush off some mud on my freckled skin.

"I mean, I almost died in a mudslide. But I survived so, I guess I'm doing okay."

James frowned. "I was really worried there for a moment. I thought you might go under the current, and I'd never see you again."

"You can't get rid of me that easily," I joked with him, hoping to lighten the mood because I really didn't feel like dishing out the emotional and heavy right then.

He smiled, letting out a soft chuckle.

"I'll have to think up a better plan then," he winked, and I was surprisingly put at ease by our banter.

But then I remembered the way I bantered with Obsidian. It was always entertaining and felt dangerous like I was doing something I shouldn't. Playing with fire and risking getting burned. The memory made something painful clench in my heart.

Why was I comparing? They were two completely different people.

I berated myself for even thinking of Obsidian in that moment.

Dealing with the ghost of Obsidian was worse than having him right next to me. I would discover small pieces of him, sections of his existence that I'd memorized. It hurt worse to be surprised with these fragments—like shrapnel from an explosion. The pieces were burrowed inside my soul, and difficult to remove. Some may never be fully retrieved, destined to remain buried beneath my skin forever and to cause me to wince when touched at just the right angle.

"Sunn, could you search for some rocks to make a fire pit?" Mid called over to me, breaking me from the spell I seemed to be under.

"Sure," I took the excuse to leave James, hating that a sad look had overtaken his face like he'd just seen where I'd gone in my mind. James was too observant.

I gave James a weak smile before running off to find some big rocks to make a fire ring with.

I headed further than I probably needed to, and I ended up around a bend of big rocks twice my size.

I dug around at the base of the rocky terrain, trying to find one that wasn't too heavy for me to carry back down to the others.

Just then, I heard voices, and I paused in my tracks.

"Have you thought about telling Sunn?" It was Sabeara's voice. I recognized it almost immediately.

I looked down the mountain at our camp and noticed that both her and Shar were absent from the group.

Maybe they were also grabbing rocks.

I was about to turn the corner to reveal myself when Shar's words froze me in my tracks.

"She's already been through so much. If I tell her I'm her father. . ."

"It's never going to be the right time," Sabeara said gently. "You need to just get it over with."

FIFTY-ONE

SABEARA

After the mudslide ordeal, we made it to a rocky area where we could dry out and set up camp for the night. I went out on my own to look for kindling, needing a moment to think to myself after what Mid had said to me down in the mud hole.

Why was he pushing me to talk about my feelings? Did he really think I was being silenced by Dusane? It was stupid and silly. Dusane was helping me. Not hindering me.

I heard some rocks crunch behind me and turned to find Shar on my tail.

"Why are you following me?" I asked, irritation lacing my tone.

"He said something to you down there, didn't he."

I sighed. "It doesn't matter."

"I want to make sure you're alright, Ehren. You've been going through a lot."

"I'm fine, Shar. You don't have to worry about me."

I continued to look for small sticks for the fire and reached for one trapped between two boulders when Shar grabbed my upper arm, pulling me to a stop.

"Sit down," he said. I glared at his hand on my arm but obeyed. Sitting on the boulder, I narrowed my eyes at him.

"What do you want."

"Talk to me," Shar said.

"About what?" I asked.

"Midennen."

I stayed quiet, unsure if I should respond to him.

"I know you're obviously still torn up by something he said."

"He thinks Dusane is trying to control my emotions. That I'm burying my feelings and that it's bad for me."

Shar didn't say anything for a moment, then sighed. "It's a fine line between burying your emotions and controlling them."

"So you agree with him?" I asked, my eyes narrowing.

"Not exactly," Shar said, raising his hands as if telling me to relax. "You learned to control your emotions as an Envorydian, and I know what happens when you take that too far. You stop being able to connect with people, you bury parts of yourself. You become like stone."

"Aren't you in agreement with the way Envorydians live? You are one after all," I scoffed in an almost angry retort.

"Of course, I believe in controlling emotions, Ehren. But you can't sacrifice everything good in life simply because you're afraid to feel."

"I'm not afraid to feel." I stared at him, stunned for a moment. "I don't have anything to let go of."

"Are you sure?"

"Why are we talking about my problems? Shouldn't we be talking about yours?"

His brow furrowed. "What do you mean, my problems?"

"Mid thinks he's figured out something about you and Embrosine. He thinks you are Sunn's father."

Shar cursed under his breath and put his head in his hands.

"Second-guessing cornering me now?"

Shar looked up, his green eyes pained. "It was bound to come to light at some point."

"So you are her father?"

Shar nodded. "Yes."

"Have you spoken to Embrosine? What are you going to do? Keep living this lie and letting Sunn believe that Ashelor is her father?"

He sighed. "We've talked about telling her, but it's complicated."

"Does Ashelor know everything? What does he think about this?"

"He knows. But we haven't spoken to him about telling Sunn yet. We haven't had the chance. He's been away for so long, and the curse has been so pressing that everything has fallen to the side for now."

"Shar. You need to figure this out. You all can't keep living this lie."

"She's already been through so much. If tell her I'm her father. . ." he trailed off, and I could hear the fear in his voice.

"It's never going to be the right time," I said gently. "You need to just get it over with."

FIFTY-TWO

SUNN

Betrayal is a funny thing. It hurts deeply the first time you feel it. But the second time is even more agonizing.

When I heard the words. *She's already been through so much. If tell her I'm her father. . .* my entire world changed.

I couldn't stay quiet then, I had to say something.

"You're my father?" I whispered, unable to speak the words louder.

"Sunn. . ." Shar stood, turning around in surprise to see her standing there listening in on their conversation. His face took on a mixture of pain and guilt. "I didn't know you were listening."

"You're my father!" The words came out louder, and Sabeara came over to me, her eyes wide with panic.

"Sunn, he couldn't—"

"Ehren, please leave us," Shar said, his jaw clenched. "I don't need you making excuses for me."

Sabeara nodded somberly, then left around the bend where I'd come in from.

"How long were you going to keep it a secret?" I asked him, fury laced in my every word.

"As long as I needed to," Shar admitted. His green eyes were filled with guilt but also a specific type of determination. He genuinely believed he was right in keeping it a secret.

"Does my father know? Does Ashelor know?" I had to correct myself, realizing Ashelor wasn't my real father, actually. The reality stung, but what was even crazier was that it all made sense.

How often my father was away. And how Shar basically raised me. My mother and her relationship with Shar. . .they'd kept things complacent in front of me. But now that I knew the truth, I could see the lines clearly. The ones that had greyed and somehow I'd missed.

"He knows," Shar admitted, and he sighed. "He's always known."

"Why? Why aren't you with her?" I asked, immediately wondering what could have caused all of these lies.

"Your mother was betrothed to Ashelor because Ethydon needed the Isles for strength. Without the marriage, Ethydon would have been overtaken years ago."

"What about now?"

"The Sappherine tribes and their values run deep. There was always a risk that they'd refuse to help us in battle if they found out."

"So you just decided to keep this from me? That can't possibly be the only reason."

"There were a lot of reasons we decided to keep this a secret, Sunn. But the biggest one was to keep you safe. We wanted you to grow up in a world where you were protected. And the isles gave that protection to you. And we knew it was unfair to you to make you keep our secret too."

"I could've! I could've kept it a secret!"

"Really, Sunn? The illusion we've maintained is far more elaborate than you even realize. Could you have handled pretending at such a young age? Pretending that Ashelor was your father when I was standing a couple feet away in the background?"

I cursed under my breath, not believing this was really happening.

"My mother never loved him did she?" I whispered, and his jaw clenched.

"She loves Ashelor," Shar said.

"But not the way she loves you!" I cried. "She's suffered for how many years? In an unwanted marriage? And I've had all these years where I've never really even gotten to know you."

"You know me," he said, "I've been by your side your whole life."

"But I had no idea you were my father!" I shrieked. "I wished every day to have my father around! I always felt like I was missing something. When really I wasn't missing anything. You were right next to me the whole time!"

Shar sighed, and a sheen of tears came into his eyes. "I can't take back what's been done."

"No, you can't," I seethed.

"This wasn't easy for me, Sunn. You think I wanted it this way?"

A sob tore through me.

"Please, don't cry," he said desperately.

His arms came around me, and as much as I wanted to push them away, I didn't have the strength.

I let him hold me. Because a small part of me felt like my childhood self needed to be held by her real father. Not the one that had posed as one for my entire life.

I knew he had done it to protect me. Shar always acted in a way that kept everyone else safe. It was part of his selfless nature. He protected at all costs, even if it ended up hurting more than it helped.

I wanted to blame him, to hate him, to fight him. But instead, I melted into his arms because it was easier to sink then to try and fight against the waves that were crashing against me.

FIFTY-THREE

SABEARA

Sunn finding out that Shar was her father only added to the overall tension that seemed to permeate the air.

Sunn would barely look at anyone, and I didn't blame her. I knew how hard it was to feel betrayed and lied to. I only hoped she'd find it in herself to forgive Shar someday. To forgive all of us.

We left the rocky terrain the following day, and Rosen assured us we were close to where he'd last stopped before he gave up on his journey to Pendilore. He hoped we'd be able to figure out what he couldn't.

The large boulders were tricky to maneuver through, but eventually, we made it down the other side of the mountain and came upon what appeared to be a sea of rocks.

It went on for miles, endless grey stones stretching on and on ahead of us. We all convened together, gazing out at the rocky blanket of grey and slate.

"This is where I stopped," Rosen said, and he looked almost

afraid, staring at the horizon of infinite rocks and boulders. It was flat but definitely would take some time to journey through.

"You didn't go further than this?" Shar asked.

"No, I gave up. According to the map this was where Pendilore was supposed to be located. I was discouraged when I ended up here so I turned back around."

"This is where you were led to?" Dusane asked, staring in disbelief at the discouraging landscape. He took the map from Rosen's out stretched hand, and examined it again. "There's nothing here."

"I has to be here though," Rosen said, his brow furrowing. "Somewhere."

"A whole kingdom?" Mid asked, his eyes widening. "I don't see anything but rocks."

"Did any of you ever consider that maybe it isn't in plain sight?" Sunn asked, her voice causing a chill to go down my spine. She sounded pretty monotone like she was tired and numb. She'd been through so much over the last several weeks.

Everyone turned to look at her.

"Not everything is right in front of you. What if it's being cloaked by magic?"

The silence was deafening. I guessed no one had considered it because no one tried to say the thought had crossed their mind.

"How far did you walk past the rocks, Rosen?" Sunn asked.

"Only a couple hundred yards before I turned around," Rosen said.

"Then we walk further, and maybe we will hit a barrier or something." Sunn started walking through the rocks, carefully navigating the jagged landscape. She didn't even look back as she started maneuvering through the stones.

"I don't know, Sunn. That would be wonderful if that were the case, but—"Shar trailed off when Sunn suddenly got about twenty feet away and suddenly vanished from sight.

I heard Rouix gasp beside me. Where did she go?

"Sunn!" Shar called, panicking. He ran across the rocks to the place she'd disappeared.

Then she appeared again, and Shar grabbed her fiercly by the shoulders, worry lacing his features.

"Where did you just go!"

She had a look of surprise and shock on her face. "I found it." She gulped and pointed behind her where she had disappeared. "I found Pendilore."

It was then that we all watched in awe as the barrier that Sunn had passed through seemed to slowly disintegrate. The landscape rippled like a picture in the reflection of a lake and slowly faded away, revealing a new landscape on the other side.

It was so much more than just rocks now.

The first thing that came to mind was how colorful it was.

A beautiful kingdom, settled on the edge of an ocean, came into view. Bright tropical foliage bloomed for miles, and grass blanketed the hillside almost endlessly.

In the distance, I could make out homes, animals, and an entire establishment on the coast. It looked like paradise.

My jaw was agape, staring at the hidden kingdom that was revealed behind the cloaked barrier. And then I spotted a small group of people walking towards us.

A woman occupied the center position, smiling brightly at us as she neared. She wore a loose-fitted shirt and flowing pants in a bright shade of amethyst. Her heart shone beneath the material, a lovely shade of blue.

"Well, hello, you've finally arrived. We've been waiting for you," she said kindly. Her short blonde hair was neat and delicate around her dainty features. And her big brown eyes gazed at us all with wonderment like she had been eagerly awaiting our arrival. But I didn't know how that could've been possible. How could she have known we were coming?

"My name is Shar Vell. These are my friends and family. We are searching for Pendilore." Shar immediately took the role of leader and stepped forward to take the woman's hand and bowed respectfully.

"My name is Tasnim. And you're in luck because this is indeed Pendilore, the place you've been seeking."

Rosen looked utterly stunned. "I must be dreaming," he said, and that was indeed what it felt like.

Did we really arrive in Pendilore? I reached out to take Dusane's hand, and he squeezed back reassuringly.

"You are lucky to have this young woman in your midst," Tasnim smiled at Sunn brightly. "She found the barrier, and when she passed through, it alerted me to your presence."

"I've searched in the past for this very place, but I gave up before I could find the barrier," Rosen said, still gazing in awe at Tasnim.

"Well, I'm glad you tried again. We've been waiting years for you all to come. To save us."

Mid looked at Tasnim with confusion. "Save you?"

"We came to you for help, actually," I said, my voice shaking slightly. "If anyone needs saving, it's us."

Tasnim's smile softened.

"Seems this meeting was destined then. Because you're not the only people in need of saving. Why don't you all follow me, and we can speak in a more comfortable setting. It appears some explanations are in order."

FIFTY-FOUR

SUNN

I discovered Pendilore.

I hadn't expected it to be so easy. To be able to pass through a magical barrier of sorts and be delivered to the other side. But it had really been that simple. To think that for so long, no one had been able to find it.

The Tasnim woman guided us through the luscious green forest toward the main hub of their miraculous kingdom. It was all so beautiful it felt almost like I was in a dream.

It was right on the edge of the ocean, and everything seemed to glisten in the water's sparkling reflection.

People appeared as we neared the buildings and homes, and they eyed our caravan with curiosity.

I could only hope that we weren't being guided to our deaths. We knew nothing about this Tasnim woman and whether or not she was trustworthy.

I was momentarily able to distance myself from the news about Shar being my father. Instead, my attention was captivated by the kingdom before me, and I welcomed the distraction.

Tasnim guided us through the townsfolk. It was bustling with life, and I could tell the people were happy. Some people shared smiles and waved, and it was oddly peaceful.

I couldn't remember the last time I felt a place so at peace. With the kingdoms being at war, everything had felt constantly in chaos. It brought back a sentimental feeling in my chest. I reminisced about such a time in Ethydon when things were peaceful, and the people were genuinely happy and safe.

What would it feel like to be safe again? I thought. It was something I'd taken for granted as a child.

"Right this way," Tasnim said as we neared a beautiful mansion. It was draped in vines and had gorgeous glass windows. No guards stood out front which I found to be odd. Tasnim waltzed right through the front entrance and guided us into the foyer.

Many people were inside, bustling about as if this place were more of a school than someone's home. There were bookshelves everywhere and people studying at tables. Their noses pressed into the pages of old ancient manuscripts. I was only able to take this all in at a glance, though I wished to assess my surroundings even more, but Tasnim didn't seem to be giving us a tour. She was moving as if she had a specific place she wished to take us.

Many people smiled respectfully when Tasnim passed, and she gently bowed her head in response to their greetings.

We were guided up a twirling staircase, past more bookshelves and rooms with people studying, and then we finally ended up in an empty study.

Tasnim gestured for us to sit at the long table in the middle of the room.

I tentatively sat in one of the dark cherry wood chairs, and the others did the same, eyeing Tasnim skeptically. Everyone seemed to still think they were dreaming.

"It's wonderful to finally have you arrive. I can't tell you how long we've all been waiting. It's truly felt like a lifetime," Tasnim beamed at us all before letting out a nervous sigh. "Well, I guess this must feel like a lot to you all. You are probably wondering what this place is and how I knew you were coming."

"That's exactly what we are wondering," Sabeara said, looking at Tasnim with skepticism in her eyes.

"I don't really know where to begin," Tasnim took a seat at the head of the table.

"How about at the beginning. How does this place exist?" Rosen asked.

"Pendilore was created hundreds of years ago. Right after what my people call The Fall." Tasnim let out a breath. "A few of our kind escaped a large massacre and fled to this location. They took ancient records of the Stone-Hearted people with them and have been building up the kingdom ever since. Waiting for when the Chosen would discover our location and help us redeem Midennen."

"Midennen?" Mid said, his eyes widening. "Redeem me?"

Tasnim looked at him and let out a giggle. "Is your name Midennen?"

"It is."

Tasnim grinned. "Well, I am glad to see not everything had been lost." Tasnim gestured with her arms as if to encompass everything around us. "Midennen is the name of this realm."

Silence emanated throughout the room as we all stared with wide eyes and jaws slacked.

"You mean to tell me I'm named after our realm?" Mid asked.

"Indeed. The name would not be known to all of you because you don't have the true records since most books were destroyed in the massacre."

"What massacre occurred that made your people relocate here?" Shar asked, the only one able to speak it seemed, after the wild assumption that our world was named Midennen.

"Yes, the ancient kings killed off almost every Stone-Hearted to reestablish society and inflict their own history onto them."

"What do you mean reestablish society?" Rouix asked.

"Well, they wanted to oppress the people, make them believe in a curse so they could effectively control them. So they killed off everyone except those who were children, wrote the Ethirical to be the governing piece of literature, and then put the color system in place so that hearts would have degrees of power."

"Excuse me, but that's insane," Dusane said. He looked appalled. And my stomach was suddenly sick hearing Tasnim's explanation of their world's history.

"It's not nonsense. It is true. The few that managed to escape were led to this location, and slowly we have been gathering our lost history that the ancient kings had attempted to scatter. We know from the real records of our past that a select few would come and save us from the affliction of the kings and restore peace once again."

"You think we are those people?" Sabeara asked, her voice shaky.

"I know you are," Tasnim smiled, so confident it was impossible not to believe her.

"And I know you are." Another voice entered the conversation, and we all turned to see a man enter the study. He wore long white robes and had a violet heart. He smiled at us all, and a few wrinkles were present in the corners of his eyes that signified his age. Though he still looked middle-aged, he showed the faintest signs of aging.

"Elsmith?" Sabeara turned white as a ghost. She pushed back from the table, standing and knocking her chair to the ground.

Dusane stood beside her, putting his hand on her back to steady her.

Rosen also stood, a similar look of shock covering his features.

"Father?"

Sabeara and Rosen looked at each other.

"You know this man?"

"He's my father," Rosen said defensively. "How do you know his name?"

"He's the Reminant," Sabeara was shaking, tears forming in the corners of her eyes. "He's the Reminant that granted my sister her powers and then guided me to the Spirit Tree to visit my mother when I burned down the tree." Sabeara put a hand over her mouth as if not believing her eyes. "I thought you'd died. I thought I'd killed you in that fire." Sabeara paused and looked back at Rosen. "Wait, he's your father?"

Elsmith smiled calmly and walked over to Rosen. "Son, I'm glad to see you made it. I didn't know if you'd ever return to me."

"I didn't think I'd ever see you again," Rosen said. He was choked up too.

"I knew we'd meet again," Elsmith said gently, hugging his son to his chest.

Then when they pulled apart, Elsmith turned to Sabeara and smiled.

"Alive and well, my dear. No need to feel sorrowful anymore." He took her hand.

"What are you doing here?" Sabeara asked.

"Well, you see I knew that Pendilore existed for quite some time. I've just been waiting for you to discover your destiny and join me."

"Destiny?"

I was unsure what was going on. Rosen's father was suddenly in the room, and Sabeara also knew him. I looked to Rouix beside me, and she shook her head like she had no clue what was happening either.

"Yes, Destiny. I had to wait until you were able to find your brother. To free him from the Sethen Courts, and then I had to let you find your way here on your own. The way it was intended to happen."

"Hold up, did you just say brother?" Sabeara said, a coldness entering her voice that was borderline scary.

Elsmith sighed and then nodded as if he felt guilty.

"Rosen is your brother, Sabeara."

FIFTY-FIVE

SABEARA

"Brother?" I looked at Elsmith, complete shock written on my face. I had to be dreaming. Rosen, my brother?

"That's not possible," Rosen said, laughing darkly at the thought. But I could see the hint of fear in his eyes as if he worried Elsmith might be actually telling the truth.

"It's true," Elsmith said, sighing. He placed a hand on Rosen's arm. "You are the oldest of the Aigoviel children."

"How is that possible?" I asked, still processing the idea that Rosen could be related to me.

"Your mother Ehren became pregnant before she was married to your father. In order to keep the scandal from ruining Casimir's reputation, Casimir's father, King Tilan, made him give up the child."

Rosen looked as pale as a ghost now. I must've looked the same.

"Casimir and Ehren came to me. And as I am her father, I felt obligated to agree when she asked if I'd raise you," Elsmith said, looking at Rosen. And the pieces started falling into place before he even said his next words. "I am your grandfather, Sabeara."

Rosen shook his head as if refusing to believe it.

"Why wouldn't you tell me I had siblings?" Rosen asked angrily.

"I wasn't allowed to," Elsmith said. "It was King Tilan who made me promise never to reveal who you were to anyone."

I felt slightly weak hearing all of this. "So you're really my grandfather. . ." Taking this all in was proving to be extremely difficult.

“If you knew about Pendilore all this time, why didn't you tell me? I've been looking for it for years!"

"There is so much more you both don't understand. Things you were supposed to do on your own. I only ever spoke of Pendilore to Rosen as if it were a myth so that he'd have the idea in his mind. It was his and your Destiny to find it."

"Destiny? That's why you sent me on a wild chase for answers about my powers that I'd never find?" Rosen yelled, obviously angry. "Because of Destiny?"

"It's always been about Destiny, can't you see?"

"So how much of what we've known is a lie? Because according to this Tasnim lady—" Rosen gestured to Tasnim, who simply smiled at him. "The curse is a lie."

"Everything you've ever learned about the curse, our powers, and our entire realm has been a lie. That is true."

Everyone stayed silent then, waiting for Elsmith to continue.

He fetched a book from one of the bookshelves and placed it on the table. It made a loud thud as it smacked against the wood. It was the Ethirical.

"Everything in this book is a lie."

Dusane laughed, slightly hysterical. "This is crazy."

"Is it?" Tasnim challenged him, staring him down with her intense blue eyes.

Dusane's eyes widened, and he crossed his arms over his chest.

"You mean to say that the Ethirical is all a lie? Why would everything in it be a lie if we have four of the five tokens with us now?"

Tasnim grinned. "Oh sweet, Reminant. I thought you were supposed to be good at recognizing power and its source."

Dusane's eyes narrowed.

"Who's to say that the tokens are really even magical? Aren't their ways to infuse power into objects? Aren't the tokens just that? Objects infused with Stone-Hearted light?" Tasnim challenged.

"But I've sensed the power in the tokens, it's not the same power as the woman we know that can create those kinds of objects."

"Tsk, tsk, tsk," Tasnim reprimanded. "You, of all people, should know that there have been more people like your friend in the past. Your friend is not the only one that's ever figured out how to grant objects with power."

Silence filled the room again as we all contemplated this. Could the tokens not be tokens at all?

"But what about the curse? The book says that. . ." Shar trailed off, as if he was finally seeing what Tasnim and Elsmith were pointing out.

"You're saying we've been made to believe all these things?" Rouix chimed in. "But the Ethirical has been around for a long time. Wouldn't someone have figured out it wasn't real?"

"What a very unique idea, isn't it? To make a curse for people to fear so that they never turn against one another, create a caste system based on the heart colors so they are always suppressed, and are forced into believing the things that the king of Aveladon wants them to believe. If there is never contention, how can there ever be change?" Elsmith asked rhetorically. His eyes sparked with something. Something unnamable but so powerful everyone in the room felt it.

"You're saying the color system, the Ethirical, the curse, were all things ancient kings put in place to control everyone," I said, my breathing more erratic now as the reality started setting in.

"Oh, they did more than just control everything. They erased the past."

"How do you know this. How do you know they massacred an entire people?"

"Because we have the real books," Eslmith said. "We have them here in Pendilore, and we've been waiting for you all to come so we could bring the truth to light."

Elsmith walked over to the bookshelves and pulled down several volumes with cracked and worn leather bindings. He laid them out on the table and opened them for us to see.

"These are only a few of the books we've discovered that tell of our history. There are even more we have yet to translate."

"You mean there are books in more languages?" Rouix asked, curiosity furrowing her brow.

"This realm is thousands of years old. And there is so much for us to discover. ."

"So if the Kings created the fictional curse and fictional tokens, why are our powers fading if the curse isn't real?" Dusane asked.

Tasnim let out a snort and tried in vain to stifle it.

"Isn't it obvious?" she asked. "You burned down the Spirit Tree. If you take away the very thing that gave you power, it will gradually fade away."

Silence. It was deafening.

"There is so much for you all to learn," Tasnim said, barely managing to hold in her amusement. We must've looked like complete idiots.

Of course, we'd lose our powers without the tree. Why had my mother told me to burn it then?

"You told me to follow my Destiny," I said, looking at Elsmith. "And my mother's spirit told me to burn down the tree."

"It was always meant to happen, Sabeara. If you hadn't burned down the tree, no one would've believed in the curse, and things in our realm wouldn't have progressed to the dire stage they needed to be in. And none of you would've gone searching for the tokens."

"And none of us would've found Pendilore," Rosen finished.

"So, as you can see, it was all about Destiny."

"But you could've just told me it was all a lie. You could've just led us to Pendilore on your own and explained everything. Why send us on a wild goose chase for tokens that didn't exist?" I asked, anger flooding my veins.

"Because Pendilore is still in danger. And we couldn't just put up a flag letting everyone know where we were without fortifying ourselves. So all these years, we've been building up our army so we could defeat our enemy."

"Elysian?" Sunn asked, confusion furrowing her brow.

"No. Wesoltinece. The last living king. Our remaining tormentor."

"Wesoltince is still alive?" Mid asked.

"You think Elysian is dangerous. Wesoltinece has him and all of his Envorydian soldiers on little strings. They are his puppets. And the scariest part is they don't even know he's the puppeteer. They are oblivious to the author that controls them."

"How do you know that he's still alive? I thought all the kings died. Which also leaves the question of how they could have created the Ethirical if they were all dead," Rouix asked. I remembered the Galloway and the tunnels filled with Envorydian history engraved on the stone. I remembered the statue of the war king in the middle of the arena and pulling the hammer from the statue's stony grasp. He was still alive?

"That information is according to your Ethirical. But they all remained alive for many, many years. Behind the scenes, hidden in the shadows. Controlling from afar. Just because their people thought they'd died did not mean they were actually gone. And we know because of our books. Wesoltinece remains because he found very intense stone magic that has extended his life. The type of magic that none of you have even heard of. Which is another reason they wanted to suppress the people. So they wouldn't learn that there is more magic in this world than any of you could possibly imagine. Now, most of them have passed, but Wesoltinece still remains, and we have many pieces of evidence that have convinced us he's most definitely still alive and trying to stop us from bringing the truth to light."

It was terrifying to hear that the war king was still alive. That we were in the dark about our Stone-Hearted powers. That there was more that we didn't even know existed. The idea of ancient kings that once massacred an entire people made Elysian seem like child's play.

"So we've been stalling for you?" Rosen asked, disgusted.

"Not exactly. It is also written in our books that the Chosen would come to us. That we must wait for them to save us."

"There is that word again. The Chosen," Mid said with a groan.

"You forget you've been raised in a world without a god. But are you even sure of who created you?" Tasnim asked.

"A god?" Shar asked, his eyebrows raising.

"There is much you don't know and much you must learn," Elsimth gave Tasnim a warning glance like maybe she'd gone too far.

"You will have access to our libraries, and once you read the real history of our realm, you'll begin to understand. But all you need to know right now is we've been waiting for you. Timing is everything. We now must prepare ourselves for something even more concerning."

"Wesoltinece and his followers will be on their way here now. A battle will take place, and we will have to prepare ourselves," Elmisth said.

Fear rippled through the room. We all glanced at one another.

"How do you know they are on their way now?"

"We have spies throughout the kingdoms. Some even inside Obscurum's ranks. They've informed us of their plans. We have but a few days to prepare."

"We'll have to send word to the others," Shar said, talking about those from Knadiel who went to hide in the mountain caves.

It chilled me to think that we thought we'd made it to the location of our final token, but now our salvation was turning out to be the invitation to what sounded like our impending doom.

More questions were about to come out of my mouth when someone came bursting through the study door.

"Elsmith, there is an urgent matter outside." A man also in white robes appeared, bewildered and afraid.

"What's happened, Calel?"

"There are people from the Mer kingdom coming onto the shore, and there is a man with them. He's demanding to speak with our king."

"We're a democracy," Tasnim grumbled, and Elsmith shot her an exasperated look.

"I will go out to meet them," Elsmith turned to us. "We all will."

~

The unexpected interruption had us all leaving the big stone building that I was calling the library in my head. Together in a group, we walked towards the beach on which the giant mansion library rested. We descended the hill, and in the distance were hundreds of mermaid tails glistening in the dark blue waters. Memories of our time on Tetheria rushed back to my mind, and I wondered why they were here.

As we met them on the sandy shore, they transformed one by one, and their fins were replaced with legs. It was a unique sight to behold.

Some of the merpeople were gathered in a cluster with a few Pendilore soldiers, speaking with the man that had brought the mermaids to the shore.

"How did you find our location?" one guard asked.

"Please let me speak to your leader. I have important information."

As we got closer, I realized who it was and gasped. James and Shar both reached for Sunn.

"Obsidian?" Mid asked, seeing the dark hair and eyes that would be impossible not to recognize.

He turned at the sound of Mid's voice. Then his gaze landed on Sunn.

FIFTY-SIX

SUNN

He was there. On the beach. Surrounded by a bunch of mer people.

His eyes met mine and we stared at each other for several long seconds. I wasn't snapped from the spell until James shifted me partly behind him, and I realized he was shielding me from him.

"What are you doing here?" Sabeara asked, speaking for me. I had no words. I could only stare at him. So many questions and emotions flooded my body.

"Good to see you too, Cuz," Obsidian's eyes shifted from mine to hers, and he let out a typical, wicked sweet smile. "I brought some assistance."

"Assistance?" Dusane growled.

That was when I saw the beautiful woman just to his left. Wearing a gown made of sheer gossamer seaweed, her hair was flowy and decorated with shells.

"I'm Emiress, Queen of Tetheria." She bowed to everyone, and Elsmith walked over to her and returned the gesture.

"I have heard of you, Queen Emiress. It's a pleasure to finally meet you."

"She tried to take the token. I wouldn't call it a pleasure," Mid said darkly.

My eyes widened, looking at the mermaid queen and wondering why Obsidian had brought her to us. Then the realization that Obsidian was standing before me hit me all over again, and I felt my knees almost give out.

He was here. He came back. *But not for you,* my inner thoughts instantly whispered.

"Hold up, she's not here to take anything," Obsidian said, raising up a hand as if to tell everyone to simmer. "She's here to help us fight against my father and his army."

"Help us?" I could tell this was hard for Sabeara and the others to believe. Tasnim and Elmisth were the only two that didn't seem utterly appalled by this idea.

"We have only ever wished for our people to have freedom again. To be free of the hunting that has been inflicted upon our people. We do not want to be made weapons anymore," Queen Emiress said.

"I promised them that if they helped us defeat my father and his army that they could live freely among our kingdom without risk of being slaves to our people."

"Of course," Elsmith said, reaching out to grasp Emiress's hand. "You are safe here with us. We appreciate you being willing to give us aid."

"Woah, hold up. Do you know who these people are?" Mid asked, gesturing towards Obsidian and Emiress. "He's the son of the person who's coming after us."

"I'm well aware, Midennen," Elmsith said. "But it seems he no longer wishes to be on that side, is that right?"

Obsidian glanced in my direction, and Shar made a sound in the back of his throat akin to a growl.

"Look at her again, and I'll kill you here on this beach," Shar threatened.

"Easy now," Sabeara stepped over to Shar and put a hand on his chest. "Last thing we need is a pre-battle before the real battle. Calm down."

"I don't want him fighting with us. He took advantage of my daughter. And for all we know, he's known all along about Wesoltinece and is still working for him," Shar spat, angrier than I'd ever seen him. Hearing him call me his daughter shot lighting through my bones.

Obsidian's gaze turned serious, and his jaw clenched.

"I don't know anything about Wesoltinece. From my knowledge, he's been dead for thousands of years. To be honest, I don't even know what you're talking about here."

"Your father never mentioned working for him?" Sabeara asked, obviously not believing he didn't know about this bigger enemy. "He's still alive, Obsidian. And apparently, your father works for him."

"I can see a lot of history has happened between all of you," Elmsith said, speaking softly like at any moment, a fight might literally break out on the beach. "But I think we should consider that working together might be the best thing for all of us at the moment. I have read many wonderful things of the ancient merpeople in our histories and know they would be a great asset in battle."

"I knew that we would need them to defeat my father, so that's why I left."

"You left to see if you could get the merpeople to help us fight? Even if I did believe you, how did you know we'd be in Pendilore?" Sabeara asked, skepticism in her voice.

"I didn't. They did." Obsidian gestured towards Emiress.

"You've been spying on us?" Sabeara asked, glowering now at Emiress.

"Something like that," Emiress said vaguely. "But that's not the only way we knew about Pendilore. We also have always known about Pendilore because our people are one of the most ancient species in this realm. And because of the War King, we've waited until we knew for sure we could take down our adversary to come to join in the fight with the Pendilore people. I knew we'd need the compass to do it, and when Midennen arrived, the very name of our ancient realm, I knew he was the key to unlocking the compass. I knew if we didn't find the ancient king and kill him, more evil would eventually take his place and enslave my people."

"We offered you the very same option, though. We told you our kingdom would not enslave you," Mid said angrily. "Why would you try and take the compass if we offered to help you!"

"I worried you wouldn't keep your end of the bargain," Emiess shrugged. "I knew I needed the compass, and that's all I cared about. I needed to free my people."

I watched Sabeara reach for the token in her pocket.

"He promised you the token, didn't he? That's the real reason you're even here."

"Not a token, my dear," Elsmith spoke gently to her, putting a hand on her shoulder.

"What did you do to me?" Mid asked, looking at Emiress like she was some sort of spirit, fear and awe in his expression. "You changed my heart." He gestured to his golden chest.

"That, my dear prince, I'm unsure of," Emiress said. "Unfortunately, I was only made aware by my ancestors that an enchantment would need to be performed to unlock the compass. And when you appeared and told me your name, I took a wild guess that it must be you who could unlock the compass. I hadn't heard that name since it was spoken by my great great grandmother." Emiress gazed at Mid with a sparkle in her eye.

"It seems that this is all a misunderstanding. Queen Emiress sought out the compass to defeat Wesoltinece so her people can freely live on the lands of this realm. And all of you have sought the compass to defeat Elysian who in reality, is being controlled by Wesoltinece. The real enemy in this situation is all of our enemies," Elsmith said.

"So it would seem," Emiress mused.

"No need to fight then," Tasnim said calmly.

The only sound for many minutes was the waves crashing into the shore, and my eyes were pulled back to the view of hundreds of merpeople standing on the beach.

"How do we know we can trust each other?" Dusane asked.

"We can't," Shar said, his glare still locked in on Obsidian. "We will just have to hope all of us are telling the truth."

My eyes narrowed in on Obsidian's wrist, where the band was still on. He didn't care about getting his powers back. He left to get us help. I should've been thrilled that he had done something so heroic but some part of me was still feeling betrayed and angry that he hadn't warned me. Why wouldn't he just tell me about his plan? Why did he have to leave me?

"Seems we must prepare then. Why don't you all come onto land, and we will find you lodging and some food. Our people are ready to welcome you."

"Thank you," Emiress curtsied and gestured to the guard at her side.

A tension was felt all around the group as we made our way back up to the library mansion.

I kept my eyes on Obsidian, the only thing on my mind being that I needed to speak with him.

I deserved an explanation.

He didn't turn back to face me as we returned to the front steps of the building. But I couldn't look away. I waited until we were inside the lobby to turn to Shar.

I tugged on his sleeve, and he turned to look at me.

"I need to speak with him," I said. I did my best to sound natural, but a little bit of desperation crept into my tone. Shar's eyes narrowed.

"I'm not allowing it," he said in a fierce whisper.

"It's not your choice, Shar."

A growl reverberated from the back of his throat, and he took a step towards me, his hand falling on my upper arm. He gripped me so tightly it was painful.

"I'm sorry, Sunn. But I saw what happened to you when he left, and the last thing I need right now is you getting more hurt."

"Shar—"

A hand landed firmly on Shar's shoulder, pushing him away from me. It was so unexpected it startled me.

I gasped softly as Obsidian put himself between us.

"I would be careful if I were you," Obsidian warned, his voice eerily controlled.

"Obsidian," Sabeara came over to intervene. "No one wants a fight right now."

"I don't want you anywhere near her," Shar said. "I don't need her getting hurt again."

"I don't plan on harming her," Obsidian said darkly, and Shar's eyes narrowed on him even further, hatred seething in his expression.

"I need to speak with him. Can everyone please just back off?" I said, my voice rising.

Everyone was looking over at us now. I spotted James, and I couldn't ignore the disappointment in his eyes. I knew he didn't want me to follow Obsidian either. But I needed to speak to him. The whole foyer was frozen with intense silence.

"Can we talk? Outside," I said to Obsidian, ignoring everyone else.

Obsidian nodded, his jaw clenching, and then he backed away from Shar.

Shar took a step towards me as if he were going to attempt to stop me, but Sabeara put her hand on his chest. "Shar, let her go," she said softly.

"I'll be right back," I said, giving Shar a gaze that hopefully told him that he had nothing to worry about. Then I turned on my heel and headed out the door. Not even looking back to see if Obsidian was following.

FIFTY-SEVEN

SABEARA

Queen Emiress showing up with Obsidian was only adding fuel to the fire. I would lose my mind if any more insane things occurred that day. Already it was too much. Learning that the curse was a lie, that Rosen was my *brother*. Now Obsidian was back with the mermaid queen that tried to steal the compass from us.

We reconvened in the study, Shar a ball of nerves knowing that Obsidian and Sunn were outside talking. I could tell he was livid. He was a father looking out for his daughter, and he'd just let her walk outside with a killer.

But Sunn deserved to make her own decisions. And if he had brought Emiress and her people to help defeat his father, I couldn't think of more proof to believe he was on our side.

I still didn't approve of the relationship. I still hated Obsidian with every fiber in my being for the things he'd done. But I couldn't inflict those opinions and feelings onto Sunn. She deserved to make those decisions for herself. She knew the truth about him; that was all I or anyone could give her.

"We'll need to make a battle plan. Decide how we're going to defend ourselves when Wesoltinece's puppets arrive," Tasnim said to everyone in the room.

"I think we should take a bit of a break, don't you think? A lot has happened today." Rouix said, rubbing her temples.

"I think Rouix is right. Maybe we let our guests rest from their long journey, and then we can discuss more battle strategy in the morning," Elsmith said.

"I'll have to send word to the rest of our people to meet us here," Mid said, speaking of the others who went to hide in the mountain caves.

"Of course. You can send word. Hopefully, they'll arrive soon enough to help us fight," Elsmith said.

"I don't think they'll attack for another few days," Tasnim said, but she didn't sound confident. "Or I hope not."

"We have plenty of rooms available here in the atheneum. And then, if we need to, we can seek out help from those in the kingdom. I'm sure there would be many willing to share their homes. That way, you can all stay here while we plan our next move," Elsmith said. He walked over to me then and put a hand on my shoulder.

"My people can rest out in the ocean," Emiress said. "We don't need to take up any rooms here."

Elsmith nodded and then turned to the rest of us. "Well, I'll show the rest of you to your rooms then."

Elsmith guided us to a section of the atheneum that felt more like the mansion back in Knadiel that we'd left behind. Long hallways with dozens of rooms were available, and everyone quickly sought out a place to sleep. It had indeed been a long journey, and it was beginning to get dark.

I ended up at the end of the hall with Dusane and my grandfather, which felt so odd I was still struggling to process it.

"I know we still have a lot to discuss about your brother and me," Elsmith paused, letting out a sigh. "I'm sure you have lots of questions, and we will have time for that. But for now, you should get some rest." Elsmith gave Dusane a nod, and then with one last lingering glance at me, he turned and left back down the hallway.

By that point, the others were already dispersed into their rooms, and it was soon just Dusane and me.

I felt odd looking up at him, trying to understand everything that had just happened.

"I know this is a lot for you," he said gently. "I'm going to give you some space, then I'll be back later tonight. If you don't open the door, I'll know you don't want my company."

He was too perfect. Allowing me my space. And as much as I wished I had the strength to ask him to come inside with me. I didn't want him to see me break apart. Because I could already feel myself breaking at the seams. I hadn't even gotten to really talk to Rosen about our familial ties and what that all meant. And I needed a moment to try and understand everything that was just revealed to me that day because it was a lot.

So I simply nodded my head, barely holding back the tears that were pricking the corners of my eyes. *Stay strong,* I told myself. *Just for a few more seconds. Then you can break apart when no one is looking.*

"I love you," he said gently, leaning in to kiss my forehead, worry creasing his brow.

I simply nodded. Knowing that if I spoke aloud, I would just break into a sob.

He didn't say anything else then. He walked away, back down the hall to his room, and I stepped into the guest room I'd been given.

I closed the door and leaned against the wood, fighting the part of myself that wanted to succumb to my emotions and the other that wanted to be stronger than my trembling heart.

I thought I'd be used to coping when my world started crumbling. After so many moments of my sanity being chipped away and learning to patch the holes.

But there was only so much I could take. I'd lost a lot. My home. My family. Friends. Even part of myself. And now my identity, my reality.

Everything I'd thought to be true had been a lie. Rosen my brother? The curse not even real? The tokens all a ruse?

I sank slowly to my knees, my palms flat against the door. A sob ripped through my chest without my consent. It felt so good to let it leave me. I gasped for air. I just needed to remember that I was indeed really alive, that I could breathe. Tears dribbled down my cheeks, and I could taste the salt on my tongue.

I curled up into a ball on the plush carpet, and it was soft. So soft.

The sensation reminded me of a place that I'd escaped to a few times in the past. In reality and in my mind.

I conjured up the image of the grove in my mind. The rose petals on the forest floor, the sweet smell of the supple crimson petals. I sobbed harder, picturing the beautiful paradise in my mind.

I clenched my eyes harder, hoping I could transport myself there if I tried hard enough. That maybe it could become reality.

And I cried for hours.

One.

Two.

Three.

Four.

Soon the room grew pitch black, and night consumed everything. It was comforting to be bathed in the blanket of darkness. It felt so much safer.

A knock at the door sounded, and I knew it was Dusane. Promising to come back and talk to me. But I ignored it. I couldn't talk to Dusane. I couldn't control myself at that moment. I couldn't let him see me breaking like this. Not when we were about to go and fight a bloody battle. I couldn't have him think I was breaking. Because I was. After all the things I'd just learned, I couldn't be strong at that moment.

More knocks came, but I bit my lip, forcing myself to be quiet, so he knew I wanted to be alone. I shook silently as my emotions continued to tear me up inside.

Soon the knocking stopped. And he received the message. That I wanted to be alone.

For what felt like another small eternity, I stayed on the floor of the guest room.

Then another knock came this time with a voice.

"Ehren?"

Chills rippled down my spine, not expecting the new intrusion.

It was Mid.

I stayed silent. But my eyes opened.

"Open the door, please."

I didn't move. I couldn't.

"Sabeara. I know you're in there."

This man, I thought. This arrogant prince with no boundaries. He was relentless and positively obnoxious at times. So why did a small part of me hope he would open the door? That he'd push my boundaries, force his way inside, and see me like this? When I couldn't even handle the person I was in love with seeing me in such a state?

"Go away," I croaked, surprised I could find my voice.

I thought for a moment that maybe he'd listened because silence followed my command.

But then the door knob turned, and he pushed it open an inch, running into my hunched, curled-up form on the ground.

"No," I begged, pushing back against it, and another sob broke free.

"Sweetheart," he said gently.

"I don't want you to see me like this," I hiccuped, needing to wallow in my misery. I needed to break apart by myself.

"I don't care what you look like," he said through the crack in the door.

"Do you not understand the word no?" I growled, tears streaming down my cheeks. I was angry now, the agony slowly morphing into fury.

"Unfortunately, it's one that I struggle with," he said, and I couldn't believe he had the audacity to be sarcastic at such a time.

I stood up, wiping the tears from my cheeks, and then took a step back so he could fully open the door.

"You need to talk to someone after what just happened," he walked in, closing the door behind him, and his eyes searched mine. I hated that nothing was keeping him from seeing the pain in my expression. He could see right through me. It felt too invasive— too exposing.

"I don't want to talk to you about anything," I gritted my teeth and glared at him. "You're sly and quite vicious when you want something. And you have this arrogant princely attitude that really gets on my nerves. You shouldn't just barge in on people."

"What else?" he asked, taunting me. "What else do you despise about me?"

I clenched my fists at my sides. "You're the most infuriating man I've ever met."

"Go on," he took another step towards me, closing the space between us.

"You have this way of creating chaos in my life, and I think you're reckless and delusional."

"Cut to the chase, Little Bear." He took another step.

My spine went rigid, and I gasped at the nickname that left his lips.

"Don't call me that," I said, my tone cold as stone. How dare he?

But it was too late. I wasn't expecting it. And it was like an arrow straight to the heart.

"Little Bear. . ."

Something akin to a growling scream escaped me. "Don't call me that!" It echoed off the walls and made everything inside me feel free. It was like he'd unlocked a door I'd buried deep inside. And now that it was open, pain was surfacing that I hadn't even known I'd been burying.

Who knew something so small had the power to shatter me.

A flood of emotions consumed me. The same helplessness I felt when my mother died. The desperation I felt when I'd been kidnapped at Jasper's gala. The utter fear I'd experienced when I saw my kingdom burning to ash—the spirit tree crumbling down around my body.

I never wanted to be her again. I never wanted to be weak like that.

"That's it, Little Bear. Scream. Cry. Let it out."

"Stop goading me!" I charged toward him, shoving him several feet back and into the wall with as much force as I could muster.

He didn't fight me. He allowed his head to whip backward and slam into the wall. The mirrors and the picture frames in the room rattled with the impact.

"Little bear," he said, wincing in pain.

"Stop."

"Little Bear." He reached up and ran the back of his hand across my cheek.

I lifted my hand to slap him as hard as I could, but he was quick to react. He captured my wrist and spun us around.

Then he crushed his lips to mine.

It was aggressive. And exactly what I needed. His one hand slid into my hair, the other gripping my waist. He pushed me into the wall, pressing us so close together I could barely breathe.

Nothing about our reunion was sweet or soft. It was bruising and angry. All of our pent-up feelings bled into the kiss. His teeth scraped my bottom lip, and I nipped at his, then he pulled back for a moment, both of us panting.

"I'm not the only infuriating one. You're so stubborn you'd rather die than let me help you."

He took my lips again, successfully causing me to fall apart into a million little pieces in his arms. I'd been denying myself of him for so long that I was starved for his touch, his affection, his everything.

"Little Bear," he murmured against my lips. "I feel the way you tremble for me when I touch you. Tell me does he make you tremble like this?" His hand slid up my sides to grasp my fingertips in his. My hand was shaking, giving me away immediately.

A moan escaped me. "Mid," I said, not expecting such a sound to leave my lips.

"That's it." His lips found my neck, and goosebumps washed over my body. "I want to hear you say my name. I want to know that it's me who unravels you— *Little Bear,*" he whispered, leaning in to brush his nose against my cheek.

"No..." I said, gasping for breath in between kisses. I knew it was wrong. Kissing him was wrong. But everything was out of orbit. My whole world had been turned upside down, and for some reason, he was the only one anchoring me, as much as I hated myself for it.

"Little Bear," he repeated over and over again.

"Please," my anger slowly became desperation. He was unraveling me. Thread by thread.

He continued to murmur Little Bear until my knees gave out. He caught me around the waist and lifted me into his arms.

I sobbed into the crook of his neck as he walked us over to the bed in the center of the room.

"Rosen is my brother," I sobbed.

"I know," he murmured gently, running his hand through my hair.

"It was all a lie. The curse. The tokens. The kings."

He held me tighter, pulling the covers over us and kissing my temple.

"I know."

"Everything was in vain," I gripped his shirt in my hands. "All of it was in vain."

He continued to reassure me. Speaking softly and affirming each and every thing that was tearing at my heart. I talked until my voice was hoarse. I talked about my parents, my childhood, and my time in the Sethen Courts. Losing Conland, discovering the curse wasn't real, knowing that Rosen was my brother and everything that had been causing me anguish.

Eventually, I ran out of tears, and I fell silent in the safety of his arms.

"Where do you want to go?" he asked, already knowing I wanted to escape.

"Take me to the grove," I whispered.

He nodded, his golden light enveloping the two of us, and everything else fell away.

FIFTY-EIGHT

SUNN

I was so angry, an emotion I was all too used to feeling when around Obsidian. How could he leave? Leave and then return like a grand hero with Queen Emiress?

He left to save the realm. The thought came into my head, but I pushed it aside. He still left me. Without an explanation. After we'd finally gotten to a point where I felt we'd figured things out.

"Sunn, stop," he called after me.

I'd been walking for some time now. He'd been following me after we'd left the atheneum. I'd wandered through the front gardens and into a section of willowy trees to a more secluded area where we could talk privately. Many people were on the grounds at the atheneum, and I didn't need anyone to overhear our conversation.

Finally, I ended up in a small circle of trees, and a sort of stone dais came into view, with withered columns on the four corners of the slab of rock. Engravings were etched into the stone, and I didn't know what language it was. It looked to be old. Ruins from the past.

I slowed down instinctually at the sight of the stone pillars, staring thoughtfully at the unusual sight.

"There is so much we don't know. I saw books on the shelves in that library, and I could just feel that if I opened those books, everything I've ever known about this world would change."

"Sunn—"Obsidian said cautiously, like he was afraid to push me.

"It's hard to discover that everything we've been chasing isn't real. That this life we've been living has all been a lie. Did you know your father was being controlled by this War King? Did you know Wesoltinece was the real enemy, and you've just been lying?" I took another step, and he made a strangled sound in the back of his throat.

"Please," he pleaded, "I don't know anything about Wesoltinece. If my father works for him, he's never mentioned it to me. You have to trust me. Please, don't run from me." I could hear the honest desperation in his tone. The honesty I'd waited so long for. I believed him when he said he didn't know. But *he chose the wrong time to be the good guy.*

"Run from you? You're the one that ran away from me!" I spun around, too confrontational of a person to allow myself just to walk away. I always knew I'd turn around. That was the problem with being desperately in love with someone. Even when you know you shouldn't give them any more chances, you give them anyway.

When I faced him, I took a moment to admire his black eyes, which were just as insidious and beautiful as I remembered. Then my gaze drifted to the spot at his neck where my necklace hung in the curve of his throat, the little sun pendant glistening.

"I had to do something," he said, his gaze pleading for me to understand.

My eyes snapped back up to his, and I clenched my fists at my sides.

"You couldn't have warned me? Told me you were leaving that you had this elaborate plan to get Tetheria involved?" I couldn't hold them back anymore. The angry tears fell onto my cheeks without my consent.

"I knew you would have followed me. And I couldn't. . ." He growled, running a frustrated hand through his hair. "I couldn't allow myself to—."

"To what?" I whispered angrily to keep myself from yelling.

"You and me—" he struggled to get his thoughts into words. He gestured between the two of us. "We're the two most unlikely people to ever fall for each other."

"So?" I asked, breathless that he had basically just admitted he'd fallen in love with me.

"So, it's not meant to happen this way."

"Tell me how is it supposed to happen then?" I crossed my arms defiantly over my chest.

"Just like you said." He seemed to struggle to say his next words. "You'll fall for some charming nobleman with good intentions and a kind heart. Someone that will take care of you."

"Obsidian—" I started to argue, but he interrupted me.

"I am not noble, Sunn. Or good, or kind, or any of the things you deserve."

I shook my head, hating every word spewing from his beautiful lips. "Stop. . ."

"No, I can't stop," he said, his chest starting to heave with haggard breaths as he tried to get me to understand. "I may have come around to a new side of things and recognized my father's ill intentions, but when it comes to you." He closed the distance between us, his hands reaching to cup my face in his palms. I gasped at his touch, my heart soaring as it was reminded that he existed, that he wasn't just a beautiful nightmare. "I will never be worthy of your light. I have a penance to pay. And the only punishment that can satisfy the price is denying myself the one thing I want in this world."

I felt my breath leave me, the tears falling onto his pale fingers that held me.

"You." His hands fell away as he took several distancing steps back from me.

"Well, I hate to break it to you, but you don't get to be that selfish. I deserve a say in this too. And I can't be happy without you."

His eyes looked pained as I said the words.

"You can refuse to believe that you're worthy of me. But no matter how many times you push me away, I will always want you. I love you, Obsidian. Despite all of your sins and all of your darkness."

He groaned as if in agony.

"Why won't you let me walk away," he asked, his voice a guttural whisper. "Why won't you let me do right by you?"

"Stop fighting me, Obsidian," I whispered, reaching out to him to pull him towards me again. I stood on my tiptoes, pressing our foreheads together, and our breaths mingled between us. My eyes started to close on their own accord. Wanting him, needing him. "Stop fighting this, and love me the way you were always meant to."

I attempted to close the distance, wanting to place my lips against his. But before our mouths could meet, he shifted his body away from mine and pulled away.

"I can't."

I opened my eyes slowly, my mind processing his rejection.

"You can't?" I whispered, trying to keep my voice steady. "Then why did you kiss me back in Knadiel?"

"Because I had a moment of weakness, Sunn." He sighed in exasperation. "I'm only so strong."

"Why did you take the necklace?" I was more than angry— I was furious that he was blatantly ignoring how he felt for me.

"This has nothing to do with me not wanting you," he said, reaching up for the necklace and removing it gently from around his neck. He reached out, took my hand in his, and placed the golden chain in the palm of my hand. He proceeded to close my fingers around it. "I want you more than you could possibly know. But I would never forgive myself if I hurt you."

I clasped the necklace, clenching it tightly in my fist, and let out a shaky breathe,

"Well, it's too late for that. You've already hurt me."

FIFTY-NINE

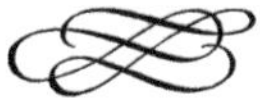

SABEARA

The morning came, and it took me some time to take in my surroundings.

I was in an unfamiliar room, wrapped in a set of sheets that smelled like clean soap. The windows gave a view of the beautiful ocean, and morning light poured in, touching everything with warm, yellow rays.

I'd slept in the supple petals of thousands of roses in my dreams. Pain, and fear, and anguish vanquished for a brief reprieve.

But I was awake now, and reality was taking hold, and it seized my chest.

I sat up quickly, only to finally notice the weight of someone's arm curled around my waist. I panicked for a moment, still disoriented. I let out a scared gasp and turned to find Mid in the bed with me.

"Woah, easy," Mid said, sitting up and putting a hand on my shoulder.

I struggled to breathe for a moment as memories of the bruising kisses and violent words we'd shared came rushing back to me. Then the way he'd held me and taken me into the illusion away from everything I'd been feeling.

I put a hand up to my mouth, self-loathing consuming me.

"What have I done?" I whispered aloud, hatred for myself taking over as the realization of the betrayal I'd just performed dawned on me.

Dusane.

"Shhh—hey. Take a breath, sweetheart," Mid instructed, reaching up to brush back my hair from my face. I continued to look at him in shock, not believing what I'd done.

"I kissed you," I said, my eyes wide.

"I kissed you too," he said, a small, guilty smile coming to his lips. "Are you regretting it?"

I opened my mouth but closed it again. Because I didn't regret it. Not in the sense he was thinking. I only regretted the fact that it was going to hurt Dusane when he found out.

The problem was I'd enjoyed the kiss. Mid had opened me up last night in a way that no one else had been able to for months. Despite the anguish I'd felt last night I finally was feeling slightly better after letting myself *feel.*

What was Dusane going to say? He was going to be so angry —so upset with me.

"I don't regret it," I finally said, and Mid visibly relaxed.

"I know I pushed you last night, so I wouldn't blame you if you did."

I reached out, putting a hand on his shoulder. "No, I needed it."

Mid paused, pursing his lips. "You're worried about Dusane."

I nodded, looking down at the sheets. I groaned and put my head in my hands.

"This is a mess."

His fingers felt under my chin, forcing me to look up at him.

"Hey, you don't have to make any decisions right now if you don't want to. I can pretend it never happened if that's what you need from me."

"No," I shook my head, leaning my forehead against his. "No, I would be lying to myself if I said I did that."

Mid leaned in then, kissing me gently. Fire burned in my core and rippled through my bones. The feelings I'd been burying were now set free, and I couldn't remember the last time I'd felt so alive while being touched by someone.

I let out a whimper before forcing to pull away from the kiss.

"I can't think straight when you do that."

"I'm sorry," he said, biting his lip to fight a smile.

"I have to tell him."

Mid nodded, his expression suddenly serious again. "If you want to tell him, I won't object." His hand cupped the side of my face, his eyes earnestly seeking mine. "I want to be with you, Sabeara."

I closed my eyes, allowing myself a brief moment to enjoy the feel of him touching me, then I forced myself to untangle myself from the sheets.

I stood up, my legs shaking as feelings bombarded my chest. I stumbled over to the vanity and took in my tear-stained face. My eyes were bloodshot, my skin sallow and hollow looking. I appeared sick. Because maybe I was. Perhaps something was wrong with me, making me act and do things that weren't in character.

I couldn't love them both. I thought. *At least, not in the same way.*

And I knew which one I loved more fiercely.

I didn't want to hurt Dusane. And just the thought of the pain I was about to cause him caused more tears to leak onto my cheeks as I sucked in a sharp breath.

"Little Bear," Mid said from behind me, his breath washing across my neck as his arms came from behind me to hold me against him. "It's going to be okay."

"I love you," I said, a sob catching in my throat. I turned around in his arms, and buried my head in his chest. "I love you, Mid. I'm sorry it's taken me this long to see it."

His arms enveloped me, "You have nothing to apologize for. I haven't been perfect in this either." He held me so tightly it was like he was holding me together. "I love you, too, Sabeara."

He kissed my hair and then pulled me back so I was at arm's length. He leaned down so he could look me directly in the eyes. "Go talk to him."

For some reason, he knew parts of me that Dusane would never know. The darkest, most vulnerable parts. And I couldn't share them with Dusane. Why I couldn't share them with him, I didn't know for certain. But it was just the nature of our relationship.

I didn't want to face that fact, but everything else in my life was coming to light. Secrets and lies, and buried truths. It was all resurfacing. Including the lies I'd been telling myself.

I didn't want to lie anymore. I didn't want to try and force something. It wouldn't be fair to myself, or to Dusane.

I needed to tell him the truth, no matter how much it was going to hurt the both of us.

I finally nodded, feeling weaker than I'd ever been, and forced myself to dress and braid my hair. Mid helped, passing me my things as I got ready. Before I stepped out into the hallway, Mid kissed me one last time, his eyes giving away the uncertainty in his expression.

"You'll be okay?"

I nodded. "Yeah, I'll be fine."

"I'll see you soon then."

I walked into the hallway, and the door closed behind me. I was alone and consumed with so many fears. I forced myself to head down toward Dusane's assigned room, but when I knocked, there was no answer. So I walked down the halls and checked different rooms in search of him. I passed others in the athenaeum, and people from Penidlore that worked and studied inside the walls of the grand building gave me soft smiles as I passed but didn't stop me.

Eventually, I ended up in the foyer and spotted James sitting next to Rouix on a sofa. They were talking quietly together.

"Have you seen Dusane?" I asked and Rouix looked up, her eyes widening at my appearance. I must've looked awful.

"He went outside. I think he went to check out the grounds."

"Thanks," I said, and I didn't bother explaining myself. I simply turned on my heel and headed outside.

The grounds were beautiful in Pendilore. Lush greenery, bright flower beds, and tropical plants bloomed along the pathways created. But I couldn't help but feel sad knowing that a battle would soon occur. It was possible the entire kingdom would be destroyed just as all the others had in the past. If we couldn't win the fight, this beautiful land could also be taken and demolished.

I pushed that thought aside, hating that my inner thoughts were so dark and cynical.

I ended up finding him near a small pond outside one of the

gardens. He was kneeling in the grass, sharpening one of his knives.

He must've been waiting for me.

"I'm sorry I didn't answer the door," I said, not even bothering with an introduction. I knew I'd kept him waiting for me, and the guilt was almost too much to bear.

He looked up at the sound of my voice and stood, putting the knife in the sheath at his side.

"It's alright." He looked me up and down, obviously noticing my still puffy and red face. "What is it, Envorydian."

"I'm sorry," I whispered, hating myself for what I was about to do but knowing it couldn't go on any longer. My hands shook as I held them in front of me, clasping my fingers together so tightly it was painful.

"Hey, what's the matter?" He came over to me, taking my hands in his, and leaned down so he could meet my gaze. "Talk to me."

He must've thought it was about Rosen and Elsmith, or about finding out about the curse being a lie. But harder than even those things was the truth I would have to admit to him in that moment.

"I love you," I said, tears leaking out onto my cheeks. "I love you."

"Shhh. . .Envorydain, what is the matter?"

"I can't be with you." I forced the words out and let out a sob that I'd been holding in. I looked into his cerulean eyes and saw the realization take over his expression.

"Ehren. . ." he said softly.

"I've been lying to myself. Lying to you," I said, my whole body shaking now. He took me into his arms and hugged me tightly, which only caused my heart o break even more.

"I know." He said suddenly, running his finger thorough my hair. "It's him, isn't it?"

I stayed silent, letting the quiet confirm his assumption.

"I love you and him differently." My voice broke, and I don't think I'd ever hated myself more than in that moment.

Dusane pulled back, holding me at arm's length. He continued to look at me, his expression not at all upset or angry.

"I know you do. I've seen it all along. Though I wished it weren't that way."

I paused, unsure if I was hearing him right. Was he saying he understood?

"Dusane. I'm sorry. You have every right to be angry with me."

"I'm not angry, Ehren." He said, letting out a sigh. "I've known the way you feel for him for quite some time." A small, sad smile tugged at the corner of his lips. "I just hoped it wasn't true."

I opened my mouth to speak again, but I found no words. I wasn't expecting. . .*that.*

The understanding in his expression jarred me. I looked up at him, my brow furrowing.

"I don't want to hurt you. I never wanted to hurt you."

"I know," he said again, tucking a strand of hair behind my ear. "I know you would never intentionally hurt me."

"But—"

"But nothing." He sighed. "As much as I love you, Ehren. I don't want you to be with me if you love someone else more."

My heart felt like someone was squeezing it too tightly.

"Despite the fear you have about being with Midennen. You need to be with the person who you can give everything to. And admit it. That's not with me."

More tears coursed down my cheeks, and more pain radiated through my heart.

"I think it's hurting more knowing that you understand."

"It's one thing to fight him for you. It's another to fight *you*." He sighed. "If this is truly what you want, there is no point in me starting a fight. Because I will always want you to be happy."

"You're too good," I said, still shocked that he was being so understanding about my confession.

"I'm not good, Envorydian. Far from it," he said, letting out a sigh.

I shook my head and reached out to take his hand. "You are."

He smiled a rare smile. "Let's go inside. We need to talk with the others about the battle."

I nodded, hating that time was always so limited.

"Are you sure—"

"Everything is going to be okay, Ehren," he said, reassuring me yet again. "Like I said. I think I always knew this was coming."

"I just was expecting more of. . ."

"A fight?" He chuckled softly as we started walking back together. "You always are looking for a fight, little Envorydian, aren't you?"

~

Even as we walked up to the athenaeum to meet with the others, I knew something was wrong.

The way Dusane had simply accepted my decision to be with Mid.

It was too easy. Too simple.

All the time we'd shared together, all the moments we'd

created—settled in a matter of minutes? I'd expected him to demand an explanation.

I had a feeling something was missing. That something wasn't right. But I ignored it in hopes that maybe we could just end things in a manner where it wouldn't be so messy and hurtful to one another. Because that was the way, I wished it to be—an ending where nobody got hurt. Where everyone understood one another and things weren't painful.

But I should've known by then that things were never so easy and simple and almost always never exactly the way I wished them to be.

SIXTY

SUNN

"We have to take the cuff off."

We were all back in the study. Tasnim had called us all together so we could discuss more battle strategies for when our enemy arrived.

I tried to avoid looking at Obsidian the entire time the conversation was happening, but I was dragged right back into it all when this was brought up.

"We can't take his cuff off," Shar said. "He could kill us all."

"But he can't help us at all with it on," Sabeara said, trying to reason with him.

"She's got a point, grandpa," Obsidian said, and Shar looked about ready to boil over his face was so red with anger.

"Shar, I know you don't like this, but she's right," Sabeara said, interrupting before Shar could erupt. "We need his help, and that means taking off the cuff."

"I can do it," Dusane said. He walked over to Obsidian, and the tension in the room was palpable.

Dusane reached for the cuff, and Obsidian looked rather bored as he sat and waited for Dusane to remove it.

A click sounded, and within seconds it was off. Everyone in the room held their breaths.

"Well, that was easy," Rosen said sarcastically.

Obsidian rubbed his wrist, and there was a red mark where the cuff had been.

"If you even think about trying to hurt anyone—"Shar threatened.

"I'm on your side," Obsidian said, his jaw clenching. "If I wanted to hurt you, trust me, I could've done it without this cuff."

Everyone in the room seemed to relax a little more at that.

"Well, now that Obsidian has his power back, that will help us, but what other advantages do we have in fighting Elysian? We need something more than just the magical objects we have," Liony said.

"You have the Chosen," Tasnim suddenly said.

Everyone looked at her in confusion.

"Tas, this may not be the time," Elsmith said.

"It's who they are," Tasnim argued. "They should know before going into the fight. It could help them."

"What could help us?" Sabeara said.

"Well, some of you have been Chosen. Do you remember me saying that."

"Yes, as much as I dislike the term," Mid grumbled.

"Well, some of you have Amberidium hearts, and those Amberidium hearts were granted to you for a reason."

"Let me guess," Sabaera said. "Destiny."

"The Amberidium does more for you than just look pretty in

your chest," Elsmith said. "It lets you pull on other people's powers."

"What?" Mid asked. "Like the amulet?"

Tasnim's brow furrowed. "What amulet?"

"This one," Sabeara took the amulet off her neck and placed it in the middle of the table.

"Well, I wouldn't believe it if I weren't seeing it with my own eyes." Elsmith looked at the necklace in awe. "It's your mother's necklace."

"It has power," Sabeara said. "It lets me pull on other people's powers for brief amounts of time."

Tasnim lifted up the object curiously. "This chain is made of Amberidium. And so is the pendant the jewel is placed in. That's why it allows you to do that."

"So Aberidium is what? A siphon?"

"Amberidium can do a lot of things," Tasnim said. "We only know a few things it can do, but it's got a lot of power within it. It's what ran through the veins of the Spirit Tree to grant powers. I believe it even runs through the very fabric of our realm. In our books, these sorts of individuals, granted with Amebridium hearts, are named Chosen. It was prophesied that a select few would be granted them by Ennen to defeat our enemy."

Rosen, Mid, Obsidian, and Sabeara all looked at each other.

"No pressure," Obsidian said, letting out a sigh.

"So how do we know for sure if we are the Chosen?" Mid asked.

"We test it out," Sabeara said. She sat up in her chair a bit more and gestured to Mid. "Here, try to use my powers." Then unexpectedly, she pulled a dagger from her hip and gave herself a tiny cut. "Go on," she urged.

Mid looked at the cut skeptically for a moment, then closed his eyes. After several minutes of concentration, the wound started to close.

I gasped, not expecting it to work.

Tasnim grinned. "See."

Rosen tried it next, then Obsidian. They all seemed to be Chosen.

"So we can pull on each other for power. That sort of gives us four an extra ability. That will help alot," Rosen said.

"Then we have the mermaids and, of course, any other Pendilore villagers willing to assist in the battle," Elsmith said.

"And we have faith," Tasnim finished.

It didn't sound like a lot, but it was all we had. I just hoped it would be enough.

~

James stopped me on the way back to my room, pulling me off to the side and into one of the study rooms.

"Can we talk," he said, shutting the door behind us.

"If this is about Obsidian, I don't want to—"

"It's not. I just want to make sure you're alright."

His blue eyes were imploring. He seemed sincere.

I let out a sigh. "We talked. But we didn't get anywhere. We argued a bit, and that was it."

"I'm sorry, Sunn. I truly am."

"I know you hate him, James. You don't have to pretend."

He sat down on one of the sofas in the little room and gestured for me to sit next to him.

"Still. Even though I don't like him, and I wish that the feelings you had for him could be the feelings you had for me, I don't want to see you hurt."

I took in a sharp inhale as he admitted his feelings for me.

"James—"

"You don't need to say anything, Sunn. I just needed to say it out loud before we went to battle. Just in case."

"Don't talk like that." I reached over and clasped our hands together. "You're going to be okay."

"Still. I had to let you know. And I also need you to know that I'm here for you. Even if you love him."

I looked down at our entwined hands, feeling guilt nearly consume me.

"You're my best friend, James."

He nodded and smiled sadly. "I know."

"I wish things could be different." It was painful to say it to him, but I needed him to know the way I saw him was not the way I saw Obsidian.

"That's okay. We can stay friends. As long as you're okay to keep dealing with me."

"I don't deal with you. You deal with me," I said, giving him a playful shove. "You're too good to me. I don't deserve you."

"He doesn't know how lucky he is. You're the most forgiving person I've ever met."

"He may not deserve it. But do any of us deserve forgiveness?" I felt my throat tighten. "We've all made mistakes, James. It's how we change after making those mistakes that make us who we are."

He smiled and gave my fingers a squeeze. "All this stuff about our realm is pretty crazy, isn't it? Do you think it's all real?"

"I think it is," I mused. "It makes more sense than what we've been made to believe all this time."

"I really hope we will be able to have the truth now. Though it's weird to hear all these things about Chosen, and Gods, and Amberidium."

"It's a lot to take in. But I think we'll get used to it with time."

A thoughtful furrowed his brow. "Let's hope time will be on our side. We're going to need lots of it."

I nodded in agreement. "If what Tasnim says is true. I think we have to succeed. Because why else would a god create Chosen individuals if he didn't believe in them?"

"Your guess is as good as mine," James said. "I don't know what it's like to be a god."

SIXTY-ONE

SABEARA

Something wasn't right. And that feeling didn't leave me. I was still worried about Dusane and how he'd taken the news about Mid and me.

He seemed fine as we had our meetings. But I could just feel it in my gut.

But despite wanting to talk to him more about it there was hardly any time for anything other than preparing for the upcoming battle.

I'd found out that I could now pull on other people's abilities without even needing the amulet. I was Chosen according to Tasnim, and it was a whole new power that I was trying to discover and master before the battle occurred.

Mid and I were out practicing in the courtyard behind the library when we got word of Knadiel's arrival.

"They've arrived, Princess," one of the Pendilore guards informed us.

I looked to Mid, both of our expressions changing to surprise.

"Already? That was faster than I expected," Mid said.

We headed towards the library, and once we got inside, I spotted my sister and Oli in the foyer among the big group. Sunn was already in her father Ashelor's arms. Embrosine was standing next to him, tears in her eyes as they embraced their daughter. They must have met up along the way.

"I can't believe you're here," Sunn said, also crying.

"I was on my way to Knadiel when I received word they were headed to the caves. I was able to meet up with your mother there."

I rushed over to them, hugging Jasper first and then Oli.

"I'm so glad you made it," I said.

"Me too. This place is incredible," Jasper said in awe.

"Where are the villagers?" I asked, and Jasper gestured behind her in the direction of the main city. "The Pendilore citizens have been kind enough to house our people for the time being. As well as those from the Isles."

I turned to see Ashelor still hugging Sunn. The Sappherine tribe was also there to help us. I felt a lot better about the whole situation now that the rest of our army was present.

"Pendilore has been very gracious to us so far," Oli said, and just then, Tasnim came down from the staircase, taking in the reunion before her.

"It's nice to meet the rest of you," Tasnim said, reaching out to shake Ruby and Knadian's hands. "I'm Tasnim. Welcome to Pendilore."

"I've already introduced them," Elsmith said with a smile, coming through the front doors. "But we will need to bring them up to speed."

Jasper looked at me, her brow furrowing. "Bring us up to speed on what?"

I sighed. "Follow me."

~

We told them everything about the war king, the curse, the chosen, and all the details in between. Jasper looked stunned after we'd delivered the message, and so did the others.

"So Rosen is our brother?" She looked over at Rosen, who was also in the study.

"I guess so," Rosen said.

"And everything that we've ever known about the curse and the Ethirical is a lie?" Oli said, and Tasnim nodded.

"That's correct."

Silence filled the study.

"This is a lot to take in," Ruby said, running a hand through her long auburn hair.

"It will take some getting used to. But I believe it is true," Knadian said, confident. "It fills in the holes we've been missing."

"It's easier for me to believe the curse wasn't real rather than the fact I have a brother I didn't even know existed," Jasper said.

Elsmith sighed. "I wished I could've told you girls earlier. So badly I wanted to be part of your lives, but it was impossible at the time."

"Well, we have the truth now. That's what we have to be thankful for," I said. "I'm glad I at least have the truth now, even if it was a little late."

"Which reminds me, can we speak to you, Sunn?" Shar asked,

looking over at Sunn, who had been quietly observing for most of the conversation.

"Sure," she said, her brow furrowing skeptically.

Her father Ashelor stood and nodded toward Shar like they'd already discussed something.

"We'll be back," Embrosine said, and the four left the room.

I looked over at Mid; he was watching the door with a furrowed brow.

"Well, I think we better let you all get settled. You've had a long journey. We can discuss more about the battle tomorrow," Tasnim said.

Everyone stood to disperse.

I tried to catch Dusane's eye, but he was effectively avoiding me. He said he wasn't angry, but he had yet to look at me since the incident.

I opened my mouth to say something to him as he passed, but nothing came out.

~

"He'll come around," Mid said to me as we entered my room later that evening. Jasper wanted to talk to me about some things and asked if I'd stay up and speak with her. I was waiting for her, and while I waited, Dusane got brought up again.

"He said he wasn't upset, but he's obviously being weird if he won't even look at me."

"You two were together for quite some time. It's going to take some getting used to."

Mid rubbed this hand up and down my back soothingly. I relaxed a tad and sighed.

"I wish I could've found a way not to hurt him."

"I know," Mid said.

He leaned into me then, kissing my lips gently. I reveled in his soft touch, getting lost for a moment and forgetting about all my problems for the brief moment of reprieve his kiss offered.

I reached up to tangle my hands into his curly locks when a knock sounded at my door, and we both abruptly jumped apart like two teenagers caught kissing.

"May I come in?" Jasper asked, peeking her head inside.

I cleared my throat, cheeks burning, and gestured for her to enter.

"Yeah, of course."

She stepped inside and smiled politely at Mid.

"I'll just be going then." He gave me one last kiss on the forehead before turning to leave. "I'll see you soon."

I nodded, and when he slipped out the door, I turned back to Jasper, so grateful to finally have her in Pendilore too.

"Do I even want to ask about you two?" She said with a small smile, gesturing towards the door Mid had just walked through.

"It's complicated," I said. "But if you want to know, I'm in love with Mid."

"I always knew you were," she said, sitting beside me.

"Did you now?"

"I'm your older sister. I see more than you could possibly know."

"Well, glad you could see it. It took me a while to figure things out."

"Love can be complicated like that."

"Well, enough about my love life. How are you doing?" I asked her, and I let out a shaky laugh. I hated talking about myself. Especially when it involved Mid and Dusane.

"I'm gathering it all slowly," she admitted, spinning the golden coin in her lap. "So Rosen is our brother?"

"Yeah," I said. "I can't believe our parents lied to us."

"Unfortunately, I can," Jasper said. "Our family has always been complicated."

"Did you see that Obsidian's cuff is off?" I asked her, and she nodded.

"I did. Who decided that he was on our side?"

"Well, it was a collective decision. He brought Emiress and her merpeople to Pendilore to help us with the fight so everyone thought we could trust him."

"It's dangerous."

"I know. But he also has feelings for Sunn."

"Sunn?" Her eyes widened.

"Yeah, I think it's another reason he's on our side now. The two have. . . bonded, I guess."

"I bet her parents aren't very happy about that revelation."

"Not particularly," I said with a sigh. "This fight could happen in a few days, Jasper. I'm afraid."

"We all are. But you can't think the worst."

"It's hard not to when we're up against something so severe. To think that Elsyain used to be our enemy and someone so much more wicked is controlling him?"

"I wish I could help you fight him. But that's one of the reasons I wanted to talk." She looked down, fiddling with her coin nervously. "Sabeara, I can't fight in the battle."

"Why? Are you hurt?" My brow furrowed. I was counting on us being able to have her wind abilities during the fight.

"I'm pregnant."

My jaw dropped, and I felt my heart stop in my chest.

"What?" Tears filled my eyes, and I reached out to embrace

her. "Oh, Jasper, this is incredible."

She sniffed, also in tears now. "It's wonderful, isn't it?"

"Yes." I nodded, wiping away my tears. "It's so wonderful. I'm so happy for you two."

"But Oli doesn't want me to fight in the battle now."

I pulled back to look at her. "I agree with him. You need to stay back for the baby."

"I don't want to stay back. I want to help."

"I know you do. But Oli won't be able to focus if you go to fight."

I took her hand and gave it a squeeze. "You'll be helping by staying back. Then he won't be worried about you the whole time."

"That's what he said."

"I'm happy for you. This is a good thing, even though you won't be able to fight."

"I know. I just wish it was happening under better circumstances."

"Me too," I said, hugging her tightly again. "But soon, this will all be over, and you and my niece or nephew will be in a safer world."

"You're going to be an aunt," she smiled with watery eyes.

I smiled back, something fierce seizing my chest.

"I'm going to be an aunt!"

We needed to get through the battle. For the sake of Jasper's baby and for all the other future plans we had yet to live.

I wanted to live in a world where we could all be safe. Where we could be together as a family and not be afraid of having to uproot our lives and fight wars.

I needed to stop our enemy, so we could live the life we all deserved.

SIXTY-TWO

SUNN

The door shut behind Shar, and I felt like I was going to suffocate.

The last thing I wanted to do was talk to my parents and Shar about how they'd lied to me for my whole life about who my real father was.

"We don't have to do this," I said, turning towards the window and looking out at Pendilore. So many people were being housed in the small little kingdom now. Preparing for a battle that could very well destroy us all. There were many more important things to worry about than the blood that ran through my veins. Another part of me knew that I was avoiding such a talk because it hurt too much to discuss it.

"Honey, we need to talk about everything. It's important," my mother said, her motherly tone making the edge of her tone firm yet somehow soft.

I clenched my fists at my sides, trying to remain in control. I didn't want to get angry again. I was tired of being angry.

"Now that the truth is out, we want to make sure you're alright," Ashelor said. It had been so long since I'd seen him that when he'd arrived with the others, I'd run to him. At that moment, I'd forgotten that he wasn't actually my father. And it hurt to know that the feelings I felt for him though real still, were somehow also a lie.

"I'm fine," I said, turning around to face them.

They all were looking at me with hesitance in their eyes. Like they knew that I was, in fact, not alright at all.

"We know this is hard for you to understand—"Shar began, but I cut him off.

"It's not," I said. "My mother couldn't be with you. Because she had to marry for the kingdom. They needed more military, and the Isles were willing to give it to them if they married. It's not hard to understand at all."

Shar let out a sigh, and I watched Ashelor's jaw clench.

"Honey—"

"No, don't treat me like a kid. I completely understand why you two had to get married. I even understand why you had to keep what you and Shar had a secret from me. I have a firm grasp on it. Trust me."

I felt the anger begin to boil beneath my skin.

"But, what I think you all don't understand is that I'm human. And I deserve to be upset that I was lied to for the past eighteen years of my life."

They all were silent. Their little attempt to have a family talk wasn't going the way they'd planned.

"So, please. Let me adjust, okay?" My tone softened, a bit of the sadness in my heart creeping into my tone. "I just need some time. I know that eventually, I'll feel differently, that one day I won't be mad. But right now, I am. And that's just how it's going to be for some time."

"You're right," Ashelor said. "We need to give you your space."

My mother looked over at Ashelor with a bit of panic in her eyes.

"We can't expect her to forgive us so easily," Shar agreed.

"I'm not saying I won't," I said quickly. "I mean, I already know I'll forgive you."

"But you're not quite ready yet," Ashelor said. And I nodded, grateful that he understood.

"I love you all," I said, my words coming out choked now, a thick lump forming in my throat. "I love you all so much, and that's why this hurt so badly. But I love you enough that I know I'll get past it someday too."

My mother wiped tears from her eyes and sniffled. "I'm sorry, Sunn."

"I'm sorry too," I said, because I knew what this must've done to her, loving someone else for so long from afar—loving someone she couldn't have.

Because I'd felt that sort of pain. The same impossible love for someone, and it was more difficult than words could explain.

My mother walked over to me, pulling me into a hug.

I held her for a long time. And her tears fell onto my neck, and I closed my eyes and relished in her embrace because as angry as I was, I knew we were headed into a fight. A battle that some of us might not recover from.

So I ignored the feelings tearing me up inside because of the lies that were told to me. I pushed them aside so I could savor what mattered most to me.

"But we do have more to take about than just what happened

between your mother and me," Shar said, and he broke the spell that I was under.

I stiffened in my mother's embrace and pulled back to turn and face Shar.

"Obsidian," Shar said, and my eyes moved to Ashelor to see his hands curled into fists.

"There's nothing to discuss," I said, and my mother reached for me, but I pushed her hands away. "No, don't touch me," I growled.

"Sunn, we can't pretend that we don't know what's happening between the two of you," my mother said.

"Nothing is happening," I let out a laugh. It sounded sort of crazed. "Literally nothing is going on," I said, remembering Obsidian's words from only days before. He refused to allow himself to be with me.

"We know something's going on. Shar has seen you kiss him, and you've told him you had feelings for him," my mother said, and it sounded like she was struggling to say the words.

"He kissed me to get Shar to fight him so he could start that battle at the Dark Fell. It was all part of his plan! It had nothing to do with him having real feelings for me!" I lied.

"We just want to make sure it's over," Shar said, his green eyes darkening. I hated myself for talking with him back in Knadiel, for admitting to him that I fell for Obsidian. I felt betrayed all over again.

"What more do you want from me?" I asked, glaring. "I already told you he tricked me. And trust me, I have seen the error of my ways."

"That's all we need to know. That nothing is going on anymore between the two of you," my mother said, trying to defuse the situation.

"Well, you can sleep peacefully tonight," I said bitterly. "Because nothing is going on between us."

I turned my back to them and left the room. No longer able to handle being interrogated.

They called after me, but I ignored them. I could barely understand everything that had happened with Obsidian. Even now, I was conflicted and torn up, and a whole torrid of emotions were going through me. I didn't have the capacity to explain it to them. And most of all, I didn't want to tell them any more lies.

~

I felt tears burn the corners of my vision as I went back upstairs to the guest corridor.

I was just turning the bend to go up the staircase when I spotted a large figure coming towards me through the blur of my tears.

I blinked back the watery film, only to discover it was Obsidian.

"Sunn, what happened?"

I panicked, turning to the first door I could touch. I opened it and flung myself inside. I slammed the door, my chest heaving with gasped breaths.

No. Please don't follow me, I thought.

I'd stumbled into a little room. It was a sitting room, bathed in darkness except for the faint pale light of the now rising moon. It had become dark so quickly. Time was always going so fast.

"Sunn, open the door," Obsidian's voice was muffled on the other side of the wood.

I felt my heart beating like a hummingbird's wings in my chest. Fear and an array of other emotions flooded my veins.

It would be worse if my parents found him in the hall, searching me out.

Cursing, I opened the door and ushered him in quickly before shutting and locking the door behind him.

"You shouldn't be following me," I hissed in an angry whisper.

"You're crying," he said, his hands cupping my face and inspecting me as if he were worried a piece of me was physically harmed. "Who hurt you?"

"No one hurt me," I said, pushing his hands off of me and glaring at him. "Would you even care if someone had?"

"Sunn, don't," he warned.

I shook my head and tried desperately not to look him in the eyes.

"Go. Please," I said. "My parents just decided to have a little talk with me about how they don't want me around you. I told them that things were ended between us. So, please. Go."

"Good. I'm glad they worry about you. You *should* stay away from me," he said, and I wanted to slap him. I think he could tell I was barely holding in my rage, and he let out a frustrated sigh. "You're so stubborn," he murmured, and he reached for me again, successfully grabbing my wrist this time when I attempted to back away.

It was the hand that used to have a cuff on it. He was more dangerous now than ever before.

"You still want me, even after everything I've done to try and dissuade you?"

I shoved my hand free from his grasp, wishing I could actually hurt him as much as he was hurting me. "You're a monster."

"Yes, I am."

"You think this is entertaining? Watching me pine after you? Is that it?"

His eyes widened as if he were surprised I'd say such a thing. "No. I'm just amazed that after everything I've done, you could still manage to feel something for me."

"I love you," I said, shocked and appalled by his words. "I'm in love with you, Obsidian. And that's not just going to go away."

His jaw clenched, and his nostrils flared. "I wish I was a better man."

"What—"

"I wish I could stay away from you," he murmured, and then he was pushing me up against the wall.

His hand wound in my hair, the other grasping my waist, and our mouths coming together in an aggressive, desperate dance.

I whimpered in surprise and in pleasure at the suddenness of it. Yet, I accepted each and every grasp of his lips against mine.

"I want to stay away from you," he said against my mouth. "But I can't."

I rejoiced in the words he spoke, though they held no significant promise of anything. I was just content to have his lips finally on mine.

I couldn't stop the little noises leaving me as his hands traveled up my sides, along my spine, up my neck, and into the tresses of my red tendrils. My body was on fire. And I wanted to burn.

"My sweet girl."

I knew I was getting caught up in him, knew that at any moment, he may stop, back away, and I'd be hurt all over again. But I was greedy, desperate for even the smallest touch he was willing to give me, no matter how forbidden or wrong it was to accept it.

"Don't stop touching me, please," I begged, my voice breathy with tortured gasps as his lips moved down to my neck and to the space on my collarbone.

"I need to," he said, his gasping breaths accompanying mine. "I need to stop," he said, but his hands and his lips were not obeying.

He reached for my waist and lifted me up like I was nothing more than a feather. I wrapped my legs around him with ease, and then he was lying me down on the plush rug in the sitting room, his body hovering above mine as he continued to unravel me with his kisses.

"Obsidian," I said, needing to speak his name like a soft prayer as he devoured me.

I ran my hands into his hair, the locks tangling between my fingertips. I wasn't even thinking anymore. I was lost. Senseless with desire. It could've been hours, days that we'd kissed. I'd lost track of everything around me.

When he pulled away, I had to take in my surroundings. It was a moment before I realized we were both on the floor, his top three shirt buttons undone and showing a sizable amount of chest, while my shirt was pushed up a bit around my waist, and my hair was a tangled mess from the work of his hands.

His lips were red and bruised, and I could feel my skin still flushed from where he'd graced me with their touch.

He groaned and leaned his forehead against mine. "I shouldn't have done that."

I didn't say anything, not wanting to scare him away. I wanted to stay there with him, in that room, forever.

His hand cupped my cheek, and he kissed my forehead, his

lips lingering for a moment. "I can't seem to stay away from you."

"Then don't," I said simply.

His gaze turned thoughtful for many moments, and I held my breath. Literally held my breath waiting to hear what he was going to say. Waiting for him to reject me all over again.

"Sunn, breathe," he said, noticing I was no longer letting out air or taking any in.

I forced myself to inhale.

"I can't promise you what you deserve."

"I never asked you to promise me anything," I said, my voice a mere whisper.

His dark locks were almost inky blue in the moonlight, and he tucked a wild strand behind his ear.

"Your parents—" he said, and the memory of the conversation I'd had with them earlier made my anger resurface.

"Don't ruin this with talk of them. They lied to me for years, Obsidian. I'm not exactly happy with them right now."

"Lied to you?"

"He's my father," I whispered, "Shar."

His eyes widened, and he sat up, helping me to a position beside him. "And you had no idea?"

"Turns out my parents never actually loved each other. It was all arranged and for political gain."

He paused as if taking in this news. "I'm sorry," he finally said, his brow furrowing.

"It's okay," I said with a sigh. "I'm sure I'll get over it eventually. They didn't mean to hurt me. As twisted as it sounds, they were trying to protect me by lying to me."

"Funny how that works, right?" He sighed. "One day, when this is all over, I hope you'll be able to rest," Obsidian said thoughtfully. His fingers ran a trail down my arm causing shivers to course up my spine.

"Will you come with me?" I asked, imagining a place where things were quiet and no threat was being harbored against our lives and our people. Where things were simple and easy.

"Come with you?"

"To rest? Will you come with me to a place where we no longer have to worry about anything hurting us or anyone judging us?"

His eyes softened, and he reached out to grasp my hand.

"I'll come with you if you want me to."

"I want you to."

"It's always been futile for me to stay away from you, hasn't it?" He was still conflicted with himself, sitting there with me on that rug in the sitting room, hidden away from everyone else, nestled in our little space of chaos. But despite feeling like things weren't entirely resolved, that things were still as twisted as they'd always been, after the kiss we'd just shared, things *were* different somehow.

It was like he'd surrendered.

"You'll stop running from me then?" I whispered, needing reassurance after so long of fighting him.

"I'm right here, sweet girl." His knuckles brushed my cheek, and I closed my eyes. "I'm not going anywhere."

SIXTY-THREE

SABEARA

I could feel that it was coming.

It was in the air, all around me. The tension, the foreshadowing of a horrific event. I could tell it was coming soon, and I hated being at a standstill.

I didn't want to focus on the bloodbath that would happen when Elysian arrived, and I was more fearful of facing the war king that was his puppet master.

I didn't want to think about Dusane or how weird he was acting, and I most definitely didn't want to think about all the other self discovers that had taken place over the last several days. I was successfully avoiding the more complex realities and instead decided to explore.

I'd always been curious. And I was *very* curious about all the things Pendilore had that we'd been denied for so long. Knowledge and history existed here that we'd been without, and once I learned the truth, I had a feeling nothing would ever be the same again.

So far, Elsmith had refrained from giving us much detail. It was weird enough to learn that I had a heart that could pull powers from the other Chosen. How the Amberidium worked was still a little confusing for me. In my head, it was just this all-powerful stone that bled into everything.

Tasnim explained it like it was this life source and that we'd been given a small chunk of that life source to help defeat the war king.

I was still grasping the idea that I could do what Obsidian could do. I could pull from anyone if I needed to and use their powers. Elsmith explained that it was my destiny to have this ability. And that it was Rosen, Mid, and Obsidian's destiny too.

But I wanted to understand more about our world, the things I'd been denied. I heard Tasnim speak of gods, and Elsmith had told her not to get ahead of herself, but I felt deprived. I needed the truth.

I made my way towards the lower levels of the library in search of Tasnim. I asked around until I found out where she might be. Most told me she was most likely at the gate.

What that meant, I was unsure.

I traveled down a set of staircases until finding a large room with stone walls. It was covered in symbols etched into the walls and columns that held up the space. It seemed like we were underground.

I looked around, taking in the ancient writing on the columns and walls, when a voice startled me.

"Who told you I was down here?" Tasnim asked. She was sitting at a table with a book open before her. Behind her study desk was a large gate. It was silver, with winding bars and intricate vine designs. It was placed between two columns. What was behind it, I wasn't certain. But I was immediately drawn to it.

"Someone told me where to find you," I said, my eyes still glued to the unusual gate. "Are we below ground?"

"Yes. Sort of. The library was built over these ruins so we could protect them and study them better. We did our best to preserve the walls and columns."

"These ruins were here before you settled Pendilore?"

"It is one of the main reasons we decided to stay here. These symbols have a lot of information on our past."

"I've never seen anything like it."

"That's because any other ruins like these have been destroyed."

I thought back to the galloway and the the walls that held ancient Envorydian symbols, and it felt similar to me. I couldn't tell if the symbols were the same or not, but they were definitely cousin languages because I noticed things that were the same.

"I don't know about that. I swear I've seen these before. In the Sethen Courts."

Tasnim nodded. "You're right. The galloway does have them. You know more than I would've guessed."

I went to sit beside her and glanced at the book before her. "What are you doing down here? "

"Studying and translating. It's all I ever really do these days." She let out a sigh.

"Is it just one language?"

"No, there are multiple. From what we can tell, there are many species that used to exist in this realm, and they had a variety of tongues. It's hard to decipher them all. It's a tedious process."

"No one with the power to just translate something, huh?" I asked, and Tasnim's brow furrowed.

"We did at one point, but he's no longer with us."

I was surprised to hear that there was actually such a power that existed. "I had no idea that was even possible."

"Anything is possible, princess. You just have to have the right circumstances."

I glanced over at the gate again. "What's that?"

Tasnim looked behind her, and realization dawned when she saw I was looking at the gate. "That is the Tempus Gate."

"Where does it go?"

Tasnim laughed. "I wish I knew so I could tell you. But we haven't been able to open it."

"Do you know anything about it?" I asked, my curiosity getting the better of me.

"We've translated a few passages that reference it. We think it may have something to do with time."

"Time?"

Tasnim nodded. "Whether that means it leads to a different time period, I don't know. It's still all very vague."

"Interesting."

"I can see that you want to learn about the truth of our realm," Tasnim said thoughtfully. "You seem eager for knowledge."

"I want to know what's been kept from me all these years."

Tasnim seemed glad that I was interested. Her eyes brightened a bit. "What do you wish to know? I can try and give you what little I do have knowledge of."

"You mentioned gods. Do they really exist?"

"They do. And the one that governs our realm is a very special being. His name is Ennen." Tasnim closed the book to give me her full attention.

"That sounds familiar." My memory of our time in Tetheria

came rushing back to me. "I think that name was used in the enchantment on Mid."

"It was a prayer, Sabeara. Not an enchantment." Tasnim said. "The life is Enn, and the life is en."

"Ennen," I said, and it clicked. "The name of our god."

"We're never alone. He's always watching over us."

She let out a sigh. "But as much as I wish I could tell you more about him, I'm sure Elsmith wouldn't want me to overwhelm you."

I didn't want her to stop giving me information, so I pushed aside my questions about the god of our universe and moved to easier subjects.

"Are there more stones? More trees?"

"Yes and no. More stones exist that you've not been given access to. But as for trees, the only Spirit Tree I know of that exists is the one that you burned down."

"Have I doomed us?" I asked, fear seizing my chest.

"A tree can be regrown, Sabeara," Tasnim smiled softly. "There are ways for the Spirit Tree to exist again, which is something that our books mention. I'm confident one day we will have the tree back."

I sighed with relief. "You don't know how badly I needed to hear you say that."

Tasnim waited patiently for my next question.

"You say there were more species, what kinds?" I asked.

Tasnim hesitated. "I only know of a few for sure. And one of them was people with wings. The others were tiny, with pointed ears. I'm still trying to translate the names."

"Like the mermaids, there are others?"

Tasnim nodded.

"And they all had access to Stone-Hearted power?"

She nodded again.

"We are not the only beings that have access to Stone-Hearted power. Our aniamls can be Stone-Hearted too."

"Animals?" My eyes widened, and memories of the ice snake in the caves with a glowing heart filled my head. "So many things make sense."

"It may take some time, Sabeara. To learn all the things about our god and our realm. Especially because we are still discovering it as we speak. But you have been living this lie for so long it will be difficult to take it all in. I would go slow."

"You aren't going to tell me any more?" Disappointment threaded through me.

"I've already given you a lot to think about. Maybe you should take a few books we've already translated and read those over. Start small."

She stood up and walked over to another part of her desk and found a small book, she passed it to me, and I flicked through the pages with wide eyes.

"Thank you," I said, genuinely taken aback by her kindness.

"As much as I wish I could tell you everything. It would take weeks. And Elsmith would kill me if I overwhelmed you right before a fight like this."

"Well, could you maybe just tell me if the books say anything about this battle?"

Tasnim tensed. Like she wasn't expecting me to ask that question.

"Is it predicted what will occur?"

"There is no certain answer to what our outcome will be. But I have faith that we will defeat Wesoltinece. I have read passages that give me confidence that we will be able to defeat him with help from our god."

"This is more spiritual than I would've thought it to be," I admitted, my mind sort of feeling overwhelmed with everything she'd told me. Maybe she was right. I needed to take this slow.

"You've got lots of time to understand it all," she said. "Hundreds of years, hopefully."

"That's if I survive this battle," I said, a new fear taking hold, thinking about what was about to take place.

Tasnim looked about, ready to say something else, when someone came running down the stairs into the room we were in. We could hear the patter of frantic feet, and then a guard stumbled into the basement ruins.

He looked right at Tasnim, his face pale as if he'd seen a spirit.

"Tas, we need you," he said, his eyes wide. "Elysian and his army have arrived."

SIXTY-FOUR

SUNN

They had spotted them several miles from the border, but they were coming.

The battle was going to happen as soon as they crossed over that threshold and passed through the veil that hid Pendilore.

Fear and panic seemed to surge throughout the entire kingdom.

We all reconvened in the study we'd originally discussed our plans in, and as everyone came into the room, it became charged with tension.

It was odd to see everyone in one place. My grandparents, my parents, Olivine and Jasper. Sabeara and all her Envorydian friends. Obsidian and Queen Emiress. It was a large group of us, and we barely fit inside the study room.

So many of us had come together. Even Emiress was there to help us fight. We had Knadiel, the Isles, and the people from the sea, but would it be enough to defeat King Elysian? And then Wesoltince, who we now knew was behind it all? Would he make an appearance? Or would he continue to move his puppets until he successfully ended everything?

I went to stand next to James.

"You alright?" he asked, and I nodded, but really I wasn't. My stomach felt like anxiety was going to burn a hole through it. I looked across the room and spotted Obsidian. Our eyes met, and my anxiety eased a bit.

"We need to get to our locations. As talked about before. Emiress will stay with her people beneath the water and emerge when Elysian and his army least expect it. Olivine will guide the rest of the army to the open fields, hopefully leading them away from the villagers. We'll bring all those unable to fight into the library to keep them safe," Knadian said, talking out the battle plan like it was already memorized.

"I think we need another spot to attack from," Sabeara interjected. "Somewhere from up higher on the hillside. Maybe a few of us could come down from a higher point that Elysian won't be expecting."

"Good thinking," Dusane said. "I will go with you to scout out a place."

"I'll go as well," Mid added, and I could feel the tension in the room. The three of them still had things they were obviously working through. But they'd have to set aside their differences for the battle.

No one argued about the second point of attack, and then more discussion took place. Everyone was talking, making sure we hadn't missed any crucial details of the plan, and a hum spread throughout the room as things were discussed. I felt out of place, not knowing my role, just knowing I needed to help.

"You'll stay here with Jasper, Sunn," my mother said suddenly.

"We need to make sure you don't get hurt," Ashelor said, and everyone in the room fell silent.

"What?" I felt my breath leave me. "I have to fight," I struggled to get the words out, seeing the determination suddenly forming on both their faces. They wouldn't try and stop me from fighting in this, would they?

"You're human," Shar interjected. "No way are we allowing you to fight on that battlefield. Especially with your limited fighting knowledge."

"You can't stop me from fighting!" The words left me, and I hadn't even realized I'd yelled at them until I saw the surprise on everyone's faces.

"Sweetheart, we don't want to see you get hurt," Ruby said to me, and I had never remembered a time I was angry with her. But hearing those words now, I was livid.

"Sunn, don't fight them," James said gently, and I shook him off, seeing red now as I realized they were telling me I wasn't allowed to fight in the battle.

"I can help!" I said desperately. "I may not be the best fighter, but I know I can help you all."

I could see the pity in Mid's eyes as he looked at me like he knew I was trying to fight a losing battle, and it only spurred me to more anger.

"Maybe we should give them some privacy," Knadian said, eyeing the room with the intent to get everyone to vacate.

Everyone picked up on the cue and followed Tasnim outside, leaving me with my parents and Shar.

"Don't do this, please," I begged, desperate now.

"It's not up for discussions," my mother said, rarely did she get stern, but I could see the decision had already been made. "I'm not losing you, Sunn."

I felt tears burn the corners of my vision, despite knowing they would not help my case. I was so angry that they just came, a few drops trickled down my cheeks, and Shar had the decency to look guilty.

"You can't do this! I need to fight with you all! I have to help!"

"You'll be more helpful staying here, where we know you are safe," Shar said.

More tears blurred my vision as I realized I was again useless. That without my powers, I was simply a mortal that dragged everyone else down because they would just worry about me if I was there.

But I couldn't just sit behind and wait to hear if they'd defeated our enemy or not. I had to help them win this. I didn't want to be the only one left behind.

"You can't stop me from fighting!" I nearly shrieked. I was fraying at the edges now. Everything must've been building up, and I couldn't hold it back anymore because I felt sort of like I was losing my mind. I was not helping my case by breaking apart like a child throwing a tantrum, but I couldn't stop. I was so angry, so upset that my mother was understanding only weeks before and allowed me to leave to journey to Pendilore. She'd treated me like an adult and let me choose for myself. And now, suddenly, she was treating me like I was a child again.

I growled in rage and slammed my hand down against the table.

"I'm coming, and none of you are going to stop me,"

Shar walked towards me and tried to reach for me, but I slapped his hand away.

"If you don't want me to come, you'll have to lock me away," I said angrily, and he looked more than ready to take me up on the offer.

But I struggled against him as he tried to grab me, knowing he would do anything to protect me, even carry me up to my room and keep me captive like a prisoner.

"Stop fighting, Sunn."

I struggled against his hold and let out another cry of anger as Ashelor assisted. I kicked and fought like it was all I had left in me.

"Sunn, stop."

"LET GO OF ME!"

"Let her go," I heard someone say, and it was his voice. My eyes popped open, and Obsidian walked through the door again.

"Get out of here," Shar growled, still holding me against him so I couldn't escape.

I sobbed, using all my strength to rip free of his grasp, and ran for Obsidian.

I wrapped my arms around his neck, and his arms encased me.

"You're alright," he murmured into my ear.

Ashelor and Shar both took a step towards me, but I held on even tighter to Obsidian, and he shielded me with his body.

"Stop this. Can't you see she's had enough?" Obsidian said darkly, his hand outstretched, and they all froze.

His power could bring them to their knees. And they all knew it. I didn't know if Obsidian would actually use his power to stop my fathers at that moment, but he seemed threatening enough to halt them in their tracks.

"She can't fight in this," Shar said.

"Let me just speak with her."

"I don't need you speaking to my daughter anymore," Ashelor growled.

"If you want her to stay, you will."

Everyone fell silent, and I held on tighter to Obsidian's neck.

"Let her go," my mother said to both my fathers. And I was grateful for her surrender. "Maybe he can talk her into staying."

It wasn't likely. But I didn't want to be in that room any longer. I needed to get away, and Obsidian was the only person I wanted around at that moment.

No more was said. I didn't look back at them as Obsidian took me from the room. He walked with me toward my guest room, and when we entered, he locked the door and turned around to face me.

"You're a spitfire, you know that?" He kneedled down so he could look at me more fully.

Tears stained my face, and I must've looked like an angry, puffy-faced child.

"I need to fight," I said, but my voice quivered.

"I know, sweet girl. I know you need to fight," he murmured, reaching up to brush the tears from my cheeks. "But what can I do to make you stay?"

"Nothing. I'm coming. I don't care if I have to fight you too."

He sighed.

"What if I ask nicely?" his lips quirked up into a teasing smile. "Will you please stay here, Sunn?"

"No."

"For me?" He tried again, running his hands through my hair and causing shivers to course down my spine.

"How would that be fair to me? To be held up here worried that you're hurt?"

"I'm not going to get hurt," he said, standing then and pressing his lips to my forehead.

"You don't know that."

"My love," he said, cupping my cheeks and tilting my chin so I would look at him. "I need you to listen to me."

I sucked in a breath, seeing the seriousness in his gaze.

"If I lose you to him and his army, I will never forgive myself." His voice was strangled with emotion. "As much as I know it's your choice to fight, I'm asking you to choose to stay. Because if I lost you, I would never recover."

I opened my mouth to speak, but he shook his head.

"No, let me finish." He swallowed thickly. "If you stay, I'll be able to focus on the fight more. And the better chances I'll have of surviving this knowing that it's you I'll be coming back to. So please—"

"Okay." I finally said, choked up with emotion hearing his confession. "Okay, I'll stay."

I didn't want to. I desperately wanted to fight him more on it and force my way onto that battlefield. But how could I deny him when he was telling me that it was me he was basically living for?

"If it means you'll come back to me whole..." I whispered, leaning down to kiss him gently. "Just, please. Come back."

SIXTY-FIVE

SABEARA

There must've been thousands of us. Yet we would still be significantly smaller than the army coming for us.

It was a sight to see, the droves of soldiers and everyday citizens from Pendilore and Knadiel, arming themselves to fight and take their stance together on the battlefield.

Emiress and her army were submerged within the waters just a mile or so from where the battle would take place. I could see the reflection of their scales even from a distance. If I didn't know they were there, I would've mistaken the flickering of the rays of light to be just the sun.

I was hiking up the hillside, Dusane and Mid at my side. We were searching for a place where we could ambush from above. We wove through the trees, not much conversation being passed between us.

It was still awkward, and I could feel the tension in the air.

I ignored it the best I could as I stepped over branches and maneuvered across the rocks until we finally came to a more open area that overlooked where our soldiers were lined up on the battlefield. I could see them below well enough still that I could make our Shar and Oli at the front lines. But hidden enough in the foliage at such a distance, I didn't think our enemy would see us coming.

"This is a good spot," I said, putting my hands on my hips. I struggled to catch my breath for a moment. It was a bit of a hike, but it was the perfect location to come down from.

"We're hidden in the trees," Dusane said, glancing around at the little cleaning. "Elysian won't be expecting you to not be on the main battlefield. It will throw him off a bit, I think."

"Good. " Mid said, giving me a look. He glanced at Dusane.

"You two good here while I go see if there's a place higher? Just to make sure we're in the best spot?" Mid asked, and we nodded.

Mid gave me a lingering glance before slipping back down through the path in the trees.

It was just Dusane and me then, and he chuckled when Mid was gone.

"He's very obvious."

"He knows I've been trying to talk to you."

Dusane sighed and walked over to sit on a large boulder. He gazed out at the army forming below, his brow furrowed.

"What's there to talk about."

"Well, I think things aren't exactly resolved between us," I admitted.

"With you choosing Mid?" he asked, and I nodded.

"Dusane, are you sure you're alright?"

"You're not the first woman to break my heart," he said, "I've had relationships before, Ehren. I'm not a child that can't handle a little rejection."

"But, Dusane. . ."

"Ehren, don't you think there are much bigger things we should be concerned with? Like the battle that's about to go down?" he asked, raising his eyebrows.

My cheeks heated with shame and also a bit of anger. "I want to make sure things are resolved between us before we go down on that field. In case we don't get the chance."

"You worried we won't make it?"

"It's a very real possibility some of us are not going to make it out of this," I said, my jaw clenching as I tried to swallow the fear that was always just below the surface these days. I was worried it might rise up and consume me if I wasn't careful. I didn't have room to be afraid right now.

"Ehren, I think you're overthinking the way that I feel about this," he said, his blue eyes assessing me thoughtfully.

"I think there were some things not said," I pressed.

"You really want the truth about how I feel?" he asked, and I nodded.

"Yes, that's exactly what I want!"

"Sabeara. . ." he paused as if catching himself saying my real name was weird for him. "You and Mid—"

I waited, needing to hear the truth from his lips because we were about to fight our enemy, and I wanted to know if things were alright between us. I needed it. I hated that I'd hurt him.

"Well, you see." His cerulean eyes remained impassive, their usual emotionless mask. "I really don't care who you love, darling."

I paused. My heart paused. Everything paused.

My eyes widened, taken aback. "What?"

"The reason I don't care. . . is because I never really loved you." He sighed, standing from the rock he was sitting on and facing me. "But that's not what you wanted to hear, was it?"

SIXTY-SIX

SUNN

I paced my room.

I couldn't stand still. Not knowing that Obsidian was out there, fighting in a battle against his father's entire army.

I wanted to be with them. I wanted to help. But I'd promised to stay.

My heart hurt, and my nerves felt frayed. I felt like I was going insane.

I let out an angry growl, itching to grab the vase on the nightstand and throw it across the room.

Guards were stationed outside my door, and I knew I wasn't going to be able to outrun them if I tried to leave.

I stopped in my tracks and looked towards the window. I hurried to the doors and pushed them open, walking out onto the veranda. I leaned against the railing, searching the fields for the army approaching, and when I saw it with my own eyes, I gasped.

It was much bigger than our forces. Fear seized me, and I put my hand over my mouth, a sob threatening to escape me.

Hundreds, if not thousands, of soldiers came up over the hills to meet our army. They looked like ants from my view, but I could see them, and seeing them made it so much more real.

I had to help. I couldn't just be stuck in my room knowing I could help even helped take one of the Obscurum cloaks down.

I looked back at my door one more time, then I made a plan.

SIXTY-SEVEN

SABEARA

It took me a second to process his words. Because at first, I didn't know if I'd heard him right.

"You never. . . loved me?"

He took several more steps toward me, and I backed away from him, feeling something dark and sinister overtake the air around us.

"I was always out, for one thing, Sabeara." He pulled the golden hammer off his belt and swung it a couple of times in his hand. "To be the king of this realm."

"K—king?" I stuttered, fear making my blood run cold. "Dusane, what are you talking about? Are you joking around with me?" He had to be playing with me. This couldn't be happening.

But then he smiled, letting out a chuckle, and I realized it was indeed real. "You were so easy to manipulate. I almost wish it could've been harder."

"Who are you?" I took several frantic steps back and tripped.

He reached out to catch me, then turned me around, pulling me against his chest. I felt the tip of his hammer come up to meet my neck. The golden tip was cool against my skin, and I froze.

"I'm the creator of this hammer, little Envorydian."

My whole world came crashing down at that moment.

I thought I knew betrayal, I thought I knew heartbreak. I thought I knew pain and sorrow and agony.

But I had never known it like this.

Elysian wasn't the enemy. No, the enemy had slept beside me, kissed me, and pretended to love me.

The real enemy was staring next at me the entire time, and I had been too blind to see it.

"Wesoltinece."

SIXTY-EIGHT

SUNN

The wind blew through my hair as I clung to the horse's mane beneath me. I could feel the panting breaths of the creature against my thighs, and my eyes were stinging from the wind.

I squinted, keeping my gaze on the army ahead.

I stayed in the line of trees as much as possible. Not wanting to be noticed. I just needed to be able to see what was happening and be able to step in if I needed to. That's what I told myself, at least. I told myself I wouldn't fight unless I had to.

When I neared the open field, I halted my steed and dismounted.

Then I ran. I ran until my lungs burned and my muscles ached.

Finally, I made it to the edge of the treeline, and I hid behind a large tree, observing the scene before me.

Elysian was at the head of his army line. They were a mass of white and black cloaks, and he rode in on a black horse in the very center. Next to him was a man on a white steed that had to be the king of Severesi. This king had long white hair and milky eyes that were so sinister it gave me chills. I didn't know this leader. But I knew they were alliances with Obscurum.

They were a terrifying front, but I didn't see anyone that resembled the terrifying war king Tasnim claimed to be the true enemy.

I wondered if this king would appear or if he wanted Elysian to fight his battles for him.

The two armies came head to head but didn't charge at each other.

Knadian, Oli, and Shar were on the front lines, and they walked up to meet Elysian and the Severesi King.

We had our soldiers from Knadiel, the soldiers from the Sappherine tribe, and the soldiers from Pendilore. But it looked small in comparison to Elysian's side.

I spotted Obsidian, who was standing next to Rosen and Rouix. His eyes were set on his father, his gaze dark and angry.

I could barely hear their conversation from the distance I was at, but I could pick up on bits and pieces.

"You've run out of places to hide," Elysian said. "You can surrender and hand over the tokens, or we will destroy you."

"We won't surrender to you," Knadian said boldly. "I'll die before allowing my people to be subject to your tyranny."

"So noble." Elysian sighed. "Well, so be it then. If you won't surrender, a fight we will wage." Elysian looked to his son, and his eyes narrowed. "You are on the wrong side, my son."

Obsidian didn't say anything in response. He simply raised his chin up higher as if daring Elysian to take another step.

Elysian raised his fist, then with a dramatic sweep of his arm, he lowered it. And it was like he had cut an invisible rope holding back all his soldiers.

Both armies erupted, charging toward one another with war cries and angry bellows.

I gasped, pressing myself even more against the tree, watching with wide eyes as a sea of chaos unfolded before me.

Knadian was the first to take on Elysian, while Shar, at his side, fought the Severesi King. Knadian used his water power to fight the glowing dagger Elysian was wielding. He shot streams of sharp water like swords at Elysian's chest, and the glowing dagger glided through the water, cutting the watery weapons in half.

My mother was also in the fight, using her electric blue light to shock and take out many soldiers in her path. She was a sight to behold. Rarely did I get to see her use her incredible ability, but it was miraculous thing—the blue sparks shooting from her fingertips like little lightning bolts.

My eyes shifted to Obsidian; he was using his power, draining the hearts of those around him that got too close. He was also using Rosen's power, the two pulling on each other's powers as Tasnim told them they were capable of.

It was unlike anything I'd ever seen, all the powers colliding together.

Oli was wearing the cloak and was using his super strength to lift and throw those that came in his path. Ruby used her power to produce plants from the ground, and much like our time on the Night Fell mountain with Mid, she captured their legs and tugged them to the ground so they were immobilized.

I watched from the sidelines, fearing for their lives. Because they weren't the only ones with powers.

Our enemies had them too. I saw a man moving so fast that

he was a blur. He fought with Rouix, who disappeared and reappeared, avoiding the fast man with her vanishing gift. It was hard trying to locate her throughout the masses.

My gaze returned to Obsidian amidst the chaos, and I was reminded of the time on the ship when he'd taken down the Oculor. He was even more vicious than that day, his dark locks whipping in the wind while he zeroed in on his opponents, taking them down one by one.

Despite the force we had on the front lines, it didn't take long to see that we were outnumbered.

I felt my stomach drop and fear nearly consume me as the black and white cloaks began to overtake our small force.

The battle wouldn't last very long at the rate they were overtaking us, especially if the war king decided to join in.

Just when I was about to step out onto the battlefield to help, a conch horn sounded, and everything around me seemed to slow down.

I turned my head towards the ocean waves in the distance and spotted the mermaids coming up out of the water.

It made chills erupt down my spine as they emerged from the turquoise waves, water glistening on their florid scales as their fins turned to feet and they walked across the sand.

Elysian and his men turned with stunned expressions toward the merpeople, and that's when I felt a glimmer of hope.

SIXTY-NINE

SABEARA

"It's not possible. You can't be him," I said, gasping for breath. "You helped us for so long. Why would you do that if you were after us the whole time?"

But the blade at my throat proved that he was telling the truth.

"Oh, my sweet little Envorydian. The best place to be when trying to defeat your enemy is right next to them. I kept you close so that I knew exactly where you were and what you were planning."

"But you were kidnapped by Elysian—" A sob escaped me, the reality too much for me to handle. I quivered in his grasp, too terrified to scream.

"And as for the kidnapping. Well, that was all staged too. I needed to speak with Elysian, and that was the easiest way to escape for a while. It was all planned. Just like everything else from the very moment I laid eyes on you."

I shook my head, tears leaking onto my cheeks. "No, no. You're lying."

"It doesn't have to end like this," he crooned, his breath hot on my neck. "You can still save yourself. You can stay with me and be my queen. We can rule this realm together."

I tried desperately to keep my knees from giving out. Realizing that in the last several years, every moment spent with him had been planned and calculated. It was like someone was breaking every bone in my body. I'd cared for him. Kissed him. *Loved* him. I'd fallen for the person trying to ruin me and my people.

"You think I would want to rule by your side? After everything you've done?"

"Our world is better when everyone inside of it is under control. The color system keeps people in check. Trust me, Sabeara. You don't want to live in a free world."

I clenched my eyes shut, trying to wake myself up from the nightmare I was currently living.

"You can't honestly believe that."

"I do. I believe it wholeheartedly. Over the last several hundred years, I've gained power that you wouldn't even begin to imagine. There is so much more to this world. More stones, more magic. And we don't have to share that with anyone. That is power, Sabeara. Control is power."

I shook my head, trying to block out the part of me that wanted to curl up and sob on the ground. I needed to fight back. I couldn't let him win this.

"You're wrong."

"Well then, if you won't join me, then that means you're no longer on my side." He sighed, pressing the tip of his hammer a bit more into my flesh. I winced as the blade started to draw blood. "I'm sorry you couldn't see things the way I see them. Now you have to die with them."

SEVENTY

SUNN

The mermaids joined the battle, Emiress at the head. I watched in awe as they raised their spears and swords and charged toward the white and black cloaks that met them on the yellow beach.

It split the battle in two. Some in the waves, the rest on the grassy hills. It felt like in every direction, there was fighting.

Emiress used the compass to summon creatures in the water. Crykon raised their glimmering heads, and an array of other sea creatures like sharks and stingrays could be seen taking down the soldiers that were lured into the water by the merpeople.

They were skilled fighters and added to the numbers. I felt less hopeless as they assisted in taking on a portion of the black and white cloaks.

My attention turned to Liony, who was coming up on Knadian, still fighting Elysian.

The water coming from Knadian's hands was starting to slow down. He was getting tired.

"Hang on," I found myself saying even though no one could hear me "Don't give up."

Elysian swiped, landing a blow with his purple dagger to Knadian's shoulder. Knadian cried out in pain and stumbled to the ground.

"No!" I yelled.

Liony cut in front of Knadian, just as Elysian raised his dagger to finish off the rest of him.

I took a step forward, almost breaking through the treelike as fear consumed me. But then Elysian stilled.

He looked down at Liony, a new expression taking over his features.

I watched as the chaos around them continued, but the two of them froze. He must've remembered her from when she'd pretended to be the ambassador. When she'd infiltrated his kingdom to get the cloak.

But just when I thought he would take a swing at her too, thinking he would surely want revenge after what she'd done, I saw something unusual in his expression.

Mercy.

Why would King Elysian hesitate to kill Liony?

And then, before I could even answer my own question, she lifted her dagger and sent it straight through his heart.

I gasped, stumbling back as I watched the horrific sight before me.

Elysian stilled, and fell to his knees. The light from his eyes drained, and suddenly our enemy was defeated.

Before I could even register what had happened, the king's auxiliary Sylvester raised his sword and pointed it in Obsidian's direction.

Obsidian was gazing down at his father's body in the grass.

He was distracted, a blank look in his onyx eyes.

Liony tried to warn him, but before he could turn, Sylvester landed the butt of his sword into his shoulder, and Obsidian fell to the ground.

I screamed, running out from the treeline towards him.

I somehow remind unscathed, passing unharmed through the fighting. I lifted my small knife from the hidden spot in my boot and let out a war cry, landing it in Sylvester's arm.

Sylvester hissed in pain and turned around, backhanding me across the cheek.

I fell to the grassy earth and felt blood on my tongue.

"Sunn!" I heard Liony shout in panic. I sat up, disoriented, to find Obsidian with Sylvester in a chokehold. Then he drained the life out of him, the color in Sylvester's heart extinguishing.

Sylvester slumped to the ground, and relief filled me.

Obsidian turned to me, a new fear taking over his dark expression at the sight of me.

"What are you doing here?"

SEVENTY-ONE

SABEARA

I closed my eyes, gathering my will to fight back when suddenly Dusane's hold loosened, and he let out a painful cry.

I spun around to find Mid in the trees several yards away. His hand was outstretched and glowing. He was causing Dusane pain with an illusion.

Dusane fell to his knees, cradling his head in his hands.

"Sabeara, are you okay?" Mid asked, and I was never more grateful to see him than at that moment.

"Mid, he's Wesoltinece! He's the war king."

"I always knew something was off about you," Mid growled, increasing his power and causing Dusane to cry out even more. "It's going to be a pleasure to kill you."

I thought he was going to end it then and there when suddenly, Dusane's cries of pain stopped, and he stood up from the ground. It was like one second, the illusion affected him, and the next, he was perfectly fine.

Mid grunted, trying to use his power, but it was like suddenly it stopped working.

"I've lived for a very long time Mid. You can't hurt me the way you think you can."

Mid grunted, trying harder, it seemed, but the illusion was futile. It was like Dusane had figured out how to block it, and Mid had just caught him off guard unexpectedly when he'd come out of the trees.

Before we could get our bearings, Dusane slammed the hammer down into the earth, causing it to quake so severely that the earth cracked and quivered and sent us tumbling down the hillside.

I groaned in pain as I hit several rocks, sliding and rolling down the hill toward the field below.

The rocks pierced my skin, digging into me and causing cuts and bruises. I moaned with every blow until I landed at the bottom, covered in rocks and foliage. I stood up shakily, spitting out dirt and pulling out sticks that had become embedded in my skin.

I looked over to find Mid in a similar condition. He'd fallen down the hill, too, and had several gashes on his body from the falling rocks and debris.

I looked up to see Dusane, but he was no longer where we had left him.

Then something flickered above us, and I looked up to find him soaring through the air.

He floated down from the sky, light as a feather, landing in the field gracefully.

"Did you really think it would be so easy?"

Fear shot through every cell in my body. He was more powerful than us. He had access to things we didn't even understand. He could have hundreds of powers at his disposal, and we didn't know what we were up against.

Mid lifted his glowing hands and ran towards Dusane, not giving up.

The two collided. Mid used everything he had, creating vines, animals, and any other illusion he could muster, and even used his sword. Then he pulled on my power to heal himself as he attempted to strike even a small cut onto Dusane's skin.

I joined in, pulling from Rosen, who was in the distance fighting Elysian's army, and produced the Amberidium shield on my skin as I raised my daggers and tried to land a blow on Dusane's shoulder.

He turned on me before I could even touch him with my blade. He grabbed me by the neck and lifted me like I weighed nothing, tossing me to the earth like a ragdoll.

I groaned, thankful I'd had the shield as it protected my skin marginally from the blow I experienced as I crashed into the grassy earth.

I used all my strength to stand again. My arms and legs shook with pain and exhaustion.

Mid swung his sword, abandoning the use of his powers to fight with his brute strength. But with a wave of his hand, Dusane moved the sword to the side, displacing it with his mind.

Mid growled in frustration, and then Dusane, with another wave of his hand, sent him sprawling twenty feet backward. Mid hit the ground so hard his body went still in the tall yellow grass.

"Mid!" I screamed, my heart stopping in my chest. I wanted to run to him, make sure he was alright, but then Dusane was advancing toward me, his hammer raised.

"You should've joined me when you had the chance, Little Envorydian. It didn't have to be like this."

SEVENTY-TWO

SUNN

"You shouldn't be here," he said, reaching down to lift me up. "Leave, now."

James came running towards us now, spotting me amongst the chaos.

"I couldn't just stand back and watch you get hurt!" I said.

"Sunn, what are you doing?" James asked, pale as a ghost at the sight of me.

Obsidian looked about ready to argue more, but then the Severesi king came running towards us.

Obsidian shoved me towards Liony and James. "Don't let her die," he commanded them.

Liony and James obeyed, putting me behind them and making themselves my shield.

I was just about to try to fight through them, wanting to push past with all my strength to assist Obsidian, when my attention was brought to something on the hillside.

Two people came tumbling down the mountain, and the

residue of an earthquake made the ground tremble beneath our feet.

It was Mid and Sabeara.

Someone came flying down from the sky. Landing in the grassy field a couple hundred feet away from the main battleground.

All three of them stood to face one another, and that's when Mid charged toward Dusane.

They were fighting one another.

Why were they fighting?

"Look," I said, pointing toward them.

James let out a gasp, watching the fight unfold. Dusane was using powers that I was pretty sure he shouldn't be capable of. He was a Reminant. He couldn't fly? Could he?

"It's him." Tasnim came running up beside us. Blood was streaming down her temple—a sword in her left hand. She looked more intense than I'd ever seen her. "It's Wesoltinece,"

It all came crashing down then, the reality of that statement.

Dusane, Wesoltinece?

We didn't even get time to understand it, couldn't even take a breath to try and process it because the Severesi king landed a hit to Obsidian's leg.

"Obsidian!" I screamed, needing to help him with everything in me.

I pushed against Liony and James again with all my strength, but they were strong and pushed back with just as much fervor.

"Stay back, Sunn," Liony ordered.

It was agony. Watching him fight and being immobilized.

Obsidian used his power against the king, trying to drain his heart. But the Seversi king was a fierce fighter, and he had an insane ability to predict every move Obsidian was about to make. Like he was always one step ahead of him.

"He's reading his mind," James concluded, and my heart sank. How could Obsidian win if the king knew his every move?

But despite the Severesi king's predictive powers, Obsidian somehow landed another blow to the king's side.

Tasnim joined in, trying to help Obsidian. The two were using everything they had to take down the white-haired mind-reading king.

Obsidian lifted his sword and tried to hit the king in the side. It would've been the final blow.

But he wasn't quite fast enough. The Severesi king predicted his move and shifted to the side just as Obsidian could land the final strike.

And that's when I saw the blood. Seeping down the neck of the sword now embedded in Obsidian's chest. It dripped like crimson rain onto the tall blades of grass, and it took me a moment to realize who it belonged to.

Obsidian gasped, freezing in place as he clutched at the sword now buried deep within his heart.

Everything stopped.

And time stood still.

Then my whole entire world shattered.

SEVENTY-THREE

SABEARA

I swung my daggers, using all my force against the hammer in Dusane's hand. He grunted and then shoved, sending me sprawling backward. Thankfully I withstood the blow, regains my footing, but only barely.

I looked over to Mid, hoping he was still alive. Then almost cried out with joy when I saw his body move a bit, he was stirring.

A new determination swelled in my chest, and I desperately tried to use the other Chosen's powers to fuel me as we were all connected, all our powers surging to make us more than we could've been alone. Mid's power was the hardest to use though, and it was almost impossible for me to understand it. His power swirled in the back of my mind, begging me to take it, but it was almost like another language. Rosen's and Obsidan's were much easier to use, and I tried desperately to use Obsidian's ability to try and drain Dusane's heart. I knew the only way this would end was if I killed him.

But I could feel Obsidian's connection beginning to fade. And it was almost like it was slowly disintegrating.

I looked over to see Obsidian and Sunn further away. In the grass a couple hundred yards away, I could see her kneeling over him and knew that he must be hurt.

"No," I whispered.

Then the hammer hit the ground again, causing the ground to break again and send jagged pieces of earth unfurling in my direction.

I hurried to my feet and jumped out of the way, barely missing the massive crater in the earth that almost consumed me.

"I know you have more in you, Envorydian," Dusane taunted, and I glared at him, so much hatred in my blood that it would probably remain forever inside me. I had never been so severely betrayed, and the love that I'd felt for him had now morphed into a hatred unlike any I'd ever felt for anyone.

"Come one. Show me what I created you to be." He stalked towards me, his blue eyes so vicious and eager for violence. So different from the passive, kind blue eyes I'd come to know. There was no emotion left in his voice. All that remained was a trained, cold-blooded killer.

I growled, getting to my feet and taking up a battle stance. I tugged on Rosen's power, shielding my body with the golden Amberidium connecting our very beings at that moment.

I thought desperately for a way out, feeling Obsidian slipping away and knowing all I had left in me was my healing ability and Rosen's shield to help me end this.

I tried to use the last of Obsidian's power again, letting out a battle cry as I tugged the life from Dusane's heart. He broke out into laughter, so wicked and vicious it was chilling.

The power was gone before I could even take another breath. He was basically immune, filled with so much Stone-Hearted power that it would take days to drain him of all that ran through his veins.

I hoped someone would come to my aid, but the others were still in the middle of the fighting. We were severely outnumbered, and this was my battle to fight. I had to end this.

I knew I could never beat him, simply because he had taught me everything I'd ever known, and he was more powerful than any other Stone-Hearted, practically immortal now due to the power he'd accessed. I would never get the upper hand.

I needed help. From something bigger than myself. Something or someone more powerful than the enemy in front of me.

We're never alone. Ennen is always watching over us.

Tasnim's words were like renewed hope as they came to my mind. Could it be true? Could there be a greater power, a god that could save us?

I looked all around at the bloodshed surrounding me, then back at the man before me. And I decided to stop fighting. I decided that if there was a god, this god would save me.

"The life is Enn, and the light is en," I whispered, "The life is Enn, and the light is en. The life is Enn, and the light is en." As the words left my mouth, something shifted in the air.

I closed my eyes, continuing to chant the prayer. And then, miraculously, something happened.

A soft wind swirled around me, so soft I barely felt it at first, and then when I opened my eyes, I was no longer alone.

Spirits surrounded me, appearing amid the bloodshed like radiant angels.

My eyes widened, and I stumbled back, unsure of how I'd summoned them.

Dusane's face fell, his eyes suddenly wide with fear.

"How did you summon them?" He looked frantically from left to right as more and more spirits appeared before him, and soon I was surrounded on all sides.

I felt tears come to my eyes as my mother was suddenly at my side and my father on my left.

"You are not alone," my mother spoke, her voice like a soft breeze.

"We will help you fight," my father said. The relief I felt at the sight of them could not be named. I knew I was safe now. I knew they were going to help me.

"Time to end this," I heard the voice behind me, and I turned in surprise, finding Conland standing there in his spiritual form.

"It's so good to see you all again," I said, my chest aching and my bones aching from fighting. But with them in my presence, it was all suddenly bearable, like they were lifting me up.

"You can't be here!" Dusane yelled, backing up as the spirits started to close in on him. "This isn't possible!" He looked panicked now, raising his hammer and slamming it into the ground, but it didn't affect the spirits, in the slightest. The ground shook but I only could feel its trembling. The spirits around me remained unphased.

"It's time for this realm to return to what it was always meant to be," my mother said, looking at Dusane with pity in her eyes. "Free."

All the spirits moved towards Dusane, surrounding him much in the way I'd once seen them around the Spirit Tree. It was like a tornado. I stared open-mouthed, my heart beating so fast as I watched them consume him.

They prayed in an unknown tongue, but it was so beautiful it had tears streaming down my face.

Then they all gradually began to vanish once again. Disappearing back to where I could no longer see them. The battlefield was no longer occupied by their souls, and what they left was Dusane, on the ground, drained completely of power.

He laid on the earth, gasping for breath and grabbing at his now empty chest. He was mortal. They'd taken everything from him.

Everyone on the field had halted. The chaos brought to a standstill. I'd barely noticed that it was suddenly so quiet. I looked around me to see wide eyes staring over at us. They must've all seen what had happened, and all were too stunned to keep fighting.

I took my dagger in my hand again, and I walked over to Dusane, a sob tearing out of my chest.

I kneeled beside his crumpled form and could hear his struggling breaths.

"It didn't have to end like this," I said, not bothering to hold back the tears as they fell to the ground next to him.

He spat blood, coughing. He looked to be aging. All the years he'd managed to bury slowly consuming him now and catching up with him. The hairs on his head turned grey and began to seep across his whole head, wrinkles marrying his beautiful flesh.

He glared at me, withering away to nothing. He would soon be dust.

"We could've had everything."

"I don't need everything." His form blurred in front of me as tears overtook my vision.

His form disintegrated before my eyes, and soon he was a pile of dust in the wildflowers.

SEVENTY-FOUR

SUNN

Tasnim let out a battlecry, lifted her dagger just as the Severesi king was pulling his weapon from Obsidian's chest, and she sliced a clear cut across his neck.

The pale king fell to the ground beside Obsidian. The Seversi king was deathly still, but Obsidian was still gasping for breath.

I broke free of Liony and James's grasp, running toward him.

I fell to my knees at his side, and reached my hands to his chest.

The blood seeped onto my hands, so warm and a dark crimson that I would never be able to rinse off my skin completely.

"Obsidian!" The world stopped around me—the fighting and the chaos becoming a muted thundering in the background. A fear so strong constricted my lungs, freezing my very muscles.

He groaned, his head tossing back with the agony of the wound.

"Obsidian, tell me what to do." I didn't know how to stop the bleeding. I searched blindly beneath his black cloak for the source of the wound and felt only more flesh and more blood.

"S—Sabeara," Was all he could manage to say through clenched teeth.

I tore my eyes from him and looked across the battlefield. I tried to spot her in the chaos, then there she was, fighting Dusane. The two head to head in a fight. Too far out of reach. She wouldn't be able to reach us in time.

"She's too far away," I whispered, and that's when the reality settled in. The pain of it tore through me like a hot branding iron, searing my bones and blood. I would be scarred forever. "Can you use her power from here. Can you heal yourself?"

He shook his head, already fading. "I can't, I'm too weak."

"Please, Obsidian. You have to try, please!" I begged frantically.

"Sunn, look at me," he groaned. I looked down at him, his beautiful onyx eyes gazing at me, an expression in them that I would never forget. Acceptance.

"No. . ." The tears blurred my vision, brimming over onto my cheeks. I knew what it all meant. I knew what this moment was bringing me. And I couldn't stop it. I was powerless. So powerless.

"Shhh, sweet girl," he struggled to say, his jaw clenching with the pain it was inflicting to try and hold on.

"You're going to be okay, I promise. Don't you dare start saying goodbye," I begged him—desperation unlike I'd ever known overwhelming my fragile heart. I brushed back a strand of black hair from his sweat-slicked forehead. He was so pale, so much paler than normal. He was slipping away from me.

"Listen to me," he said. I shook my head, biting my lip to hold back the sob threatening to overtake me. "I need you to know—" I could see his onyx depth become glassy, tears I never thought I'd see coming into his eyes.

I shook my head, clenching my eyes shut. Too weak to hold myself up I fell against his chest, a sob wracking through my body, tearing my soul open.

"No, please," I cried.

He stroked my hair with frail fingers and struggled to finish speaking.

"You have a light in you, so bright." He gently felt for my chin, forcing me to look at him. "Don't let anyone extinguish it."

"I can't live without you."

He smiled sadly, a lone tear slipping onto his pale cheek.

"You can," he murmured. Then pulling me down to him, he pressed his lips to mine.

The kiss was painful and beautiful. Much like the way we loved each other. Had I known how we felt about one another would lead to such destruction, maybe I would have walked away when I had the chance. But as his lips brushed against mine, agony in every remaining kiss, I knew I'd do it all again. Because what kind of love would it have been if he hadn't been the one to break me?

He pulled away, his hands shaking where his palm cradled my cheek. His eyes were drooping closed, struggling to stay open.

"I love you, Sunn," he whispered. And it was the first time he said the words to me, and a tortured sob fell from my lips, knowing it would also be the last.

I leaned my forehead against his, and we stayed that way as

his breathing became even more labored, his palm falling from my cheek as the tendrils of death began to take him.

"I love you, Obsidian," I whispered.

"Always and endlessly," he said as his eyes fluttered closed.

The last of his breaths left him, and the golden light in his chest faded as his body went still.

SEVENTY-FIVE

SABEARA

I ran over to Mid, my chest burning from exhaustion. I fell at his side just as he was sitting up again.

I hugged him desperately, so glad that he was alive.

"You're okay," I said, a sob escaping me.

"I'm fine, I'm fine," he murmured, kissing my cheeks and my forehead. Anywhere he could touch his lips, he peppered me with sweet kisses, tears also in his eyes. "Are you hurt?" he asked.

"No, I'm okay," I said, still clinging to him.

Oli, Rosen, and Rouix ran over to us, their clothes covered in splashes of blood and dirt.

"You two okay?" they asked. And we turned to see that the white and black-cloaked army were all kneeling down in surrender. They'd dropped their weapons, and our soldiers were taking those who remained into custody.

"We're okay. Where's Elysian?" I asked. Oli kneeled down beside me, brushing back blood-stained hair from my cheeks.

His green eyes grounded me, keeping me from completely breaking apart there in Midennen's arms.

"He's dead," Oli said, his jaw clenched.

"So is the Severesi King," Rosen said.

We'd killed their leaders. And we'd taken out Dusane. There was no reason for them to keep fighting.

Rouix looked behind her at the pile of ash where Dusane had once been.

"I'm so sorry, Rouix," I said, another sob escaping me.

She looked back at me, a fierceness in her red eyes. "Do not apologize. You did what you had to do."

"Did you have any idea? "I asked, and she shook her head.

Just then, we heard a wailing cry in the distance, and we turned to see Sunn. She was kneeling over Obsidian, Shar and her mother were trying to pull her away from his body, but she was fighting against them.

"He's gone," Rosen said softly. "Obsidian didn't make it."

We'd just gone through hell and back. And some of us didn't survive.

I knew some of us wouldn't make it out of the battle. But never would I have guessed it to be Obsidian—or Dusane.

Another sob choked me, and I desperately tried to take in a breath.

"It's going to be okay," Mid murmured, pulling me tighter against him. "I know it hurts right now. But you did what you had to do."

It didn't feel like I'd done the right thing.

The world was closing in, despite the fact we'd just defeated our enemy. And it was impossible to revel in a victory when so much had been broken.

"It's over," Oli said. "It's over."

As I was wrapped in Midennen's arms, looking out at the field of wildflowers, now full of death and blood. I knew, even at that moment, that someday, we all would heal.

The war was over. And we could now be free.

And it was just as my mother's little storybook had once said. After the princess had defeated the dragon king and won her kingdom the victory.

We were now satiated in our ascendancy, the days no longer waiting for salvation and the nights suddenly still.

EPILOGUE

SABEARA

Healing.

That was what I was supposed to be doing after the war—after we'd defeated our enemies and freed our people from the lies we'd been living for hundreds of years.

But healing wasn't so easy. It took time. It wasn't quick or simple. It was often times agonizing.

I walked through the fields that day. Six months after losing Obsidian. After losing Dusane.

I breathed in the salty air that Pendilore's ocean landscape provided and let it fill my lungs until I couldn't take it anymore. Then I let it out, hoping to expel some of the hurt I still harbored in my body.

But no matter how much I breathed. My heart still ached.

"Are you ready?" Mid's voice came from behind me, and I turned to see him walking toward me.

Over the last six months, we'd grown closer than I thought

was possible. And I don't know where I would've been without him.

His dark curls were swept back from his eyes, and I could see their emerald-scarlet color so clearly in the noonday sun. I reached for his hand when he got close enough.

Our fingers entwined, and he leaned down to kiss my lips gently. I reveled in the assurance he offered, in the feelings he evoked. He was everything to me and continued to anchor me over the last six months of grieving.

He pulled away with a soft sigh and looked around at the field of tall yellow grass dotted with wildflowers. Everything was blooming with spring colors.

"Is this where you want it?" he asked, and I nodded.

It seemed the only place it belonged. Where so many lives were lost, and so many realities altered, we needed something in this spot to give hope to those of us who were still healing.

"I asked Tasnim, and she thinks it's a good place."

"Did Jasper give you the coin?"

I nodded. Reaching into my pocket, I pulled out the little coin she'd moved between her fingertips her entire life. Little had we known it was made of Amberidium.

She'd given it to me for this very moment, and I felt my fingers shake as I knelt down in the tall plains of grass beside Mid.

He helped me dig a couple of inches down, moving aside soil until the perfect groove in the ground was created to house the little coin.

I placed it in the soil and covered it up. Patted the top gently and then laid some wildflowers over it.

"The life is Enn, and the light s en," I whispered softly to the little coin now nestled in the earth.

And just as I spoke the prayer, the ground started to move. A soft hum vibrated the ground around us, and Mid and I looked at each other with wide eyes.

Then the humming stopped. We looked down at the spot where our Amberidium seed rested.

And that's when a bright green sprout pushed up from beneath the soil— peeking out to meet the sun.

EPILOGUE

SUNN

I stared down at the book before me, the symbols on the page no longer symbols. But words. Ones I could understand now.

I'd been granted my power after the Spirit Tree had been regrown. When I discovered I could translate ancient languages, I'd immediately taken to the ancient books in Pendilore's library.

I'd been studying the ancient ruins and the Tempus gate. Because I knew that the answers to everything were inside of it.

"What does it say?" Tasnim asked over my shoulder. She'd been my mentor as I'd been searching the ancient pages for the answer I so desperately sought.

A way to get back the love of my life.

"It mentions the stone again. The stone that can bring back the dead."

"Sunn, if you go through that gate to find that stone. There's no telling how we'd get you back."

"I need to find him," I said determinedly. Closing the book, I grabbed the key from off the table that was littered with books and handwritten note pages. I'd uncovered the key weeks ago. After translating another ancient text, the key's location had been revealed.

"Are you sure you want to do this?" Tasnim asked, coming around the side of the table. She put a hand on my shoulder to stop me. There was uncertainty in her voice. Tasnim was usually the one pushing for more knowledge, more discovery, to find the things our realm had lost. But when it came to the Tempus gate, it was impossible not to see the fear in her eyes. It was one thing to translate books. It was a whole other thing to go through a magical gate we still barely knew anything about to find a stone that could bring back the dead.

But I had no other choice.

My heart had been broken since he'd taken his last breath.

And I knew that if I could find a way to give us a second chance, I would take it. Because I had nothing to lose.

So I took the large crystal key in my palm and walked over to the twirling silver gate pressed snugly between the stone pillars.

I inserted it into the slot that I knew would wake the gate from its ancient slumber, then I took a deep breath—and turned the key.

ABOUT THE AUTHOR

Kendra Thomas is from Mapleton Utah, a small town pressed against the beautiful Rocky Mountains. Kendra has been an aspiring author since she was in sixth grade. She has a passion for fairy tales and fiction books. Along with songwriting, horse riding, and playing the guitar. Kendra Thomas is a Dental Hygienist by day and a writer by night. She earned her bachelor's degree at the Utah College of Dental Hygiene at the young age of nineteen years old. She is also happily married to her best friend, Cade Thomas, who is always pushing her to be ambitious and creative.?Her most wanted dream is for others to love her stories and characters as much as she cherishes them. She hopes to inspire other young authors to pursue their dreams, and to write about the worlds inside their heads as she was once inspired to do as a young girl. She hopes that the Granted Series might be a place of sanctuary for those seeking a whimsical getaway and a thrilling adventure

www.ingramcontent.com/pod-product-compliance
Lightning Source LLC
Chambersburg PA
CBHW070542310726
48982CB00010B/1437/J

9798986098746